# Catch as Cat Can

# RITA MAE BROWN

## & SNEAKY PIE BROWN

Illustrations by
Michael Gellatly

**Thorndike Press • Waterville, Maine**

Copyright © 2002 by Rita Mae Brown

Illustrations by Michael Gellatly

Published in 2002 by arrangement with Bantam Books,
an imprint of The Bantam Dell Publishing Group,
a division of Random House, Inc.

Thorndike Press Large Print Basic Series.

The tree indicium is a trademark of Thorndike Press.

The text of this Large Print edition is unabridged.
Other aspects of the book may vary from the original edition.

Set in 16 pt. Plantin by Elena Picard.

Printed in the United States on permanent paper.

**Library of Congress Cataloging-in-Publication Data**

Brown, Rita Mae.
 Catch as cat can / Rita Mae Brown & Sneaky Pie Brown ;
 illustrations by Michael Gellatly.
  p. cm.
  ISBN 0-7862-4045-8 (lg. print : hc : alk. paper)
  ISBN 0-7862-4044-X (lg. print : sc : alk. paper)
  1. Haristeen, Harry (Fictitious character) — Fiction.
 2. Murphy, Mrs. (Fictitious character) — Fiction.
 3. Women postal service employees — Fiction. 4. Women
 detectives — Fiction. 5. Women cat owners — Fiction.
 6. Virginia — Fiction. 7. Cats — Fiction. 8. Large type
 books. I. Title.
 PS3552.R698 C44 2002b
  813'.54—dc21                                    2002018036

Dedicated to
John Morris and Robert Steppe
When they're good, they're good
but when they're bad, they're better!

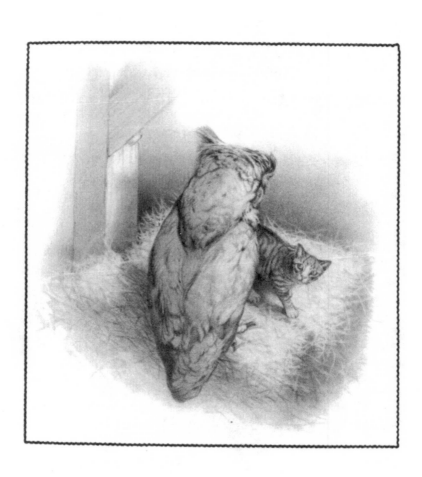

# Cast of Characters and Events

*Mary Minor Haristeen* (*Harry*)   The young postmistress of Crozet.

*Mrs. Murphy*   Harry's gray tiger cat.

*Tee Tucker*   Harry's Welsh corgi, Mrs. Murphy's friend and confidante.

*Pewter*   Harry's shamelessly fat gray cat.

*Pharamond Haristeen* (*Fair*)   Veterinarian, formerly married to Harry.

*Mrs. George Hogendobber* (*Miranda*)   A widow who works with Harry in the post office.

*Susan Tucker*   Harry's best friend.

*BoomBoom Craycroft*   A tall, beautiful blonde who irritates Harry.

*Big Marilyn Sanburne* (*Mim*)   The undisputed queen of Crozet society.

*Little Mim Sanburne*   The daughter of Big Mim, struggling for her own identity.

*Tally Urquhart*   Older than dirt, she says what she thinks when she thinks it, even to her niece, Mim the Magnificent.

*Rick Shaw*   Sheriff.

*Cynthia Cooper*   Sheriff's deputy.

*Herbert C. Jones*   Pastor of St. Luke's Lutheran Church.

*Lottie Pearson*   Assistant Director for Major Gifts at the university. She is in her mid-thirties, ambitious, well connected, looking for Mr. Right. If she can't find Mr. Right she might weaken and take Mr. Right Now.

*Thomas Steinmetz*   Second-in-command to the Ambassador from Uruguay. He is suave, very wealthy, and always ready for a good time. He doesn't discuss his age but he's probably in his mid-forties.

*Diego Aybar*   Under-Counsel to the Ambassador of Uruguay. He most often assists Thomas Steinmetz. He is as handsome as a swarthy Apollo; women fall all over him.

*Sean O'Bannon*   The proprietor with his brother, Roger, of O'Bannon Salvage. Taking over the business after his father's death a year ago, Sean has increased profits by catering to the restoration trade. He's a good businessman, single, late thirties.

*Roger O'Bannon*   Outgoing, raucous, besotted with Lottie Pearson, he works hard at the salvage yard but he plays hard, too. He tries Sean's patience at times.

*Don Clatterbuck*   He repairs leather items such as tack or leather sofas. He also practices taxidermy as a hobby. He's a low-key working-class guy.

*Pope Rat*   A disreputable rat living at the O'Bannon Salvage yard. He knows how to steal food out of the vending machines.

*Abraham*   A very old, courtly bluetick hound.

*The Dogwood Festival*   A spring celebration with wine tastings, parties, and parades organized by many communities in central Virginia. Crozet hosts a parade.

*The Wrecker's Ball*   A fund-raiser for a charity selected each year by members of the salvage and building trades. The O'Bannons are currently in charge of the ball.

# 1

Long, low strips of silver fog filled the green hollows and ravines of the Blue Ridge Mountains. The mists feathered over the creeks and rivers at six-thirty in the morning. Redbud was blooming, the tulips had opened. The white and pink dogwoods would explode in another week.

Mrs. Murphy, awake since five-thirty, snuggled next to Pewter, whose small snore sounded like a mud dauber at work, a low buzz. The two cats rested in the hollow of Mary Minor Haristeen's back while Tucker, the corgi, stretched out to her full length, most impressive, on the hooked rug next to the bed. She, too, snored slightly.

Murphy loved spring. Her undercoat would shed out, making her look sleeker and feel lighter. The robins returned, indigo buntings and bluebirds filled the skies. Down by the creek the redwing blackbirds snatched insects, gobbling them in one swallow. The scarlet tanagers flew into the orchards for their forays. The rise in the bird population excited the tiger cat even though she rarely caught one. Both she and Pewter dreamed of killing the blue jay who made their lives miserable. Hateful and aggressive, he would dart at them in a nosedive, scream as he got close, then pull up at the last moment just out of paw's reach. This particular blue jay also made a point of pooping on the clean clothes hung on the line to dry. Harry hated him, too. Harry was Mary Minor's nickname, which often surprised people upon meeting the young, good-looking woman.

People assumed her nickname derived from her married name but she had earned it in grade school because her clothes were liberally decorated with cat and dog hair. Her little friends hadn't yet mastered spelling, so hairy became harry. To this day some of her classmates remained on uneasy terms with spelling but rarely with Harry.

Outside the opened window, the cat heard the loud *rat-ta-tat-tat* of woodpeckers. She couldn't remember a spring with so many woodpeckers or so many yellow swallowtail butterflies.

The giant pileated woodpecker, close to two feet in length, proved a fearsome sight. This bird, found throughout the hickory and oak forests of central Virginia, was a primitive life-form and in repose one could almost see his flying reptile ancestors reflected in his visage.

The smaller woodpeckers, though large enough, seemed less fearsome. Mrs. Murphy enjoyed watching woodpeckers circle a tree, stop, peck for insects, then circle again. She noticed that some birds circled up and some circled down and she wondered why. She couldn't get close enough to one to ask because as soon as they'd see her, they'd fly off to another juicy tree.

As a rule, birds disdained conversation with cats. The mice, moles, and shrews happily chattered away from the safety of their holes. "Chattered" being a polite term, because they'd taunt the cats. The barn mice even sang, because their high-pitched voices drove Mrs. Murphy crazy.

The tiger glanced over at the clock. Harry, usually up at five-thirty, had overslept. Fortunately, today was Saturday, so she wouldn't have to rush in to work at the post office in Crozet. A part-time worker took care of Saturday's mail. But Harry, an organized soul, hated to waste daylight. Murphy knew she'd fret when she awoke and discovered how late it was.

Pewter opened one chartreuse eye. *"I'm hungry."*

*"There are crunchies in the bowl."*

*"Tuna."* The fat gray cat opened the other eye, slightly lifting her pretty round head.

*"I wouldn't mind some myself. Let's wake up our can opener."* Murphy laughed.

Pewter stretched, then gleefully sat, her back to Harry's face. She gently swept her tail over the woman's nose.

Mrs. Murphy walked up and down Harry's back. When that didn't produce the desired effect she jumped up and down.

"Uh." Harry sneezed as she pushed the tail out of her face. "Pewter."

*"I'm hungry."*

*"Me, too,"* Murphy sang out.

The dog, awake now, yawned. *"Chunky beef."*

"You guys." Harry sat up as Murphy stepped off her back. "Oh, my gosh, it's six-forty. Why did you let me sleep so late?" She threw off the covers. Her bare feet hit the hooked rug and she sprinted to the bathroom.

*"I'm standing vigil at the food bowl."* Pewter zipped to the kitchen.

Murphy, in line behind her, jumped onto the kitchen counter.

Tucker, much more obedient, accompa-

14

nied Harry to the bathroom, looked quizzically while she brushed her teeth, then quietly followed the human into the kitchen, where she put a pot of water on the stove for tea.

"All right, what is it?"

*"Tuna!"* came the chorus.

"M-m-m, chicken and rice." She put that can back on the shelf.

*"Tuna!"*

"Liver." She hesitated.

*"Tuna!"*

*"Tuna,"* Tucker chimed in. *"If you don't feed them tuna they'll make a mess and it will take me that much longer to get my breakfast,"* she grumbled.

Harry reached into the cupboard, lifting out another can. "Tuna."

*"Hooray."* Pewter turned little tight circles.

"Okay, okay." Harry laughed and opened the can with the same hand opener her mother had used. The Hepworths, Harry's mother's family, thought fashion absurd. Buy something of good quality and use it until it dies. The can opener was older than Harry.

The Minors, her father's family, also practical people, proved a bit more willing to let loose of money than the Hepworths. Harry fell somewhere in the middle.

After feeding the cats and dog, she turned on the stove, pulled out an iron skillet, and fried up two eggs. Breakfast was her favorite meal.

"Well, I've got Mr. Maupin's seeder for the weekend so I'd better overseed those pastures," she said to the animals, good listeners. "I was lucky to get it. Anyone with a seeder can rent it out for good money, you know. I'd love to buy one but we'd need almost twenty thousand dollars and, you know, I'd rather stand in line and wait to rent Mr. Maupin's. Even a used one is expensive and you only use it in the spring and, in the fall, depending . . ." Her voice trailed off, then rose again. "The trouble is, when you need it, you need it. We were lucky this year." She reached over to stroke Mrs. Murphy's silken head, as the cat had joined her at the table. "I just feel it's going to be a lucky spring. Worms to turn and eggs to lay."

She washed her dishes, walked out on the screened-in porch, and threw on her barn jacket which hung on a peg. The temperature was in the forties but by noon would near sixty-five.

As Harry stepped outside into the refreshingly cool air the first thing she noticed was the fog on the mountains. The sun, rising,

16

reflected onto the fog, creating millions of tiny rainbows. The sight was so beautiful that Harry stopped in her tracks and held her breath for an instant.

The cats noticed the rainbows but their attention was diverted by a huge pileated woodpecker, lying in the dust, just off the screened-in porch.

*"Cool."* Pewter hurried over, tried to pick up the freshly dead bird in her jaws. It was quite heavy. She gave up.

*"I could help you with that,"* Tucker offered.

*"Touch my bird and you die,"* Pewter hissed.

Mrs. Murphy laughed. *"It's not like you brought it down, Pewter."*

*"I found it. That's almost as good."*

*"Yeah, the great gray hunter."* Tucker curled her upper lip.

*"I don't see you catching anything, fat bum."* Pewter's eyes narrowed to slits.

*"I'm not fat. I don't have a tail. That makes me look fat,"* Tucker replied sharply. *"Bubble butt, you should know."*

Pewter lashed out, catching the dog squarely on the nose. *"Weenie."*

*"Ouch."*

"What is going on with you two?" Harry walked over to the fighting animals. "Oh, no." She knelt down to examine the giant woodpecker. "You hardly ever see one of these up close."

*"I found it first."* Pewter put her paw on its plump breast, claws out for emphasis.

"Pewter, let go," Harry commanded her.

*"Only if I get my birdie back."* She swished her tail.

*"You'd better let go, Pewts,"* Mrs. Murphy advised.

*"Oh, sure, so you can grab my wood-pecker."*

*" 'Cause she's top dog,"* Tucker wisely noted.

*"I'm not a dog."* The gray cat said this with a supercilious air.

*"Good, because I'd hate to claim you."*

*"You're being a real snot,"* the cat said but she relinquished the bird, retracting her claws.

Harry first felt the woodpecker's neck because a bird will sometimes fly into a windowpane and break its neck. The woodpecker's neck was fine and wood-peckers usually don't fly that close to houses. She turned the bird over. Not a mark.

"This guy is heavy."

*"Tell me,"* Pewter agreed.

"In perfect condition. Strange. Really

18

strange." Harry lifted the bird by its feet as she stood up. "Taxidermist," was all she said.

*"I can pull the feathers off a stuffed bird as well as a live one."* Pewter smiled.

*"Indulge her, Pewter,"* Tucker growled, her nose still hurting.

The cat said nothing, following Harry closely as the human located her old large cooler, filled it with ice, wrapped the wood-pecker in a plastic bag, then placed it in the cooler. She would visit the taxidermist after overseeding.

She then walked to the barn, turned the three horses out, picked stalls, scrubbed water buckets, and was on the tractor in no time, happy as she could be.

The animals had no desire to run after the tractor as Harry monotonously rolled up and down the fields, so they reposed under a huge white lilac bush, blooms half-opened. Pewter and Tucker called a truce.

*"It was weird — that woodpecker."* Mrs. Murphy watched a swarm of ladybugs head their way.

*"An omen. Found treasure,"* Pewter purred.

Tucker rested her head on her paws. *"A bad omen if you're the woodpecker."*

# 2

"What do you think?" Harry leaned over the heavy wooden table where Don Clatterbuck studied the recently deceased pileated woodpecker.

"I can do it. Sure can." His smile revealed teeth stained by chewing tobacco, a habit learned from his maternal grandfather, Riley "Booty" Mawyer, who was old but still farming.

She folded her arms across her chest. "Lots?"

"Not for you." He smiled again.

"Well — ?"

"Oh, how about a hundred dollars and you give my card out when foxhunting starts again? At the meets."

"Really?" Harry knew she was getting a good deal because stuffing birds was more difficult than stuffing deer heads.

"Yeah. We go back a ways, Skeezits." He called her by a childhood nickname.

"Guess we do." She smiled back and

pointed to coffee tables, the tops covered with old license plates, some dating back to the 1920s. "These are good. You ought to carry them up to Middleburg and put them in those expensive shops there."

His shop, a converted garage, overflowed with hides, knives to cut leather, and a heavy-duty sewing machine to sew leather, though usually he employed hand tools even for sewing. Donald repaired tack, leather chairs, car upholstery, even leather skirts and high-fashion stuff.

He made a decent living from that and his taxidermy but he also exhibited a creative streak. The license-plate-covered coffee tables were his latest idea.

"Not satisfied. I want to make some using the color for design. The old New York plates used to be orange so what if I used orange and, say, the old California plates, black. I don't know. Something different."

"These are good. The ones right here. Where do you get these cool old plates?"

"Yard sales mostly. Junkyards. Scratchin'."

As they'd known one another since they were toddlers, they employed a shorthand. Scratchin' meant he'd scratch up stuff like a chicken scratches up grubs. Many of Harry's friends did this, as they all had

21

known one another all their lives. In the case of the older generation, this shorthand contracted into orders. The Virginia way was that older people gave orders, young people carried them out. "Worship of youth is for other parts," as Virginians said. And what any true Virginian would never say was that those "other parts" of the country didn't count.

Another fundamental of Virginia life was that society was ruled by women. The entire state was a matriarchy, carefully concealed, of course. It would never do for men to know they were being directed, guided, cajoled, or sometimes openly threatened to do what the Queen wanted, the Queen being the reigning woman of every locality.

What the men never told the women was that they knew that. Hunting, fishing, and golf provided a respite from the continual improvements of the ladies. Despite the occasional irritations, interruptions, and exhaustion of pleasing women, Virginia men bore this burden for reasons they did not share with those same women. The men felt they were bigger, stronger, and more inclined to fight, which also meant they could protect those who were smaller, weaker, and who needed them. They declined to let the women know that those ladies needed them or that they knew full well what the ladies were doing.

The system worked most times. When it didn't there was hell to pay.

Harry and Don, in their late thirties, actually believed they weren't part of this dance. Of course they were, and in time they'd understand just how much they'd been influenced by their elders and by the very ethos of Virginia.

"You're the craftsman." She smiled.

"I get by." He wiped his hand across his chin, leaving a faint streak of light brown stain, as he'd been coloring calfskin before Harry came into his shop.

"You've always done good work. I don't know where you get your ideas. I remember the Homecoming float with the stallion that bucked. I still don't know how you built that bucking horse. No one's ever topped that."

"Wasn't bad." He grinned.

"Where do you get all this stuff?" She pointed to a broken pediment, good stone, too; a huge pile of ancient license plates; an old gas pump, the kind with a whirling ball on the top; a massive enameled safe with a central lock like a pilot's wheel; and a beautiful old Brewster phaeton, badly in need of repair but an example of the coach builder's art.

Mrs. Murphy and Pewter sat in the cracked, deep green leather of the phaeton seat. The body of the coach itself was dark green enamel with red and gold piping, quite lovely even if faded and cracked.

"O'Bannon's."

"The salvage yard? I haven't been there since the old man died."

"Opened up four acres in the back. The boys are good businessmen. Sean really runs the business and Roger runs the garage, old cars. He still spends half his time at the stock-car races. You ought to go over there." Don carefully put the woodpecker into a large freezer he had for game. "They've even got a caboose on the old railroad siding. Must have been fun in the old days when businesses all had railroad sidings."

"When did Sean expand?" Harry asked, knowing Sean O'Bannon was the older of the two brothers and seemed more commanding than Roger.

"He started about a month after his dad died. Said he could never get his father to see how the business could grow. He borrowed some money from the bank. It's a big expansion."

"Thought I knew everything." She scratched her head.

"You gonna be another Big Mim?" Don laughed, naming Mim Sanburne, in her late sixties although not broadcasting her age. Mim was wealthy, beautiful, imperious, and prepared to rule Crozet and all of Virginia if permitted to do so — and even if not permitted. She had to know everything.

"Thanks," Harry dryly replied.

*"Mom likes to give orders as much as Mim, secretly,"* Pewter giggled.

Murphy disagreed with her companion. *"I don't think so. I think she likes to go her own way but if she has to work in a group of humans she wants to get the job done. Mother doesn't want to hear a lot of personal stuff about people's lives — girl talk. Hates it."*

*"I think she could run Crozet every bit as much as Big Mim."*

*"She has the ability but not the desire."* Mrs. Murphy sat up and thought how civilized it would be to travel in a phaeton on a perfect spring day such as this.

*"Don't forget Little Mim."* Tucker, who had been inspecting every item on the floor of the shop, walked over.

*"True."* Pewter considered the social and political ambitions of Mim's sole daughter. *"She's vice-mayor now, too."*

Jim Sanburne, husband to Mim, father to Little Mim, was mayor and had been mayor since the middle of the 1960s. His daughter challenged him for the mayoralty in the last city election but they compromised and she became vice-mayor, appointed by her father, approved by the City Council. Had she gone through with the campaign it would have divided the community. This way harmony was preserved and she was mayor-in-training.

"Go over to O'Bannon's," Don suggested. "Artists go there. Not just motorheads. BoomBoom Craycroft is there once a week, sifting through scrap metal."

"What?"

"She's welding artistic pieces. Says it grounds her."

"Give me a break." Harry grimaced. "BoomBoom can't stick to anything and every new activity is her salvation and ought to be yours, too. Well, at least she's out of her group therapy phase."

"Ready for the Dogwood Festival next weekend? Our mid-April rites of spring?" He changed the subject.

"No." She pursed her lips. "Damn that Susan. She suckers me every time."

"What do you have to do this time?"

"Parade coordinator."

"Yeah?"

"Means I have to line everyone up at the

starting place, Crozet High School, space them correctly, use the bullhorn, and get them marching. It's easy enough until you consider who's marching in the parade. The clash of egos — our version of *Clash of the Titans*."

Don laughed. "BoomBoom especially. Your favorite person."

Harry started laughing so hard she couldn't talk. "She's leading a delegation of disease-of-the-week. I forget which disease."

"Last year it was MS."

BoomBoom Craycroft, a beautiful woman and an ambitious one, each year selected a charity. She would then lead this group in the annual parade, a celebration of spring and Crozet. It wasn't just that she wished to perform good deeds and help the sick, she also wanted to be the center of attention. She was too old to be the head majorette for the high school, obviously, so this was her venue.

"I suppose we wouldn't laugh so hard if we had whatever illness it was but I can't help it. I really can't. I think she should lead a contingent for breast reduction." Harry giggled. BoomBoom carried a lot of freight upstairs.

Don gasped. "Don't do that."

"Spoken just like a man. You twit." She made a gun out of her thumb and forefinger and "shot" him. She walked over to the huge safe. "Got your millions in there?"

"Nah, just half a million." He laughed, then thought a moment. "Give me two weeks on the woodpecker. You've hit me at a good time."

"Great." She gave him a high five and picked up her brood to head to O'Bannon's. "See you at the parade."

## 3

With the exception of the interstates, the roads in Virginia were paved-over Indian trails. They twisted through the mountains, leveled out along the riverbeds and streams, proving a joy to those fortunate enough to own sports cars.

Harry, on the other hand, was the proud owner of two trucks. One truck, a dually F350, was expensive to run due to its big engine but she needed the power to pull her horse trailer. Thanks to a long-term loan she could afford the payments. She had three years left.

For everyday use she drove her old 1978 Ford half-ton, ran like a top, was cheap to operate and repair.

Today she curled around the hills and valleys in the old Superman-blue Ford, the two cats and Tucker cheerfully riding in the cab, commenting on the unfolding countryside.

Don Clatterbuck's business rested just past the intersection with Route 240 on

Whitehall Road. The O'Bannon Salvage yard was located east of town on that same Route 240, tucked off the highway so as not to offend intensely aesthetic souls. To further promote good community relations, the O'Bannon brothers had put up a high, solid, paled fence around the four acres, a considerable expense. A large, pretty, hand-painted sign swayed on a wrought iron post at the driveway, right by the big double gate. A black background with white lettering read "O'Bannon Salvage," and a red border completed the sign. What made everyone notice the salvage yard, though, wasn't the sign but the black wrecker's ball hanging from a crane positioned next to the sign. Each morning Sean or Roger opened the heavy chain-link fence gate and each evening they locked it, the wrecker's ball and crane standing like a skeletal sentinel.

As the postmistress of Crozet and born and bred there, Harry knew every side street and every resident, too. There was no shortcut to O'Bannon's. She'd have to go through town. Don had aroused her curiosity. She wanted to see Sean's improvements.

She no sooner turned east than she passed the supermarket and spied Miranda Hogendobber, her coworker and friend, in the parking lot. Her paper bags of groceries were perched on the hood of the Ford Falcon, an antique that Miranda used daily, seeing no reason to spend money on a new car if the old one operated efficiently.

Miranda seemed upset. Harry turned into the parking lot, found a space, and hurried over to her friend, the animals behind her.

"Oh, Harry, I'm so glad to see you. Look. Would you look!" Miranda pointed to her tires, hubcaps missing. "I've never had anything like this happen — and at the supermarket."

"*It's all right, Mrs. Hogendobber.*" Mrs. Murphy rubbed against her leg, feeling certain this would calm the lady.

"*What's the big noise about a hubcap?*" Pewter shrugged.

"*Car's from 1961. How can she replace them?*" Tucker replied.

"*The car runs fine without hubcaps.*" Pewter struggled to understand human reactions, since she often felt they missed the point.

"*You know how she is. Everything has to be just so. Not a weed in her garden. She doesn't want to cruise around with her lug nuts showing, you'll pardon the expression.*" Murphy circled Miranda, rubbing on the opposite leg.

31

"Did you call the sheriff?"

"No. I just walked out this very minute." Miranda, crestfallen, stepped back to view her naked wheels again.

"Tell you what, you stay here and I'll run over to the pay phone." Harry started to move away, then stopped. "Do you have anything that needs to go into the freezer? I can take it home for you."

"No."

Harry called the sheriff's office and before she hung up the phone to rejoin Miranda, Cynthia Cooper, a deputy with the sheriff's department, pulled into the lot.

"That was fast." Harry smiled at the young, attractive deputy.

"Just around the corner at the firehouse going over the parade route for the thousandth time."

"Look." Miranda pointed to her car as Cynthia, notebook in hand, walked over.

"That's just heinous." Cynthia put her arm around Miranda. "Do you have any idea how much they're worth?"

"Not a clue." Miranda's pink lips, shiny with lipstick, pursed together.

"That's probably why someone stole them. Because they're hard to find. They must be worth something," Harry thought out loud.

*"Why can't she put on new hubcaps?"* Pewter, irritated, wanted to get on the road again.

*"Not the same."* Tucker sniffed the wheels hoping for human scent but the perpetrator had pried off the hubcaps with something other than his hands.

*"Piffle,"* the gray cat yawned.

"Are we keeping you up?" Harry noticed the large yawn accompanied by a tiny gurgle. "Why don't you go back and sleep in the truck?"

*"Ha, ha,"* Mrs. Murphy laughed.

*"Aren't we the perfect puss?"* Pewter growled at the tiger cat.

*"Don't start. I'd like to have one Saturday where you two don't fight."* Tucker sat between the two cats.

"Tell you what, while I write this up, Harry, pick up the mobile in the squad car and call O'Bannon's. Ask Sean if he has any Falcon hubcaps."

"Funny, I was just on my way over there." Harry trotted over to the squad car, slipped behind the wheel, and dialed on the mobile unit. She punched in the numbers feeling envious. She'd love a mobile phone herself but thought it too expensive. "Hi, Sean, Harry."

"How you doing, Harry?"

"I'm just fine but Mrs. Hogendobber isn't. Someone this very minute stole the hubcaps off her Ford Falcon. Coop's here at the scene of the crime, if you will, and she told me to call you. You wouldn't have any Ford Falcon hubcaps, would you?"

"Yeah," Sean's voice lowered. "I just bought them from the dude who must have stolen them. Dammit."

"We'll be right over." Harry clicked the end button on the phone. "Hey, Coop. He's got them."

"My hubcaps?" Miranda's hand fluttered to her throat.

"He said he just bought them off someone. If they aren't yours it's an odd co-incidence. I said we'd be right over."

"Mrs. Hogendobber, do you feel settled enough to drive your car over there? I'll follow in the squad car."

"Of course I feel settled enough." Miranda couldn't believe the deputy thought she was that ruffled by the theft.

"I'll tag along, too, if you don't mind." Harry picked up Pewter, who was wandering in the direction of the supermarket. "I was going that way anyway."

"Fine." Cynthia opened the door to the squad car.

Mrs. Murphy sat in Harry's lap as she

34

backed out of the parking space. *"First the woodpecker, now the hubcaps. What next?"* *"Extinction by death ray."* Pewter giggled.

# 4

*"Like ants at a picnic."* Mrs. Murphy marveled at the humans, about twenty, walking through lots of elaborate broken columns, pediments, sarcophagi all neatly divided according to function.

The short drive to the building was dotted with large terra-cotta, stone, and ceramic pots. Next to the stone lot was a marble lot with large sheets of roseate marble that must have come from an old hotel lobby, smaller pieces of veined green marble, a bar top perhaps, which rested next to jet-black marble, again all neatly stacked. The largest outdoor lot was filled with rubble from stone walls, building foundations, some blocks hewn square and others natural.

The indoor rooms of the main building contained wooden cornices, fireplace mantels, pilasters, handblown glass, hand-hammered nails, a cornucopia of treasures.

A railroad siding ran parallel to the main building. A flatcar filled with heavy stone cornices, lintels, and copings was near the building. Flatbeds delivered materials and perhaps an old car once a week. Behind that was an old red caboose which stayed as yet unrestored.

Sequestered in the rear of the four acres was Roger's garage shop. Fast-growing pines shielded it from view. Dotted around the various outdoor lots were small neat buildings. They looked like garden sheds and contained tools, old tractor parts, and other items needing protection from the elements.

The animals found the debris less fascinating than the humans but occasionally a whiff of a former occupant, another dog or cat, lingered. Such olfactory information was recent, of course. No such signature wafted from shards saved from the late seventeenth and early eighteenth centuries.

Harry was amazed at the salvage yard's transformation into a kind of architectural dumping ground. The last time she had visited, Sean's father, Tiny Tim, who was tight as a tick with his money, jovially presided over the place, one big yard filled with rusting cars. Tim collected old gravestones as he was interested in the stonemasons' carvings. He'd talk about the tombstones, then move to the broader subject of death.

Tiny Tim vehemently opposed autopsies. When he died his wife and sons did not request one so no one knew exactly what he died from, but a lifetime of smoking, drinking, and eating anything that didn't eat him first probably did him in.

Sean, long and lean, wore a faded orange canvas shirt tucked into carpenter's pants. Grease was not ground into his hands, no smears of oil or dirt besmirched his shirt. He could have been a greengrocer except for the carpenter's pants.

One wall displayed specialized tools used in restoration: elegant chisels, small hammers, larger ones, tiny butane torches for peeling back layers of leaded paint. The choices were overwhelming and expensive.

Cynthia and Miranda approached the counter.

Sean asked his assistant, Isabella Rojas, to take care of the customer he was serving and he strode across the expanse to greet the two women. "Welcome. I think you're in luck."

Harry caught up with them, the three animals lagging behind. "This is wonderful."

"Thanks." He focused on Miranda. "Mrs. Hogendobber, follow me."

The humans and animals left the main building, walking about four hundred yards to the rear where thousands of hubcaps, sparkling in the sunlight, hung on wires. They were organized according to car model and year.

The glare from the shiny surfaces caused Mrs. Hogendobber to shield her eyes with her hand. "My word, I had no idea there were this many hubcaps in the world."

*"Let's cruise the outbuildings."* Tucker wagged her nonexistent tail. *"Bet they're full of vermin."*

*"You're a ratter, are you?"* Pewter sashayed, a superior air exuding from her gray fur. *"You couldn't catch a comatose mouse."*

*"Look who's talking,"* the corgi called over her shoulder as she sprinted toward the garage building followed by Mrs. Murphy. A trail of fading beer cans gave evidence of Roger O'Bannon's progress. Sobriety was not a virtue associated with Roger.

Pewter declined. For one thing she really didn't care much about mousing or Roger O'Bannon. Birding was her game and she was still put out that Harry had saved the woodpecker for Don Clatterbuck's skills. She wanted to pull the feathers off. Truth be told, Pewter had never killed a bird but she picked up those who died or fell from the nest. She liked yanking out the feathers. She wouldn't eat one. Pewter wouldn't eat anything that wasn't well cooked except for sushi. Something about the darting and dodging of birds excited her and she dreamed of killing the blue jay housed in the maple tree. One day the arrogant fellow would fly too close, run his mouth too loud. She knew her day would come and she'd end his foul abuse. But for the moment she was content to sit at Harry's feet and listen to the tale of the hubcaps.

"My hubcaps!" Miranda reached for the only set of Ford Falcon hubcaps on the line.

"Now, Mrs. H, if you file a theft report I have to impound the hubcaps as evidence. If you don't file, you can put them right back on your car," Cynthia counseled her.

"No!" Miranda shook her head in disbelief.

"That's the law."

"How long will that take?"

"It depends on whether we find the suspect or not. If we do and he comes up for a hearing and then a trial, it could take months — many months." Cooper sighed, for the clogging of the courts wore her out as well as her sister and brother officers. She often thought to herself that people would be far better off trying to solve problems themselves instead of running to the sheriff's department or a lawyer to do it for them. Somehow Americans had lost the ability to sit down and talk to one another, or so it seemed to her.

"Oh, dear, what will the girls at church say?" Miranda worried about driving around undressed, as it were. "Well . . ."

"Maybe we can solve this together." Cynthia focused on Sean, now removing the hubcaps from the line. "The obvious question: who sold you the hubcaps?"

"Usually Roger takes care of the car end of the business but he's not here at the moment," Sean said. "I just happened to be outside when a kid drove up with the hubcaps."

"Know him?"

"No. Never saw him before in my life. I knew the Falcons were rare so I paid fifty dollars for them, wholesale. I priced them at one hundred and twenty and hung them right on the line. If I'd taken a moment to think about it, I might have realized they were Miranda's but the kid said they came off his grandmother's Falcon that had breathed its last."

"What did he look like?"

"Slight. Early twenties. Sandy hair, a pathetic attempt at a mustache." Sean sported a red mustache and closely clipped beard of luxurious density but the curly hair on his

41

head was black and long. He tied it in a ponytail at the nape of his neck. Harry called this a dork knob behind his back.

"Any distinguishing features? Do you remember his clothes or his car?"

"1987 GMC truck. Gray. Virginia plates. Uh, a Dallas Cowboys windbreaker maybe as old as the car and — yes, there was one distinguishing feature. His left eye sagged, an old wound. It was half-closed and a small red scar ran from over the eyebrow to below the eye itself."

"Runny nose? Jumpy?" Cynthia was looking for a fuller picture of the "perp," as she called him.

"No. Calm. Didn't smell alcohol either."

Miranda took out her checkbook as Harry held the hubcaps that Sean had handed to her. The older woman fished around in the bottom of her purse. "I've got a pen in here, I know it."

"Put that away," Sean chided her gently. "I'm not having you pay for what's yours."

"But you paid the thief."

"My problem. I mean it, Miranda. You put that checkbook away right now."

Cynthia thought a moment. "Why don't we do this? You put the hubcaps back on your car. I'll fill out this report and I'll look for the kid. If Rick Shaw" — she mentioned her boss, the sheriff — "wants to see the evidence, I'll send him to you. I just don't see the point of impounding your hubcaps where they'll sit until God knows when. Just let me handle this."

"I don't want to get you in trouble." Miranda appreciated Cynthia Cooper's concern. She had become friends with the young deputy over the last few years.

"A little trouble won't hurt me." She smiled.

"I'm sorry about this." Sean genuinely liked Miranda, as did most people in Crozet.

"Times change and it would appear not for the better. You had nothing to do with it." Miranda smiled back at him.

"If you all don't need me anymore I'll get back to the store. Saturdays are always our busiest day." He took a few steps, then stopped. "You all are coming to the Wrecker's Ball, aren't you? First Saturday in May. It's our fund-raiser for the project Building for Life, which helps poor people who need homes."

"Wouldn't miss it." Cynthia closed her notebook.

"My ex-husband asked me to your ball months ago. I was so proud of him for planning ahead but," Harry laughed, "it's

43

foaling season so for all I know right in the middle of the dance his beeper will go off. The perils of veterinary medicine, I guess."

Fair Haristeen, Harry's former mate, was a much-sought-after equine practitioner. He'd built up a fine practice, constructing a modern clinic with an operating room.

*"Eradicating vermin. Ha,"* Pewter cackled, trying to direct Harry to her furry pals.

Harry looked down at the gray cannonball of a cat. She would have scooped her up but her arms were full of hubcaps.

Miranda whistled for Tucker.

A yip told them where Tucker was and also that the dog was in no hurry to return to the humans.

"Let me put these by your car, Miranda. I'll even put them on for you but I'd better find those two first. Do you mind?"

"Of course not. I'm taking up your Saturday afternoon."

"I was coming here anyway, really I was." Harry walked briskly back to the Falcon, parked in front of the new main building. She stacked the hubcaps by the driver's door.

"Hey, I'll put the hubcaps on. How do we know someone else won't pick them up or try to buy them?" Cynthia came over. "You get the kids."

Harry put Pewter in the truck cab, careful to roll down the window partway even though it wasn't that warm, only in the low fifties. She then hurried back to the garage. "Tucker!"

*"I've got a rat!"* Tucker crowed.

*"A rathole. Be accurate,"* Mrs. Murphy corrected the dog but she, too, knew the rat was in the hole and her tail fluffed out a little. A rat could be a formidable enemy, with teeth that could tear a hunk of flesh right out of you.

Harry opened the large sliding door and slipped in. Three old cars, in various states of interior and exterior rebirth, sat side by side. The walls were hung with tools, an air compressor sat in the corner, and the pièce de résistance, an expensive hydraulic lift in a pit, bore testimony to Roger O'Bannon's passion. Just as Sean loved old buildings, Roger loved old cars; and fortunately for both brothers, the market for old cars and trucks was soaring just like the restoration business.

One wall was filled with tools, vises, rubber fan belts hung on pegboard. Everything was organized and neat except for the garbage can overflowing with beer cans.

Tucker and Murphy crouched in the back right-hand corner of the shop.

"Come on. Time to go," Harry ordered.

*"He's in here. He's got a bag of popcorn."* Tucker's nose never failed her.

*"Wonder where he got the popcorn,"* Mrs. Murphy said.

A voice much deeper than expected startled them. *"The vending machine. I know how to get in and out. Now leave me alone before I tear your face off."*

*"I'll rip your throat out first!"* Tucker ferociously replied.

*"Listen, you nipshit, I've got lots of ways in and out of this joint. If I want to I can just slip out and you won't even know it. But this is my living room and I want you out."*

*"You can't talk to me that way. I'm Tucker Haristeen!"*

*"Yeah, and I'm the Pope. Look, Tucker, you're on my turf, I'm not on yours. And take that cat with you before I get really mean."*

"You two are pushing the envelope!" Harry grunted as she lifted an uncooperative Tucker. "Now we're going and I mean it. Mrs. Murphy, if I have to come back here for you, no catnip tonight. Is that clearly understood?"

*"Mean. You can be so mean sometimes,"* Mrs. Murphy grumbled.

*"Pope Rat, I will come back here and get*

you! *Your days are numbered,"* Tucker promised.

*"Dream on."* Laughter emanated from the hole.

Two disgruntled creatures joined a languid Pewter on the front seat, the driver's window rolled down partway. Miranda had waited for them. Cynthia had left to respond to a fender bender at Wyant's store in Whitehall.

"Thank you again, Harry."

"Please." Harry waved her hand as if to say it was nothing. "What are you going to do for the rest of the day?"

"I'm going to plant pink dogwoods at the edge of my front yard. It needs an anchor. Did you know that the Romans planted quince trees at their property corners? It's a good plan but I'm going to plant dogwoods, pink." She drew out the word "pink" until it sounded like "pa-ank."

"Pretty."

"What are you going to do?"

"Plow the garden. It's about time."

"We might have one more frost but I doubt it. Although I remember one year back in the fifties when we had a frost in May. Don't forget to plant okra for me."

Before either woman could get in her vehicle, Roger rumbled through the opened front gates. A shiny trailer rolled behind his Ford dually. Unlike a horse trailer, this one had no side windows, slats, or side doors.

He screeched to a stop. "Hey, babe."

"Am I the fourteenth woman you've called 'babe' this morning?"

"Nah, the ninth." He pulled over so traffic could get in and out, cut the motor, and stepped out of the rig. "Mrs. Hogendobber, you're a babe, too, but your boyfriend would knock my teeth down my throat so how about if I just say, 'Hi, lovely lady.' "

"Roger, you're an original." The good woman smiled.

They filled him in on the hubcap episode. He was delighted the hubcaps had been recovered immediately.

As the humans chatted Pewter remarked, *"If he'd lose twenty pounds, trim up his hair, and take a little more care about his person he'd pass."*

*"As what?"* Mrs. Murphy snickered.

That made Pewter and Tucker laugh. Tucker stuck her nose out the slightly opened driver's window.

*"Kinda chilly."* Pewter ruffled her fur.

*"Yep,"* Tucker replied, watching Roger drop the tailgate to proudly display his stock car. They stepped up the tailgate ramp for a closer look at this latest incarna-

48

tion of the Pontiac Trans Am.

"— someday." Roger crossed his arms over his chest.

"Well, I hope you do get into big-time racing but, Roger, it's so dangerous."

"Your green Hornet is impressive." Harry admired the brilliant metallic-green Pontiac.

"Oh, I love this machine, I do, but it's kind of the difference between" — he thought a minute — "a real nice horse and a great horse. NASCAR is the top of the top, you know. I'm down here in the bush league."

"You've got a lot of horses right here." She patted the long hood of the car, then stepped back onto the ramp. "Grease monkey."

He turned up his palms, grease deep in the skin. "Daddy had me swinging that wrecker's ball by the time I was twelve. In the blood. 'Chines." He looked up at the steel giraffe. "Still works." Then he looked at Harry. "Come on."

If it had a motor in it, Harry was enthralled. She clambered up the metal steps ringing with each footfall, up to the operator's cab.

*"What is she doing?"* Pewter crossly complained, paws on the dash as she peered up-

ward through the windshield.

Mrs. Murphy and Tucker followed her example. They heard the motor fire up.

"You know," Miranda said out loud, "I believe I'll move my car."

*"If she's getting out of here, we should do the same."* Pewter headed for the open driver's-side window.

*"Worrywart."* Mrs. Murphy barely got the words out of her mouth when the wrecker's ball swung over the roof of the truck, over part of the new main building's roof.

*"Adios!"* Pewter flew out the window.

*"Damn."* Tucker scrambled to the window; it was a long drop for the dog.

*"Don't worry, Tucker, I can open the door."* Murphy leaned hard on the door handle, pressing with all her weight.

Hearing the click, the corgi pushed against the door, which opened, Tucker nearly tumbling out. Once on the ground, cat and dog bolted just as the ball passed over on its way back.

*"Every cat for herself,"* Pewter called from under a neatly stacked crosshatched pile of railroad ties.

Miranda crouched in her Falcon, which she'd parked next to those railroad ties. "Tell you what, I hope that boy is sober." She emerged from her car thinking if any-

thing did go wrong she'd have a better chance on foot.

*"Me, too,"* Pewter concurred.

Up in the operator's cab, Roger brought the ball back up to the nose of the crane. "Your turn."

She sat on the cracked black leather seat, warm from Roger. "Ready."

"If you want the ball to go down — no, don't grab them yet — you squeeze these calipers. Closing them completely dumps the ball straight down. Smash.

"If you want to swing the ball use this set of calipers here, here on the left, and the wheel" — he pointed to the steering wheel — "will move the whole deal, turn the cab and the crane, see. Got it?"

"Piece of cake." She smiled as she swung the ball, slowly, over the other side of the fence, keeping her eyes glued to the ball. "Bet you get to a point where you can work the calipers, the wheel, the pedals kind of like a drummer."

" 'Zactly, but I say if you can drive a tractor you can learn to do most any heavy equipment work."

She brought the ball back up, let it down a little bit, then brought it up to the nose. "This is so cool."

"Yeah."

Sean strode outside, looking upward along with his customers who were outside. He shouted, trying to be heard over the heavy diesel motor, "Roger!"

Roger leaned out of the cab, saluting his brother, then he swung back in. "He is so old. Turned into an old man. I'm telling you, I love my brother but, Jesus H. Christ, he is such a pain in the ass. Like this business is the center of the universe. Ever since Dad passed. Okay, okay, everyone has to make a living but Sean thinks he's the indispensable person. Hey, the cemeteries are filled with indispensable people, you know what I mean, Harry Barry?" He sighed. "Miss seeing you around."

"Thanks, Rog. What a nice thing to say."

He shook his head. "We've got the yard on an even keel. Working like dogs but all I ask" — he waved again to his gesticulating brother, then cut the motor — "is to go to the tracks Friday and Saturday nights." He glanced down. Sean hadn't moved. "Big Brother is watching you. Well, babe, lesson's over."

"I loved it."

As they climbed down, the three animals hurried back to the truck, jumped in, and together using the armrest pulled the door back.

Tucker had to jump onto the floorboard first but she scratched up on the seat and helped pull the door back with the kitties.

*"She doesn't need to know I can open the door."* Mrs. Murphy raised her long silky eyebrows.

*"What she doesn't know won't hurt her."* Pewter giggled.

*"I'm thrilled to be alive,"* Tucker exhaled. *"Seeing that black ball swoosh over my head did not inspire confidence."*

Harry, enthusiastically reporting her lesson to Miranda, didn't notice the animals shutting the truck door. She hadn't even noticed it was open in the first place and she was so excited when she was up with the wrecker's ball she missed the people scattered below.

Sean fired off a few choice words to Roger, who shrugged. Sean turned on his heel, stalking back into the main building.

Roger smiled at the two women. "The only question worth asking yourself is, 'Am I having fun?' "

Harry drove home feeling the day had improved considerably. As she turned down her long farm road to the house she noticed a gleaming BMW 740il parked in front of the barn. The car belonged to BoomBoom

Craycroft, a marvelously beautiful woman who had had an affair with Harry's ex-husband, making her a least-favorite of Harry's. Granted, BoomBoom had slept with Fair Haristeen after Harry had separated from him. Still, the affair had lasted for about six months. Harry was devastated. Of all women, BoomBoom! She had competed against the tall beauty since grade school. Harry usually won the athletic and intellectual events, although BoomBoom ran a close second along with Harry's best friend, Susan Tucker. But where no female classmate could compete with Boom was her effect on the male of the species. Most men, especially when they were young and not wise in feminine wiles, fell for BoomBoom like the proverbial ton of bricks.

The two women had managed an accord over the last few years but that was the extent of it.

"Damn, damn, damn," Harry whispered under her breath.

*"If you'd let me catch that rat she would have come and gone,"* Tucker unhelpfully suggested.

*"Tucker, shut up. You know how they can get. It's all hands on deck."* Mrs. Murphy put her paws on the dash.

## 5

"I'm so glad you're here. I was just about to leave," BoomBoom effused as the three horses watched her from the paddock.

"We're in luck," Harry dryly replied as Mrs. Murphy, Pewter, and Tucker scrambled to see who could get out of the truck first.

Pewter won only because she used Mrs. Murphy's back, banking off her to touch the edge of the seat, then slide down, front paws onto the running board and onto the ground.

*"I don't believe you did that!"* Murphy was furious.

*"Toodle-oo."* The gray cat made a beeline for the house, where she knew a large bowl of crunchies waited on the kitchen counter.

*"Pretty good for a fat girl."* Tucker eased herself down.

*"Don't take up for her."*

*"I'm not but it is amazing."*

The cat replied with a laugh, *"You're right,*

*though, she can be agile when she has to be. After all, she is a cat."*

"Self-regarding, *you cats."* Tucker walked over to greet BoomBoom, who leaned over, petting the dog's glossy head.

Mrs. Murphy, now out of sorts, thumped into the barn, walked into the tack room, sat down hard, and shouted at the tiny mouse-hole in the wall, *"I know you're in there. I tell you, you'll be mouse soufflé before Memorial Day."*

The mice, sound asleep, didn't reply. Further agitated, the cat returned to the house, where the humans had now repaired. Maybe she could irritate someone in there.

Despite her antipathy, Harry had minded her manners and invited BoomBoom into the house for tea or a soft drink.

BoomBoom sat in the living room, ensconced in one of the old wing chairs Harry's parents had bought forty years ago for five dollars apiece because they were circa 1930s, unfashionable at the time, and beat-up. Since then they'd been re-covered five times; the last time, before her death, Harry's mother had had them redone in soft green leather, an extravagance on the one hand but a prudent expense if one considered the long run. The chances were that Harry would never have to re-cover the chairs in her lifetime.

"I have a teeny-weeny problem." BoomBoom cast her eyes downward, which meant the problem had just increased in size. "I'm hoping you'll help me."

"Oh. Why not ask Susan?" Harry volunteered her best friend, who got along with BoomBoom better than Harry did.

"Susan is married."

"Ah." Harry was getting the picture.

Mrs. Murphy strode into the room, sat down on the coffee table, and yelled, *"Everybody is horrible! Only I am perfect."*

"Murphy, what's the matter with you?" Harry swatted at her to leave the room.

The tiger cat eluded this clumsy effort by jumping onto the wing chair, taking up residence on the back behind BoomBoom's beautiful, long blond hair, held up in a simple swirled French twist. Having just left the hairdresser's, BoomBoom's tresses were lighter than usual. *"BoomBoom has big bosoms. Bet she blacks her eye when she jogs. Bet it's hard to bend over and stand up again. Maybe her face just hits the floor,"* she warbled, quite pleased with herself.

"Boom, push her off of there. She's being naughty."

"I don't mind the noise. The tuna breath is what gets me." BoomBoom laughed.

58

*"Tuna breath?"* Mrs. Murphy's eyes widened, the beautiful electric color seemingly brighter. She unleashed one dagger claw, expertly hooking it into the pretty tortoiseshell clip holding up Boom's hair. With a flick she dislodged half of it so Boom's golden hair fell out of place.

"Now that is enough!" Harry, angry, stood up, grabbed the cat — who offered no resistance — and dropped her to the floor. "One more stunt like that and you're sleeping in the barn tonight."

Pewter, observing the display, coolly said, *"She's only doing what you'd like to do, Mom. You can't stand BoomBoom."*

*"Right."* Mrs. Murphy, emboldened by the support of Pewter, emitted another yowl.

*"First you fight and now you're best friends. You two are infantile."* The dog rolled her eyes. She had squeezed next to Harry on the sofa.

*"Big word, Tucker. Congratulations,"* Mrs. Murphy said sarcastically as she turned her back on the company and lifted the tip of her tail in her right paw, bringing it to her lips for grooming.

*"Hee hee."* Pewter couldn't resist laughing because it was funny to her but also because it would make the dog mad.

Tucker ignored them, placing her head in

Harry's lap, looking as adorable as possible.

*"You know what I'm doing, I'm venting. Humans vent all the time,"* Murphy said.

*"I wouldn't imitate humans."* Pewter thought about grooming but then decided she was too tired. *"It's a species that has as its motto: I can't always do it the hard way but I can try. They make everything so complicated, no wonder they vent, bitch, and moan. It's their own fault."*

*"There is that,"* the tiger cat agreed with her.

BoomBoom had just finished an elliptical tangent that finally returned to its starting point, her need of Harry's help — ". . . so you see Susan wouldn't be quite right and Lottie Pearson is too eager, if you know what I mean. She parties in D.C., Richmond, and Charlotte, all in search for a man of means. She's beginning to get panicky about marriage, I swear. Of course she says she's canvassing for contributors to the university. Her job as a fund-raiser covers a multitude of sins, I swear." Lottie Pearson was a social acquaintance of BoomBoom's, whom she sometimes liked and sometimes didn't. Today was a didn't.

Harry, fearing what was coming, quickly interjected, "But Lottie Pearson is single and Susan is not. That's a plus." Harry echoed BoomBoom's earlier dismissal of turning to Susan for help. She wished BoomBoom would get to the point. Exactly what did she want?

"Lottie Pearson will complicate things. I really don't want my friends interviewed about their net worth."

"Boom, you're losing me here. What friends? What net worth?"

After a long, refreshing draft of steaming-hot Plantation Mint tea, the tall woman placed the china cup in the matching saucer and laid them on the coffee table. "Your grandmother's china. I remember your grandmother."

"Mom's mom." Harry smiled, an image of a lean, silver-haired lady crossing her mind.

"She was a good teacher. Pony Club."

Pony Club teaches young people all aspects of horsemanship. Riding is but a small portion of one's skills.

Harry leaned forward. "Remember when she made us take apart a bridle, strip it, dip it, put it back together, and she inspected everyone's work? Susan tried to cheat and used a toothbrush to clean around the bit instead of totally dismantling it?"

BoomBoom laughed. "And then she gave that lecture on shortcuts. Hey, I can still hear her voice when I'm considering the lazy way — 'the shortest way around is often the longest.' "

As they neared forty both women were slowly realizing that shared experiences were binding. Time possesses the greatest power. Men who fought on opposite sides in a war, in old age, often felt closer to their former enemies than people of their own nationality who were younger.

"You know." BoomBoom lowered her voice, a sweet, dark soprano, a counterpoint to Harry's liquid alto. If the two had sung together they would have sounded heavenly. "I've been seeing this divine man. He's so interesting. He's urbane, speaks four languages, and he's tremendously intelligent. He's coming down this weekend and at the last minute his assistant at the embassy said he could come and —"

"Embassy?"

"Yes. He's Under-Secretary to the Ambassador for Uruguay."

"Who?" Harry was fighting exasperation.

"My friend, Thomas Steinmetz, is Under-Secretary." BoomBoom threw up her hands. "I'm going in circles. Will you escort my friend's friend? That's what I'm trying to ask."

Now this was interesting. The two cats

and dog turned their heads to stare at Harry, who blinked.

*"Say something,"* Mrs. Murphy suggested to Harry.

"Uh —"

BoomBoom tried to be more organized now that the cat was out of the bag, so to speak. "Handsome. Fun. A lot of fun really. Recently divorced."

"How recently?"

"U-m-m, a year."

"Why are you asking me, really?"

"Because you're fun, you're very attractive, and because, well, you never know." She held up her hand, her large diamond reflecting the light.

"Know what?"

"When lightning will strike."

Harry scrunched down in the sofa a bit. Tucker refused to budge. "Tucker."

*"I don't want to miss a thing,"* the bright-eyed corgi replied to the complaint.

*"Ha,"* both cats giggled.

"Harry, you need to get out more." BoomBoom picked up the teacup once more.

"How ironic coming from you."

When Harry and Fair separated and filed for divorce, his brief affair with BoomBoom kept tongues wagging in Crozet. It was like the small-town version of being splashed across the front page of the tabloids.

Harry always felt that Fair could have picked someone out of town or that BoomBoom could have refused him. The fact that both Fair and BoomBoom were great-looking people, in the prime of life, escaped her.

"You're still angry with me and I've done all but grovel, and I repeat for the thousandth time, he was separated from you. Separated."

Ignoring this because she didn't believe BoomBoom's version of the timing of the affair, Harry plunged in. "Well, it hurt like hell. And just why didn't you stay with him?"

"I could never be a veterinarian's wife."

Truer words were never spoken. Not only could BoomBoom not stand the schedule of an equine vet, those calls for colic coming right in the middle of a romantic evening, she needed more position, more power, more money.

BoomBoom's affair with Pharamond "Fair" Haristeen, DVM, owed something to putting herself back together after the shock of her young husband's sudden death. To her credit, though, she never used her loneliness as an excuse.

On Fair's part, the affair was a flight from responsibility, pure and simple. He realized it. Broke it off after six months and went into therapy — a tremendously difficult thing for him to do, to ask for help. After the first year of therapy, he begged his ex-wife's forgiveness. He still hoped to win Harry back. She was the best mate he could find and he knew it. She understood horses. She understood him. She expected to work hard in this life and what she asked in return was a partner who also worked hard, remained faithful, and had a good sense of humor. He knew he could do that now.

She remained diffident, although at times she would be pulled back toward him not just emotionally but physically, and that only stirred the pot. Not that she told BoomBoom but Susan knew, of course, and Mrs. Hogendobber suspected.

The animals remained discreet on the subject.

Harry, silent for a while, finally spoke. "What I don't get is why you won't leave me alone? Why is it so important that we be — something?"

"Because we're part of one another's lives. We grew up together. And because we're women and women are smarter than men about these things."

"I don't think I'm smarter than a man about infidelity."

"But he wasn't unfaithful, Harry. You were separated." BoomBoom made this point again, as though speaking to a slow child.

"Can we table this?" Harry rolled her eyes heavenward.

"You've been tabling it for years. Surely we can coexist. We work on all the same projects."

"So does everyone else. It's a small town," Harry said peevishly.

"We hunt together, we play golf and tennis together."

"I hardly ever play golf and tennis. I haven't got the time." Harry fidgeted.

"Okay." BoomBoom took a deep breath. "Will you be Diego Aybar's date?"

"That's his name?"

"Diego Aybar. And trust me, he is handsome, full of energy — even if lightning doesn't strike, you'll enjoy his company. Please say yes, Harry. I know he'll like you and it will be an unforgettable weekend for all of us."

"Fair asked me to the Wrecker's Ball. I could go to everything but that and I'm parade coordinator for the festival" — she paused — "but you know that. 'Course once that last float pushes off —"

*"Say yes,"* Pewter meowed. *"A little shake-*

up in the status quo can't hurt."

"All status and no quo." Mrs. Murphy watched her human struggle with conflicting emotions, the most obvious being mistrust of BoomBoom.

"Harry, if you don't like this, if you suffer through the weekend I'll buy you that new Wilson tennis racquet everyone is raving about. Then you can beat me."

"I beat you anyway. You don't have to bribe me, BoomBoom."

"Well?"

"Clothes?"

"God, she's a hard nut to crack." Pewter exhaled.

"And lacking in all spontaneity but I love her," Mrs. Murphy purred as she leaned into Pewter who'd come up right next to her.

"Don't you two make a pretty picture, but I'm next to Mom and you aren't."

Rising to the little dog's challenge, the cats leapt onto the back of the sofa. They plopped down behind Harry's head.

"It will be fun. All you need is a spring dress for the tea. Your white evening gown looks lovely on you. You need only one new dress. I know how you hate to shop."

"That evening gown was Mother's."

"Classic. Christian Dior classic. Your mother had fabulous taste."

"And no money. She won the gown." Harry smiled, remembering her mother and her pride in the gown that she had, in fact, won in a contest to design the Christmas Ball for the United Way. Christian Dior, a friend of Tally's — Big Mim's aunt who knew everyone and anyone — put up the gown as a reward.

"Come on. It will wake up Fair. He has no competition."

Harry uncrossed her arms. "That's a fact." Her eyebrows twitched together a moment. "All right, BoomBoom. I'll do it. I don't exactly know why I'm doing it but I'm doing it."

"Thank you."

*"Spring fever,"* Pewter laconically said, a small burp following.

*"Excuse yourself, pig."* Mrs. Murphy reached out and touched Pewter on the shoulder.

*"Excuse me. Spring fever."*

*"Pewter, what are you talking about?"* Tucker wanted an answer. She hated it when the cats got "airy," as she called it.

*"Spring fever. That's why Harry is going out with this new guy."*

*"You might be right,"* Mrs. Murphy agreed. *"This will get Lottie Pearson's knickers in a twist. She's on the man hunt and BoomBoom*

68

*ignored her in favor of Mom. She'll have her revenge. Just wait."*

"On whom? Mom or BoomBoom?" Tucker lifted her head.

*"Both, if I know Lottie. Her social ambitions seethe. Being escorted by a handsome man working on Washington's Embassy Row is her idea of perfect. She'd get to meet more important people and she'd look important. She cultivates people, I guess that's how you put it, before she asks them for hundreds of thousands of dollars for the university. She'd like to run this town someday, too. Never happen. Big Mim will live to be one hundred and fifty. Look how old Aunt Tally is. They never die, I swear. But you mark my words, Lottie Pearson is smart and devious. She'll get her revenge."*

*"It's so petty!"* Pewter exclaimed.

*"Precisely but that's the way people are. They're further and further removed from nature, and they get weird, major weird."* Mrs. Murphy watched as Harry walked Boom-Boom to the back door in the kitchen.

*"Spring fever."* Pewter marched back into the kitchen for more crunchies.

69

# 6

The work week rolled along without incident. Harry and Miranda sorted mail, light this time of year. Big Mim made pronouncements about how to improve the Dogwood Festival before Saturday's parade. Everyone smiled, said, "You're right," and went about their business.

Fair, Harry's ex-husband, was just wrapping up foaling and breeding season. Upon hearing that Harry would be accompanying Diego Aybar to the tea party and then the dance, he fumed; but Fair had committed the mistake of thinking he didn't need to ask Harry. He assumed she would be his date if he could shake free of work. Usually a low-key and reasonable man, he slammed the door to her kitchen, upsetting the cats and secretly delighting Harry.

Miranda glowed for her high-school beau, who would be returning from Hawaii, where he had finally settled his estate, would be her escort for all festivities. She was to pick him up at the airport Friday morning and she figured he'd bounce back from his travails and travel by Saturday, the big day. Tracy Raz, former star athlete of Crozet High, class of 1950, was a tough guy and an interesting one, too.

Reverend Herbert C. Jones, pastor of the Lutheran church and parade marshal this year, was the most jovial anyone had ever seen him, which was saying something as the good pastor was normally an upbeat fellow.

Little Mim, as vice-mayor of Crozet, used this opportunity to insist more trash barrels be placed on the parade route. She endeared herself to the merchants in town by having flags made up at her own expense for them to hang over their doorways. The flags, "Crozet" emblazoned across a French-blue background, also had a railroad track embroidered on the bottom right-hand side. As Crozet was named for Claudius Crozet, former engineering officer with Napoleon's army, she hoped out-of-towners would ask about the tracks. Crozet, after capture in Russia, again rejoined the emperor for Waterloo, managing to escape the Royalists and sail to America. He cut four tunnels into the Blue Ridge Mountains, an engineering feat considered one of the wonders of the nineteenth century. His work — sans dynamite, using only picks, shovels, and axes — stands to this day, as do the roads he built from the Tidewater into the Shenandoah Valley.

The town itself never became a glamorous depot but remained a quiet stop before one plunged into the mountains themselves. Most residents worked hard for a living, but a few enjoyed inherited wealth, Little Mim being one, which is why she paid for the flags herself. She thought if merchants hung the flags out it would create further color for the day, showing pride in the community. Not that residents of the small, unpretentious town lacked pride but rather, in that quiet Virginia way, they didn't speak of it. The surrounding countryside, dotted with apple orchards, drew tourists from all over the world, as did Albemarle County itself, laboring under the ghosts of Jefferson and Monroe, to say nothing of all the movie stars, sports stars, and literary lights who had moved there, enticed by the natural beauty of the place and the University of Virginia. As it was only an hour by air from New York City, some of the richest residents commuted daily in their private jets.

Crozetians, although part of Albemarle County, more or less ignored Charlottesville, the county seat.

Little Mim, a Republican, and her father, a Democrat, now ran the town together. He was grooming her as well as pressuring her to jump parties. So far, she had resisted.

The merchants adored her, not just because of the flags. Like her father, she had a natural flair for politics.

Lottie Pearson assisted Little Mim. Both women were five feet six inches, slender, and well-groomed. Since both favored bright spring sweaters, khaki slacks, and flats, the only way you could tell them apart from the back was that Lottie's hair was honey brown while Little Mim's was ash blond this week. Lottie was much in evidence throughout the week as she climbed on a ladder watering and inspecting the huge hanging baskets at each street corner. Like Fair, she wasn't thrilled about Harry escorting Diego Aybar but she put a good face on it. Little Mim was so busy preparing for the festival that she really hadn't the time to tell anyone what she thought even if she was so inclined. Little Mim, divorced, was beginning to feel lonely. Diego would have been a suitable escort for her, too.

The last task before the parade was hanging the bunting. Everyone pitched in, so the blue and gold colors streamed across

Route 240 and Whitehall Road. Bunting hung from buildings. Blue and gold flags and streamers waved from people's windows. Blue and gold were the colors of the French army under Napoleon, or so the town felt. White and gold with the fleur-de-lis was the emblem of the Royalists, so there wasn't a fleur-de-lis in sight.

In addition to the big wrecker's ball crane, which the O'Bannon brothers used to carry the heavier items through town, they owned a smaller, second crane. Roger perfected the knack of appearing wherever Lottie happened to be, always using the excuse that he had a job to do. He asked her to be his date at the Wrecker's Ball, held the first weekend in May, but she put him off, saying she needed to get through the Dogwood Festival first.

Since she didn't give him a flat no, he felt hopeful. Sean told him to give it up, as did Don Clatterbuck, his fishing buddy. Roger swore he'd win her over.

By Friday night Harry crawled home. She'd womanned the post office by herself since Miranda had to go to the airport. She also thought Miranda and Tracy would have a lot to talk about, so she forbade Miranda from coming back to work. The irony was that Miranda wasn't a postal employee. Her

74

long-deceased husband had been the post-master and she helped out now to keep busy. When George died she drifted in and out of the post office through force of habit. Harry performed many small services for Miranda but felt she could never adequately repay the older woman's boundless generosity.

Determined to go to bed early, Harry slipped into bed by nine; Mrs. Murphy, Pewter, and Tucker, too.

Just as the animals fell asleep, Pewter murmured, *"I have this feeling it's going to be a big, big day tomorrow."*

*"The Dogwood Festival's always big."* Tucker rolled over on her side.

*"Something more."* The gray cat closed her beautiful chartreuse eyes.

Mrs. Murphy, on her back next to Harry, turned her head up to look at Pewter reposing on the pillow. *"Cat intuition."*

# 7

Saturday dawned bright and clear, the temperature at five-thirty a.m. being forty-seven degrees Fahrenheit. The redbuds opened in full bloom, although those in the hollows where it was cooler stayed the dark raspberry color before full flowering. The apple trees still had some blooms but the pear trees were finished, as were the peaches. Tulips and pansies filled gardens in town. But the glory, the highlight, the beauty of spring resided in the dogwoods, which fortuitously chose that exact day to open. The mountains were filled with wild dogwoods. Creamy-pink flowering trees dotted bright green lawns. White and pink dogwoods lined driveways. Everywhere one looked dogwoods bloomed, and to complete the perfection, the azaleas opened, too. Hot pink, soft purple, flaming orange, pure white, and radiant pink azaleas announced their presence heralding high spring in Virginia. The wisteria swaying from doorways and pergolas added lavender and white to the unbelievable color. Old ruins, smothered in wisteria, became a focal point for photographers.

Spring had arrived but not just any spring, spring in the Blue Ridge, the apotheosis of springs.

Harry smiled as she drove to her old high school at nine a.m. The parade would start at ten. Her concession to this task was to apply mascara and to iron her jeans as well as a crisp white shirt. A red crewneck sweater kept her warm. The temperature was fiftyish. Mrs. Murphy, Pewter, and Tucker, old hands at the parade, had been groomed to perfection.

When Harry parked the old truck the temperature had climbed to sixty degrees. By noon she figured it would reach seventy degrees and stay close to that comfortable temperature throughout the day.

Despite the jitters, everyone was smiling as they lined up on the tarmac at Crozet High School. On a day like today not smiling was impossible.

Mrs. Murphy and Pewter sat on a wooden milk crate placed in the bed of the truck. As Harry had parked by the head of the parade, they had the best view. Tucker couldn't stand not being with Harry so she tagged along at her human's heels.

"How do I look?" Reverend Jones held out his arms full-length, a blue and gold marshal's sash covering his chest.

"A million bucks." She smiled. "Are you ready?"

"What do I do but wave?" The older man laughed.

Sean and Roger O'Bannon walked up. Roger, a touch shorter than his brother, had obviously just buzz-cut his sandy hair.

"Time?"

"You've got time." Harry smiled at him. "Like your new haircut."

"Make time." Roger snapped his fingers, ever the younger brother, slightly rebellious. "Do you know this is the fifteenth year I've driven a float? Do I get a medal?"

"No, Roger. It means you're a glutton for punishment." Harry laughed at him.

"Ever since I got my driver's license."

"Liar." Sean poked his brother. "You drove before you had your license."

"Not a float."

"If Dad were here he'd settle this."

"Well, he's not." Roger smacked Harry on the small of her back. "Talk to Lottie for me."

"Why?"

"She's playing hard to get."

"Smart girl." Sean laughed.

Roger growled at him, baring his teeth as fangs. It startled Tucker, who growled back. "I want her to be my date at the Wrecker's Ball."

"You're upsetting my dog," Harry said to Roger.

"Same effect he has on Lottie."

"Sean." Roger threw up his hands in mock despair. "What do women want?"

"Ask us one at a time," Harry swiftly replied.

Roger laughed, "Good answer."

Sean spoke to Roger. "Be persistent and send presents. Always works for me."

"Oh? Since when?" Roger pulled Sean's ponytail.

"You're driving her float. That ought to spike your hormones." Sean readjusted his ponytail. "Make her special."

"Guys, would you like me to leave?"

"I said hormones. I didn't mention his sperm count." Sean smirked. "No help for that."

Harry threw up her hands. "Too much information! Go back to your respective floats."

"You're worse with women than I am," Roger swirled right back at his brother.

"Well?" Harry crossed her arms over her chest.

"I'm going." Roger turned on his heel.

"I'm not." Waiting until his brother was out of earshot, Sean whispered, "Do you think it would do any good if you spoke to Lottie?"

"Hell, no. She's pissed because BoomBoom fixed me up with someone she wanted to go to the dance with."

"Who?"

"I don't know. A friend from Washington. Lottie doesn't know him either but he's new and he has a good position at an embassy. Guess the idea excited her. Anyway, she won't listen to me. Ask Little Mim to help you, since Lottie's been working with her for the festival. Worth a try."

Sean smiled weakly. "Thanks, Har." He took a few steps, then turned back to her. "He's an okay guy, a little rough around the edges. Typical motorhead."

"I know." She winked as Sean set out to find Little Mim.

Harry checked her watch, then her clipboard. She scanned the floats. The O'Bannon Salvage float was an elaborate reconstruction of Monticello made out of salvage.

"They'll win the prize for sure," Reverend Herb whispered in her ear, coming up behind her.

Harry returned to her list. "Herb, you look terrific and you'll pull out in about fifteen minutes. We've got the St. Elizabeth band right behind you and the Mah-Jongg Club."

The Mah-Jongg ladies, most of them in rickshaws being pulled by sturdy-legged youngsters, wore Chinese clothes. The club had been running strong since the 1920s and these were the survivors, Aunt Tally Urquhart among them in an electric-blue dress.

Harry grabbed the bullhorn as she ascended the three-foot-square wooden stand that served as her command post. "Hey, gang." They chattered still. "Earth to parade. Earth to parade." Slowly the assembled, perhaps five hundred strong, quieted. "We are ten minutes from blastoff. If you have to go to the bathroom, do it now." A titter of laughter followed. "Remember, the parade always takes longer than we think it will. There are people with buckets filled with ice, bottled water, Gatorade, along the route. They are there for you. If you feel even a tiny bit thirsty, call out and they'll bring you your drink."

"Scotch on the rocks," Aunt Tally hollered, her voice strong and youthful for a woman in her nineties.

"Oh, you spoiled my present." Reverend Herb Jones trotted over, handing her a bottle of good scotch as everyone around screamed with laughter and the news was passed down the line, with more laughter following in ripples.

*"I could use some catnip."* Pewter was grateful that Harry had put a huge bowl of water in the truck as well as crunchies but she wanted catnip, too.

*"Get in a rickshaw then. Your chances will improve."* Murphy laughed.

*"I just might."* The gray cat leaned over the edge of the truck.

Harry checked her watch again. "Eight minutes."

An athletic figure jogged alongside the assembled floats.

"Welcome home!" Harry beamed, seeing Tracy Raz.

"Hey, girl." He kissed her as she leaned down. "I'll catch up with you later. Cuddles is nervous. I think she's blown every note on her pitch pipe." He laughed at Miranda, whom he sometimes called Cuddles, her high-school nickname.

Miranda was the lead singer for the Church of the Holy Light and the choir was arranged on a float called Stairway to Paradise, which was just what you would expect.

"Have you seen Boom?"

"I did a minute ago. Primping." He smiled.

"Big surprise. Hey, you'll be at the tea dance. I'll find you there."

"You got it." He kissed her again and jogged back down the line, where Miranda could be seen in her choir robes, her back turned toward Harry. The other choir members were taking their places on the stairway to paradise. A few appeared as though their Maker might call them soon enough.

*"Mom, don't forget to drink water yourself,"* Tucker, ever solicitous, barked.

Harry stepped down, lifted the dog, and climbed back up. She didn't understand a word the corgi had said.

Jim Sanburne and Little Mim sat in an open convertible behind Herb's float.

Harry smiled at them and they smiled back. "Little Mim, Sean's looking for you."

"He found me. I'll do what I can," came the unenthusiastic reply.

Lottie was on the third float, Daughters of Time, sponsored by the United Daughters of the Confederacy. Lottie's hoopskirt was so big a stiff wind would send her airborne. Roger was driving that float while Sean was driving the O'Bannon float.

"Four minutes," Harry called out.

A tug at her jeans behind her turned her around. BoomBoom, dressed as a 1920s flapper for the Heart Fund float, said, "I want you to meet Diego before the tea. Mary Minor Haristeen, please meet Diego Aybar."

Harry's mouth moved but nothing came out. She was staring into the liquid brown eyes of one of the most gorgeous men she had ever seen. "Uh — welcome to Crozet."

"My pleasure. BoomBoom tells me I should meet you at Aunt Tally's" — he said "Aunt Tally's" with a Spanish accent and a hint of good humor — "garden. She says everyone falls in love in the garden."

"With the garden." Harry smiled.

"No, in the garden," BoomBoom corrected. "Listen, I've got to get back on my float. Diego, the two best places to see the parade are from the back of Harry's truck or on the corner of Route 240 and Whitehall Road."

"Try the truck," Harry stammered. "The two cats are good companions."

The two cats at that very moment were laughing at their mother, who was in a state. Neither could ever remember seeing Harry like that.

"The best friends come on four feet," he said in his beguiling light baritone.

*"Now there's a man with sense."* Mrs. Murphy walked forward to greet him as he gracefully bounded into the truck bed.

"One minute," Harry called into the bullhorn.

Reverend Herb Jones straightened up, took a deep breath. In the car behind him, Little Mim leaned over and kissed her father on the cheek. The drivers started their motors. Some band members threw back their shoulders, others licked their reeds, while the drummers spun their drumsticks in anticipation.

"Ten, nine, eight, seven, six, five, four, three, two, one — showtime!" Harry called.

The drummers clicked their sticks in rhythm. The four different high-school bands interspersed throughout the parade marched in place. The Reverend Jones cruised first, slowly out of the school lot. The St. Elizabeth band, first with the music, initially walked out to bass drums only, *boom, boom, boom;* then the snare drums kicked in and within a minute they all burst forth with the ever-popular theme song from *Rocky.*

Harry waved as each group passed her. She heard the roar from all the people crowded along the path. Tears sprang into her eyes. She felt as if her own life were parading before her. The sight of Tally Urquhart in her rickshaw, participating in her ninety-second parade (Tally was a star even as a toddler) brought the tears rolling down.

What great good fortune to be where you know people, you love people, and hopefully they love you. The fact that her family had nested here immediately after the Revolutionary War, having drifted over from the Tidewater, where they'd lived since 1640, only deepened the experience of home.

Tucker crowded next to Harry. Tucker loved music. The cats had leapt to the roof of the truck so as not to miss a single thing.

Harry waved as friends and neighbors passed, and then she glanced back at Diego. His smile was five thousand megawatts. She smiled back at him, grateful that this small slice of Virginia pleased him. It hadn't occurred to her that she pleased him, too.

Harry felt as though her chest would burst. The joy, as high as grief was deep, nearly overwhelmed her.

# 8

Although covering less than two miles from the high school to the town's main intersection, the route was hilly. The float builders, knowing this, had devised railings and props such as fake boulders with little handholds on them, so that the people on the floats could grab them when the floats rolled downhill.

Lottie Pearson forgot this. When the Daughters of the Confederacy float dipped into the decline just before the fire department, she lurched off the float, saved only by the metal in her hoopskirt, which hit the pavement first. Unhurt, she was helped back on the float by friends standing along the parade route. Roger couldn't leave the truck. Lottie's skirt was bent, which meant her pantaloons showed. Each time she pushed the skirt back into place it popped up on the back side. The result drew cheers and laughter but not of the sort she hoped to hear. As she was the leading lady on the float, the one right up front, she was loath to relinquish her position. If the choice was between obscurity and showing her ass, Lottie bravely decided to show her ass.

As the last band marched out of the parking lot, the black and red of Albemarle High, Harry hopped down from her perch.

*"Mom's got a little tan. Looks good against her white T-shirt,"* Pewter noted as Harry removed her sweater with the day's warming. Pewter giggled, remembering the sight of Harry ironing her jeans and T-shirt.

*"Nobody looks better in jeans than Harry,"* Tucker called out from behind her mother. *"I mean, if this fellow likes a fit body then he has to like Mom."*

Mrs. Murphy loved her mother, but she realized that not all men like natural women. Many, attracted by artifice, want lots of hair, preferably blond, boobs pushed up to the max, long fingernails, expensive clothes, and perfect makeup. In a word, BoomBoom.

Harry actually was a beautiful woman but she had no sense of it. High cheekbones accentuated wonderful facial bone structure. Her long black eyelashes drew attention to her soft brown eyes. She rarely wore lipstick on her full lips. Her hair, short and black, curled just above the nape of her neck. But one had to study Harry to recognize her beauty. A woman like BoomBoom hit one over the head with it.

As Harry had no vanity she was able to concentrate on whomever she encountered. She didn't think she was pretty. She didn't worry about the impression she was making. Her focus was on the other person. This quality beguiled more men than her looks once they got around to really studying her. There was an innocence about her. It never occurred to her, not once, that she might be attractive to men. She had known her ex-husband since kindergarten. The art of flirting, of luring men, seemed irrelevant to her since she had always loved Fair. When he left her she assumed she'd never love again. She didn't launch into tirades about how awful men were, how they used women and dumped them, the usual cry of the abandoned female. Harry had seen women behave execrably toward men. As far as she was concerned one gender was as bad as the other.

Fair's attempts to reconcile touched her. She truly loved him but now in quite a different way. At first she felt she could never trust him again. Lately, she thought maybe she could. He'd learned and she'd learned but the difficult part was that she didn't know if she'd feel romantic about him again.

Certainly she could go to bed with him. She knew his body the way a blind woman knows Braille. However, that didn't constitute romantic desire.

She didn't share these thoughts with Susan or Miranda. Harry kept her deepest thoughts to herself, sometimes asking the animals for their opinion.

As Mrs. Murphy watched Harry approach the truck she felt the lightness in her step, the surge of energy that illuminated her human's face.

*"How could Diego not like Mom . . . but is he good enough?"* Mrs. Murphy stretched. *"After all, we are better judges of character than humans. We need to check out this situation."*

*"You're right and I should have thought of that straight off."* Tucker felt guilty.

*"You would have eventually."* Mrs. Murphy hopped into the bed of the truck just as Diego, of average height and muscular, hopped out.

*"Oh, balls,"* Pewter disagreed. *"One human is pretty much like any other. They make a big deal out of these tiny, tiny differences but as a species they're all cut from the same cloth."*

*"Mother's better."* Tucker defended Harry, whom she loved with all her heart.

*"They do fuss over nits and nit-picking but I think they're very different from one another*

and that's their challenge. They are herd animals and they need one another to survive but they can't build communities to include everyone. It's a real mess. They don't understand their fundamental nature, which is to be part of the herd," Murphy stated.

"I'm not part of any herd." Pewter proudly jumped down next to Murphy.

"Of course not. You're a cat," Murphy said.

"Murphy, this herd idea sounds good but you once said that dogs are pack animals and here I am — not with other dogs." Tucker waited for Harry to put her in the cab of the truck.

"We're your pack." Mrs. Murphy drove home her point. "The fact that we're cats plus one human is beside the point."

"H-m-m." Tucker pondered this as the humans chatted. "I never thought of that."

"Mrs. Murphy, Cat Supreme." Murphy pushed out her chest, then laughed.

". . . merrier." Diego finished his sentence, which had started out "The more." He had agreed to ride in the cab of the truck with two cats, one dog, and Harry. He didn't seem to mind at all.

Harry drove them around the back way. They parked near the main intersection, walking the last block. The cats remained in the truck with the windows open. Neither one liked crowds, although they usually rode on Harry's shoulders if they had to enter a fray. Pewter complained about the marching music. She preferred Mozart. Furthermore, the trumpets hurt her ears. Mrs. Murphy thought it was time for her noon nap.

Tucker eagerly accompanied Harry and Diego. As they reached the main intersection the people lined the road four deep, a lot for Crozet. At five feet ten inches, Diego could see over most of the crowd, but Harry, at five feet six, had to stand on her tiptoes.

Diego gently worked his way to the front, reached back for Harry's hand, and pulled her up with him. When people saw it was their postmistress carrying Tucker they gladly gave way.

They'd no sooner reached their place than the United Daughters of the Confederacy float rolled by, with Lottie and her pantaloons evoking comment.

Harry heard Roger O'Bannon yell to a bystander, "Give me twenty bucks and I'll dump them all on the road."

Laughter greeted this offer. Lottie ignored it, of course.

Spurred on by the laughter Roger stuck his head farther out of the truck, artfully concealed by the float. "Hey, Lottie, why don't you ditch the hoop?"

"Shut up, Roger."

"You'd better be good to me. I'm driving this boat." He laughed loudly. She ignored him again so he catcalled, "Lottie, oh, Lottie Pearson."

"Roger, for God's sake, watch where you're going."

They were cruising close to the side of the road.

"Just trying to get you girls a nice cold drink."

Danny Tucker, Susan's son, rushed up, two drinks in each hand. The ladies eagerly reached down.

"How did women wear these things?" one young lady grumbled, for the finery was heavier than anything she had ever worn before.

"They didn't wear them every day," Lottie snapped, then remembered her attention should focus on the crowd. She smiled big and waved, then she saw, really saw Diego Aybar. Her smile froze. She recovered and continued to ignore Roger, whose suggestions grew ever more risqué.

By the end of the parade the mood of the participants and the crowd was even more elevated than at the beginning. The reason for this was that the Veterans of Foreign Wars had a small brass band with two snares and they peeled out of the parade as it ended, marching and playing all the while. They marched straight into a small bar where they continued to hold forth.

BoomBoom was taking a Polaroid of Don Clatterbuck and Roger at the float. The "belles" had all fled. The minute she clicked the picture both men made a beeline for the bar.

"Is it always like this?" Diego asked.

"More or less, which means either they're more drunk or less." Harry smiled.

"Ah yes." He smiled back at her and it was obvious he liked her. There weren't a lot of women like Harry hovering about the embassy. She intrigued him. "You know for us the seasons are opposite. Spring fever comes in late October and early November."

"I imagine it's beautiful in South America."

"Yes — not every centimeter but — yes."

"Did BoomBoom give you today's schedule?"

"We are to go to a tea party. BoomBoom wanted me to meet you in the garden. She suggested I see the parade and meet you afterward but I wanted to meet you as soon as possible and I'm glad I did."

"Me, too. I guess BoomBoom wanted us to meet in the garden because I'd have a dress on. I rarely do." Harry blushed for a moment. "The truth is I'm 'most always in jeans."

"Señorita, you are beautiful no matter what you wear." He bowed his head slightly.

*"Oh, this is good."* Tucker happily drooled.

Harry burst out laughing. "Mr. Aybar —"

"Diego."

"Diego, you are very kind." She took a deep breath. "We have a few hours before dressing for the party. If you'd like I could drive you around, show you a bit of the county. I don't think there's any way we could get to Monticello and back on time, though."

He held up his hand. "I have seen it. Mr. Jefferson has my full admiration."

"Cruise?"

"Cruise." He echoed her word. Diego was a quick study.

And cruise they did, chatting all the while. She drove by estates, apple orchards, cattle farms. To her delight she learned that the Aybars maintained a residence in Montevideo but the family had an *estancia* where they bred cattle.

Diego, educated at Duke, studied law at

Yale and then studied back home in Uruguay. His father propelled him toward diplomacy but his heart was in farming.

"I'm at a crossroads."

"And your father will be upset?"

"Ballistic." Diego smiled wanly. "Family is, oh, I can't say more important in my country but tighter, a deeper sense of obligation, perhaps. Here the job comes first — or so it seems to me. Home, it's family. And like everything, that's both good and bad. You see, we have ruling families and they ask not what is best for Uruguay but what is best for the family."

"I think I understand. And you come from such a family."

"My father and grandfather would like to think so."

"Perhaps the weekend can take your mind off your crossroads."

"Or help me make a decision. One hates to disappoint one's family, no? — but one hates to violate one's self."

"Entire novels have been written about that." Harry turned back toward the mountains. "Where is Thomas Steinmetz?"

Diego replied, "He had some business to attend to but will be at the tea. You must know that your county is overflowing with retired ambassadors, diplomats, senior officials, and senior officers of the military."

By the time Harry dropped Diego back at the guest house at BoomBoom's place, they had learned a lot about one another. Perhaps the most important thing was that they both had a sense of humor.

The phone rang as Harry struggled with her panty hose.

"How do you like Diego?" BoomBoom asked.

"He's handsome and charming."

"I thought you'd like him. His passion is farming."

"Yes, we discovered that. Are you calling me just to find out if I like him?" Harry remained suspicious of Boom.

"Well, no. I need your help. Roger O'Bannon insulted Lottie Pearson and she's mad at me anyway — all the more so since she laid eyes on Diego. I asked Aunt Tally if she might disinvite Roger and she wouldn't hear of it, but you know how Aunt Tally likes a scene. I thought you might speak to her. She likes you better than she likes me."

"BoomBoom, since when are you solicitous of Lottie Pearson? There's more than you're telling me."

"No, really there isn't. I was hoping to spare Aunt Tally a scene."

"For God's sake, BoomBoom, as you said,

Aunt Tally lives for a scene." Harry started to laugh.

"You're right. I contradicted myself." BoomBoom sighed deeply. "I was hoping to spare myself."

Aunt Tally was about to get her scene all right but it wasn't the one BoomBoom anticipated.

# 9

In order for a Virginia party to be a success certain things must occur. First, someone has to leave in tears. Second, someone has to pass out due to overindulgence. Third, there has to be a fistfight, and last, someone has to fall in love.

If pressed on these qualities most Virginians would decry the fistfight, the tears, and the drunkenness, but not Aunt Tally. Forthright about life being theater, or at least her parties being theater, she mixed her guests like water and sulfuric acid, then waited for the explosion.

Her advancing years only whetted her appetite for drama. Her beloved yet criticized niece, Big Mim, said it was because Aunt Tally had no sex life. She stirred up other people's hormones.

Upon hearing this, Tally snapped, "Of course I have no sex life. There are no men over ninety and those under ninety won't look at me. You find me a beau and I'll wear him out. I'm still hell in bed, Marilyn, and don't you forget it!"

"Dear God, spare me," Big Mim murmured through her frosted-bronze lipstick.

This was said in front of Reverend Jones, Miranda, Susan and Ned Tucker, as well as Lottie Pearson, who arrived early so as to mix with the older crowd, ever trolling for major donors to the university. There was no way Big Mim could be spared.

"Well, what are you all staring at with your mouths hanging open? Catch flies that way." Tally flicked out her silver hound's-head cane at the assembled. Before she could further berate the small gathering, the doors were flung open and everyone else seemed to arrive at once. The O'Bannons, extremely merry, roared in. Roger wore a sprig of mint in his sports coat for reasons known only to himself and Jim Beam. Sean kissed Aunt Tally repeatedly. She was loath to let him go.

Ned Tucker realized that Aunt Tally's servants, almost as old as the great lady herself, would never be able to pass the hors d'oeuvres and drinks fast enough. He hastily directed people to the bar, a temporary measure. He then called the band director of Crozet High School, an old friend, telling him to send a couple of kids over to pass food around. He'd make a contribution to Crozet High.

He no sooner hung up the phone when BoomBoom swirled in, the diaphanous skirt of her spring dress, a pastel lavender, catching light and the breeze. Next to BoomBoom, in line to meet Aunt Tally, stood Thomas Steinmetz, blond, middle-aged, impeccably dressed. This was a man who flew to London at a whim to be measured for shirts at Turnbull & Asser, suits from shops on Jermyn Street, and shoes from Lobb's or Maxwells. Standing behind Thomas was Diego, also impeccably turned out, a bright turquoise handkerchief in his silk-and-linen jacket breast pocket.

Tally's sharp eye missed nothing. "Harrow?" she asked Thomas.

"Yes." He nodded slightly to the American, who recognized his old school tie from England. Most Americans hadn't a clue.

"Well, you're a wise man then — wise enough to escort one of the most beautiful women in Virginia." She was taking his measure.

"Madam, I am speaking to one of the most beautiful women in Virginia." Thomas bowed low and Tally pursed her lips, all ready to say something about being The Ancient of Days, but at the last minute she decided to enjoy the praise.

"You are very kind, Mr. Ambassador." BoomBoom had given Tally his bio before, of course, but she bumped him up from being counsel to number one. He didn't mind. She turned her attentions now to Diego, being introduced by BoomBoom. When she took a moment to focus on him, his light brown eyes, his jet-black hair, she breathed in. Oh, if only she were young again!

She and Diego chatted and laughed as two cats and one dog tore through the house.

*"Quick. Let's get past the receiving line!"* Mrs. Murphy led her friends. *"Aunt Tally will insist we do tricks."*

*"I smell ham biscuits."* A dreamy look came over Pewter.

*"Later. We've got to dodge the humans."* Tucker nudged Pewter with her nose, for the fat kitty had slowed down.

*"They can just get out of my way,"* she replied with a saucy toss of her gray head, but she did move.

Tally said, "Where's Harry?"

BoomBoom called over her shoulder for Tally was now greeting Tracy Raz, who'd stopped off to buy an orchid corsage for Miranda as well as one for Aunt Tally.

102

"She's in the garden."

"She can't go in the garden before she goes through the receiving line. You tell her to get her bucket back here or she'll hear from me."

"I will but —" BoomBoom glanced around, then walked back, whispering something in the old lady's ear.

"Oh, well, all right, but tell her she has to come back here then." She smiled a moment. "Harry. H-m-m."

Diego strode into the garden, where Harry waited in a simple but very becoming dress. She leaned against a handsome bench built in the eighteenth century, worth a small fortune. Tally believed things should be used. Her only concession to the bench's value was to bring the outdoor furniture into the huge mudroom each night. Her George II silver, her Hepplewhite sofa, chairs, all the paraphernalia of old Virginia wealth pleased her, but she wasn't possessed by her possessions. Nor did she call attention to them. Only new people did that.

Diego bowed, then kissed Harry's right hand, brushing the back of her hand with his lips, the proper way. "In the future, I shall equate spring with you."

"Diego, you know how to turn a girl's head." She laughed.

"May I bring you a drink?"

"I think you'll have to because Aunt Tally's butler probably can't make it from the bar to the garden." She noted his puzzled look, then she pointed out the butler, who happened to be slowly passing the opened French doors.

"Ah, a gentleman in the fullness of his years."

"Before you fetch me a drink I must pay honors to Aunt Tally. I ran around the back of the house and didn't go through the receiving line because I wanted you to find me in the garden. I guess I spoiled the effect by telling. I was running late because my neighbor's cows crashed through the fence and I had to drive them back. My neighbor knows next to nothing about farming plus he's in Seattle on a photo shoot for Nordstrom's. I just made it!"

"A photographer?"

"A model. Little Mim was mad for him. You've met Marilyn?"

"Only just, on my way to you."

Harry stood up, a little unsteady on her heels. "I don't know why I'm talking so much. I'm actually a fairly quiet person. Everyone will tell you that and lots else, I guess." She smiled, her white teeth enhancing her clean, open features.

"I'll walk you back to the grand Aunt Tally. I take it she earned her name hunting?"

Harry positively beamed. "Oh, you know about foxhunting?"

"Tally champagne." He called out as they passed the bar and Ned Tucker held up a bottle of violently expensive champagne.

They both laughed as Roger said a bit too loudly, "Come on, Ned. Stop telling me how great it is and pour, dammit."

"An artist?" Diego noted Roger's attire ... just off, despite his wearing a sports coat. The cowboy boots didn't help.

"Uh, a mechanic. He and his brother Sean own a salvage yard filled with architectural pieces, columns, that stuff. It's quite interesting." They'd reached the line for Aunt Tally. Big Mim had rejoined her aunt on the receiving line.

No sooner had Harry and Diego taken their place than who should walk up behind them but Fair, at six foot five towering over everyone.

"Harry." He leaned down and kissed his ex-wife. He knew thanks to BoomBoom that she was "helping out" with the South Americans as BoomBoom put it, but of course Boom had neglected to describe Diego. When Harry introduced them, Fair struggled to contain his surprise and dismay. He collected himself. "Welcome to Crozet."

"Thank you." Diego firmly shook his hand.

At that moment Harry reached Aunt Tally and Big Mim. Both ladies took in the situation. A sly smile crossed Aunt Tally's lips, Lancôme lipstick generously but not sloppily applied.

"Aunt Tally, I cheated."

"I know you did but in a good cause." She turned her cheek for Harry to kiss her. "I saw your animals rip through here so I knew you couldn't be far behind. That cat of yours, the gray one, will eat me out of house and home."

"Be glad she doesn't drink."

Tally laughed. "There is that. And Mr. Aybar, you may kiss me now, too, since you've met me." She turned her other cheek and Diego kissed it, then kissed the back of her hand.

He bowed and also kissed Big Mim's hand. She brightened considerably.

As they moved away both Aunt Tally and Big Mim made a fuss over Fair, how good he was to forgo a date with Harry so the Uruguayan gentleman wouldn't be lonesome, how's foaling, how are you, etc.

As Fair moved away, quickly intercepted by Lottie Pearson wearing a flowered hat, Tally whispered to her niece, "I just lo-o-ove my parties. Uh-huh."

"You're incorrigible." Big Mim laughed, then reached out to greet Deputy Cynthia Cooper, herself in a spring dress. "I don't think I've ever seen you look so lovely."

The tall woman replied with humor, "Mrs. Sanburne, I don't think you've ever seen me in a dress."

"Well . . . yes."

"You're a tall girl. You'd look good in anything, even chain mail," Aunt Tally said. "Is your boss coming by?"

"The sheriff said he'd try to make it but he's a little behind today."

"It was good of him to let you join us." Tally let go of her hand and Cynthia headed for her friend Harry.

Big Mim whispered, "Security. You didn't tell me you hired security."

"I didn't. I like Cynthia Cooper." Tally beamed at Lynne Beegle, a prominent local rider, as she moved up in the receiving line.

Harry, Diego, and Cooper chatted away, soon joined by Miranda Hogendobber, Tracy Raz, Susan Tucker, and Ned. They celebrated Tracy's return, found out that Diego had a great sense of humor, and thoroughly enjoyed one another.

Over in a corner, Lottie Pearson fended off Roger O'Bannon. She had a smile on her face as she refused his advances. She'd never admit it but she liked the attention. Fair, not being her date, had gotten her a drink, then circulated. He was currently talking to Little Mim about zoning ordinances, not his favorite subject but one of hers.

Lottie pulled a cigarette from her small beaded clutch bag. "Damn." She couldn't find a light.

Roger pulled a brightly colored matchbook from his sports coat, struck a match, lighting her cigarette. "Here, take the pack." He paused. "I'll pick you up at eight," he declared.

"No, you won't." She tossed her head back.

"I'll take you to Mim's dance tonight, too. You don't have a date. And I'll escort you to the Wrecker's Ball."

"Who told you that?" Lottie crossly said. "I have a date for tonight."

"A little bird."

She eyed BoomBoom across the room. "A big robin redbreast. Wait until I get my hands on her."

"I'd rather you get your hands on me."

Eavesdroppers stifled a giggle, making

certain not to stare at the impending drama.

"Roger, dream on."

"You know what's wrong with you, Lottie? You're a goddamned snob. And you know what else? I've never seen a snob who was really happy because there are so few people they can lower themselves to be with, you know? And you need friends in this world. You need friends. It's a cruel world sometimes. You need friends and you need a drink."

"You've had enough to drink, which is why I'll forgive you calling me a snob. If you want me to go out with you, Roger, you're sure going about it in a bizarre manner."

"I'm not drunk." A whiff of belligerence filled his voice. "And I'm getting rich. You forget that. How many F.F.V.'s have money? Look at Harry. Great blood and not a penny." He liked Harry but he didn't mind using her as an example of First Families of Virginia. "Business is booming. I'm not a poor man. Didn't your mother tell you it's just as easy to fall in love with a rich man as a poor one? Well, I'm rich."

Lottie at the moment wasn't pleased with Harry because she thought Diego should have been her date. BoomBoom was heartless in assigning Diego to Harry. After all, Harry could have gone to the parties with her ex-husband. Everyone knew he was still in love with her and was dying to get her back.

"Lottie, maybe you've had too much to drink." Roger touched her arm as she was lost in thought.

"Huh. No!"

"Well, let me get you one. The world looks a lot better after you've belted back some Jim Beam."

The John D'earth band started playing out in the garden. Aunt Tally had set up her outdoor dance floor. People drifted outside.

Sean, wearing a sports jacket and tie, walked over. "Roger, lay off for a little bit or you'll be useless by tonight."

"Big Brother is watching you," Roger said with no malice as Sean moved away, Lottie in tow.

"Thank you, Sean," Lottie said, her voice low.

"He's always had this crush on you, Lottie. I wish you could see past his exterior. Roger is a good man and he'd be a good provider, solid. He needs a woman to anchor him. He drinks because he's lonely."

"This is said by a man still single." Lottie thought Sean the better-looking of the brothers.

"The business has taken up so much of

my time, a lot more than I thought. I'll tell you, I've sure learned to respect my father and grandfather. They started the business and they changed with the times although at the end Dad was set in his ways. Rog and I have to put everything we've got in the business. But you know, I like the challenge." He exhaled a long deep breath. "But I do have to get out more. I'm not going to find a wife in the junkyard."

"Oh, if BoomBoom, now the artiste, comes to your lot I imagine other women do, too."

"You'd be surprised at the people who come out there." He grinned in semi-agreement. "BoomBoom surprises me. She really is welding." He held up his hand. "Honestly. She's making sculptures out of scraps and they aren't bad. Kind of whimsical. But I still don't think I'm going to meet the love of my life at the salvage yard."

"BoomBoom with a welding torch." Lottie's eyebrows rose.

Aunt Tally followed her guests into the garden as the marching-band members served drinks and hors d'oeuvres. "Where did all these children come from? Have people been reproducing behind my back?"

"Ned Tucker called for some extra help," Big Mim told her.

"He should run for office. He's a smart man."

"What kind of office?" Big Mim wanted no interference for her daughter's career. She was relieved that Marilyn finally had some direction in life.

"Congress."

"Yes, he'd be good but let's see how Little Mim does."

"She's vice-mayor and she's young. Give her time."

"But Ned's young, too," Big Mim said.

"He's in his late forties. Marilyn's in her thirties. Let Ned pave the way." Aunt Tally rapped the brick path with her cane, betraying her impatience as well as her intelligence. If Ned ran for Congress and won, then Tally and others like her could push him toward the Senate someday and Little Mim could inherit his seat. It would be less of a fight and that way they'd have two politicians in their pockets. A lot of ifs but most endeavors started that way and Tally paid little mind to ifs.

"May I have this dance?" Reverend Jones held out his hand to Aunt Tally.

"I thought you'd never get me away from her." Tally laughed as they stepped onto the floor. "She hovers around me. What does she think? I'm going to keel over in her presence because I'm older than dirt?"

"She hovers over you because she loves you."

"Oh, that," Tally answered the Reverend.

Diego held Harry. She felt a chill run down her spine. Fair, dancing with Lottie, glared.

Thomas Steinmetz made the rounds of the ladies, always returning to BoomBoom, as was proper.

"You're making a lot of women happy." BoomBoom smiled at him.

"So long as I make you happy." He smiled at her as one who is accustomed to getting his way with women.

Roger wandered over, a bit more sober. "Are you really an ambassador?"

"Thomas Steinmetz, Roger O'Bannon, proprietor with his brother of O'Bannon Salvage," BoomBoom said.

"Pleased to meet you." Thomas held out his hand.

Roger blinked, then shook it. "Likewise. You guys have tin mines in Uruguay?"

"Bolivia has more of those than we do." He noticed Aunt Tally being led back to a table. "If you will excuse me, it's my turn to dance with Aunt Tally."

"Lucky dog," Roger replied noncommittally.

Lottie passed by BoomBoom and hissed. "You're a real shit to fix up Harry with Diego. You want Fair back."

BoomBoom turned on her heel. "Lottie, you are so small and so off course. I ought to smack you right in the mouth."

"You've got a violent streak. You had it in high school. Go ahead. Just go ahead," Lottie baited her.

Roger grabbed Lottie by the elbow. "Come on, Lots. Let's talk."

"No." She shook him off.

Roger stood there for a moment, indecisive, then walked away, a slight sway to his gait.

"Lottie, don't be an ass. I put Harry and Diego together because I knew he loved farming. How was I to know they'd hit it off? Because you're unhappy you don't want anyone else to be happy."

"Bitch." Lottie's voice rose a bit.

"Yes," Susan answered as a joke for she could overhear part of the exchange. "I can go from zero to bitch in three point six seconds. Ask my husband."

Lottie fixed her gaze on Susan standing with Cooper, then decided to allow Roger to lead her away. The two women joined BoomBoom.

"You certainly have an effect on women."

Cooper laughed at BoomBoom.

"Usually negative." She smiled, though, as Thomas was returning to her.

"She'll wear us all out." He indicated Aunt Tally.

"First woman to fly a plane in Albemarle County as well as other things," Susan remarked.

Under the long table inside the house Pewter had fallen fast asleep. Stuffed with turkey, ham, smoked salmon, and other delicacies, she needed a snooze to aid her digestion. Tucker lay beside her, a little bubble escaping her lips.

Murphy sampled everything but she wasn't a big eater. She'd walked back into the kitchen.

The caterer's assistant fussed over the large silver samovar, filling it with coffee. He sniped at one of the kids. "Keep the coffee coming — for obvious reasons."

*"Crab."* Murphy curled her tail around her as she watched.

"Be sure and put out the raw sugar. I noticed most of it was gone."

"Yes, sir," Brooks Tucker, Susan and Ned's daughter, said. She walked through the pantry filled with china and silver to go back to the kitchen. She carried the near-empty silver sugar bowl, which she filled with raw sugar, hurrying back to the dining room to put it on the table. Another sugar bowl with cubed white sugar was on the table. That, too, was getting used up fast. Honey was also on the table. She wondered if Aunt Tally would mind if she filled up a few nonmatching bowls with sugar to meet the demand but forgot about it as Chef Ted, the caterer himself, called for her to come back in and take a tray of moist carrot cake out.

"Want to help me, Mrs. Murphy?" Brooks asked.

*"Sure."* The cat trotted after Brooks, then remained in the dining room sitting on the fireplace mantel so she could see everything.

Back out on the dance floor, Diego inadvertently bumped Fair as the dark man danced yet another dance with Harry.

"Watch it, buddy, and while you're at it you could move away from my wife."

"I am not your wife." Harry was appalled.

Fair then tapped Diego on the shoulder. Diego quizzically looked to Harry, who indicated she'd dance with Fair. They didn't dance so much as they quietly moved back and forth. Neither one said a word.

Diego joined BoomBoom, Thomas, and Susan, who gave the men a two-sentence

116

description of the marriage and its un-raveling.

"They were high-school sweethearts. They got married and, well, it didn't work."

"Ah, I see," Diego said with some feeling. "He seems still to care."

"He does," Susan flatly stated. "He wants her back. She was the best thing that ever happened to him and he lost her. Those things happen."

"To lose Harry would be quite a loss," Diego murmured.

"Everyone grows at their own rate." BoomBoom had no desire to remain on this topic.

Susan understood, of course. Their attention was diverted by Sean propelling his brother back into the house.

"She's not interested," Sean said with the little group overhearing.

"She is, too. You don't get women, Sean," Roger said.

The music ended and Diego walked out, taking Harry's hand. Fair stood there a moment.

"M-m-m, I can see steam coming out of those ears," Aunt Tally noticed, but then she noticed everything, most especially that Miranda Hogendobber was happier than she'd seen her since girlhood and Tracy Raz looked twenty years younger. They were obviously in love.

Sean sat Roger down and got him a cup of coffee. Many people crowded around the table for coffee and tea. The desserts had been brought out.

Mrs. Murphy thought about waking up Pewter and Tucker but they were sound asleep. She noted from her high position how many of the men had bald spots.

Roger was loaded, but not as loaded as Sean made out. After all, he could still recognize people, he could still speak. He drank his cup of coffee in silence.

Sean bent over, whispering to Lottie now at the desserts. She glanced at Roger, then sighed.

"It would mean so much," Sean said. "And he could use a second cup."

Mrs. Murphy watched as Lottie picked up a piece of Black Forest cake, then moved over to the samovar, poured a cup of coffee. She reached for the cubed sugar in a silver bowl. She paused for a second, and Thomas just behind her handed her the china bowl with raw sugar. He had just dipped a spoon into it but being a gentleman he handed it to Lottie first. She dumped three heaping spoonfuls of sugar into the cup and turned to hand it back to Thomas just as he reached for it. She lost her grip and the bowl clattered to the floor, breaking and spilling sugar all over the random-width heart-pine flooring.

"I am sorry," Lottie said.

"I'm the clumsy one. This gives me the opportunity to ask you for a dance when you're finished with dessert." He smoothed over the incident.

"I won't be long." Lottie smiled and hoped it would upset BoomBoom.

People noticed and approved as she walked over to Roger, handing him the coffee and the cake. "Roger, I'm sorry I was cross but sometimes you're a pest. Try to think of less blunt ways to approach women, all right?"

He liked the idea of being served and said in a low voice, "I'm like a bull in a china shop. But really, Lottie, we'd have a good time if you'd go with me to the ball. I promise not to drink. I'll buy you a corsage and, well — it took me a long time to work up my nerve."

"It did?"

"Yes, you scare me half to death." He sipped the coffee. "Just because I'm a pest doesn't mean I'm not scared."

"Well — let me think about it while I dance with Thomas Steinmetz."

"I'll sit right here. I won't move." He smiled genuinely for the first time that afternoon.

*"Some men really don't get it,"* Mrs. Murphy thought to herself. *"It's one thing to show a woman you like her. It's another thing to push her. Men need to be a little mysterious. They ought to study cats."*

The party rolled on and a few more men asked Lottie to dance. Aunt Tally danced every dance.

When Lottie returned to Roger he was fast asleep, his head resting on his chest.

"Roger. Roger." She shook him. "Roger, you lazy sod, wake up," she said lightheartedly. "Roger." Lottie stepped back. "Oh, my God."

Little Mim came over and without thinking said, "What'd you put in his coffee? He's out cold."

"He's either passed out or — dead." Lottie's face registered horror.

"Oh, Lottie, don't be a drama queen. He's been drinking since the parade." Little Mim grabbed his arm to pull him up. "He's warm. Really." With a touch of disgust and determination she gave him a yank and he pitched forward, falling flat on his face.

Little Mim looked at Roger and back at Lottie. "Roger!"

Mrs. Murphy jumped off the mantel, ran under the table, and woke up Pewter and Tucker. Tucker hurried over to Roger, sniffed, then backed away.

Cynthia Cooper was brought in from the dance floor. She walked into the room thinking he was out cold. She felt for a pulse in his neck. Nothing. She tried again. By now other guests were gathering around. She pressed her forefinger and middle finger on his neck again. Nothing. "He's dead."

# 10

"Why does everything happen to me?" Tally grumbled as she watched her guests struggle with the situation.

Then again, what does a hostess do when someone dies at her party? Dispose of the corpse after the festivities? Haul him out and dump him on the lawn so no one has to look at him? Comfort the family members? But years of cotillion plus years of running Crozet before stepping aside for her niece had given Tally a sure touch.

She listened as the ambulance wailed about a mile away. In the quiet of the country sounds carried.

"Ladies and gentlemen, if you would all repair to the garden, please." She nodded to Ned Tucker, who shepherded them out the opened French doors. Then she walked over to Sean, leaning against the chair in which Roger had been sitting before Little Mim yanked him off of it. Sean's mouth hung slack. "Sean, come over here and sit with me." The nonagenarian led the tall, lean man into the formal living room. Big Mim helped her as they gently sat him on the peach-colored satin Hepplewhite sofa.

"Aunt Tally, I'll get the door."

"Thank you, dear."

But Cynthia Cooper reached it first, opening it for Diana Robb and her Crozet Rescue Squad assistants, Dick and Susan Montjoy. Big Mim joined them as they walked over to the body.

Diana said under her breath to Cynthia and Big Mim, "I knew the coke would kill him sooner or later."

"I had no idea," Big Mim whispered, surprised since she thought she knew everything about everybody.

Cooper shrugged. "People use the better part of their intelligence hiding their habits. I see it every day."

"Yes, I guess you do," a troubled Mim replied. "Sean's in a state of shock. I wonder if he knew."

As Diana and Dick carefully lifted Roger into the body bag and then onto the gurney, Big Mim quietly walked into the formal room.

"Sean." Aunt Tally patted his hand. "Sean, honey, they're taking Roger away."

Big Mim leaned over. "I know this is difficult. Is there a funeral home you —"

He jerked his head up. "Hill and Woods."

"Yes. I'll go tell them." She paused a moment longer. "For the sake of your health, Sean, you might want to request an autopsy."

He dropped his head into his hands. "No. I don't want anyone cutting my brother."

Tally and Big Mim exchanged glances and then Big Mim returned to Diana Robb and the Montjoys. "Hill and Woods. Tell them Sean's in no condition to make decisions at this moment."

"Okay." Diana rolled out the gurney as Susan opened the door.

When the door shut, Big Mim folded her hands together, her seven-carat emerald ring shining like green fire. "I wish he'd order an autopsy. When young people die like that you want to know. It could run in the family."

"Yes, but when young people do drugs, especially cocaine, it wreaks havoc on the body," Cooper said.

"The only thing I ever saw Roger do was drink beer and bourbon, a bit too much of it." The older, perfectly groomed woman stared out the front window, watching as Diana shut the ambulance door.

"That's just it. You don't see people do

these things. Albemarle County is a wealthy, wealthy county, Mrs. Sanburne. You can buy anything here and there's a group that does drugs. They know one another and they protect one another," the deputy whispered.

"But surely we'd have some sign, Cynthia. A deterioration of behavior. A sudden drop in weight or the reverse. He seemed so normal. Not the most brilliant man but well — normal."

"He was." She sighed. "Now, I can't prove he took cocaine, but we have Diana's word on it and she's rarely wrong." She thought a moment. "Some people can take a line or two of cocaine and enjoy it just like some people can take a drink or two. One of the reasons the anti-drug campaign doesn't work is it really doesn't tell people the truth. It just demonizes drugs instead of explaining that different people have different chemistries. One person can drink and not become an alcoholic and another is lost with one drink. There's so much we don't know and it would appear we don't want to know."

"Are you condoning drugs?" Mim was incredulous.

"No. But aren't we hypocritical? One drug, alcohol, is legal. Either legalize them all or ban them all. That's how I see it, and it would make my job a great deal easier."

"I'll have to think about that. In the meantime I'd better find someone to take Sean home. And I'd better release the guests from the garden. This will put a crimp in my dance tonight." She said this without rancor but more in the spirit of how life throws curveballs to everyone from time to time.

"I'll tote Sean home," Cynthia offered.

"Thank you."

As Big Mim headed for the garden, Mrs. Murphy, Pewter, and Tucker emerged, breaking their silence.

Pewter crossly complained, *"You didn't wake me up in time. Lottie Pearson's shrieking woke me up. You saw the whole thing!"* Mrs. Murphy had told her what happened.

Mrs. Murphy padded over, not focusing on the spilt raw sugar, a small amount, that had fallen into the cracks on the floor. *"How was I to know he'd just died? I didn't know until he flopped on the floor. As it was I did come get you two."*

Tucker blinked. *"He just keeled over?"*

*"Here today, gone tomorrow."* Pewter giggled.

*"Diana thinks the cocaine did him in. Humans lower their voices but it's so easy for us*

to hear." Mrs. Murphy ignored Pewter's merriment. *"I never smelled cocaine on Roger, though."*

*"Easy to determine. Bitter. They sweat it out."* Tucker wrinkled her nose.

*"Pope Rat would know."* Pewter mentioned the rat in Roger's shop. *"He lived with Roger . . . not that Roger knew."*

*"It really doesn't matter."* Tucker watched Sean being helped to his feet by Fair Haristeen and Reverend Jones. *"He's done for and that's the end of it."*

But it wasn't, of course.

# 11

Bumblebees buzzed around the wisteria, their fat bodies a triumph over physics and logic. Yet there they were, a squadron of them, their black and yellow bodies purposefully darting here and there in the late afternoon sun.

Harry and Susan sat out on the lawn. Mim's dance for charity would be in two hours. Both women were bemoaning the occasion. Mim had little choice but to go forward since it was a fund-raiser. Then, too, it wasn't a death in her family. No one expected her to cancel.

"We have to do it," Susan said.

"I know. We do. Everyone will be there but it's going to be leaden. And you know how Big Mim gets if a fund-raiser doesn't take off."

"She'll be sensible about this party. After all, no one can control these things." Susan plucked out the mint leaf from her tea and chewed it. "Love mint. You have the best mint patch."

"I grew those mint plants on the window-sill. It will be another month before my herb garden does much." She shielded her eyes to watch her three horses in the meadow. She'd turned them out in the larger pasture.

"It was kind of awful that Little Mim pulled Roger off the chair." Susan lowered her eyes, which produced a giggle from Harry. "Harry, you're horrible."

"Well — it was funny. Who said death couldn't be funny? Not that I wished him dead," Harry hastily added. "After all, he showed me how to run the wrecker's ball and he could be fun when he wasn't — you know what I mean. If he could have seen his death he'd have a sense of humor about it. *Really*."

"You're terrible."

"No, I'm not. I'm honest. Lottie Pearson screaming her silly head off just added to it, you know. And I'll give BoomBoom credit." She smiled knowingly at Susan. "She hauled Lottie's silly ass out of the room. If Lottie had screamed any louder, she would have shattered the crystal."

Susan considered this as Mrs. Murphy rolled over in the freshly cut grass. "Murphy, what a lovely tummy."

*"Mine's better."* Pewter rolled over, too.

*"Fatter."*

130

*"Better."* Mrs. Murphy closed her eyes.

*"Mine's whiter."* Tucker rolled over as well.

"Would you look at that. Three spoiled children. Oh, to be one of my animals." Harry smiled. "What a life."

"No bills. No taxes. No stress. No unrealistic expectations about the future. They live in the moment." Susan sighed. "I'd be better off if I could be more like them."

"Me, too." Harry shifted in her seat. "Miranda and Tracy said they'd take food over to Sean and then go on to Big Mim's. Think we should take food?"

"Tomorrow. This is going to be hard on Ida O'Bannon. She hasn't fully recovered from her husband's death. I don't know if Sean can handle all this. Men usually aren't too good at these things."

"No." Harry squinted as a bumblebee flew up to her, decided she wasn't a flower, then zoomed off. "Lottie Pearson's mad at BoomBoom." She didn't need to explain since Susan knew why. "But she let Boom lead her off. She wants something but I can't figure out what it is."

"Your mind is a grasshopper."

"I know. Always was. I didn't mean to change the subject, and I am sorry for Ida and Sean."

"Do you think Thomas Steinmetz is married?"

"Now who's changing the subject?" Harry touched Susan's leg with her foot.

Susan laughed. "Well, anyway, do you think he's married?"

Harry shrugged. "I don't know. If he is, he's bold as brass coming down here and staying with Boom. Washington's not that far away. He strikes me as the bold type anyway."

"Honey, with the telephone, e-mail, and television, nothing is that far away. It's both wonderful and dreadful."

They sat in silence for a few moments as the killdeers called on the meadows, their high-pitched voices distinctive.

"Did Roger have any enemies?"

"Harry." Susan's voice rose, filled with humor and a touch of censure. "You watch too much *Mystery Theater.*"

Sheepishly, the slim woman replied, "It's good."

"Who would want to kill Roger O'Bannon? If he had any enemies it would be himself. He sat back there in his garage like a doodlebug in its hole. His socializing was at the stock-car races. I mean he was pleasant enough but you can't be covered in grease and expect someone like Lottie

Pearson to fall for you."

"Lottie's a snob."

"So is half of Albemarle County."

"I guess." Harry exhaled. "Anyway, it crossed my mind, that's all. Oh, did you notice the flying blue heron sculpture in Aunt Tally's garden?"

"Yes."

"BoomBoom made it out of scraps. Kind of amazing."

"H-m-m." Susan enjoyed another long sip. "Diego Aybar." Given the length of her relationship with Harry, Susan didn't need a transition. She could hop around subjects as rapidly as Harry, although her concept of herself was as a logical, linear person.

"Yes?"

"You're smitten with him."

"You're soft as a grape."

"I suppose I'd have to be to be your best friend. Share a little, Harry, it's part of friendship, you know."

"Oh — he's handsome —"

"Gorgeous."

"Okay, Susan, he's gorgeous."

"And charming."

"Yes, but you know he has a quality, a sweetness, really, I can't think of another word but sweetness. I wish American men would get over trying to be so, uh, manly and just be themselves, you know."

"Well, that was a little outburst," Susan laughed, "for you, anyway."

"But Diego has" — she thought hard but couldn't find a substitute word — "sweetness." She inhaled. "But I hardly know him."

"True."

"Do I detect something acidic in your voice?"

"No, you don't actually. I'm only hoping that someday you'll fly. You'll let yourself go. Anyway, I don't believe in mistakes anymore." Susan set her glass down hard enough to make the ice cubes collide.

"Huh?"

"Mistakes. There are no mistakes. No matter what you do, no matter how awful it seems at the time, it's not a mistake because you needed to learn that lesson so — let go."

"I don't believe that."

"Harry, I knew you'd say that."

"Well, I don't. Murder is a mistake. You can't murder someone and then say you needed to learn that lesson. The lesson being, I suppose, that human life is valuable and no one has the right to take it except in self-defense, naturally."

"We aren't talking about murder."

"I'm carrying forward your theory about

mistakes to its extreme conclusion."

"Thereby proving my point." Susan threw her head back, peals of laughter filling the fragrant air. "You need to let go."

Harry sat quietly for a moment, considered Susan's thought, then smiled slowly. No need to reply.

# 12

Flaming torches lined the long, curving driveway to Dalmally, Mim Sanburne's estate. The pinpoints of red-orange against the twilight created the eerie sensation of going back in time. Cool night air arrived with the sunset. The temperature plunged to fifty-two degrees Fahrenheit and would probably wind up close to freezing.

BoomBoom arrived shimmering in a raspberry chiffon evening gown, with a silver fox stole wrapped around her shoulders. Thomas would have cut the motor and leapt out of his Mercedes sports car to open the door for her, but Mim, leaving nothing to chance, had hired a valet parking service from Charlottesville. She demanded that no car jockey take the expensive cars for a joyride. The valet company signed a contract to that effect. Mim always made a point of marshaling staff before a party and reading them the law, the law of Virginia and Mim's law. Her Aunt

Tally and her mother had taught her this.

Not all the guests wallowed in riches. Tracy Raz drove Miranda in her Ford Falcon. People laughed, saying that Miranda would be buried in that car, which itself was over forty years old. Slimmed down, a smiling Miranda emerged from the car. She wore a red gown, almost medieval in style, which looked fabulous on her. She wasn't afraid to show off a bit, now that she had lost so much weight. As she passed along the receiving line, Big Mim, Little Mim, Jim, and Aunt Tally murmured to one another how youthful Miranda looked. Tracy, too, had lost some weight, scaling down to one hundred and seventy, what he had weighed when he made All-State from Crozet High.

As Miranda and Susan had helped Harry make up and dress up, the young postmistress dazzled as she glided along the receiving line. A simple royal-blue sheath, with a plunging neckline made all the more daring by long sleeves, was perfect on her. Diego, in white tie at her shoulder, couldn't take his eyes off her.

Nor could Fair Haristeen. Vowing to himself that he would win his ex-wife back before midsummer, he smiled, walked over, and made a point of engaging Diego in conversation.

As they chatted, Lottie Pearson arrived with a subdued Donald Clatterbuck in tow. Uncomfortable in white tie, obviously rented at the last minute, Don smiled sheepishly as people recognized him, which took a moment. Don hadn't even dressed up for his high-school graduation. As Roger O'Bannon had been a buddy, Don was dumbfounded by the news of his death. He wasn't at all sure he should be at Big Mim's. Lottie threw a fit when he tried to back out so he reluctantly accompanied the forceful woman.

Thomas bent over and breathed into BoomBoom's ear, "Americans must learn never to rent evening wear. Good clothes last your whole life."

"Provided you stay in shape, which you have," she breathed right back into his ear, the color rising in his cheeks.

"Ah, Diego." Thomas waved him over. "I didn't see you come in." He bowed low to Harry. "The beauty of Virginia's countryside is exceeded only by the beauty of her women."

Even BoomBoom, mouth slightly agape, blinked and said, "Mary Minor, if only your mother could see you now."

Harry laughed. "I'm not sure she'd believe it." Noting Thomas's and Diego's puzzled expressions she hastily added, "Mother despaired of transforming me into a proper lady. She would have been happier with a daughter like BoomBoom."

"Harry, don't say that. Your mother loved you."

"Boom, she loved me but she would have rather gone shopping with you."

They laughed as Lottie Pearson, dragging Don, flounced by. Not able to resist Diego's handsome face, she stopped and made a point of introducing Don. The two Uruguayans made Don feel immediately at ease. They even pretended interest when Don held forth on the wonders of taxidermy. Lottie ignored him. He was occupied anyway. She wanted to corral Diego but had to settle for talking to him with Harry. She'd never thought much about Harry one way or the other but at that precise moment, Lottie loathed Harry Haristeen. Even the sidelong, knowing glances to Fair fell short of their intention. Fair did not pull Harry away from the dark handsome man nor did he make an effort to assist Lottie in her flirtations.

"I know you all are wondering how I could come here tonight after Aunt Tally's but, well, I called Reverend Jones and he said I should follow my heart. After all, the

O'Bannons aren't close friends and Roger, poor fellow, could be a pest. It's not like he was family and, well, people do die. What about all those football players who drop before they're forty?" Her hand fluttered to her throat. "And you know how Big Mim gets if you miss one of her parties."

"We know," Harry and Fair said in unison, then blushed. The years together often meant their thoughts were similar.

"Is Big Mim such a dragon?" Thomas's pleasant voice coated each word like honey. "She's so gracious."

"As long as you do things her way." Lottie's lips formed a pout.

Don, running his finger under his neckband, said with sense, "Ought not to criticize the hostess when you're enjoying her hospitality."

Thomas bowed his head slightly to Don. "A Virginia gentleman."

"Don?" Lottie said with surprise.

Harry deflected the conversation, speaking directly to Don Clatterbuck. "How's my woodpecker?"

"Frozen stiff." He laughed.

"Woodpecker?" Thomas inquired.

"When I woke up a few days ago, I found, well, actually, my gray cat, Pewter, found a pileated woodpecker. One of those huge woodpeckers. Dead. She pretended it was her kill, which if you know Pewter is absurd, but I finally convinced her to give it to me. Made a beeline for Don. He's the best. You should see his work." She paused and said, "Museum quality."

Don blushed as Lottie's eyes darted about. How would she ever extricate Diego from Harry? She wanted to ask him to accompany her to a huge alumni fund-raising dinner and dance, but he was glued to Harry. She believed Harry would look much less attractive if he could see her covered in grease as she repaired her ancient tractor. Harry was just too butch.

"What's a peel— ?" Diego smiled, groping for the next syllable.

"Pileated woodpecker." Fair Haristeen's deep voice finished the word. "The largest woodpecker in America, close to twenty inches. You've seen the Woody Woodpecker cartoons?"

"Yes." Diego laughed.

"They're based on the pileated woodpecker, which has a brilliant red crest and red mustache as well as a distinctive loud call. Woody Woodpecker borrowed a bit of that, too."

"Can one see such a bird?" Thomas asked.

"Actually, you can. They don't hide. And they fly in an odd manner." Fair, as a vet, held the floor, which he liked. "They flap a few times, gaining speed rapidly, then fold their wings flat to their sides and zoom like a rocket. You'll hear them before you see them. They're noisy."

"Rapping into dead trees echoes in the woods. Fair's right. It's loud." BoomBoom was glad they'd steered away from Roger O'Bannon's demise. She'd felt a bit detached about it as he moved in a different circle. But when Lottie brought up the subject of Roger, BoomBoom decided she was both stupid and vain.

"They eat ants in the trees." Harry smiled at the two visitors. "You fellows don't really want to know about woodpeckers, do you?"

"I do. I'm an amateur naturalist. North America has many unusual animals."

Jim Sanburne strode by, clapping Fair on the back. "Going coon hunting tomorrow? Jack Ragland's bringing out Red Cloud."

"Red Cloud?" Diego was thoroughly enjoying himself, as this really was different from Embassy Row.

"Fabulous hound, brother, fabulous hound. Won about everything there is to win in this country in hunt trials." Jim's voice carried over the room.

"Like foxhunting?" Diego asked curiously.

"Oh, you don't want to go coon hunting. It's so country." Lottie rolled her eyes.

Jim Sanburne cleared his throat. "Music." The one word explained coon hunting to the locals. Jim loved the sound of the hounds, those deep, high, and middling voices. It was music.

Lottie grimaced. "You can break your ankle running around in the dark."

"That's what flashlights are for." Harry found Lottie as welcome as prickly heat.

"Women coon hunt?" Thomas wondered.

"Yes. Anyone can go so long as the hound owners invite them. It's not like foxhunting where an engraved card is sent out. You know?" Thomas nodded that he was familiar with foxhunting so Harry continued. "People can hunt one hound or two, called a brace. They can even hunt coon with a pack, it's up to the hunter or hunters. They'll often run their hounds together so the sound is better and oh, how the sound carries at night. It will make the hair stand up on the back of your neck."

"What happens when you find the raccoon?" Diego thought he'd like to see this unique Southern practice.

"Coon climbs up a tree, sits there, and

144

looks at you. You can shoot him down or leave him be. I leave the coon alone so I have the pleasure of his or her acquaintance another time." Jim folded his arms across his chest, then added, "Never sporting to kill a female, especially in spring. She might have babies back home."

"Ah, yes." Diego smiled.

"Does one have to pay to participate?" Thomas wanted to go.

"Not at all, brother, not at all. Tell you what, I'll call Jack right now and ask him if you all can come along tomorrow night. What about you, Harry? Fair?"

They nodded yes.

"You'll hate it," Lottie declared.

"I'm going, too." BoomBoom, for all her perfect fingernails, clothes, etc., was a country girl, after all.

"All right. Jack should have been here tonight along with his wife, Joyce, but when I told him it was white tie he begged off. He said if I put a gun to his head maybe he'd wear a monkey suit — actually, Joyce would be the one to make him do it — but he's not wearing tails." Jim's deep laugh rumbled. "Tell you one thing, the man can hunt. Wife can, too. And gentlemen, I'll bring along a little something to cut the night's chill, a little something we do better in the mountains than they do anywhere else."

"Better keep your voice low." Fair winked. "Cooper's right behind you."

The deputy was talking to Tracy and Miranda and turned when she heard her name. "I didn't hear a thing."

"Good. Always thought a deaf woman would be an advantage." Jim winked.

"You mean dumb, don't you? One who can't talk." BoomBoom winked back.

"Is that what I meant?"

"Sexist pig." Harry stuck her finger in Jim's stomach.

"Awful. You can dress me up but you can't take me out. Come to think of it, I'm not out. This is my home." Jim roared with laughter, then shambled off to the telephone.

"How can he say that?" Lottie fumed.

"He's pulling your leg, our legs." Harry's eyes returned to Diego. "Every woman in this room knows that Jim Sanburne would do anything to help; his heart is bigger than he is."

"That doesn't excuse sexism." Lottie pursed her lips. "You make excuses for men, Harry." The "you" was loaded with innuendo.

"Lighten up." Don stifled a giggle. "Otherwise I'll have to give you a stuffed shirt."

At this they all laughed except for Lottie.

Miranda and Tracy joined the group just as Gretchen, the majordomo, butler, servant, you name it, strolled through playing the glockenspiel. She repeated the same three notes, which meant time to go to the dining room.

Mim and Jim Sanburne enjoyed the resources to host a sit-down dinner for sixty guests, seven courses, each with a different wine, champagne, sherbets, and cakes at the end. Mim had grown up with wealth, never knowing anything but abundance although she'd suffered bouts of emotional famine. She married Jim Sanburne on the rebound. He was big, strong, handsome, poor. Over the years he'd proved hot as a forty-balled tomcat. His licentiousness had as much to do with his sex drive as the fact that having a rich wife isn't all it's cracked up to be. In time they worked it out. He stopped running after women, she stopped giving him orders.

After dinner the orchestra played in the ballroom, which was decorated with dogwoods, pink and white, and viburnum, providing fragrance as well as beauty. Lottie sat next to Don, who didn't ask her to dance. Finally she pulled him onto the dance floor, hissing, "Getting cold feet?"

"No, I'm just not much of a dancer," Don replied.

Miranda had left her purse in the Falcon. Needing her lipstick, she rose from one of the small tables arranged on the sides of the dance floor. "Honey, do you have the car ticket?"

Tracy reached inside his cutaway, the inside pocket. "I do. But you sit right here. I'll get your bag, sweetie."

"Why don't we get it together?" She winked.

The older couple strolled through the rooms to the front of the house, where they gave the attendant the ticket. He picked up a cell phone and called in the number. In the distance they heard the old engine fire up.

When the car was delivered, the parking lot driver emerged, a young, slender man with sandy hair and a thin mustache.

"Wait, don't get out. I just need to grab the lady's purse. You can take the car right back."

"All right, sir."

As Tracy reached in for her small, beaded purse Miranda fixed her gaze on the young man driving her precious vehicle. She noticed that his left eye sagged and there was a red scar over his eyebrow running through to below the eye. It took a moment for this to register, then she blurted out, "You, you stole my hubcaps!"

He blanched, shot out of the car, running flat out into the darkness.

Tracy tore out after him. He hadn't been a star halfback for nothing and he was still in great shape. Although the kid had a head start he was no match for the older man. When he turned to see Tracy gaining on him he misstepped and rolled, got up, tried to pick up speed, but Tracy knew how to throw a block. He leaned down and pushed off his right foot, sailing into the back of the young man. Tracy hit him so hard that the kid's body flew up in the air like a rag doll, then fell to earth with a sickening thud. Tracy was on him fast, squeezing his head in a hammerlock. A heavy object on a chain around the young man's neck popped out of his shirt when he was blocked by Tracy. It was a Mercedes star hood ornament.

"I didn't steal nothin'."

"We'll see about that."

# 13

As Tracy forced the young man back toward the house, he took no chances. Holding the kid's left arm up behind him with his other hand on the young man's collar, his grip was tight. Each time the kid tried to shake free, Tracy jerked the bent left arm upward, which evoked a howl. In the cool night air thunder over the mountains presaged an approaching spring storm.

The main attendant had the presence of mind to find Big Mim, who in turn corralled Cynthia Cooper. The two women were waiting with Miranda Hogendobber as Tracy delivered his quarry.

"It's the man Sean described," Miranda said. What upset her as much as anything was the fact that a young person would steal.

Cynthia stepped forward. "I'm Deputy Cynthia Cooper. Cooperate and maybe we can make this less unpleasant."

"I didn't steal nothin'," he sullenly defended himself.

"Why don't we start with your name?" Cynthia then turned to Tracy. "You can release him. And thanks."

The scared youth grumbled, "Fast for an old man."

Miranda couldn't help but smile. "Son, you've been brought down by one of the best halfbacks this state ever produced."

The youth warily studied Tracy, who beamed thanks to Miranda's praise.

"What's your name?" Big Mim betrayed irritation.

"Wesley Partlow."

"Mr. Partlow, your address," Cooper methodically asked.

"Got none."

"You must sleep somewhere," she pressed.

He shrugged. "When I get tired I —"

"Come on. Where do you live? You're clean. You're wearing a white shirt and black pants," Big Mim said.

"They gave me the shirt." He nodded to the head attendant. "Company policy. All valet attendants wear a white shirt and black pants. The logo is over the pocket."

"So it is." Mim crossed her arms over her chest.

"Let's try this again. Where do you live?" Cooper patiently repeated her question

151

knowing she'd hear more lies. She'd seen this type many times before: young, sullen, rebellious.

"No place."

"You're homeless?"

"Yeah," he smirked.

"Where's the 1987 GMC truck you drove to O'Bannon's Salvage yard? The one with the Dallas Cowboys jacket in it."

His eyes opened wider.

"Where is it?" Cooper wished she could slap the smirk right off his white face.

His eyes dropped to the ground.

"Are you hungry?" Miranda, kind even under these circumstances, thought food might help him.

"No, ma'am."

"I know you didn't mean to upset me but my Falcon means the world to me. If you'd cooperate with us we can settle this . . ." Miranda's voice trailed off.

Tracy put his arm around Miranda's waist. "Honey, don't fret over it."

"There's a quick way to settle this before I take Mr. Partlow into custody. I'll run him over to Sean O'Bannon's."

Wesley's eyes darkened, his jaw clamped shut.

Big Mim, not realizing that Cooper was laying a trap, said, "Cynthia, you can't do that. Not tonight. Not now. After all, Roger's not even cold yet. I don't think Sean is in any condition to identify a thief."

Wesley's head jerked up, senses alert, a flicker of fear in his eyes now. "Who's dead?"

"Roger O'Bannon. Did you know him?" Cooper inquired.

"No," he unconvincingly answered. He became even more wary.

Cooper sighed. No more dancing for her. "I have the strangest feeling, Mr. Partlow, that you and trouble are well acquainted. Tracy, will you stay with him while I call in for a squad car? I can't trust him to stay in the Jeep. He'd be out at the first stoplight."

# 14

The Dogwood Festival, celebrating the state tree and springtime, provided ample opportunity for revelers to overindulge each mid-April. Automobile accidents, property destruction, and fights kept the sheriff's department busy.

Sheriff Rick Shaw had the whole force out working tonight. When Cooper called him concerning Partlow he drove out in a squad car himself. It would never do for Big Mim to be unhappy. His presence as the highest elected law-enforcement official in the county usually mollified the grand lady. He'd also learned when he'd been elected twenty years ago to call Mim first when something broke. It made his life easier but also with her wide net she often could help him.

As a man ages his judgment usually improves. If it doesn't he's either dead or a drunk. Rick Shaw had learned to trust his judgment. He followed procedure to the letter of the law but he also trusted his instinct. In the past, when Mary Minor Haristeen would blunder onto a crime scene accompanied by her animals, he used to fume. Over time he had learned that help comes from unusual quarters. Once the corgi found a human hand, which eventually led him to a murderer. Harry and her furry cohorts had a funny way of blundering onto things.

So he wasn't surprised when he drove up to Mim's front door to find Big Mim, Miranda, Tracy Raz, Harry, and Diego, to whom he was introduced.

Harry couldn't resist an event. When she saw Mim head for Coop she knew something was up so she followed the deputy. Diego found her curiosity amusing.

Rick smiled at his favorite deputy. "Coop, enjoy yourself. This is the only night off you've had in two months. I'll take the perp back."

"You can't lock me up for stealing hubcaps — which I didn't do." He snarled as he put the Mercedes star, which had slipped out again, back under his shirt.

"Boy, I can lock you up for just about anything." Rick genially pulled Wesley's arms behind his back, cuffing his hands together.

BoomBoom and Thomas happened to walk out front.

"Mim, there you are. We had a wonderful time." BoomBoom noticed Rick pushing Wesley into the back of the squad car as she finished her sentence. "What's happening?"

"Miranda thinks he stole the hubcaps off her Falcon earlier," Harry said.

"We're lucky he didn't steal our jewels." BoomBoom's hand protectively covered the priceless sapphire and diamond necklace at her throat.

"The jewels are nothing. The woman is everything. I'd be afraid that he'd steal you." Thomas kissed her on the cheek after casting a jaundiced eye at Wesley, who cast it right back.

"That would be a first," Mim wryly responded, as Thomas gave the head attendant his parking ticket.

Diego whispered to Harry, "Silver tongue."

"How long have you known Thomas?"

Diego shrugged. "Our families know one another. He's a bit older so we didn't go to school together. Since working at the embassy I've gotten to know him. Before that," he shrugged again, "social. Like tonight."

"A lady-killer," she whispered, eyebrows lifting upward.

"He thinks so," Diego giggled back, a giggle that made him irresistible, especially since American men rarely allow themselves a good giggle.

"BoomBoom eats it up."

"There is a type of woman who does, and you're not that type," Diego said with insight.

"Well — no."

Their attention was drawn away from one another as Wesley Partlow turned around in the backseat of the squad car and with his handcuffed hands managed to shoot the bird as Rick started the motor.

"What an asshole," Coop muttered under her breath.

Tracy, next to her, said, "Used to see guys like that all the time in the service. We had the draft back then so there was always a small percent who thought the rules didn't apply to them. Usually that was beat out of them during basic training. Seems to me that Wesley Partlow will miss the experience of being in the armed services. Too bad. Makes a man out of punks like that."

"Well, there's one thing for sure, he's going nowhere." Cooper removed her left high heel to shake out a small pebble. "Miranda, I didn't think we'd find your hubcap desecrator so soon."

"Me neither. I bet he stole the truck, too."

"That's a given." Cooper rubbed her bare arms as the lightning flashed on the side of the mountains. "Looks like the storm finally rolled up over the Blue Ridge."

# 15

Within seconds the wind roared through Crozet at forty miles an hour, lifting party tents into the heavens, shredding striped awnings, sending Big Mim's guests shivering to the fireplaces as the temperature dropped violently.

Overhead, black clouds, blacker than night, scudded over treetops; white, pink, and even bluish lightning ripped through the swirling clouds to strike below. A brilliant bolt hit the tin roof of Mim's gardening shed, the flash temporarily blinding those who beheld it. Luckily the shed didn't catch fire.

The usual quota of car accidents for the Dogwood Festival dropped, because most people had the sense to get off the roads. Those few that stayed out skidded into guardrails. The sheriff's department and the wrecker services were working as fast as they could.

Although she had looked forward to this

night, Cynthia Cooper, overcome with a sense of duty and knowing that Rick Shaw would be on overload, bid her host and hostess good-bye, hopped in her Jeep, and drove to headquarters. She changed into her uniform and grabbed the lone squad car remaining, driving out into the lashing rains.

"Coop to Sheriff Shaw."

"Hey," came the familiar, tired voice.

"I'm heading out to Boonesville. Accident at the crossroads."

"What are you doing at work?"

"All hands on deck on a night like tonight. Yancy's squad car was lonesome. Where's Yancy?"

"In the hospital with a broken jaw."

"What?"

"Stopped a speeder, Din Marks, weaving all over the road. Guy got out of the car, Yancy shined the flashlight in his face, and the guy hit him broadside with a hammer. Held it behind his back, black as pitch tonight and Yancy never saw it coming."

"Damn."

"Filthy night. But Yancy will be okay. With his jaw wired shut he's bound to lose weight."

"There is that." She smiled. "Did he nail the perp?"

"Oh yeah. Sitting in the same cell with that

little asshole, Partlow. Hey, I don't know when we'll wrap up this night but I'll buy you coffee and a doughnut when we do."

"Best offer I've had all week."

"Over and out," he replied.

As Cooper headed up to Boonesville, a small community north of Charlottesville proper, Harry and Diego danced the last dance at midnight. Big Mim invited everyone back to the library for coffee. Her eagle eyes noted if anyone was beyond driving. Her husband whisked off those few to the apartments above the stable. Jim's size and bulk guaranteed little resistance.

Thunder roared overhead, the lightning illuminated the fields with eerie colors. The horses sensibly retreated to their run-in sheds. Even the cattle withdrew to the run-in sheds, standing patiently with the horses, who felt superior to cattle.

Tucker covered her eyes in the bedroom at Harry's home. Pewter made a big show of not caring about the storm.

Mrs. Murphy, curled up on the bed, said, *"This is a bad one. I'm surprised there isn't hail."*

The words were no sooner out of her mouth than a tremendous rattle pelted the roof. Hailstones the size of golf balls pounded down, bouncing high off anything

161

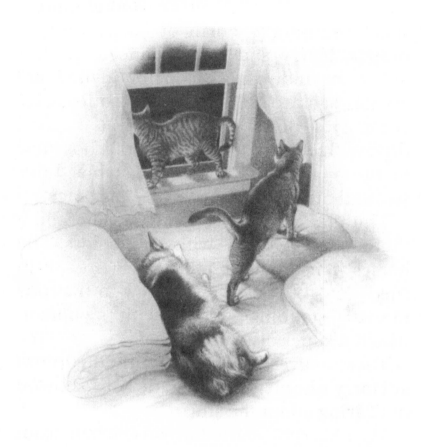

they hit.

*"Wow!"* Pewter hurried to the window.

*"It was a dark and stormy night,"* Mrs. Murphy chanted in a ghostly voice.

*"That's not funny."* Tucker shivered.

*"Wimp."* Pewter tossed her head in the air.

*"Don't pick on her. She really hates these things and this is a hateful storm. Bet the horses are glad Mom opened their outside stall doors. She's got a sixth sense about the weather."*

*"She watches the Weather Channel."* Pewter, never one to be impressed with humans, jumped as a big hailstone smashed against the window.

*"Wasn't on the Weather Channel. I watched it with her. This is one of those wild storms that comes out of nowhere."* Mrs. Murphy knew how swiftly weather could change in the mountains. *"People are lucky their crops aren't high enough to beat down but this will tear the dogwood blossoms right off the trees."*

The sound of Harry's truck coming down the driveway sent them all to the back door. She floated through the door heedless of the weather. "Hello, babies."

*"I'm glad you're home,"* Pewter confessed.

Tucker, thrilled that Harry was home, followed her human closely. *"I hate this."*

163

Pewter decided to follow Harry, too.

Mrs. Murphy scampered ahead of them as the hail sounded like artillery fire. *"Let's be glad we're inside tonight, safe and sound."*

That was the same feeling Cynthia Cooper had when she finally pulled back into department headquarters. At four-thirty in the morning her eyes burned, her mouth was dry. It had been one fender bender after another.

She pushed open the heavy swinging door. The odor of fresh coffee greeted her.

Rick smiled. "Doughnuts right here. Krispy Kremes."

"I could eat a bug." She poured coffee, grabbed a glazed doughnut, and slumped into her desk chair. "Where is everybody?"

"Out. I called Krispy Kreme and told them to give everyone doughnuts and coffee. I'd pick up the tab. Mercifully, things are slowing down. Next shift comes on at six. Hey, want a jelly doughnut?"

"No. You don't fool me. You bought those for you."

"Uh — yes. I even bought a carton of ciga-rettes, which I am stashing in your desk."

"Why?"

"Because if my wife comes in she'll check my desk."

"Little lies lead to big ones." Coop rolled

her eyes.

"It's my one vice. I've tried to give it up and I finally decided, to hell with it. I might as well enjoy it."

"Yeah." She reached for another glazed doughnut. "My problem is I enjoy the first two puffs, then I can't stand the taste. Lot of money to spend for two puffs. I'm hungry. I think I'll call Miranda and ask her to make her orange-glazed cinnamon buns to-morrow."

"It is tomorrow."

"Oh — well, the next tomorrow." She licked her fingers. "Mim threw another grand party. She was afraid it would be subdued because of Roger O'Bannon's death but it wasn't. Not really Roger's crowd."

"I wouldn't think so. What happened?"

"He keeled over in his chair. Pretty much like you heard over the radio." She mentioned the radios in the squad cars. "Makes you think. I mean about stuff like smoking and eating doughnuts and greasy ham-burgers."

"Coop, when your number's up, it's up." Rick folded his hands over his chest as he leaned back in his big chair. "And Sean won't agree to an autopsy?"

"No, unless he's changed his mind. He

was, well, you can imagine. Held it together but what a shock."

"People have strong feelings about autopsies. If it were my brother I'd do it. In case it's something hereditary, something I could attend to."

"Now wait a minute. You just said you're smoking, to hell with it and when your number's up, it's up."

He grinned. "Me?"

"Wasn't it Emerson who said, 'Consistency is the hobgoblin of small minds'?"

"You're the reader but it sounds good to me." He cocked his head. "Christ, the storm is getting worse."

She polished off the last of her doughnut. "Who's back in the Taj Mahal?" she said, referring to the jail.

"A full house. Students. People who should know better and Din Marks, the jerk who smashed Yancy."

"Din? Well, I suppose it's better than Spirit-Moves-Us. Remember him?"

"Easy wardrobe. Bedsheets." Rick laughed. "And people give money to guys like that. Religious nuts. I'm in the wrong business. I'll shave my head, put a dot in the middle of my forehead, wear bedsheets, and chant 'Om' — instant riches. Tell people they're stressed out and need to find inner peace."

"Spirit-Moves-Us did, with prepubescent girls."

Rick grimaced, shaking his head. "Said it was part of his religion. He won't be out of jail for years."

"Is the guy's real name Din?"

"That's what his driver's license said. Oh, can't really hold that Partlow kid on hubcaps. I'll let him go later. Actually, I ought to release him now. Kick his sorry ass right out in the storm. I'll run him by the salvage yard first."

"I think I'll pay him a visit." She glanced at the clock. "A five o'clock wake-up call ought to bring a smile to his face." She walked into the cell block, Rick with her. The arrested were sprawled in cells, dead drunk, sleeping it off. Wesley, though, sat straight up, listening to the storm. "Good morning, glory," Cynthia said teasingly.

"Sounds like a tornado."

"They're louder," Rick answered him. "We're going to take you over to O'Bannon's Salvage later this morning. If Sean makes a positive I.D. your ass is grass. If not, you're free."

"I didn't steal nothin'. He'll tell you." Wesley listened as the hail intensified.

"Okay." Rick shrugged.

"Wesley, if you cooperate things will go

easy."

He glared at her. "Nothin's easy."

"Fine." She turned and walked out, Rick with her.

Once outside the cell block they paused for a moment.

Rick sighed. "I need to pay my respects anyway. I'll ask Sean if he's up to identifying the little jerk. If he's not, we let him go."

Unexpectedly, Sean agreed to do it, said he could handle it. When Rick brought Wesley to him he swore he'd never seen the kid though Wesley matched the description he'd given. Either there were two young men with a pronounced scar over the left eye or Sean was too rattled to make sense of anything. Then again, in his vulnerable state he could have figured nailing a kid for hubcaps wasn't worth it.

Rick released Wesley Partlow. He'd already run a check with DMV on the kid's license, which was current and clean. His address was Randolph Street, Waynesboro. He didn't really think too much about it. Small-fry.

# 16

At seven o'clock Sunday morning, Fair Haristeen drove through the puddles in Harry's driveway. He stopped in front of the barn because he knew she'd be feeding the horses. At the slam of his truck door, Tucker joyously dashed out to greet the vet. Tucker loved Fair.

*"Wasn't that an awful storm?"* The corgi wagged her tailless bottom.

Small tree limbs were scattered over the yard and dogwood petals covered the ground.

"You're the best dog." Fair bent over to pat the silky head.

"I'm in here," Harry called out from the center aisle of the attractive old barn.

"Figured." Fair jumped over a puddle. "You should see the roof of BoomBoom's barn. Swiss cheese."

"Your first call?"

"Not exactly. When I drove by I saw her and Thomas standing out by the barn so I pulled up. You know when Kelly" — Fair mentioned BoomBoom's deceased husband — "built that barn I couldn't believe he'd put on such a cheap roof. The man was a paving contractor. He knew better."

"Yeah, but riding wasn't his thing so he built a cheap barn. Pretty tacky of him."

Fair removed his baseball cap. "Never thought of it. He had more money than God."

"Just a little revenge on his part. Control. And to what do I owe your company?"

"Does the word 'control' have anything to do with it?"

Mrs. Murphy, lounging in the hayloft with Simon, the opossum, remarked, *"You know, I think he's gaining insight."*

*"M-m-m."* Simon evidenced scant interest in human couplings and uncouplings. *"Did I show you the beads I found?"* He rolled out his treasure.

*"Simon, those aren't beads, they're ball bearings, and if you found them around here it means a piece of Mom's equipment is about to die a horrible death."*

*"Really?"*

*"Really. Where did you find them? And I assume this had to be a few days ago. You weren't fool enough to go out in that storm."*

*"I'm not telling."*

*"All right. Don't tell but put them back —*

*maybe she'll see them before the damage is done. Something's broken."*

"I'm not putting them back and I'm not telling. Anyway, maybe I didn't find them here. They're shiny and I found them fair and square. I like shiny things."

*"Marsupials are weird."* Mrs. Murphy lashed her beautiful tail to and fro. She didn't like being disobeyed.

*"Pewter grabbing a dead woodpecker and then Harry picking it up is pretty weird."*

*"She took it to the taxidermist."* Mrs. Murphy laughed, her good humor restored. *"And you know that Pewter will tear it to shreds the minute that stuffed bird is brought back into the house."* The cat tiptoed over to the edge of the hayloft, having decided that the human conversation might be more interesting than her own. Not that she didn't like Simon, but he was a bit simpleminded at times.

Pewter reposed in the tack room on a neatly folded Baker blanket. She'd gorged herself at breakfast and would need half the day to digest.

"It's been quite a Dogwood Festival." Fair dipped a clean old towel in water, rubbed it on a glycerin bar, and began wiping down Harry's hunt saddle.

"You don't have to do that."

171

"No, but I like to be useful." He hummed a Billy Ray Cyrus tune, then cleared his throat. "You seem to have hit it off with Diego."

"Yes," came the terse reply.

Fair knew better than to expect an explanation out of Harry. He'd known her all his life and having been married to her he felt he knew her better than anyone except maybe Susan Tucker. But women's friendships existed on a separate plane from spousal relationships. He often laughed to himself when he'd hear idle chatter about the differences between men and women. Women, according to the experts, were more forthcoming about their emotions than men and they bonded through sharing emotions whereas men bonded through activity. In all the years he'd known Mary Minor she'd never volunteered an emotion. You had to pry them out of her. She'd happily tell you what she thought, read, saw, did, but not what she felt. Susan used to harangue her over it but Harry was Harry and that was that. "Take me or leave me" was her attitude and when Fair thought about it, he concluded she was right. You either accept someone or you don't and no amount of jawing about it will change them or bring you closer.

"The guy looks like a movie star." Fair flipped the stirrup iron up over the saddle seat so he could better clean the flaps. The saddle was clean but he needed a task.

"He does but you're pretty great-looking yourself." She winked.

"You say that to all the boys." He laughed, glad to be in her presence. "Lottie Pearson is on the warpath, by the way."

"Against me or BoomBoom?"

"Anyone that gets in her way but I think you and BoomBoom are, well, let's just say, hold on to your scalps."

"What is Lottie's problem?" Harry scrubbed out a water bucket in the sink in the tack room. It had hot and cold water, a nice feature in a tack room. "I mean it's not like I woke up one morning and said, 'Today I will piss off Lottie Pearson.' And I only agreed to be Diego's date after pressure from BoomBoom. She said Lottie would bore him to tears whereas I could talk about farming."

"Lottie's getting scared and she's getting bitter."

Harry tipped her head up to stare into Fair's blue eyes. "Scared about what?"

"She's in her thirties, never been married, and no prospects in sight."

Dropping the bucket in the sink, Harry

put her hands on her hips. "Oh, come on, you don't believe that."

"About Lottie I do. Man-hungry."

"Said by a man." Harry giggled.

"Hey, we may be the slower sex but I don't know any man who doesn't have radar for a woman crazed to get married. The pheromone of fear or mating or something is what she sends out. Nothing turns a man off faster than that except personal uncleanliness, I guess."

Harry resumed scrubbing. "Never thought about it but you're probably right. What's to get scared about, Fair? You can't just go out and find a mate. It's not like shopping for a car."

"No, but it is a big-ticket item." He smiled. "What I find offensive about Lottie is that she wants to get married but no one is good enough. Roger O'Bannon was crazy about her and, well, now he's dead. He wasn't right for her." Fair lost his train of thought. "It's hard to talk about him in the past tense."

"I know what you're trying to say."

"She wants someone who is First Family of Virginia. That stuff is so superficial."

"Easy for us to say because we are."

"Have you ever cared for one moment that your ancestors arrived here in 1620?

No, 1640. Good memory." He tapped his forehead.

"No. I'm proud of them but it doesn't make me better than anyone. And the slave trade really picked up at the end of the seventeenth century so as far as I'm concerned those African-American families are F.F.V., too."

"If there's one thing that I really hate about Virginia it's the great game of ancestor worship." He flipped over the other stirrup. "On the other hand, it gives us stability, I suppose. Anyway, even if Lottie marries one of us she's not F.F.V."

"No, but her children will be."

"Great. Another generation of snobs." Fair laughed again. "My favorite low moment for Virginians was when the descendants of Thomas Jefferson had a reunion and argued about whether to let Sally Hemings's descendants join when the DNA tests proved they carried Jefferson's blood. I mean here we are in the twenty-first century and someone is going to argue about this."

"You're expressive this morning." She shook her head.

"Actually," he exhaled, "I'm so glad I didn't find Diego here."

She shot him a searing look. "Oh, like I'd go to bed with him on the first date, so to speak?"

"Uh — yes."

"Fair, it's my body."

"I love your body."

"Oh, Fair —" She threw up her hands.

"I love your mind, too."

*"This is getting good."* Mrs. Murphy leaned way over the edge of the hayloft.

Even Pewter woke up. Tucker sat, tongue out, listening to every syllable.

"You can be real smooth when you want to be. Now look, I'm doing what I want, when I want, and with whom I want. Don't fence me in."

"I haven't."

"Yeah, and you haven't had any rivals either."

"Oh, now I do?"

"Might."

"I hate it when you're coy."

"Well, I hate it when you try to manage me."

"I'm not managing you." He leaned over the saddle. "I'm being truthful."

"Then I'll be truthful right back. I like Diego and I'll see him again, most likely. Other than that, I don't know squat."

"Don't go to bed with him." Fair's voice grew stronger.

"I'll do as I damn well please."

"Latin-American men are faithful to their mothers and no one else. You don't know

176

who he's slept with. You can't be too careful."

"That's pretty racist." Acid dripped from her voice.

"It's true. They're dominated by their mothers!"

"Fair, you are so full of shit." Harry laughed. He was unintentionally funny.

"I'm trying to protect you."

"No, you're not. You don't want me to go to bed with anyone but you."

"I admit that."

"Get over yourself."

"Harry, go slow. Think things through. What kind of future would you have with a man from a country full of ex-Nazis?"

"Fair, for Chrissake!"

"It is."

"So are Argentina and Paraguay and, for that matter, the United States. After the war didn't our government spirit out any German who had knowledge we needed or wanted? And furthermore, that was over fifty years ago. Somehow I think most of those dudes are dead. Now you're an expert on Uruguay?"

"Can't blame a guy for trying."

"Yeah, yeah. To change the subject, are you going on the coon hunt tonight?"

"Thought I would."

The best time to hunt coons is the fall but sometimes a hunter would train his young hounds with an older hound before then. Summer was too hot so spring often was a good time to work young hounds. The female coons, "heavy," usually gave birth in April through May to litters of between one and eight. They'd only be hunting males.

She filled the cleaned-out bucket with clean sponges, placing the bucket under the sink. "I wonder when Roger's funeral will be."

"Wednesday or Thursday. Unless Sean thinks he'll have to wait for the weekend because of out-of-towners. I doubt it though. Herb will know. Brings death a little closer, doesn't it?"

"Nah." She shook her head. "Can't think about it. It doesn't do any good. You can die at four years of age or one hundred. But you can't think about it."

"Sounds like your dad."

"It's true, though."

"I suppose, but Roger's death makes me think about it. One minute he's sitting in the chair and the next minute he's on the floor with Little Mim pulling on his arm and Lottie screaming."

"Been quite a weekend. Lottie falls off the

float. Oh, wait, it started with Miranda's hubcaps getting stolen and winding up at O'Bannon's. Then Lottie bounces off the float. Given the hoopskirt I'm surprised she didn't bounce right back or she could be our own living Taco Bell symbol. Then Roger goes to his reward. The twerp who stole Miranda's hubcaps shows up parking cars at Big Mim's party. Tracy tackles him. Then the storm from hell rips through Albemarle County. And you're worried that I'm going to sleep with someone other than you? Isn't there a Chinese curse, 'May you live in interesting times'?"

# 17

Diego and Thomas spent the day at Windy Ridge, an estate owned by the retired Ambassador to the Court of St. James's. Since she didn't need to be a tour guide for the visitors, Harry worked, suppressing her excitement about the coming evening's coon hunt. She loved to hunt. Picking up the debris around her house took two hours. Then she walked her fence lines to make certain they weren't torn up. Blair Bainbridge's cattle loved to amble over onto her lush pastures. Not that she minded herding them back but she didn't always have the time to drive them across the creek, repair the fence, check for injuries. Also, her three horses, Poptart, Tomahawk, and Gin Fizz, disliked the cattle. They'd pin back their ears, bare their teeth, hurl crude insults usually involving the fact that cows have four stomachs.

Mrs. Murphy and Tucker accompanied Harry on her rounds. Pewter declared the storm frayed her nerves; she needed to rest in the house. The offending blue jay swooped around the kitchen windowsill. Seeing Pewter asleep on the kitchen table, he unleashed a torrent of abuse.

After a day's work the tiger cat and Tucker felt entitled to participate in the coon hunt. Both waxed furious when Harry shut them in the house, closing off the animal door, then driving off in her 1978 blue Ford pickup.

*"You'll pay for this!"* Murphy threatened as the red taillights receded into the gathering twilight.

*"Pipe down."* Pewter rolled over. *"You've slept all day. Don't tell me you're tired."*

*"I didn't sleep all day. That horrid blue jay perched on the windowsill. He called me a fat gray sow, a sea cow, a ponderous pachyderm. I'll kill him!"*

Mrs. Murphy walked back from the door, jumped onto the kitchen counter, trotting to the window over the sink. *"I can't believe she left me! We worked today. We deserve a party."*

*"We were invited to Aunt Tally's tea party. Of course, that didn't turn out so good, did it?"* Tucker thoughtfully added.

*"That's not the point."* Mrs. Murphy batted at the windowpane.

Pewter jumped up on the counter, too. She headed for the large bowl of crunchies, stuck her head in, and munched away.

*"Noisy eater."* Tucker giggled.

*"Tailless wonder."* Pewter flicked a nugget on the floor for the dog. *"I've endured enough insult for one day."*

*"It's a dumb time to coon hunt."* Murphy hoped to find a way to make her loss less. She adored any form of hunting, even if only to watch from the bed of the pickup. After all, she was the best hunter in central Virginia, maybe all of Virginia.

Put out as she was, she should have been grateful to be left behind.

The sodden ground sucked the boots right off the hunters' feet. The bushes and branches, loaded with droplets, soaked each person who brushed by. Durant Creek, a tributary of Beaver Creek, roared like a diesel dump truck on full throttle.

Harry, hardened by outdoor life, didn't much mind. BoomBoom was a surprising trouper. Thomas bravely soldiered on in his expensive Holland and Holland outfit. Diego wore what Harry told him. He had bought a pair of Red Wing work boots after leaving the former ambassador to Great Britain and topped his outfit off with a pair of old jeans and a canvas shirt. Thomas

182

thought Diego's boots were too country and not English enough. He regretted it now, though, as he tried to keep up in his green wellies, a wonderful high rubber boot for country chores but not for running behind hounds. Thomas was hard put to keep up, his flashlight bobbing as he labored. Boom stayed back with him, a sacrifice for her since she liked being up front.

Jack's hounds treed two coons in rapid succession. He called them off, walked about a quarter of a mile, and set them to work again. Joyce, his wife, walked along, too.

Fair enjoyed good hound work and was pleased to see shiny coats on the hounds. He wanted to stay behind Harry and Diego but forced himself to run ahead of them.

Jim Sanburne brought up the rear along with Don Clatterbuck, both men moving at a leisurely pace, happy to listen to the music.

Harry held the flashlight as she and Diego ran behind Fair.

"They're on another one. Picked him up by the creek," Harry said, but the words were no sooner out of her mouth than a rumble overhead surprised her.

Low clouds moving fast presaged another storm. She'd felt the temperature drop but paid little attention to it. The cloudy skies held the scent down; the falling temperature, now in the high forties, made for a glorious night of hunting about to be cut short.

A flash over the creek side stopped everyone in their tracks.

"Folks, I got to pick up. We don't want to be out here." Jack put his grandfather's huge cow horn to his lips, blowing in his hounds.

Joyce peered up at the sky. "Sure hope it's not like last night."

As the people turned to head back to their trucks the thunder moved closer and a light splattering of rain began.

Impulsively, Diego reached for Harry's hand, drawing her to him, and kissed her. She kissed him back, then they broke off, racing toward the trucks, laughing.

A glitter caught Harry's eye. "Hold up."

The rain fell steadier now but she moved to the left, off the path. Diego followed her. She knelt down, picking up the Mercedes star and a snapped chain. "The hubcap thief."

"Odd." Diego studied the object.

"He wore it around his neck." A bone-rattling clap of thunder convinced her to hasten back to the truck. Running, she pocketed the hood ornament. By the time she and Diego reached their safe haven they were drenched and shivering.

They'd parked at the end of a gravel road northeast of Crozet, the boundary between Booty Mawyer's farm and that of Marcus Durant. Durant, out of town this weekend, was an avid coon, fox, and rabbit hunter. He'd hunt just about anything. He'd built a twenty-foot-by-sixteen-foot shack. With a tin roof, a wood-burning stove, and two sets of bunk beds by the walls, he could roll in and sleep if his hounds kept running late into the night. A generous man, he shared his shack with his buddies, so long as everybody cleaned up.

Fair, using well-cured wood stacked outside under a protective overhang, started up a fire. Soon the little group was thawing out, passing the jug, and telling tales in the time-honored tradition of night hunters.

Thomas and BoomBoom sat next to one another on the edge of a bunk bed, as did Jack and Joyce. The others sat on upturned milk crates and wooden chairs in front of the stove.

Jim leaned back, putting his cold, wet feet in front of the stove. Everyone peeled off their shoes, boots, socks, hoping they'd dry before they had to put them back on.

"Ever tell you about the first time I coon hunted with Mim?" Jim cast his eyes around the room. "Guess not. Well, I'd come back from Korea in one piece and I hadn't been home three days when I spied Mim coming out of Crozet National Bank arguing with Aunt Tally. I stopped my truck, hopped out, took off my hat to the ladies, and asked Mim out then and there. Heard her family broke off the romance with another fellow because he wasn't high-class enough. Hell, he was more suitable than I but faint heart ne'er won fair lady and to hell with suitability. Aunt Tally looked me over like I was a horse to buy. Well, Mim said yes. So Tally says, 'Where you taking her?'

" 'Coon hunting,' says I. 'See that's what you hunt, young man.' " He laughed, imitating Tally's voice. "A fine night. Crisp, you could smell the leaves turning. Marcus's father, Lucius, had a good pack of hounds, turned 'em loose, and what a hunt.

"Mim was a speedy little slip of a girl. She kept right up and the next thing we heard was screaming and cussing. Lord o'mighty. The hounds ran right up on Arnold Berryman, covering Ellie McIntire.

"She was screaming. He held up his coat over her. Scared the hell out of the hounds. I thought that would be my last date with Mim.

"She enjoyed herself so much she asked

when we could do it again." He slapped his thigh and laughed, the others laughing with him.

"Ellie McIntire." BoomBoom shook her head, remembering the spinster librarian who had struck terror in their hearts when they were children.

"Thank you," Thomas said as he received the jug from Fair. After a long draft he handed it to BoomBoom.

"Thomas, how do you like our country water?" Jack, who didn't drink, asked.

"Potent and smooth," the older man replied.

"Thomas, tell them how your grandfather brought the telephone to Montevideo." BoomBoom slipped her arm through his, leaning into him.

"Oh . . ."

"Tell," the others chimed in.

"My grandfather saw the telephone in London. He was our ambassador there before World War One. He formed a company and started the first telephone service in our country. Then my father, not to be outdone, founded the first television station. I remember when I was a boy being very disappointed to find out that Jojo, the clown on the children's show, emitted the distinct aroma of gin." They all laughed.

"Tell them what you did."

"My dear," he demurred.

"Thomas brought satellite technology to their communications company."

"BoomBoom, it was the logical progression. That didn't take the intelligence or courage of Grandfather or Father. Or the determination of my mother, who took over the television business. She's slowed down a bit by heart trouble but really, she's smarter than I am."

"The Steinmetzes are quick to see the future and profit," Diego said admiringly. "The Aybars are running cattle instead of satellites." He laughed.

"Nothing wrong with running cattle," Jim said. "You come on over and look at my Herefords."

"Hunting down your way?" Jack politely asked.

"Yes, and fishing. If you like deep-sea fishing, you must come down," Thomas said, a hint of pride in his voice.

"Sounds like machine-gun fire." Joyce looked up at the tin roof as the rain intensified.

The four hounds thought so, too, as they edged closer to their humans.

"You know, I'd like to come on down and go fishing." Jim smiled at Thomas. "Mim and I have never been to Uruguay. Is there something we could bring . . . like jeans? When you visit Russia you bring jeans. At least we used to in the seventies. People would pay a lot of money for jeans from the United States."

"Not a thing," Thomas replied. "We'll take care of everything."

"Some things cost three times as much and some things are extremely inexpensive," Diego added. "Now, we don't have foxhounds or coonhounds. Those would fetch a high price."

"They're my babies." Joyce laughed.

"Almost forgot." Harry pulled out the Mercedes star.

"Where's the car?" BoomBoom laughed.

"That's the only part I could afford." She laughed, too. "Actually, I found this on the path back a ways. When Tracy brought Wesley Partlow back to the house at Mim's party, he wore a star like this around his neck."

"Anyone report one missing?" Fair logically asked.

"Not that I know of," Jim answered, "but many of our guests were feeling no pain."

They all laughed.

"It can cost two hundred and ninety dollars to replace that star," Thomas said.

"Hang on to it." He stopped a moment. "Had to replace one once."

Harry didn't get home until one in the morning. She headed straight for bed, missing the shredded needlepoint pillow in the living room, compliments of Mrs. Murphy.

# 18

A series of thunderstorms crackled across Crozet for twenty-four hours. A few minutes of calm would ensue, and occasionally the skies lightened, but within a half hour clouds darkened again, the rains came down, and the roar of deep thunder reverberated throughout the mountains and valleys.

Harry sorted mail amid peals of thunder. Tucker crouched under the small table in the back of the post office. Mrs. Murphy sat on the dividing counter between the public side of the room and the working side. The broad and smooth old wooden counter with a flip-up section so the postmistress could walk in and out had seen generations of Crozetians call for their mail.

The advent of the railroad, built by the engineering genius of the New World, Claudius Crozet, brought the mail and news faster to the hamlet named for him. Residents no longer waited for the stage. They could stand at the station to watch the mail sacks being tossed off the train. The mail from Crozet would be picked up as it hung from a yardarm, the sack hooked so it could be grabbed from the moving train. Trains had cars outfitted as post stations and often money would be in the post station car, the postal employee taking the precaution of wearing a pistol.

The town had built its latest post office at the turn of the nineteenth century, altering it only to make more room for parking, since cars take up more room than horses. The pleasant structure had been rewired three more times in one hundred years, the last rewiring occurring in 1998. Small though the station was, it was hooked into the national postal computer system. Miranda resisted using the computer. Harry, much younger, mastered it rapidly. Wisely, she never instructed Miranda in its use. She waited for Miranda to ask — which, finally, she did.

Technology, so beguiling in its promises, often only delivers a new set of problems. The postal computers coughed, sputtered, and took to bed quite often with virus infections. While they could weigh packages, give an instant answer on postage at home and abroad, anyone handy with a scale, an instrument thousands of years old, could give the information in about the same amount of time. And wonderful though the blinking screen may have been, letters still needed to be hand-canceled at times, postage-due markings in maroon ink required human hands, and the process of sorting the mail once it arrived at the local postal offices was done the way it had always been done — one letter at a time.

In short, the tasks of the postal worker had changed little over the last century. And the advent of the twenty-first century still hadn't altered those tasks.

Harry owned a computer from which she sent e-mail or occasionally logged on to the Internet to look up something. She spent an evening once reading about Hereford cattle on the Internet. Then she switched to the Angus site and compared notes. But mostly she thought the information revolution was more hype than reality.

And nothing could substitute for a love letter. The sensuality of the paper, the color, the ink, the contents, the privacy of it, were inviolate and perfect.

As she sorted that Monday's mail she thought about writing Diego a letter. Maybe she'd mention their kiss in the rain or how wonderful it was to dance with him on a cool spring night. Then again she could talk about grass crops. She hummed to herself as

Miranda carefully pulled the striped dish towel off the orange-glazed cinnamon buns she brought to work. The fragrance of Miranda's best creation mingled with the pot of coffee brewing in the back.

"Heaven."

Miranda glanced at the old railroad wall clock. "Heaven at seven-thirty in the morning." A clap of thunder made her laugh. "I don't remember so many storms. One after the other. I'll get over there in a minute to help you. Oh, tea?"

"Yes, thanks. Don't rush. There's not that much mail, which is surprising. Enjoy the lull. The summer postcards will fire up soon enough. Before that we'll have the graduation notices. Never ends." She sorted postcards as though shuffling playing cards.

Miranda brought her tea. She herself poured a bracing cup of coffee. Miranda had let Mim talk her into joining a coffee club, so each month she received another type of pricey coffee from France, Germany, Spain, Switzerland. This delicious coffee was from a famous café in Vienna.

A light rap on the door, next to the animal door, brought forth a "come in" from both women.

"Hi." Susan quickly stepped in, for the rain had intensified. "Have you ever?"

"No," they said in unison again.

"What are you two, a duet?" Susan laughed, shaking the raindrops from her auburn hair, cut in a sleek pageboy.

"Hogendobber and Haristeen. Has a ring to it. How about H and H?" Harry laughed.

"That sounds like a candy." Susan breathed in the moist aroma.

"Vienna." Miranda poured her a cup.

"You'll be our expert. Next thing we know, Miranda, you'll open one of those upscale coffee shops where a cup costs three bucks."

"It is outrageous but a good cup of coffee is special, especially that first cup." A louder boom lifted all eyes to heaven. Miranda cast hers down first. "Oh, Tucker, poor baby, it's all right." She knelt down to pet the shivering corgi.

Pewter, deep in the mail cart, said in a high-pitched voice, *"I don't like it either."*

Harry walked over to give love to the rotund gray kitty.

*"Chicken,"* Mrs. Murphy tersely criticized them.

*"Hateful bitch,"* Pewter promptly replied.

"I'm glad I don't know what they're saying." Harry laughed. "Hey, we all went coon hunting last night with Jack and Joyce Ragland. Got soaked. Hunted until the storm really hit, but it was a great night anyway. The voices on those Ragland hounds are something special. Goose bumps. I didn't get home until one this morning."

"You didn't shoot any, did you?" Miranda hated the thought of shooting animals.

"No."

"Well, while you were coon hunting, I took my two cherubs to see their grandparents. Danny" — Susan mentioned her son — "wanted to see the new Audi sports car that Mamaw bought for herself. He told her she looked like a teenager in her TT. I think that's what it's called. Anyway, it's a fabulous design and drives nicely. There's my mother, seventy-one, driving a high-tech sports car. I love it! What'd you do, Miranda?" Susan asked.

"Sewed curtains for Tracy's apartment. He fixed my washing machine. Romantic. Actually, it was. We'd spent the weekend doing all the Dogwood Festival things. It was kind of nice to be home doing chores. You girls will have to see his apartment, right over the old pharmacy. He's got the entire floor for three fifty a month. It needs a lot of work but Eddie Griswald couldn't give it away. Everyone in Crozet wants their own house. Tracy's very happy for now."

"I can paint," Harry offered.

"He'd like that."

"Oh, I forgot to tell you. Look what I found last night." Harry walked over to her bag, an old Danish schoolbag, worn through in spots. She fished around in the bottom, retrieving the Mercedes star.

Susan took it from her. "Remember there was a fad in the eighties and early nineties? City kids would snap these off and wear them."

"Before my time," Harry joked.

"Oh, puh-lease." Susan's eyebrow shot upward as she dragged out the syllables.

"Where'd you find it?" Susan asked.

"Near Durant Creek, where we were hunting."

"That's what that boy had around his neck." Miranda reached for her first and only orange-glazed cinnamon bun, an act of discipline. Last year she would have had three eaten by this time but she'd cut back dramatically on sweets and had lost over thirty-five pounds in the past year. She could have worn her high-school clothes if she'd kept them.

"It might not be his," Susan volunteered. "Then again, how many disembodied Mercedes stars are there?"

*"Here comes another one,"* Mrs. Murphy

warned Tucker and Pewter as a bright flash of lightning presaged a mighty rumble.

"So," Susan's voice rose merrily, "when do you see Diego again?"

"Uh — I don't know. If not next weekend maybe the weekend after. I like him."

"That's obvious." Susan smiled. "And he likes you."

"Seems to."

"What man wouldn't?" Miranda thought of Harry as her own daughter in ways.

"What a nice thing to say." Harry blushed.

"Was Fair at the coon hunt?" Susan's curiosity bubbled over.

"He was."

"And?"

"Pretty much as you'd expect," Harry said, tossing a package onto the A–B section of the package shelf.

Miranda and Susan looked at one another, then back to Harry.

*"Jealous."* Mrs. Murphy stated the obvious, something she usually didn't do but among humans it was often a necessity.

Little Mim drove up to the front of the post office. The rain poured. She sat in her $83,000 Mercedes waiting for the rain to lighten, but it didn't. It only rained harder.

Murphy, eyes sharp, noticed the star was

missing from Little Mim's exquisite car. *"Aha."*

*"What are you aha-ing about?"* Pewter grumbled from the bottom of the mail cart.

*"The star is missing from Little Mim's silver-mist Mercedes."*

*"Really?"* Pewter clambered out of the mail cart, sending it rolling about a foot in the opposite direction of her progress. She jumped up next to Murphy. *"It is."*

The humans noticed the cats staring out at Little Mim so they looked, too.

"Oh, my gosh, the star is missing from her car!" Miranda noticed first.

"You're right." Susan giggled.

"Boy, Wesley Partlow will be sliced and diced." Harry sighed. "Guess I'd better give her this when she comes in."

"Well, what would you do with it?" Susan wondered.

"Mount it on a block of wood and put it on my bookcase. It's the closest I'll ever come to a Mercedes." Harry reached for an umbrella in the stand by the front door. "I'll go out and walk her in. You know, that kid must be dumber than snot."

"Harry, what a vulgar thing to say."

"Sorry, Miranda." She opened the door a crack. "I wouldn't want to be in his shoes."

Truer words were never spoken.

# 19

"Cut him down," Rick Shaw ordered one of his men.

The photographs had been taken, the body dusted for fingerprints, the ground under the corpse inspected.

Two kids crossing in the rough patch of land behind Crozet Elder Care, a home for the aged, had found Wesley Partlow dangling from a fiddle oak. His tongue hung down on his chest, his face was purple-black, his eyes bugged out, and his feet and hands were swollen from the fluids collecting there. The storms hadn't improved his appearance but they probably saved his eyes from the birds.

Naturally, the gruesome sight scared the bejesus out of the kids, but they had the presence of mind to call the sheriff. Although Rick and Cynthia Cooper had witnessed plenty of unpleasant sights over the years, it didn't mean they liked seeing it.

The body was lowered carefully onto the

gurney. If Wesley'd been cut down with a thud the corpse might have been even more damaged. The coroner couldn't save anyone, that's for sure, but he usually had the right answer about someone's health a day late.

As Diana Robb rolled away the mortal remains of a wasted life, Coop examined the bark of the tree. "If he shimmied up the tree, he didn't slough off bark."

"He would have made a long skid mark. The rains would have taken care of little marks, don't you think?" Rick looked skyward. "And here comes some more."

"I don't know, boss. He was light. He could have climbed up without much effort, without a lot of scraping and slipping. I looked for tire tracks."

"Yeah." Rick, too, had wondered if he'd been hoisted up on a truck bed. "Washed out."

Wesley Partlow didn't seem like the suicide type.

"I don't get it."

"Let's find Din Marks."

They drove out sloshing through ever-deepening mud holes. As they turned onto Route 240 the raindrops fell, fat ones making big splashes on the windshield.

By the time they reached Fashion Mall, some thirty minutes later, it was again pouring. They parked by the side door and made a run for the Sears store. Din Marks worked in the lawnmower section. He blanched when he saw them.

Rick spoke to the other man behind the counter. "Can you hold the fort? I need a minute or two with Mr. Marks."

"Sure." The middle-aged man nodded.

Rick motioned for Din to follow him. Together with Cynthia they walked into the center concourse of the mall. Few shoppers milled about, weekday mornings being sparsely populated.

"Would you like to sit?" Rick pointed to a bench.

"No."

"When you were locked up with Wesley Partlow, did he say anything to you? He was mad at someone or someone was mad at him? Anything?"

Din shook his head. "No."

"Did he seem depressed?" Cynthia asked.

"Not him." Din ruefully smiled. "I was drunk but I remember his smart mouth."

"Did he mention cars, hubcaps?"

"No. Said he didn't do anything. He didn't belong there and he'd get out. I said I slugged a cop and he laughed. I didn't mean to hit Yancy. Didn't mean to — well, I was drunk."

"We know," Rick replied. "Did you notice anything unusual about Wesley himself?"

"No."

"Did Wesley mention doing business with anyone in town?"

"No."

"Did he mention a truck?"

"No."

Cooper spoke again. "Would you say he was calm, agitated, surly, afraid?"

"Uh. Watchful. We didn't say too much to one another. He told me if I puked he'd kill me. When I woke up he was gone."

"By the way," Rick said, "how'd you get to work this morning?"

"Walked."

"In the rain?" Coop inquired.

"I'll be walking in the rain for a long time. I'm gonna lose my license for three years."

"Maybe you should stop drinking." She handed him an AA number. "Can't hurt to try."

"Yeah," he mumbled.

"Call the number, Din," Coop urged him. "The next time we pick you up it could be in a body bag or you'll have killed someone else."

"It'll be three years from now. I won't drive."

"Don't drink. You can't handle it," she flatly stated.

"Go on back to work," Rick told him.

Din turned to go, then stopped. "What happened to that kid?"

"Found him hanging from a tree."

Din blinked. "Shit."

"If you think of anything, call us."

"That asshole would have never hung himself," Din blurted out.

"That's our assessment of the situation, too," Rick said.

Back in the squad car, Rick and Coop wiped their faces, damp again from the rain.

Rick pulled out a cigarette and lit it. "Never received a report for a stolen truck."

"The eighty-seven GMC." She lit up as well. "Maybe it wasn't stolen."

"That has occurred to me."

"Who'd lend him a truck?"

"Someone stupid." Rick inhaled. "Or someone who's a fence."

"O'Bannons?"

"Thought of that. Tim O'Bannon would have killed his kids if they'd ever pulled a stunt like that. He was as honest as the day is long. He'd never take stolen goods."

"The old man's dead."

Rick paused. "Sean's not that stupid. Make a couple of thousand tax-free dollars but jeopardize your whole business by selling stolen goods? He wouldn't do it."

"Who knows?" Cooper opened the window a crack to let the smoke out but the rain snuck through the crack. Even though she quickly put the window up, her right thigh was wet. "Damn."

"No point driving until I can see where I'm going." He sighed. "Coop, apart from drugs, what could bring in big bucks? Moonshine can still make you rich if you're careful," he noted.

Neither one had to tell the other that they were treating the demise of Wesley Partlow as murder. It's true that people can harbor deep pain and secret losses and finally do themselves in. And sometimes a surly façade covers pain; but both officers of the law felt that wasn't the case. Someone threw a rope over that fiddle tree and strung up Wesley Partlow just like in the Wild West.

"I searched the computer for a criminal record. Wesley Partlow managed to keep his nose clean. He was smarter than I gave him credit for. I thought he was just a dumb punk."

"He goes in the ground after that autopsy." Rick squinted, the rain had let up a little. "How's your appetite?"

"Why?"

"Haven't lost it after this morning?"

"No. Have you lost yours?"

"Takes more than a hanged man to do that. Let's go to the Riverside Café."

"I'll call Big Mim on the way. The news will be spreading all over Crozet. You know those two kids will tell. They'll have nightmares for months."

"Yep." He turned right out of the parking lot, heading for the intersection of High Street and Free Bridge. "Wait a second before calling the Queen of Crozet. Did you check out the number of 1987 GMC half-ton trucks in Virginia?"

"Over twenty thousand, four-wheel drive and two-wheel, still on the road."

"How about in Albemarle County?"

"Yancy's on that since he has to sit around. Guess he'll be sitting around for a while."

"Okay."

"We don't know if the truck is registered here. Could be out of state."

"I know."

"Like a jigsaw puzzle," she said, "all the pieces have been dumped on the table in a heap."

He turned toward her. "Maybe all the pieces aren't on the table."

# 20

The word of the grisly find reached the post office by one-thirty. Big Mim stopped by after her errands.

"I feel terrible." Miranda meant it, too.

"You didn't know him," Harry hastened to comfort her. She knew how guilty Miranda could get.

"She's right, Miranda. You simply reported that your hubcaps were stolen and by chance or whatever he was parking cars at my party. And you can believe I have chastised that company. I'll never use their valet service again. Not that he did any harm but still, they ought to scrutinize their help more closely. Their excuse was he had a valid driver's license and they needed all the help they could get due to the dogwood parties." Big Mim shook out her umbrella. "I've made a mess. Sorry. I didn't think it would be so wet."

"Don't worry about it. I'll mop up the floor before I leave tonight. It's that kind of day." Harry scratched Pewter at the base of her tail.

"Do they know how long he was there?" Miranda asked.

"No. The coroner will figure it out," Big Mim replied. "Did you know our county is getting so populous we have two coroners now, full time?"

"I didn't know that," Miranda replied.

"I guess I'd better call Cynthia and tell her I found the Mercedes star and gave it back to Marilyn." Harry headed for the phone while Miranda filled in Big Mim. Big Mim hadn't seen Little Mim since breakfast so she knew nothing of the returned star.

*"I wish Mother hadn't found that star."* Mrs. Murphy sighed. The low pressure was getting to her.

*"Who cares?"* Pewter purred. *"Wesley Partlow's nothing to her."*

*"She's curious. She'll be especially curious now. You know how she gets,"* Tucker agreed with Mrs. Murphy.

*"If the kid killed himself, that's that,"* Pewter, the hard-boiled, replied. *"He didn't have much of a life to look forward to, did he?"*

*"I can't imagine a dog killing herself,"* Tucker mused. *"I think it's a peculiar thing to humans. Suicide."*

"*If it's suicide we have nothing to worry about.*" Mrs. Murphy joined Pewter on the counter. "*But if it's not suicide then this will be a stormy spring.*"

"*Oh, come on,*" Pewter said, a touch sarcastically. "*Who would risk their own freedom to kill a loser like Wesley?*"

# 21

The sodden ground could suck the shoes right off a horse. It held onto human shoes, too, as Harry and Cynthia Cooper trudged along the deer path not far from Durant Creek. Tucker, up to her knees in the mud, accompanied them. Mrs. Murphy and Pewter, left back at the farm, planned even more retaliatory destruction.

Harry pointed. "Here we connect up to the old farm road. Jeez, it's loud."

Coop stopped at the crossroads of deer path and farm road. "The ground's soaked. If we get any more rain, the creeks and rivers will jump their banks."

"Spring."

"Yep."

"We were running back. I noticed a gleam. And that's about the size of it. We walked over, I discovered it was the hood ornament. I didn't notice footprints or tire tracks. It started to pour but it had been raining before, as you know. If a car or truck had come back here there would have been deep ruts. There weren't." She moved over. "About here."

Tucker, senses much keener, sniffed around. No trace of human scent remained, although a hint of coyote lingered. She was glad her mother couldn't smell it because coyote spelled a great deal of trouble for everyone. The force of the storms beat down small branches, brush, stripped some buds off trees. She couldn't gather any more evidence than the humans.

"Where does the farm road lead?"

"To the creek."

"Any structures, sheds, anything like that along the way?"

"No. Marcus Durant's shack is the only building and that's back where we parked."

"Well, let's head back." Coop stuck her thumbs in her belt. "Whatever might have been on the ground is washed away by now, but" — she looked around again — "I've got to run down every lead I can. I just wonder what the hell he was doing out here, if he was here."

"Come on, Tucker."

*"I'm coming,"* the dog replied, irritated that she couldn't locate more scent.

A sharp breeze picked up as the two women and dog walked back.

"Sure doesn't feel like spring today," Cooper commented.

"Cuts to the bone. Coop, what's going on? You wouldn't be out here with me if you weren't worried."

"I don't think Wesley Partlow committed suicide. Marshall Wells can't get to the autopsy until tonight. I'll withhold judgment until I get his results."

"Isn't it hard to perform an autopsy on an exposed corpse that's been hanging?" Harry grimaced.

"Those guys know what they're doing. They take tissue samples. I couldn't do it. I trust their opinion because they do such a thorough examination of the body, too. Rick and I have trained eyes but we're not doctors."

"I wouldn't think a kid like Wesley could be hanged without a fight. Surely there are easier ways to kill someone than to hang them."

"Not if all you have is rope. What if our killer, assuming there was one, didn't have a gun or a knife? Right now I don't know much of anything and I sure don't know why he was out here. I would figure from the time we released him to the time you found the Mercedes star would have been five to six hours."

"He wouldn't knowingly throw away the star." Harry was thinking out loud. "He could have lost it running or in a fight. From here to the elder-care home in Crozet is about three miles."

"Yeah." Coop opened the door to the squad car.

"Shut the door, Cynthia. Let me wipe off Tucker's paws first."

*"I can wash them,"* Tucker grumbled.

Harry had had the presence of mind to throw an old towel in the squad car. She grabbed it, bending down to clean off the corgi's muddy paws. "I'd never know you had white feet, Miss Pooch."

Coop leaned against the car door. "He wasn't on drugs. That's the first thing I think about. Wesley was clean as far as we know."

"I'd have thought he'd take anything he could get. Maybe he had more sense than I gave him credit for — what little I saw of him. Some people are life's losers. It sounds harsh but it's true. Miranda gets mad at me when I say that because she believes everyone can be redeemed through the Lord. I hope she's right."

"She hasn't been quoting as much scripture lately." Coop smiled. "Tracy?"

"Yeah, though she was never what I'd call a

Bible thumper. Okay, there were times when she came close but she has toned down a little. I actually like it when she quotes the Bible. I'm learning something. I never did memorize much except for Hamlet's soliloquy, which I hate." Harry, meditatively rubbing Tucker's paws, got lost in thought.

"M-m-m, come on, she's clean enough."

"All right, Tucker. In you go."

*"I told you I could wash myself."* Tucker sat down on the backseat and began washing her paws.

As they drove down Whitehall Road, Coop asked, "Is there anything unique about the farms out here?"

"Unique? Well, some of them are very beautiful but I can't think of anything unique. Many of them were filled with wounded soldiers during the War Between the States. They'd ship them in by train and folks would pick up soldiers, ours and the Yankees, down at the train station and take them home. God, it must have been a mess. Just about every house in central Virginia had soldiers in it."

"Hard to imagine."

"You were in as much danger from the surgeon as you were from the enemy. But no, there's nothing special unless you count architecture."

"I sure wish I knew what he was doing down here."

"Did anyone pick him up from the station?"

Coop shook her head. "Walked right out and kept going."

"Creepy."

"Wesley?"

"The weekend. Kind of a weekend of death. Roger and then Wesley."

Cynthia said, "I heard Lottie Pearson hired a lawyer."

"You're kidding."

"Just in case we accuse her of poisoning Roger. Now, there's a paranoid woman. No one is accusing her of anything. It was her dumb luck to hand him coffee and cake."

"Who told you?" Harry could think of a few people who would get the news first.

"Little Mim."

"Lottie's been shining her on."

"Oh, well, Little Mim knows it. She said she called BoomBoom to tell her she made the right decision in fixing you up with Diego and not Lottie."

"She did?" Harry was surprised.

"You're a lot more fun than tight-ass Lottie." Coop whistled. "And he is gorgeous."

"Pretty is as pretty does."

"Oh, Harry, that's what you always say about horses."

"Well, it applies to men, too."

Coop laughed as she turned right, out toward Harry's farm. "Who knows what men say about us?"

"That we're beautiful, sexy, and wonderful. Right?" Harry laughed, too.

"I'm sure."

"Do you have to go to the autopsy tonight?"

"No, I get the night off. Things are returning to normal, finally."

"Miranda, Susan, and I are going to Tracy's apartment over the pharmacy to paint. Miranda's bringing all the food. How are you with a paint brush?"

"Picasso."

When Harry walked inside her house she noticed how silent it was. Not a kitty in sight. It wasn't until she went into the living room that she beheld savaged lampshades, pillows tossed on the floor, and her bowl of potpourri strewn all over the carpet.

"Mrs. Murphy! Pewter!"

*"You don't think they'll show their faces, do you?"* the dog intelligently asked. *"They're both in the barn in the hayloft, I guarantee it."*

Harry looked at the old clock on the mantelpiece. "Damn. Well, come on, Tucker, I was going to take them to Tracy's but not now."

She grabbed her old white painter's pants, a white T-shirt, then headed out the door with a bouncy Tucker at her side.

Once at Tracy's she blew off steam about the depredations of felines. It made her paint faster but she was careful with her brush and didn't make a mess. Miranda had chosen a rich, warm beige for the living room, the windows trimmed in linen white.

Once Cynthia arrived the pace really picked up. They had the living room and all the trim knocked out by eight. Miranda had set up two card tables in the kitchen. Susan went off her diet. She couldn't help it, the food was too good.

Tracy had fought in Korea right out of high school. He stayed in the army, got his college degree, and after years of outstanding service was wooed away from the army by the CIA. He wasn't a right-wing fellow; he'd seen enough government mismanagement to cure him of any blind patriotism. However, he revered the Constitution and loved his country, warts and all. He had a logical mind, a mind good at detail. When he retired to Hawaii he thought all would be well, but his wife had died three years earlier. His fiftieth high-school reunion brought him home and back to his high-school flame, Miranda, herself widowed. It was as though they had never parted. So he flew back to Hawaii, attended to business there, sold his house, and returned.

Both Tracy and Miranda were of a generation where you didn't live with a member of the opposite sex unless you married them. He could walk to Miranda's from his apartment and everything would be proper.

"When do you move the furniture in?" Susan asked. "Do you have furniture?"

"Some." He looked at Cynthia Cooper. "Did you notice the knot on the hanging rope? Not to change the subject."

"Just looked like a knot to me."

"You saved the rope for evidence, of course."

"Yes."

"Mind if I come down and look at it tomorrow? And who notified next of kin?"

"Augusta County Sheriff's Department." A cloud crossed Cooper's face. She didn't want to trespass on another law-enforcement agency's jurisdiction, but she thought she probably should have gone with someone from the Augusta department. She'd go over there tomorrow.

★ ★ ★

Already a few pounds thinner thanks to his wired-up jaw, Officer Everett Yancy hopped out of his seat when Deputy Cooper walked through the doors of the sheriff's headquarters.

"Coop!" He hustled her to his desk, sat her in his chair, leaned over, and punched in a code. "What do you make of this?"

On the computer screen appeared a message from their contact at Richmond's Department of Motor Vehicles, Carol Grossman. The DMV, efficient, processed information from satellite DMVs statewide as well as mailings from individual drivers.

The message read:

Hey, you asked for this driver's license Saturday night.
Here's our record.
Yrs, Carol

Yancy reached in front of Cooper to scroll up more text. Before her eyes was Wesley Partlow's license. But the photo on the license wasn't Wesley Partlow.

For the first time, Cooper felt the ground give way beneath her. She knew they were going out into deeper water.

She glanced up at Yancy. "These guys

219

are good — real good."

No sooner had she studied Carol Grossman's message than the phone rang for her.

"Hello."

"Deputy Cooper, Officer Vitale. I'm sorry to be a little behind. I went over to the Partlows' like you requested. No one's dead."

"Thank you, Officer Vitale." She put the phone down. "Someone sure is dead, along with my brain!" She stormed out of the room.

# 22

"You've got ants in your pants." Miranda re-inked the stamp pads, then closed the lids, sliding them under the counter.

"I want to know what's going on."

"We all want to know what's going on. That's why Tracy drove down to the sheriff's office this morning."

"Well, why hasn't he called?"

"Harry, he left a half hour ago. Will you calm yourself?"

*"Yes. It's time for my morning nap. I need quiet."* Pewter yawned.

The front door swung open. BoomBoom came in, wearing bib overalls, large hoop earrings, and a bright green T-shirt. "Good morning, ladies."

"I can see you're going to spend a day on the tractor." Harry thought she'd like to be on her old John Deere.

"No," came the brief reply as Boom-Boom slid her key in the lock of her postbox, swinging open the brass door with the glass window.

*"Bills,"* Tucker told her as the corgi helped sort the mail this morning.

"Why, hello, Tucker. I didn't notice you when I came in."

"Where are you off to in your overalls?"

"Harry, I'm not accustomed to you being so interested in my schedule." BoomBoom sorted through the envelopes as though they were cards in a deck. "What gives?"

"Nothing." Harry appeared nonchalant.

BoomBoom sashayed to the counter, leaned on it, and purred, "You want to know if Thomas has said anything about Diego."

"Not me."

*"I hate it when humans try to purr."* Mrs. Murphy stuck one leg straight up, contorted her head under it to lick the back side.

"If I made her do that people would say it's cruelty to animals." Harry pointed to the agile tiger kitty.

"You can't do that." Miranda smiled. "I know I can't. I bet the Dalai Lama couldn't do it either."

"What's the Dalai Lama got to do with it?" BoomBoom, mystified, wrinkled her nose, a habit when she was puzzled.

"Doesn't he twist himself into a pretzel, sleep on nails?" Miranda's eyes grew larger. "Walk through fire."

"No, that's a master yogi."

"Yogi Bear." Harry giggled.

BoomBoom said, "But honestly, they can do things like that. There are some who can have out-of-body experiences."

"I have out-of-body experiences when I get the flu."

"Harry, gross." BoomBoom stacked her mail on the counter, flipped it on the side, and tapped the envelopes evenly together. "Anyway, do you want to know what Diego said to Thomas?"

"Sure," she shrugged.

*"Mother, don't try to be so cool."* Mrs. Murphy still had her hind leg over her head.

Tucker walked back behind the counter when Harry tipped it up. *"Murphy, I wish you wouldn't do that. It hurts just to look at you."*

*"If you didn't have such stumps, you could do it, too,"* the tiger cat said with malicious glee.

*"Ha, ha,"* the dog dryly replied.

*"Why isn't anyone paying attention to me?"* Pewter pouted.

*"You said you wanted to take a nap,"* Murphy fired back.

*"Am I asleep?"*

*"Pewter, you are so perverse."*

*"All cats are perverse."* The little dog

headed for the back animal door.

*"Where are you going? What are you doing?"* Mrs. Murphy demanded.

*"Hey, there's nothing in here but two bitchy cats."*

*"Is that so?"* Pewter fluffed her fur.

*"Guess you won't find out what Thomas told BoomBoom."* Mrs. Murphy cleverly dangled the bait.

*"Oh, yeah."* Tucker stopped, returning to the counter.

"Well?" Miranda expectantly leaned over the counter.

"Thomas said that Diego hopes to see Harry again." BoomBoom hooked her thumb under her overall strap. "Has he called you?"

"No, Thomas hasn't called me," Harry said.

"You know what I mean. Don't be such a smart-ass, Harry."

"Yes, Diego has called me. Is everyone happy now?"

"You didn't tell me." Miranda was hurt.

"Because he called last night after our painting party. I forgot to tell you because there's so much else going on. Anyway, Diego has to fly back to Montevideo this week, but he hopes to be down for the Wrecker's Ball."

"Oh. What painting party?" BoomBoom asked.

Mrs. Murphy, bored with the humans, put her hind leg down finally, swept her whiskers forward, and stared right down at Tucker. *"What a pretty doggie."*

Tucker looked up but a fraction of a second too late because the cat swooped down on her, bowling her over. *"Oooph."* The dog had the wind knocked out of her and was rolled over by the force of Murphy's aerial bombardment.

Pewter, ears up, inched closer to the tangle. *"This looks good."*

*"Banzai! Death to the emperor,"* Murphy sang out.

*"You watch too many war movies,"* Tucker snapped as she scrambled to her feet. She bolted out the animal door, Mrs. Murphy in hot pursuit.

Pewter hesitated a moment. After all, puddles dotted the alleyway; but the screams from outside finally lured her out the animal door, where both cat and dog pounced on her, knowing she'd fall for it.

"Nonstop party." Harry laughed.

"What, painting?"

Both Harry and Miranda told her about the painting party at Tracy's apartment and Tracy asking Coop to see the rope.

Just then the phone rang. Miranda picked it up and Harry crowded next to her. BoomBoom hurried behind the counter to listen in.

"Oh, hello, Mim." Miranda tried to hide the disappointment in her voice.

"Has my package arrived from Cartier? I sent my tank watch up to New York to be fixed weeks ago." Big Mim emphasized "weeks."

"No package today. I'm so used to you being my first customer. Where are you?"

"I'm on my way to Richmond with Marilyn. I promised I'd take her to Monkey's." She mentioned a dress shop much frequented by ladies such as herself. "I'm on the car phone. Clear as a bell, isn't it?"

"You two have a wonderful time. Bye now." Miranda hung up the phone.

Lottie Pearson walked through the door. "Hello." She opened her postbox, gathered her mail, and walked right out.

"Can you believe?" BoomBoom's eyebrows shot upward.

The phone rang again. They all reached for it but Miranda was first.

Miranda picked up the receiver. "Hello."

"Hi, sugar." Tracy's baritone sounded deep. "I'm heading back. Need anything?"

"What'd you think?" Harry, leaning over,

227

spoke into the receiver.

"Did you grab the phone from my beautiful girlfriend?"

"No. She's right here. BoomBoom, too. We're hanging on your every word."

"Oh." He inhaled. "Heavy rope, climber's rope. You know when you see movies of hangings in the Old West, how the rope has a special kind of noose?"

"Yes," they said in unison.

"That's what I wanted to see. If Wesley took the time to make that noose, assuming he killed himself, or if his killer did, assuming he was murdered. The noose isn't as easy to tie as you would think."

"And?" Harry's tone raised up.

"No. A simple knot like you tie when you're tying up a package."

"Honeybunch, what does that mean?" Miranda breathlessly asked, having regained full access to the receiver.

"That either Wesley or his killer didn't know how to tie the knot, didn't care, didn't have time. Or that the climber's rope would hold."

"I don't follow." BoomBoom honestly didn't.

"One of the reasons the noose knot was used to hang people is that it would hold the weight of the body and snap the neck. It's more humane than choking to death, which is what happens if you tie a common package knot. In time the common knot will give even on good quality rope."

"This gives me chills. You come on home." Miranda half laughed.

"I will. Say bye to the girls."

Miranda hung up the phone as the three animals pranced through the animal door, best friends again.

"I didn't know that about a noose." Harry's hand instinctively flew to her neck. "Choking and swinging at the same time. What an awful way to die."

*"I think we missed something."* Mrs. Murphy quietly sat down on a chair by the table in the back.

*"We have only to wait. They're bound to tell another human. You know how they are."* Pewter jumped on a chair at the table and began biting out the mud between her toes. She hated dirt.

"All this talk of death . . ." Boom's voice faded away, then increased in strength. "Roger's funeral is tomorrow. Are you all going?"

"You know we will." Miranda frowned for a moment. "Now, why would you even ask?"

"I don't know." BoomBoom's shoulders hunched up, then she relaxed. "I'm a little distracted. Aren't you?"

"Well, it has been a strange couple of days but we may be making too much of it all." Miranda noticed the tiny mud pellets falling to the floor since Pewter was sitting in one of the chairs next to her. "Pewter, pick up after yourself."

"I'll clean it up." Harry opened the small broom closet in the back, fetching the dustpan and brush.

"Well, I'm off."

"You never said why you're wearing overalls." Harry knelt down, brushing up the mud bits.

"I'm going to work."

"What work?" Harry rather impolitely replied.

"Welding. I have an order to make a hen and chickens for Opal Michaels."

"Better make it a chicken with attitude," Harry said.

"If I were making it for Big Mim I'd put a crown on that bird." BoomBoom laughed as she opened the front door.

Miranda picked up Mrs. Murphy to pet her. "I'm glad to see you and BoomBoom are getting along better."

"She's always made more of an effort than I have."

"Well, I'm glad to see you recognize that.

Remember your Proverbs. 'A friend loves at all times, and a brother is born for adversity.' " Miranda quoted Chapter Seventeen, Verse Seventeen.

"I wouldn't go that far." Harry winked at her.

Mrs. Murphy listened as the tiny mud bits hit the floor. *"Pewter, you have more mud between your toes than an elephant."*

*"And you don't?"*

*"Not as much as you."*

*"Why aren't you grooming yourself?"* the gray cat wondered.

*"I'm waiting until she sweeps up your mess. Then I'll make another one."*

*"Murphy, you're awful,"* Tucker giggled.

# 23

St. Luke's Lutheran Church, pleasing eighteenth-century architecture with clean brick and white lintels, filled with those wishing to pay their last respects to Roger O'Bannon. The town residents crammed into the pews, the light streaming through the stained-glass windows.

All rose when Sean O'Bannon and his mother, Ida, entered by the door next to the lectern to take their seats in the front row. The once numerous O'Bannon clan had dwindled over the decades. As neither Roger nor Sean had ever married, the line might well end with Sean.

As the mother and son seated themselves, the congregation also sat down.

People were surprised at the change in Sean's appearance. He'd cut off his dork knob, gotten a good haircut, and was clean shaven. A well-cut dark gray suit gave him a substantial, solemn air. No one could remember Sean wearing a suit since high school; he'd always been low-key, counter-culture. The Reverend Jones solemnly came out of a door recessed behind the pulpit. He bowed his head before the altar, then turned to face the congregation. Herb, no stranger to funerals, tried to invest this last event with meaning. He avoided platitudes, the easy phrase.

Fair sat with Harry. Susan and Ned Tucker, Miranda and Tracy were on the other side of Harry. After the service they drove to the cemetery south of town, a pleasant site with a beautiful view of rolling pastures. When the casket was lowered into the grave, tears rolled down Sean's cheeks. He'd held up until then. His mother put her arm around his waist.

When Harry drove away with Fair, Susan, and Ned in Ned's car, Sean was still standing at the gravesite.

"Depressing," Susan tersely said.

"Harry, do you want to go back to the post office or do you have time for lunch?" Ned turned left toward town.

"Work. Miranda's having lunch with Tracy."

"Want me to bring you a sandwich?" Susan volunteered.

"Yeah. How about chicken, lettuce, tomato, and mayo on whole wheat."

"Do you have cat and dog food at the P.O.?" Ned pulled up at the post office.

"Susan, you know I do. I'll go hungry before they do." Harry smiled as she hopped out of the car.

"I've got a call at Quail Ridge Farm." Fair rolled down the window. "Take you to the movies over the weekend?"

"Sure," Harry replied.

The post office was only fifteen minutes from the cemetery by foot but she had liked being in the car with her old friends. As Harry walked in the back door she caught a glimpse of the two cats, paws fishing in the backs of the postboxes. They jumped down as she closed the back door and walked across to unlock the sliding door — like a small garage door — that separated the public section of the post office from the workers' section.

"What are you two doing?"

*"Nothing,"* both said unconvincingly.

She walked to the open backs of the postboxes, peering inside, shutting one eye for a better view. The torn ends of envelopes presented themselves. Irritated, Harry pulled them out. "Great, Big Mim and Fair. You would have to claw those two."

*"We were just playing,"* Pewter replied. *"No real harm done."*

*"For now."* Tucker rolled over on her back.

*"You're supposed to be on our side."* Mrs. Murphy pushed the mail cart into the recumbent dog.

Before a first-class fight could erupt, Cynthia Cooper opened the front door.

"Hey, I thought I'd see you at the funeral," Harry said.

"I was picking up the coroner's report on Wesley Partlow."

"And?"

"Murdered."

Harry grimaced. "By hanging?"

"Ultimately. Apparently he was a hard bugger to kill. Given the rains and the condition of the body when we found him, we shipped him right off to the cooler. But on close examination, small hunks of hair were torn from his head, there were bruises on his torso. He put up a fight. He can't be exactly sure but Marshall Wells is ninety percent certain that Wesley wasn't dead when the rope was put around his neck. Unconscious, maybe, but not dead."

"That's gruesome."

"Yep. I was quite happy not to have to attend this coroner's exam."

"I don't think I could get through one with a body in good condition."

"You get used to it. Think of the body as a

book. You open it up and read." The tall blonde pointed toward the divider.

Harry nodded, so Cooper flipped it up and walked toward the back.

"Coffee, tea, Coke. Susan's bringing me a sandwich. You're welcome to half."

"Actually, I just ate." She sat down in the chair. "No sign of the GMC truck either. I don't know if he stole it and returned it before the owner knew it, stole it and the owner didn't report it, or the owner lent it to him. I keep thinking the truck will get me on the rails.

"The other thing that bothers me is I can't find a police record. We sent out his dental information. That's often the easiest way to get something, that and the name. But Wesley Partlow isn't his real name."

"What?" Harry exclaimed as Cooper filled her in on the false photo on the driver's license.

"I'm going over the mountain to Waynesboro later today."

Harry sat down opposite Cooper as Murphy jumped in her lap and Pewter nestled in Cooper's. "It's almost as if he were a ghost, isn't it? A nameless, unknown person who" — she paused — "left no trace."

"Except for the Falcon hubcaps." Cynthia Cooper sucked in air between her teeth. "A kid like that collects bad marks, a real bad report card. I'll find it in time."

"Does that mean you have to keep the remains?"

"No. We've got photographs of the corpse. And we took mug shots and fingerprints when we booked him. There's not much point in keeping him in the cooler. A lot of times when a corpse is disfigured or decayed, people can't recognize it. Odd though, some corpses retain their features for a long time, the eyes can be gone, the lips, too, but they are still very identifiable.

"You know, I have this theory that fake boobs, plastic hips, the whole march of medicine will mean that corpses stay around longer. We don't just live longer, we die longer — sort of."

"You're punchy," Harry replied.

"A little."

"How's Rick?" Harry stroked under Mrs. Murphy's chin.

"You know how he gets when he has an unsolved crime. He's pieced together all the area topo maps and pinned them on the wall. Then he uses colored pins for the day. Day one, all the known movements of the victim are in blue. Day two, green and so on. It's a good system because Rick thinks better if he can visualize."

"He's a good sheriff."

"Yes, not that the county knows or cares." Coop sighed. "People take things for granted."

"In every endeavor." Harry started to reach across the table but it squeezed Murphy so she stopped. "The only reason to kill someone like Wesley is because he was caught red-handed stealing again or" — she stopped a second — "because he knew something."

"Revenge."

Harry thought a moment. "Maybe."

"Suppose he insulted someone on a deep level? You know, tried to seduce a man's wife or, worse, an underage daughter. Something like that can set a normal person right off. Murder is normal. That's why we don't want to look at it. The media is fascinated with serial killers, a fairly rare aberration, but most murders are run-of-the-mill affairs committed by run-of-the-mill people."

"That theory would place Wesley's killer in his own social class. Wouldn't it? People like Wesley don't have a lot of contact with people higher up on the scale."

"My, what a pretty gray tummy and so much of it, too." Cooper laughed as Pewter rolled over in her lap. "Uh — I don't know.

What if he did odd jobs on a big farm, made a pass at the lady of the manor?" She shrugged. "Who the hell knows?"

"He knew enough to sell hubcaps."

"And to park cars."

"My guess is he knew someone in Crozet. He wasn't just passing through. I mean, you don't just pass through Crozet. Charlottesville, yes, but not Crozet. We're a little off the beaten track." Harry's features brightened. She liked figuring things out.

"Route 64's not that far away, nor is Route 250."

"Yeah, but if you come to Crozet you usually have a purpose or a person in mind. We're a little bit nondescript, you know."

Cooper thought silently for a time. "I think you're right. What next?" She ran her fingers through Pewter's fur.

"I don't know but I can help."

*"No,"* Tucker said from under the table.

*"Oh, Tucker, don't be a poopface. This will liven up the spring,"* Mrs. Murphy chided her.

*"You're the one who always counsels prudence,"* the dog reminded her.

*"Maybe I'm bored."* The tiger placed her paw on Harry's forearm. *"I'm ready for a little action."*

*"Be careful what you ask for."* Pewter

turned her head so she could see Murphy from under the table.

*"And what would you ask for?"* the tiger replied.

*"Steak tartare garnished with braised mouse tails."*

# 24

Tucked on the west side of the Blue Ridge Mountains in the Shenandoah Valley sat the modest city of Waynesboro. While not wealthy like its eastern neighbor, Charlottesville, Waynesboro evidenced its own character, which was up-front, hardworking, and ready for a good time.

Cynthia Cooper liked the town, which was economically dominated by a DuPont chemical plant. Virginia Metalcrafters was also based in Waynesboro, and she enjoyed stopping by to watch the men create the beautiful brass door locks and other items for which the firm was justly famous.

She turned right past the Burger King and McDonald's, heading west. Then she turned onto Randolph Street, filled with neat, well-kept houses.

She parked in front of a brick rancher painted white with navy-blue shutters on the windows. The front door, red, had a large polished brass knocker, no doubt made at Virginia Metalcrafters.

She rapped on the knocker. Within seconds the door opened, revealing a careworn woman perhaps in her mid-forties but appearing older at the moment. Glued to her side was a pretty golden retriever.

"Mrs. Partlow?"

The woman involuntarily took a step back. "You're the second policeman to come here. My son is not dead."

"Yes, ma'am, I know that and I'm sorry to bother you. I'm Deputy Cynthia Cooper from the Albemarle County Sheriff's Department. Is your son at home?"

"As a matter of fact, he is. He works the night shift at the DuPont plant. He's asleep."

"I see." Cooper smiled at the golden retriever. "Beautiful dog."

"That's Rolex. Wesley gave her to me on my birthday. He said he couldn't afford a Rolex but the puppy would make me happier than any watch. He was right, wasn't he, Rolex?" She patted the silky head as Rolex thumped her tail.

Reaching inside her chest pocket, Cooper pulled out a license, which she handed to Mrs. Partlow. "Is this your son?"

Her eyebrows darted upward. "No. Who is this?"

"We don't know."

Mrs. Partlow studied the rest of the license. "The rest of it is correct."

"We're hoping your son will know who the man is in the photograph. Do you mind waking him?"

"No, not at all. It's about time for him to get up anyway. Please come in, Deputy —"

"Cooper." She walked through the door.

The parquet floor in the entrance hall gleamed.

"Come on in the living room. I'll go wake Wesley." Mrs. Partlow disappeared down the hall, Rolex at her heels.

Cooper heard a few grunts and groans.

Mrs. Partlow returned. "He'll be out in a minute. May I get you something to drink?"

"No, thank you, ma'am."

Wesley soon appeared, wearing a blue T-shirt, jeans, and sneakers without socks. "Hi."

Cooper stood up to shake his hand. "I'm sorry to disturb you."

"That's okay." The slight, curly-haired young man smiled.

"Here's your driver's license."

He took the stiff card from her hand. "I have my license. I think. Let me check." He hurried back to his room.

Cooper could hear metal clothes hangers

sliding on a metal closet pole. Rolex cocked her head. "Good ears, Rolex."

Wesley, perplexed, stepped back into the living room. "It's gone! I keep my license in the pocket of my bomber jacket except for when it's really hot, then I just stick it in the visor of my truck."

"Do you have any idea how long you've been missing your license?"

He thought a moment. "I remember getting gas. Had it then. Last week. I —" He paused. "You know, it's kind of hard to remember. I just never think about my license."

"Do you recognize the man in the photo?"

He peered intently at the likeness. "Kinda. I've seen him around but I don't know his name."

"Whoever he is, he can sure doctor a driver's license or he knows someone who can." Cooper smiled.

"Yeah. Looks valid to me."

"Me, too," Mrs. Partlow chimed in.

"Mr. Partlow, think. Any guidance you can give me will be a big help."

"He's dead, right? Mom said the Augusta cop came by to tell her I was dead."

"I think I surprised him more than he surprised me." Mrs. Partlow smiled tightly.

"Yes, he's dead. Could you have seen him

244

at the gas station?"

"Uh, no." Wesley cupped his chin in his hand as he took a seat. "Might have seen him at Danny's, the bar behind the post office downtown." He furrowed his brow. "Yeah."

"And when you go to Danny's, what do you do with your coat?"

"Hang it up or put it over the back of the chair."

After a few more questions, Cooper left, driving over to Danny's. The bartender, Louis Seidlitz, was just setting up, preparing for the evening's traffic.

Louis recognized the face but couldn't recall a name to go with it.

As she drove back toward Charlottesville, climbing up over Afton Mountain, she thought how quick-eyed and light-fingered the false Wesley Partlow had been. Quick enough to pilfer a driver's license. How many pockets did he touch before finding pay dirt? Apparently he rifled them without drawing attention to himself. She was reminded of that expression, "Opportunity makes a poet as well as a thief."

# 25

Although the ground remained soggy, the next day the sky, a robin's-egg blue, presaged a spectacular spring day. The late-blooming dogwoods covered the mountainside. Earlier blooms had their petals knocked off by the storms but fire stars still dotted banks with their brilliant red.

Tucker inhaled the heady fragrances of spring as she sat on the back step of the post office.

Harry often walked the four miles to work but given the rains of the past week she drove. On the way to work she'd swung by the small lumberyard outside of town. Luckily, there was enough sawdust to shovel into the truck bed. Usually by Wednesday or Thursday there was enough sawdust for the horsemen to drive down and load up. She'd filled up her truck, pulled a tarp over it, and arrived at work by seven-thirty a.m.

Tucker told the cats, once they arrived at work, that she was going on a jaunt alone.

*"Suits me,"* Pewter declared.

Murphy, a little miffed, said, *"Why alone?"*

*"Want to check in with my dog friends. Not all of them like cats."*

*"Get new friends."* The tiger turned her back to her.

With anticipation and a heady sense of freedom, Tucker took another deep breath, then trotted merrily down the alleyway behind the post office. She turned north, which meant she would swing past private homes, past the new grade school, and then she'd be in the open countryside. Despite her short legs, the corgi moved at a fast clip. In fact, she could run very fast, and on occasion she enjoyed the delicious victory of outrunning a hound, a spaniel, or once even a Great Dane. It should be noted that the Great Dane had a splinter in its paw. Still, Tucker was a confident, cheerful dog. She edged along well-manicured lawns, dogs in the houses barking empty warnings. In no time she was in farmland.

Early corn, tiny shoots just breaking the furrows, gave the red clay fields a green cast. The hay in other fields already swayed over her head. She pushed through a field of rye and timothy mix. Tucker could identify any grass crop by its odor. She reached a rutted farm road and thought she'd go down to the old Mawyer place. Booty Mawyer, seventy-seven, farmed his three hundred acres pretty much as he always had. A shrewd fellow, he sank no money into large purchases like tractors, manure spreaders, hay balers, and the like. He kept four Belgian horses and worked them in teams of two. The cost of feeding and shoeing his horses proved far less than tractor payments. And he managed to get everything done. His grandson, Don Clatterbuck, helped him in the evenings, and during hay-cutting time, Don worked full-time with him.

Tucker could hear the old man and his horses in the distance. A faint whiff of onion grass floated across the light southerly breeze. Tucker stopped and sniffed. Wind from the south usually meant moisture and lots of it, yet the day was achingly clear. Still, the dog trusted her senses. She figured she'd better get back to the post office by lunchtime.

She hurried down the road, eager to visit anyone at all, first coming to the old tobacco-curing sheds. Booty Mawyer, like many central Virginia farmers, once upon a time made a good profit from his tobacco allotments. After World War II the business slacked off, the cost of labor zoomed upward, and many farmers allowed their allotments to fall into disuse. But the accoutrements of a lively tobacco trade still stood — curing sheds, storing sheds, and in town, the old auction house.

Foxes especially like curing sheds. Just why, Tucker couldn't understand, except that having a burrow under a nice structure was always a plus. There were lots of sturdy outbuildings, yet the tobacco-curing sheds held a fascination for *Vulpes vulpes*. Tucker didn't mind foxes. Mrs. Murphy hated them and hissed with the mention of a fox's name. From time to time the cat would declare a truce, but the real reason Murphy loathed them was that they competed for the same game.

The milk butterflies flitted upward along with Tucker's thoughts as she reached the shed. She walked around the side of it and stopped. Sitting right in front of her was the 1987 GMC pickup, the faded Cowboys football team jacket jammed up on the top of the seat.

# 26

Tucker blasted through the animal door at the post office with such velocity that her feet skidded sideways and she fell over, sliding. A bump into the mail cart stopped her unusual progress.

Scrambling to her feet she shouted, *"I found it! I found the truck."*

Mrs. Murphy, who watched the dog's slide with mirth, hopped off the table. *"Where?"*

*"At Booty Mawyer's."*

*"What?"* The cat couldn't believe her ears.

Pewter, roused from yet another slumber, shook herself, stuck her head up from the mail cart in which she was sleeping. *"Tucker, what are you talking about? And you woke me up."*

*"I'm telling you that the GMC truck is parked at the old tobacco-curing shed at Booty Mawyer's place."*

*"How do you know it's the right truck?"* Pewter, skeptical, asked.

*"Has the Cowboys jacket on the seat. Like Sean said. Remember?"* The dog's eyes shone with intelligence.

*"He did say that, didn't he?"* The gray cat pulled herself up and out of the mail cart using her front paws.

"What's the commotion here?" Harry smiled down at her friends.

*"Oh, Mom, I wish you could understand me."* The corgi's ears drooped a bit, then perked back up.

Harry handed the dog a Milk-Bone. For good measure she gave the cats a few bits of Haute Feline, then returned to her task of reorganizing the carton shelves.

*"I think we'd better check this out. This just doesn't sound right."* Mrs. Murphy brushed her whiskers with her paws. *"For one thing, Tucker, Rick Shaw and Coop could have traced the truck to Booty Mawyer easily enough. License plates alone would do that and even though Sean didn't get the number all they would have to do is tap into the Department of Motor Vehicle computers for 1987 GMC trucks in the county. So something's amiss."*

*"That's just it, Murphy, there are no license plates. 'Farm Use' is painted where the plates should go. This truck is long off the records."*

*"Well, why didn't you say that in the first*

*place?"* The cat was already heading for the door.

*"You didn't give me the chance. And you know, Murphy, 'Farm Use' trucks aren't supposed to go out on the roads. Who would remember this old truck?"*

*"Tucker, I'm sorry. Come on."* She disappeared through the door, her tail swishing through last.

As Tucker hurried after the sleek tiger, Pewter wailed, *"I smell rain. I'll get wet."*

*"Stay here, fatso."* The corgi couldn't resist a parting shot.

*"Don't leave me! I hate to miss anything."* Under her breath the gray cat grumbled, *"I know I'm going to regret this."*

"What is going on?" Harry scratched her head as Pewter's gray bottom vanished through the door.

"Must be a good party somewhere." Miranda laughed. "Here, let me hold that package or you'll tip the shelf over."

The three animals streaked along the lawns. Tucker held other dogs at bay, declaring they were just crossing and would be off that particular dog's property soon enough. The corgi also advised other dogs they would probably be returning that way and she was sorry to disturb them but important business was at hand.

The other domesticated animals behaved reasonably, except for one Australian shepherd who mouthed off so abusively that Tucker told the cats to run on. She advanced on the medium-sized dog, who, seeing the determination of the corgi plus the bared fangs, decided that passage through his lawn might not be so offensive.

Tucker caught up with the cats as they entered the rye field.

*"Guess you shut him up."* Murphy brushed the slender rye blades.

*"For now."*

*"How much farther?"* Pewter sneezed as pollen tickled her nose.

*"I told you to stay at the post office,"* Tucker chided her.

*"I'm not complaining. I just want to know how far,"* she snapped back.

*"Ten minutes."* Tucker pushed through the rye.

They journeyed in silence until emerging on the farm road. The ruts seemed even deeper to Tucker this time. In the near distance they could hear a tractor whine.

*"Doesn't sound right, does it?"* Pewter noted.

*"No."* Tucker, spying the tobacco barn up ahead, put on speed. She rounded the structure, the long-distant whiff of decades of

smoke still pungently perceptible. *"What!"*

The two cats almost collided into her.

*"Where's the truck?"* Pewter caustically asked.

*"It was here. I swear it!"*

*"That tractor sounds stuck. Let's find it. Maybe Booty's using the truck to pull it out,"* Mrs. Murphy suggested.

Finding Booty proved easy enough not only because of the whine of the tractor but because he was cussing a blue streak. The animals heard words they'd never heard before.

The tractor had sunk into a soft pothole that must have been deceptive from the driver's seat. The rear wheels were mired a quarter of the way up the large yellow hubcaps. Booty, overalls shiny with fresh mud, placed stones, anything he could find, in front of the wheels, then he'd swing back up into the seat to try again.

Abraham, a bluetick hound, mournfully watched his human have fits. Abraham, two years older than God, endured some loss of hearing, stiff hips, and fading sight, but his nose stayed keen.

*"Abraham,"* Tucker called loudly to him as they approached. *"How are you?"*

*"Tucker? Who's with you? Are those Chihuahuas?"* He squinted.

*"I resent that,"* Pewter flared up.

*"Pewter, he's nearly as old as Booty."* Mrs. Murphy bumped the gray just to put her in her place.

*"Mrs. Murphy and Pewter are with me,"* Tucker answered.

*"Hello, girls,"* Abraham greeted them, his manner courtly. *"I apologize for my human but as you can surmise, he's struggling with the elements and if my nose is any good at all, we'll be wet within the half hour. He'll need another tractor to pull out this one. Oh, me."* He let out a long, long sigh.

*"No need to ever apologize for a human."* Tucker laughed.

*"He's right about the rain,"* Pewter whispered to Mrs. Murphy. *"I feel it coming. If I get wet it will take me hours to dry. I can't stand it when my hair gets matted down. Murphy, are you listening?"*

*"Stop worrying."* She edged up to Abraham, then rubbed against his chest.

*"Mrs. Murphy, you smell like nutmeg."* He chuckled. *"Pewter."*

*"Here I am."* Pewter rubbed against him also.

*"We're hoping you can help us."* Tucker sat down as Booty cursed to high heaven. *"There's a farm truck parked behind the curing shed. I chanced by not an hour and a*

half ago and now on my return, it's gone. Might you know of its whereabouts?"

"No. I didn't hear the truck being driven off but then I don't hear so good anymore."

"Do you recall Booty driving the truck to town?" Mrs. Murphy spoke up.

"Farm truck. Don't know how it would make it to town and back, really," Abraham answered.

"I thought when I came by that Booty was out with his team of horses," Tucker wondered. "And I thought he didn't own a tractor."

"What a memory you have, Tee Tucker. He worked the little field, the garden patch field, I call it, with the horses but Dimples threw a shoe. So he unhitched the horses and he was going to hitch up the second pair, you know he has the young ones he's bringing on, fine matched pair, ah, but I digress here. Well, he checked the weather and thought he'd return Marcus Durant's tractor to him. He'd borrowed it to dig fence holes. Marcus has every attachment made in the U. S. of A. and Booty's getting on in years, he just didn't feature digging fence holes with the hand digger. Luckily he finished that job, earth's soft, has to set the fence posts, of course, so he wanted to return the tractor. Now he's got to hitch up the young horses to pull out the tractor and he'd better wash off the tractor, *too. Rain'll help."* He exhaled and his flews fluttered out with his breath.

*"Abraham, would you do me a great favor?"* Tucker's pink tongue hung out slightly.

*"If I can, I would certainly not like to disappoint a lady."*

*"Will you walk over to the curing shed with us and work the ground where the truck was parked? Your nose is better than mine."* Tucker flattered the bluetick hound but in truth hound noses were the best of the best.

*"Why, I'd be delighted although I'm sure your nose is keen as can be."* He stood up on all fours, stretched, and moved toward the shed, happy to be useful. Hounds need to be useful or they sink into a torpor.

Booty turned around and beheld the four animals leaving. "Abraham, Abraham, you are useless as tits on a boar hog." He sputtered, needing to take out his anger on someone.

*"Going deaf has its advantages,"* Abraham chuckled. Once at the shed, he put his nose to the ground, working in small circles around the spot where the truck had been parked. *"Grease. Gas. Now, that's odd. Pump's down by the shed. And —"* He lifted his head, sniffed in fresh air to clear his nasal passages, then put his nose to the ground

again. *"Something, something, a chemical? Tucker, get over here."*

Tucker also put her nose to the ground as the cats watched. A stiff breeze came up quickly, blowing their fur toward their heads.

*"It's not fertilizer yet it smells organic. The man-made chemicals are harsh. This is — h-m-m, familiar."* Abraham inhaled another deep draft. *"Acidic. Natural. Ah, I have it. Yes, tannic acid. Yes. Use it sometimes on the backs of new Oriental rugs to make them look old. Use it on skins. That's it."*

*"Any association with a human?"* Mrs. Murphy asked as she lowered her head, the wind picking up considerably.

*"Don."* Abraham nodded slowly. *"Guess he borrowed the truck. Funny, though, he didn't leave his car. I can't think of anyone else with that scent. The moisture's holding it down pretty good. I don't know if Don did take the truck but I'm sure this is tannic acid."*

*"Forgive me, Abraham, I'm not an initiate into the mysteries of scent."* The tiger smiled, her green eyes glittering. *"But isn't it possible that the odor could be from the leather on the bottom of shoes or from the leather upper? It's muddy enough here for a shoe to sink in."*

*"Wouldn't be this pungent."* Abraham's deep voice reverberated. He lifted his head

south, to the wind. *"Going to be another blow. You'd better head back or stay here if you'd like. Booty will get over himself."*

*"Thanks. We'll go back. Oh, one more question."* Tucker also lifted her head. *"I don't recall Booty being a Dallas Cowboys fan. I thought he was Redskins all the way."*

*"Is."*

*"There was a Cowboys windbreaker on the back of the truck seat,"* Tucker said.

*"No one in our family roots for any team but the Redskins. I'm not a football fan myself but I can tell you that. Go on now. You haven't much time."*

*"Thanks again, Abraham,"* Tucker said.

*"Yes, thank you,"* the cats replied.

*"Glad to be of service."* Abraham turned, ambling back to the house. He'd given up on Booty and the tractor.

As the three hurried back the first raindrop splattered down behind the grade school.

*"I knew it. I just knew it,"* Pewter railed as Mrs. Murphy and Tucker forged ahead, and as the storm worsened her volume level rose. *"I should have never left the post office. I should have trusted my first impulse. When am I going to learn to do that? What do I care about an old truck? I mean I don't care about Wesley Partlow. I didn't know Wesley Partlow. I wouldn't care if half the human race van-*

*ished. All they do is make a mess. I should have never let Tucker talk me into this. I hate those two. I hate them. Really!"*

# 27

Rick Shaw stopped off at Pantops Shopping Center to grab a snack. He'd slipped back into the car with the sandwiches as Cynthia Cooper returned with drinks and two cartons of cigarettes since the price was so good.

He turned on the engine. Just as he did he heard the dispatcher's voice. "Sheriff, Sheriff Zakarios of Culpeper needs to talk to you. I've been trying to get you."

"Say what he want, Sheila?"

"No. But he said it's important."

"See if you can get him for me. I'll be in the car."

"Righto."

"Wonder what Zak wants." Coop bit into a ham-and-cheese sandwich. She hadn't realized how hungry she was until she took her first bite.

"Rick," Zakarios's voice boomed over citizen's band radio.

"Yes, Zak. What's cooking in Culpeper?"

"Albemarle resident found on White

Shop Road just about a half hour ago. Shot through the temple, slumped over the steering wheel. Don Clatterbuck."

"I'll be right there, Zak."

"We sealed off the site. You know this guy?"

"Yes."

"Damnedest thing, he has a stuffed pileated woodpecker on the seat next to him. Thing's almost two feet tall."

"He's a taxidermist on the side. Sirens on, maybe I can get to you in a half hour. I don't know, rain's looking evil."

"How far down are you on White Shop Road? This is Deputy Cynthia Cooper."

"Hi, Coop. Not two miles. We're a little off the road to the right. You'll see the yellow tape and the squad cars. Ambulance will be here, too. Thought you'd want to see him before —" He was interrupted, then returned. "John says he thinks he's been dead less than an hour."

"Be there as fast as I can. Over and out."

A gushing rivulet of rainwater poured down in front of Rick Shaw's eyes each time he bent his head. The sheriff's hat, a modified cowboy hat that he and other officers wore, shunted water fore and aft, but the rains were so heavy the hat was soaked through in fifteen minutes.

Sheriff Zakarios mourned the loss of clean vehicle tracks next to the truck. Tracks could still be seen but the rain wiped out a tread imprint. "We've gone over his truck thoroughly." He wiped his cheeks, wet; his hands were wet, too. "Not a feather off this woodpecker."

Coop leaned against the 1987 GMC truck, now wearing real license plates, her back to it. "The woodpecker belongs to Mary Minor Haristeen. He must have just finished it."

"She into drugs or anything?" Chris Zakarios asked.

"No," Coop replied. "Straight as an arrow. Why, were you going to tear apart the woodpecker?"

"Not right off the bat but I'll impound it for a while."

"Neat. Small caliber." Rick opened the door a crack again, inspecting the wound. "Twenty-two, I'd reckon."

"Whoever it was walked right up to him," Chris theorized. "The driver's window wasn't down. The door was closed. So the door had to be opened, perhaps by Clatterbuck himself, *bam,* then the killer closes the door and drives off. Swift. No sign of struggle."

"Well, Don wasn't looking for it." Rick sighed. "Your people might as well take the body away. I appreciate you calling me. You'll keep the Cowboys windbreaker for evidence, too? You see, we've been looking for this particular truck and windbreaker."

"I don't suppose there was anything in the pockets that —" Coop hoped against hope.

"A matchbook. We dusted it. Here." He handed it to Coop, who bent over to shelter it from the downpour.

Beautifully colored with turquoise, air-brushed orange, and yellow with squibbles of purple, the matchbook was expensive to produce. Three inches by two inches, shiny coated paper, the proprietor intended to make an upscale statement. "Roy and Nadine's," with the Y of Roy as a martini glass, announced the restaurant in Lexington, Kentucky. The address, Palomar Center, Harrodsburg Pike and Man-O-War Drive, was printed on the back. The phone number was printed under the address.

Rick huddled next to Coop. "Don't jump to conclusions."

"I'm not but if this matchbook belongs to Partlow maybe he's from Kentucky."

"We sent the fingerprints out nationally," Rick replied.

"Doesn't mean he's got a record." She noted that at the bottom of the matchbook, the black lip had printed in white ink, "Contemporary American Cuisine." The R in the restaurant's name was printed in yellow, the A in deep orange, and the N was hot pink. "Great design. I'll call the restaurant." She walked back to the squad car, scribbled down the information, then emerged into the deluge, handing the matchbook back to Sheriff Zakarios.

"Know much about the victim?" the Culpeper sheriff asked.

"Friendly. No record. A relaxed kind of guy."

Coop answered the good-looking, trim Culpeper sheriff. "It's hard to imagine anyone wanting to kill him."

"Half of what we do comes back to drugs." The sheriff squinted as the rain blew sideways. "Maybe he had a secret life."

"It's a damn national epidemic." Rick stepped away from the GMC as the ambulance crew pulled out the body. "Coop, get the license plate number."

"Yeah." She had written down the letters and numbers the minute she got out of the squad car. The license plate, white with blue raised numbers, appeared much older than the truck itself but it had the correct registration stickers on the upper left-hand and upper right-hand corners. She slipped inside the squad car, ran the information, and within minutes was back out. "Nothing. This license plate is from before computer records. Carol Grossman will check back in the files. But the stickers are certainly current. And there's no way you can peel them off another vehicle's plate without tearing the stickers."

"We've got a homicide. The victim was reported driving this truck."

"Kid hanging from a tree." Sheriff Zakarios stroked his long, square chin. "That's a hell of a note. So is this."

"Thanks for the call." Rick Shaw clapped Zak's back.

"I'll help in any way I can."

One of Zak's deputies called to him while wrapping the pileated woodpecker in plastic. "Good work."

"He did very good work." Cooper sighed. Don was a likeable man, clearly a man who had either been in the wrong place at the wrong time or had been involved in something she couldn't fathom right then. But she and Rick would figure it out. They usually did, and she always came to the same conclusion: it's easier to keep your nose to the grindstone and be honest. But she couldn't imagine what Don could have done that was dishonest. As far as she knew, criminals had no need of taxidermy skills.

As they climbed back into the squad car, Rick tossed his hat in the back, droplets flinging outward. Coop threw hers back there, too.

"I'll have to get my hat blocked. I forgot my plastic hat cover."

"Those things look awful." She shivered in her seat.

"Chill?"

"Yeah. Soaked to the bone."

"Me, too, but I've more protection." He pinched his spare tire, which was decreasing slowly. Rick struggled with dieting. The temptation was to roll into a fast-food joint.

"When we get back I'd better tell Harry her woodpecker has been impounded."

"This woodpecker is news to me. She shooting woodpeckers out there? Isn't that against the law?" He winked.

"Found it dead by the back porch. Actually, the cats found it."

"Those cats of hers." Rick laughed. "She'd better enlist them for Social Security numbers given all the work they do." He turned left down Route 29. After about five minutes he asked, "Any ideas?"

"The truck ties them together. Weird."

She lapsed into silence and then spoke again. "I'll track down Lottie Pearson, too."

"Why?"

"She dragged Don to Mim's charity dance."

"And wasn't it Lottie who brought O'Bannon the coffee? It was. Glad you were there. Lottie Pearson." He whistled low. "Want me to turn up the heat?"

"No. We'll suffocate. I've got a change of clothes in my locker. I'll talk to Lottie after calling Roy and Nadine's. She'll be a real treat." Coop folded her arms across her chest.

## 28

"No." Lottie frowned as the rain slashed at the windowpane in her office.

"Lottie, no one thinks you killed Donny Clatterbuck. Don't get your nose out of joint." Cynthia Cooper, tired and frustrated, spoke bluntly. "But you were in his company recently. Anything you noticed might create a major breakthrough." Cooper thought to herself how onerous it was to butter up people like Lottie.

"Well." She tapped the desk with a pencil, rose from her ergonomically correct seat, crossed the tidy, attractive office, and closed the door behind Coop. "Of course I want to help. It's just that you put me off coming to my place of work in uniform. I have a position to uphold." She returned to her seat. "The university would take a dim view of anything incorrect." She lowered her voice on "incorrect."

Assistant Director of Major Gifts, Lottie was hypersensitive to social nuance. The job suited her and the day would come when old Vernon Miller retired and she would take over. Patiently she nurtured his social contacts as well as her own.

"I understand but *you* have to understand two men are dead, Wesley Partlow and Don Clatterbuck. There's a strong possibility that their murders are connected —"

"What?" Alarm registered on Lottie's face. "And who is Wesley Partlow? I read about him being found but the paper didn't say much."

"Because no one knows much. Partlow was a kid parking cars at Big Mim's fund-raiser."

"What's someone like that got to do with Donny?"

Coop leaned forward as the rain beat down. "Don Clatterbuck was shot in a truck Partlow had driven before he was killed. Sean O'Bannon described the truck when we — Well, it's a long story involving Mrs. Hogendobber's hubcaps but Sean correctly described the old pickup. We couldn't trace the truck. We had no license plate. We now have a license plate but it's ancient. The stickers are current. Carol Grossman down in Richmond, working on this since this morning, has tracked the old license plates to a Jaguar dealer down in Newport News.

They used them as part of the decor."

"The dealer stole the plates." Lottie jumped to a conclusion.

"According to the dealer, he didn't. They turn the plates in. By law they must."

"Well, someone took them." She liked being right.

"Someone did. Someone also filched new date and month stickers. Dealers don't have those. You can't even peel them off someone's plates intact using a razor blade. As you can see, Lottie, this is becoming more and more interesting."

"I still don't believe Donny would know anyone like that hanged man." She stopped herself, regrouped, and continued, "There has to be a reasonable explanation. A coincidence. Maybe Partlow stole the truck and returned it. No one knew."

"That has occurred to us but what I need from you are details: Don's mood, did he say anything about plans for the future? That sort of thing."

"Would you like a beverage?" Lottie asked. "I apologize. I should have offered you one when you came through the door."

"A hot coffee would work wonders."

"Cream and sugar?"

"Heavy on the cream, light on the sugar."

Lottie pushed a button on her phone

system. "Franny, two cups of coffee. The usual for me and heavy on the cream, light on the sugar for the other. Thanks." She returned her attention to Coop. Lottie thought Cooper, nice-looking, could look even better. With a bit of luck a tall, lean woman like Cooper could make a decent match in a county like Albemarle, but working as a deputy destroyed her chances of moving too far up in the world. Lottie wondered why women didn't think of those things. Life would always be easier if one was attached to a wealthy man.

They chitchatted until the coffee was placed before them. As Franny withdrew, Lottie took a deep sip, as did Cynthia.

"Thank you. This is just what I needed."

"For the record, Donald Clatterbuck and I weren't dating. He escorted me to Mim's party. I liked him, of course. Who didn't? You know why I, well, I won't go into that but it still bothers me that BoomBoom didn't allow me to show Diego Aybar the sights. I love doing that sort of thing and Harry already has a beau. It just upset me. That's how I wound up with Donald." She cast her eyes at Coop but Coop betrayed no feelings of her own so Lottie continued on. "He couldn't have been nicer. You see, I'd not been especially solicitous of him. Well, truthfully I ignored him. You know, he was just a working-class guy. But he actually had some ambition, which surprised me."

"In what way?"

"He said he was taking his leather-design business on the Internet. He'd been working on a website where he would display techniques. I don't know anything about leather design and repair but I remember he said something about showing the different quality of skins. He thought if he did that he'd get orders for special items like sofas, couch slipcovers, even boots."

"He was good." Cooper sighed.

"He also wanted to go on the Internet for his taxidermy business. He said he ought to preserve rich people and call the business Stuffed Shirts. He had a good sense of humor."

"So he seemed positive?"

"Yes. He mentioned saving to buy his grandfather's farm. Said it had been a good year so he was going to make Mr. Mawyer an offer. He mentioned that no one else in the family was interested. He's lucky there."

"No clouds on the horizon?"

"No. If there were he didn't mention it. You mean was he afraid of something or someone?"

"Considering he was shot, yes, I'd —"

Lottie interrupted. "What if the murder was a mistake? What if whoever killed him saw the truck and thought he was someone else?"

"Anything is possible." Coop drained her cup.

"Would you care for some more?"

"Thank you, no. I'm finally warming up. If I hadn't had a change of uniform in my locker I'd be sitting here dripping on your floor. It's not that cold but I took a chill."

"Don't you just hate that?" Lottie asked sympathetically.

"Did you think Don wanted to go out with you again?"

"We just didn't click on that level. What can I say? No chemistry." She dabbed her lips with the small napkin Franny had brought with the coffees. "Speaking of chemistry, Harry and Diego!"

Coop smiled. "Who knows?"

"Do you think she's done with Fair forever? I mean I thought that's why Boom-Boom set her up. Boom wanted Fair away from Harry. She's like that."

"I don't know. That was a long time ago, BoomBoom and Fair. Five years . . . or close to it. I don't think she wants him back."

"She wants them all. She's not happy unless every man is circling around her like a honey pot."

"Then you would have thought she'd have kept Diego for herself." Coop shrewdly observed Lottie's reaction.

"Steinmetz is a bigger fish and probably a richer one, too. She doesn't miss a trick. I hate the way men fawn over her."

"She's beautiful."

"Artifice." Lottie sniffed.

"Don evidenced little interest."

"They grew up together. He saw right through her."

"But, Lottie, Fair grew up with her, too."

Not one to appreciate an errant detail in her argument being pointed out to her, Lottie's shoulders froze a bit, then relaxed. "Donald had more sense." She glanced out at the gloomy day, returning to meet Cooper's eyes. "I'm sorry he's dead. He was a nice person. I can't imagine why anyone would want to kill him."

# 29

"Would you look at this!" Harry followed her observation with a string of curses. One of the joints on the old disc used to break up earth had cracked, small ball bearings scattered underneath. The rain pelted the tin roof of the equipment shed. She'd just gotten home after work and decided since she couldn't work outside, she'd grease the manure spreader, the disc, check the tines on the drag, the fluid levels in the 1958 John Deere tractor.

Mostly she couldn't bear the thought of being inside for one more minute. By the end of the day at the post office she wanted to be outside as long as possible.

The cats, less enthusiastic about her work ethic in the rain, repaired to the house. Only Tucker accompanied her. The shed, tidy and tight, kept the rain out, but the wind added to the gloom.

*"Boiling black out there."* Tucker felt the electricity of the storm building.

Harry reached down, rubbing one of

Tucker's ears between her thumb and fore-finger. "I can't complain, really. This disc is almost as old as the tractor. You know on the new ones the joints are sealed after being packed in grease. I guess that works, I don't know. Wonder how much it will cost to fix it? Oh, well." She leaned against the tractor. "What we need is a drill seeder. Fat chance." She laughed because the type she needed retailed for $22,000. That was practically a year's salary for Harry.

She lifted up the hood of the dually, checked the oil, the windshield fluids, and the pressure in the tires. She repeated the process on the 1978 Ford F150 which she'd pulled into the shed. Finally satisfying her-self that everything was fine she sprinted to the barn. She'd left the back stall doors open and the three horses had wisely chosen to come in from the storm.

*"Phone's been ringing off the hook,"* Poptart told Tucker.

The corgi hopped up on the tack trunk to speak to the youngest horse eye to eye. She stood on her hind legs, sticking her head through the square opening with the big feed bucket underneath. *"Ever wish you could answer it?"*

*"No."* Poptart laughed. *"Makes more work. Every time one human calls another there's*

*usually a chore attached or something that sends Harry flying out of here. Can't see why any reasonable human would wish to be interrupted like that."*

*"And who would call you?"* Gin Fizz, the oldest of the three, asked.

*"Anne Kursinski."* Poptart laughed, naming one of the most famous show-jumping riders in the world.

*"Princess Anne would dial me."* Tomahawk put in his two cents.

*"Oh, I'm sure the next time the Princess visits America, she'll make a special request to come see workaday hunters right here in Crozet."* Gin Fizz guffawed.

*"And why not?"* Tomahawk stoutly replied. *"Most horse sports come from foxhunting. Point-to-point races, steeplechasing, hunter shows, jumper shows."* He ended with authority.

*"Three-day eventing,"* Tucker added.

*"Thank you, Tucker. I forgot that one,"* Tomahawk called from his stall.

*"I thought three-day eventing came from cavalry drills,"* Gin Fizz said.

*"Cavalry were foxhunted. Eventing is still related to foxhunting,"* Tucker declared, although the connection was slender.

Harry walked in to close Tomahawk's back stall door. The wind blew with such ferocity she thought the doors would bend. "You all are so talkative."

*"Evil out there, Mom."* Tomahawk nuzzled her.

She kissed his nose, giving him a molasses cookie. She had two for each horse.

*"Dressage doesn't come from foxhunting."* Poptart was thinking out loud. *"Haute école. Guess it's centuries old. I can't do it. I can't canter in place, half halt at the letter B or whatever. Just can't do it. I want to run!"*

*"Don't we all."* Gin Fizz eagerly awaited Harry's visit to his stall. *"The trick is, Poppy, to stop."*

At this all four animals laughed loudly, even Poptart, since she had the tendency to run right through the bridle. Young, she'd become so excited when the other horses took off that she wanted to pass everyone. This wouldn't do. Harry schooled her but it was going to take time. There are no perfect horses just as there are no perfect people. Her one flaw was small compared to Poptart's gift: the ability to jump the moon. Nothing was too high or too wide and she was clever with her hooves.

Gin Fizz admired the youngster's ability but wished he could give her some of his wisdom. Whenever she'd cut a shine the old fellow would sigh and murmur, *"Youth."*

Tomahawk, less impressed with Poppy's talents since he was fairly talented himself, usually responded, *"Mares."*

The two geldings felt that mares were emotional, erratic, and a royal pain in the ass. However, they loved Poppy despite her moodiness.

She thought highly of herself, too.

*"You'd better not run away with Mom,"* Tucker warned her.

*"I won't,"* Poppy said halfheartedly.

*"I can bite your ankles before you can kick me. Fetlocks, I should say. Well, I can bite and bite hard."*

*"Squirt."* Poptart pinned her ears but in good fun.

Harry closed the last outside door. "What's going on with you all? I've never heard such carryings-on."

*"Just shooting the breeze."* Gin Fizz laughed.

The phone rang again.

*"You'd better pick it up, Mom. It's been ringing off the hook,"* Tomahawk advised the human.

With a great sigh, Harry trotted into the tack room to pick up the phone. "Hello."

"Hey, Donny Clatterbuck's been shot dead." Susan got straight to the point.

"What?"

"It must have just happened. Lottie called me and I tried calling you first, then called Miranda. Where have you been?"

"In the equipment shed." She drew in her breath, thought a moment. "Susan, where was he? I mean, what do you know?"

"He was found in Culpeper by the side of the road. Shot through the temple. Oh, he had your woodpecker."

"What!"

"Mim said he had your woodpecker and he was in the truck Rick's been trying to find. The truck Wesley Partlow drove. Am I making sense?"

"Kind of. Who's going to tell his parents? Oh, this is really awful."

"Rick."

"Glad I don't have that job. I can't believe anyone would shoot Donny Clatterbuck. And what was he doing in the GMC?"

Tucker pricked up her ears since she could hear Susan's voice, then tore out of the tack room, down the center aisle barn, through the deluge, pushed open the screen door, then barged through the animal door into the kitchen.

*"Mrs. Murphy, Pewter, Don Clatterbuck was found dead, shot, in the farm truck."*

Mrs. Murphy, dozing on the bookshelf in the living room, raised her head, her eyes now wide open. *"I knew this would come back at us. Too close to home."*

*"You knew no such thing."* Pewter, also awake now, sat up on the sofa.

*"Whoever strung up Wesley Partlow was in Crozet. Right?"* the tiger argued.

*"Yes, but that doesn't mean they live in Crozet,"* Pewter countered.

*"No, but Donny sure did. I can't figure out what Wesley Partlow and Donny would have in common."*

*"Maybe nothing. People die without there being a connection."*

*"Pewter, they didn't just die, they were murdered and within a few days of one another. Think about it . . . and Partlow was seen in the truck. Am I right, Tucker? It was Booty's farm truck?"*

*"That's what Susan told Mom."* Tucker walked over to the bookshelf as Murphy jumped down. *"I hope Booty's not in danger. The truck's cursed."*

*"Oh, Tucker."* Pewter sniffed. *"Inanimate objects aren't cursed."*

*"The pyramids. The curse of the Pharaohs."* Tucker thought objects did, indeed, carry curses.

In a way Tucker was right.

# 30

All that evening the phone lines hummed throughout Crozet and Albemarle County. Usually a crisis would propel people to one another but the weather, increasingly awful, kept them inside.

Harry tried calling Diego but gave up, defeated by international codes. Uruguay's code was 598 but she couldn't get the number of zeros and ones right to get a line out. She'd figured rightly that he was two time zones ahead of East Coast time. That was a victory. She had enough trouble keeping time in her own time zone. Finally she humbled herself and rang BoomBoom.

"I just heard!" BoomBoom's excitable voice sounded higher than usual.

They discussed the dolorous news, then Harry felt she'd minded her manners and could ask her question. "Have you heard from Thomas?"

"This morning." BoomBoom dangled the bait, forcing Harry to ask another question.

"The reason I'm asking you is because I can't reach Diego and well . . ."

"It seems their government is having some crisis over loans to the International Monetary Fund or something like that. Diego will call you as soon as he gets a minute."

"I thought that was a problem for Argentina, not Uruguay, but then what do I know?" She sighed.

"We tend to ignore South America, which, when you think about it, is really dumb. After all, we're all part of the New World."

"He's probably got a mistress in Montevideo." Harry wasn't focusing on American shortcomings. She was focusing on Diego.

"No, he doesn't. I wouldn't do that to you . . . not if I knew. But he doesn't. Feel better?"

"Sort of." She walked to the stove, turning the flame up under the kettle. "Boom, this welding that you do — could you cut locks?"

"Of course."

"Steel plates?"

"Yes, but it would take some time. What I work with is thin sheets. The cutouts are strong enough to stand on the base I make for them but a heavy steel plate like the kind put in the back of pickups to hitch trailers, that kind of plate, that would take a long time. Why?"

"Donny had one of those huge old stand-up safes. If Rick doesn't find the combination, he'll have to cut it."

"That will be a very difficult job."

"I know but if you volunteer we'd be there first. I could help."

"Harry." BoomBoom considered this. "What do you think is in the safe?"

"I don't know but I'd like to find out, wouldn't you? Maybe it will tell us why Donny was shot. In fact, why don't you call Rick now, then call me back."

"Well — all right." BoomBoom hung up the phone. Within minutes she dialed back. "Harry, he's at Donny's shop now and said he'd be grateful for the help. I'll meet you there in fifteen minutes. I told him I need you to regulate the oxygen in the tanks."

"Did he believe it?"

"Uh — sort of."

"Okay, fifteen minutes."

# 31

As the blue flame slowly sliced into the heavy lock of the safe, Rick Shaw allowed as how the last person he thought would be wielding a torch would be BoomBoom Craycroft. He readily agreed to her offer, otherwise he'd have to wait a day while the safe company flew in an expert to open the lock. The county budget prompted him to make use of local talent even though it meant destroying the lock, which resembled the hatch locks of submarines.

"Harry, you drive me crazy sometimes, you and your amateur detective crap, but I hand it to you on this suggestion."

"Thanks, Sheriff." She stood by the oxygen tank feeding the welding torch.

*"She'll live off that compliment for a month,"* Tucker remarked as she sat discreetly next to a finished stuffed elk's head on the floor.

Pewter, frightened by the noise of the welding torch, crouched behind Tucker.

Mrs. Murphy perched on top of Donny's worktable. She remained motionless, since she didn't want to rouse the sheriff's attention either.

*"Think Harry will stuff us when we go?"* She laughed as she surveyed Donny's handiwork.

*"Vile!"* Pewter leaned harder on Tucker, who licked her head.

Coop stood well behind Boom.

Arms across her chest, Harry murmured, "Tell Booty?"

"Yeah. Rick did."

"Did he know anything about the truck?"

"Said it was his but for farm use. Never took it off the farm. Didn't much use it anyway, he said. No license plate. You know, he took it like the soldier that he was. He asked if Marge knew and Rick said that I was with her. He got in his car and drove in her driveway just as I was leaving. Poor Marge. He was her only son."

"Yeah." Harry felt bad for Donny's mom, a much-liked woman.

Rick checked his watch. "Harry, tell me about the woodpecker."

"I brought it in just before the Dogwood Festival and Donny said he'd get right on it. Business was always slower in the spring, the taxidermy business, I mean. His leather business was doing well and he was making coffee tables, too, out of license plates. One's over there." She pointed it out. "He was bursting with ideas."

"Did he seem like himself?"

"Yeah." She shrugged.

"Did he look healthy?"

"Very." She waited a moment. "Sheriff, what's going to happen to my woodpecker?"

*"It's my woodpecker,"* Pewter chirped up.

*"Shut up. Don't attract Rick's attention,"* Murphy counseled.

"For now, nothing. I told them to run it through an X-ray machine." He turned to BoomBoom, who stopped for a moment, pushing up her protective face guard to check her work. "How you doing?"

"Another five minutes, I hope." She slapped the mask down and resumed cutting.

"Find anything besides my woodpecker?"

"A Dallas Cowboys windbreaker just as Sean described it." Cooper squinted when a shower of sparks flew off the safe. "And a matchbook from Roy and Nadine's restaurant in Lexington, Kentucky. Very colorful."

"Any ideas?" Harry asked.

"That's what I was going to ask you." Rick hitched up his belt. "You've known Clatterbuck all your life. Did you like him?"

"Yeah. Always seemed levelheaded. He didn't run with a bad crowd. Didn't have a lot of bad affairs with women. Stuff like that."

"Huh." Rick grunted.

"I guess you looked for the key to the safe?"

"Yes, we did. Why?"

"Oh." Harry turned her palms up for a moment as if in supplication. "Hate to see the safe ruined."

"It's not ruined. I can put it back together if Rick wants me to." BoomBoom turned off the torch. She waited a moment, then pushed the heavy lock with her gloved hand. "Sheriff, if you grab one handle and I grab the other I think we can pull it out. I'm afraid if I try to do this by myself I'll push it into the safe and that might damage whatever's in there."

"Good thinking." He grabbed a brass handle.

They both pulled on the count of three and the heavy lock and spinning handle fell out on the floor with a clunk. Rick stepped aside as BoomBoom, gloves on, reached in and pulled open the door.

"Oh, my God!"

Each shelf contained bundles and bundles of crisp new bills, neatly stacked.

*"That's a lot of stuffed deer heads,"* Mrs. Murphy laconically observed.

# 32

The shock of finding five hundred and twenty-five thousand dollars in Donny Clatterbuck's safe was nearly as great as finding Donny himself.

Harry and the animals drove to Miranda's, a place of sanity and common sense. To her surprise, BoomBoom wanted to go, too.

They found Miranda and Tracy playing gin rummy. Tracy was winning.

"Knock, knock." Harry let herself in, with Mrs. Murphy rushing first through the door. "I'm coming unannounced and BoomBoom's about two minutes behind me."

Tracy rose, as befit a Virginia gentleman. "You look a little peaked, Harry, my girl. Some fortification?"

She shook the rain off in the little back-door entranceway. "How about a steaming cup of tea with a drop of Maker's Mark in it?" She mentioned the famous sipping whiskey distilled in Loretto, Kentucky.

"Why, Harry." Miranda stood up herself, heading to the teapot. "I don't remember you ever roping your tea."

"Well, I'm wet, I'm chilled, and I'm sorely vexed, as my grandmother used to say."

BoomBoom stepped in tight behind Harry. "Miranda, forgive me. I just had to see you."

"Are you two having another fight?" Miranda turned on the gas stove while Tracy opened the cabinet serving as a liquor chest. "BoomBoom, what can I get you?"

"A straight shot of gin will revive me considerably."

"What in the world is the matter with you two girls?" He put his hands on his hips.

Harry hung up her worn Barbour coat. BoomBoom did likewise, only her Barbour coat was new and longer. One couldn't reside in Albemarle without a proper Barbour coat, made in England and the best working raingear in the world. Tucker, anticipating treats, moved over to be near Miranda. Pewter, no fool, headed straight for the table.

"I don't know where to start." BoomBoom shook her long blond hair, droplets of water falling to the oak floor.

"I'll start." Harry pulled out a chair at the

kitchen table. "Rick Shaw and Cynthia Cooper were called up to Culpeper this afternoon because Donny Clatterbuck had been shot through the head."

Miranda exclaimed, "Oh, no! We haven't heard —"

"He was in the truck Sean described Wesley Partlow as driving to his salvage yard to sell your hubcaps, and don't feel left out, the only people who know about this are Donny's family. Big Mim probably doesn't know yet unless Rick is calling her now."

Both Tracy and Miranda sat down at the table to listen to Harry as they waited for the water to boil.

"What in the world is going on?" Miranda rubbed her cheek with the palm of her hand.

"Nobody knows. It's scary." BoomBoom also sat down as Tracy rose to pull out a chair for her, then reseated himself.

"The truck had stolen plates, old ones with new stickers. Coop told me that. The plates are from a Newport News car dealership. The dealer has no idea how the plates were stolen. No cars were missing. Coop asked if he would send over his employee rolls so she could check for criminal backgrounds. Nothing. The truck, as it happens, is Booty Mawyer's old farm truck. He says it hasn't been off the farm. Been moldering in one of his sheds. That's what he told Rick when Rick gave him the bad news. But, of course, it has. He said sometimes Don would move hay from one shed to another — but, you know, Booty's getting on in years and it would be easy to fool him. Well, he wouldn't know anything unless he saw it with his own eyes.

"And before I get to why we're together — in the back of the truck, on the seat, was the Dallas Cowboys windbreaker exactly as Sean described it."

Tracy got up to pour the tea. He motioned for Miranda to stay seated. He put the pot on the table, set out four cups, smacked the Maker's Mark bottle directly in front of Harry, then opened the refrigerator and brought out cold cuts. He figured, correctly, that Harry and BoomBoom hadn't eaten. He also put a chilled green bottle of Tanqueray gin in front of BoomBoom.

"Honey, let me do that." Miranda got up to arrange the food, bringing out the homemade seven-grain bread, fresh butter, and local honey.

Within minutes an impromptu cold supper sat before the two hungry women.

"Thank you." BoomBoom gratefully buttered a piece of bread cut thick.

Harry chattered as she, too, made herself

a sandwich, surreptitiously dropping food bits to her pets. "Coop said the only thing in the windbreaker was a matchbook from Roy and Nadine's, a hot restaurant in Lexington, Kentucky. She called the restaurant, gave them the fake Wesley's description, and the manager said he had no recollection of anyone like that, nor did it seem that would be the kind of customer Roy and Nadine's would attract. He did, however, promise to ask his employees if they remembered anyone looking like that. She's sending on the mug shot.

"But, well, Boom should tell you what happened next."

"Donny has that huge safe in his shop, the kind that's taller than I am. Harry suggested I call Rick and offer to open the lock using my welding torch. She was right because Rick couldn't get a service representative for twenty-four hours plus there was the expense of getting him here. So over I went, cut out the lock, and what do you know . . . there's a ton of money inside the safe! Five hundred and twenty-five thousand dollars. Five hundred and twenty-five thousand!" BoomBoom repeated.

"Stacked neatly. So new you could smell it. Rick says it isn't counterfeit either." Harry sipped her tea.

"Where in the world would Donny Clatterbuck get money like that?" Miranda brought both hands to her face in surprise.

"New? Directly from a bank or someone who had access to new bills, who dealt in large sums often." Tracy's mind whirred along. "Someone who either needed Donny to stash the money, giving him a cut, or someone who needed Donny."

"For what?" BoomBoom poured honey over a piece of buttered bread.

"He was good with his hands." Harry tried to feed Tucker another small piece of meat under the table. Pewter snatched it before the dog could get it so Harry tore another small piece for the corgi. The mild altercation revealed Harry's feeding the "kids" from the table — not that anyone really cared that much.

"I'm here, too," Murphy reminded the humans.

Miranda gave her a tidbit. "This is so — so hard to believe. Donny never threw money around."

"No, he didn't," Harry confirmed.

"He could have put the money in the bank but he didn't. This points to his doing something illegal." Tracy, hand poised in midair with a butter knife, said, "And it seems obvious that he knew in some fashion the young man found hanged. The question is, how and why? That kid looked as though he didn't have a dime."

"Coop can't find a trace of him anywhere. Wesley's not his real name," Harry said.

"I wonder if Marge knows about the money." Miranda thought about Donny's mother, worrying for her welfare.

"Highly doubtful, my love," Tracy replied.

BoomBoom finished her sandwich, which made her feel more conversational. "Wait until Lottie Pearson hears this."

"What's Lottie Pearson got to do with this?" Miranda asked.

"She blew him off just like she spurned Roger. She wants money and prestige or what passes for it. When she hears that Donny Clatterbuck had a small fortune in his safe, she'll pass out."

"Five hundred and twenty-five thousand dollars." Miranda couldn't imagine that much money.

"We helped count it. Had to wear plastic gloves that Rick and Coop keep in the squad car. They have to avoid blood because of AIDS so they carry these hospital gloves around." Harry thought a moment, then excitedly said, "When I took my woodpecker to Don, I noticed the safe. I asked him if that's where he kept his millions and he said, 'Only half a million.' I thought he was kidding."

" 'He who loves money never has money enough, he who loves wealth never has enough profit; this, too is vanity.' *Ecclesiastes*, Chapter Five, Verse Ten," Miranda quoted.

"What a memory," Tracy marveled.

"Miranda is a marvel." BoomBoom smiled.

"Mim really must not know what's happened." Harry's mind stayed on the murder. "Or she would have called you. Rick usually gets to her."

Miranda said, "She's in New York this weekend visiting Stafford and his wife."

Stafford was Mim's son, who rarely returned home as he loved his family more the farther away they were.

Mrs. Murphy washed her face with her paw. *"We've got work to do."*

*"I'm not going out in the rain,"* Pewter stoutly stated.

*"I didn't say we were."*

Tucker nuzzled her pal. *"What do you have in mind?"*

*"We need to get to Aunt Tally's and snoop around. I should have thought of it during the tea party but I got caught up in the commotion."*

"Aunt Tally's is a long, long hike, Murphy. Talk Harry into driving us over there."

"Sure, Pewter. She listens about as well as any human."

Tucker thought about it. "She's right, Murphy. The creeks are over their banks. We won't get across. We've got to convince Harry to drive us there somehow."

The pretty tiger pondered this, then curled her tail around her. "You're right."

"Finally, someone's giving me credit around here," Pewter crowed, then for good measure reached up and hooked a piece of bread off the table before a human could stop her. Once the bread was on the floor she knew the humans wouldn't touch it even if they scolded her, which they didn't, as they were too busy deciding if Lottie Pearson really was a gold digger. BoomBoom said yes. Harry said maybe. Miranda wanted to think the best of her and Tracy opted not to have an opinion.

"Don't let it go to your head. Listen, we'd better get over there tomorrow. If this rain would only stop."

"What's on your mind?" Tucker respected the tiger's brain power, the quickness of her mind.

"We need to examine the floor of the dining room, open the cupboards in the pantry, in-

*vestigate the places where Tally keeps food. We might have to check the outbuildings. I don't know exactly but I can tell you this, if we find what I think we're going to find, either Sean O'Bannon is in on this or he's the next victim."*

# 33

At twelve midnight on the dot the rain stopped. Mrs. Murphy had become accustomed to the incessant din on the rooftop. The silence awakened her. Curled up next to Harry, she lifted her head, then rose, stretching fore and aft.

Tucker, asleep on the rug by the bed, snored lightly, her parted lips revealing her considerable canines as well as the small square teeth between them.

Pewter, on the pillow next to Harry, was dead to the world. Her gray forehead rested next to Harry's pillow edge, her body formed a comma, her tail curled tight around her legs.

No point waking up the Princess of Sleep. Next to eating, Pewter loved sleep.

Murphy walked out of the bedroom, down the hall, careful to step on the old carpet runner. She liked feeling carpet beneath her paws. Then she bounced across the kitchen, out the animal door, and pushed open the screened porch door. The clouds, low and billowy, Prussian blue, flew across the sky, west to east. Puddles like black ice filled the small depressions in the driveway. Keeping that driveway in good working order gave Harry fits. She'd dutifully fill the holes only to have the stones eventually worm their way out to the side of the road. Every three years she would break down and hire Mr. Tapscott to bulldoze the long driveway, put down bluestone or crusher run, and then pack it as hard as possible. No wonder a large part of the state budget was siphoned off by road maintenance. If only Harry had the tiniest fraction of that budget, her road would be in tiptop shape.

Murphy often thought of human cares. Not that she thought road maintenance a foolish care. After all, she was a farm cat; she understood the importance of roads, tractors, and re-seeding pastures. But much of what humans fussed over seemed silly to her. They worried about their looks, about money, about their social standing.

Cats ignored social standing. To be a cat meant one was at the top of the animal chain. And since cats are not herd animals, each cat remained a complete individual. This didn't mean that Mrs. Murphy lacked kitty friends. It only meant that she didn't rely on them for a sense of herself. She simply was.

She hopscotched across puddles, entering the barn. The three horses, sound asleep, didn't hear her. She jumped on the tack trunk. Gin Fizz slept like Tucker, on his side and snoring. Tomahawk and Poptart slept standing up. Murphy couldn't imagine sleeping standing up.

She crept into the tack room. The mice were playing with a jacks ball, singing at the top of their lungs, "Take Me Out to the Ball Game."

She pounced, narrowly missing the fattest mouse.

*"Eeek! Mad cat. Run for your life!"* they screamed, scrambling for the hole in the wall. They all made it.

Murphy put a glittering eye to the hole shaped like an upside-down U. *"Have the decency to clean up after yourselves. My human doesn't think your games are funny. And you've left grain bits all over the floor. You'll get me in trouble and if you get me in trouble I'll nail one of you if it's the last thing I do!"*

*"Bully,"* a high-pitched voice replied.

*"We had a deal. You leave the tack room clean and I leave you alone."*

*"You surprised us. We would have cleaned up."*

*"Sure."* Mrs. Murphy batted the jacks ball between her paws.

*"Give us the ball back. We'll clean up. I promise."*

*"Maybe I will and maybe I won't."* With that she catapulted straight up in the air, turned halfway round, dropping back on the ball. She flopped on her side, kicked the ball out with her hind legs, then chased it wildly under the saddle racks and bridle hooks. She whacked it hard with her right front paw. The little red jacks ball slammed against the wall, bouncing back almost into her jaws.

Murphy carried on like this for five minutes until she tired of solo handball. She tantalizingly deposited the jacks ball about a foot from the mouse entrance. Making a great show of leaving the tack room, she tiptoed back in, silently vaulting onto a saddle. Holding her breath, she waited until she saw tiny whiskers appear in the opening.

*"She's gone,"* a voice said.

*"Oh, no, she's not. I know Mrs. Murphy. She's clever,"* the original high-pitched voice replied.

*"Mom, you worry too much. She's up in the hayloft with Simon."*

*"Bart, don't you go out there. You can play later."*

But Bart, young and full of himself, thought he could dash out, grab the ball, and roll it back in. Even if the cat happened to be in the tack room he thought he was quicker than she was. Wrong.

Bart no sooner scooted out than the full weight of Mrs. Murphy surrounded him. She'd jumped down, pinning him under her beige-striped tummy.

*"Bart! Bart!"* his mother screamed.

*"Mom."* His voice was muffled by all the fur.

Murphy, highly pleased with herself, twisted her body so Bart could stick his head out from under her but couldn't escape. *"Worm."*

*"Oh, please, Mrs. Murphy, don't kill me."*

*"I'm going to play with you, I'll let you go, then smack my paw down on your tail. When I'm tired of your foolishness, I'll snap your neck and bite your head off. I'll leave your head right here so Harry can see what a mighty mouser I am. I'll eat the rest. Yum."*

*"Take me."* Bart's mother boldly hurried outside amid screams from the other mice inside.

*"I could have you both, you know, I'm that fast."*

*"You're a fabulous athlete, Mrs. Murphy."*

307

The mother walked right up to Mrs. Murphy's nose. *"But he's young. I'm not. Take me."*

Bart was sobbing. Mrs. Murphy considered the situation. She heard a soft flutter in the rafters. The owl returned from hunting.

*"Go on. Get in there. She will eat you. I won't."*

*"Bless you, Mrs. Murphy."* The mother hugged Mrs. Murphy as best she could as Bart scurried into his home.

*"Just clean up around here. If you don't I won't be nice to you next time."*

*"We will!"* the jubilant chorus agreed from behind the wall.

Satisfied that she'd struck terror into their hearts, the tiger emerged into the center aisle, then climbed the ladder up to the loft. Simon was asleep, his treasures surrounding him.

She looked straight up into the cupola as the owl, over two feet of her, peered down.

*"Who?"*

*"You know who."*

*"Indeed I do. A saucy cat. A spoiled cat. Mrs. Murphy. What are you doing in here? Get caught in the rain?"*

*"No. I woke up when it stopped. Have you been hunting in it?"*

*"A foray when the worst was over."*

Mrs. Murphy climbed to the topmost hay bale. *"Come down here and talk to me so I don't get a crick in my neck. And I don't want to yell. Sooner or later Simon will wake up and whimper. You know how he is."*

Although not close friends, the two predators had respect for one another even though the owl did not understand domestication one bit. She glided down, silent as the tomb. Gave Mrs. Murphy the chills because when the owl hunted you didn't know what hit you until it was too late. Even sharp cat ears could only discern her presence when she was already close.

The owl's bright yellow eyes blinked. *"What's on your mind, pussycat?"*

*"I have to get over to Tally Urquhart's but I can't cross the creeks."*

*"Over the banks, debris hurtling in the water. The beavers don't even want to come out of their lodges and the lodges are getting holes punched in by tree limbs. You can hear the roar."* The owl blinked.

*"Yes, I heard it when I left the house. I suppose I could open the truck window when we pass Tally's drive and hop out of the car. Mother has to slow for the curve but I don't like her knowing I can manage the windows. It's not good for humans to know what we know."*

She chuckled. *"That's very owl-like of you."* She fluffed her feathers, turned her head almost the whole way around, then settled herself. *"Want me to fly over?"*

*"I need to get in the house."*

*"Ah, I can't help you there."*

*"You see, two humans have been murdered. One was hanged and the other was shot."*

*"I know."*

*"I guess you would. You're out and about. I didn't think you cared much about human affairs."*

*"I don't, but murder has a certain lurid curiosity. We owls don't murder one another. You cats might tussle, a bad fight, lose an eye, but you don't murder one another. It's one of those depressing curiosities about humans."*

*"So it appears."* Murphy leaned toward the large bird. *"I think there's been a third murder. Roger O'Bannon. And either his brother did it or his brother is next in line."*

*"Ah, so I am not my brother's keeper?"* She rocked back and forth on her huge feet.

*"Cain and Abel. Mrs. Hogendobber would know the exact quote from the Bible. I don't but I know the story."*

*"As do I. Cain slew Abel because he was jealous. The Hebrew God favored Abel. All religions have such a story. Being sacred to*

Athena, I'm partial to the Greek myths myself. But it would have to be a powerful motive for blood to kill blood. Either that or Sean O'Bannon is one cold-blooded creature."

"I don't think he is. I could be wrong. Crozet is so small. You think you know people but you don't. But I really don't think Sean is cold-blooded. What puzzles me the most is what the victims have gotten themselves into — over five hundred thousand dollars was found in Donny Clatterbuck's safe. So I would have to say that money is the motive and if that's just Clatterbuck's cut then we are talking about a great, great deal of money. But I can't for the life of me think of what they could be doing to generate that kind of cash. It's not drugs, at least I don't think so, and we know the money's not counterfeit. I've thought and thought. I even thought what if they've been selling state secrets but there are no state secrets in Albemarle County. The government officials and military brass retired here are just that, retired."

"Slavery."

"Huh?"

"Mrs. Murphy, there's still slavery. Children are bought and sold. People from Asia and South America are sold as domestic slaves smuggled into the U.S. Oh, it's called something else but it's slavery. When you can't speak the language, you can't go out on your own. You work for nothing or next to nothing and another human, maybe the one who smuggled you in, controls your life. There's a lot of money in smuggling people across the border."

"I never thought of that. I don't know, but it's something and it's here. This I do know, if Sean O'Bannon isn't part of it he'll be dead before too long. If he lives, I have to assume the worst."

"Can't you set a trap for him? If he doesn't fall into it, he's innocent," the owl said with deliberation.

"That's just it, since I don't know what it is that they're doing, I can't bait a trap."

"You are in a pickle." The owl chuckled. "But your human is safe. Why worry?"

"No, she's not. She was there when the safe was cut open by BoomBoom Craycroft, of all people. So now her blood is up. She's as curious as a cat but without the nine lives."

"Harry does have an odd way of stumbling onto the truth." The owl scratched her head with her foot.

"You could do me a favor. When weather permits, fly over O'Bannon Salvage. See if anything looks peculiar from the air. Sometimes land betrays things. Oh, and there's a very offensive rat that lives there, he calls *himself Pope Rat. I think he knows a lot."*

*"If I catch him and carry him aloft he'll sing like a robin."* She chuckled low and deep, the idea of swinging the rat in the air appealing to her.

*"When we find out what it is we'll no doubt wonder how we missed it,"* the cat sighed.

*"Or be completely amazed. Humans, for all their faults, can be damnably clever."*

# 34

Although the rain had stopped, the runoff slopped over highways, and culverts, jammed with gunk, backed up and overflowed. Everywhere one looked there was running water. The shoulders off the sides of the roads shone with it.

Driving slowly, Harry gave thanks that her lands rested high above the floodplain. Structures built in lowlands had flooded basements at the least.

Mrs. Murphy, Pewter, and Tucker had been arguing since climbing into the truck. Murphy was determined to jump out when Harry slowed for the curve by Tally Urquhart's farm entrance.

Pewter vowed she would not launch herself from a moving vehicle. What did she care if Sean might be in danger? Besides, the long, long driveway meant she'd get her feet wet.

Tucker moaned because she might squeeze out the window but not being as agile as the cat, she feared the drop. No point in collecting broken bones.

"*But I need your nose,*" Murphy pouted.

"*Won't do you a bit of good if I can't haul myself up the driveway. It's not a good plan, Murphy. Be patient. Sooner or later, Mom will call on Tally.*"

"*By that time it will be too late.*" The sleek cat put her paw on the window crank as the old truck didn't have electric windows.

"*No, it won't.*" Pewter was nervous that if Murphy rolled down the window and shot out of the truck, Harry would swerve and they'd slide off the road into the muck. Not an appealing prospect to a fastidious cat.

Tally's farm lay up ahead, marked by a big rectangular sign with a white rose on a dark green background and the name "Rose Hill" swinging in the light breeze. Mrs. Murphy, using both paws, started cranking down the window when to her delight, Harry turned right onto the drive.

"Murphy, what are you doing?"

"*Damn, now she knows I know how to roll down the window.*"

"*I told you not to do it.*" Pewter smugly moved over to sit next to Harry.

"*Brownnoser,*" Murphy spat.

"*That does us no good at all. What if this is a short visit? We need a plan,*" Tucker, being practical, said.

*"All right. When we get there, Tucker, go straight to the dining room. The flooring is old random-width. There are cracks between the boards. Sniff the cracks. Would be a bitter smell, I think. Pewter, go into the pantry. You do the same thing but get on the shelves. You'll have to stick your nose in sugar bowls, creamers, any small bowl, but be careful. You don't want to inhale anything into your system. Stuff would be lethal. Think how quickly it killed Roger O'Bannon."*

*"If it did,"* Pewter replied. *"We'll never know without an autopsy. He could have died of natural causes."*

*"We'd best hope he did,"* Tucker grimly said.

*"Sean should have ordered an autopsy."* Pewter eagerly moved toward the passenger door as Harry parked at the back of Tally's beautiful house. *"It's weird."*

*"Some humans feel strongly that the body shouldn't be disturbed. And no one thought of murder at the time. It's not so weird."* Tucker allowed Harry to lift her down.

The blossoms, knocked off the trees and bushes, scattered on the grass like pink and white confetti. Harry rapped on the back door as she scraped the petals off her boots.

As no one came directly to the door she

opened it a crack. "Aunt Tally, it's Harry."

The sound of footsteps reverberated through the back hall. Reverend Herb Jones appeared. "Harry, come in."

"Hi. I didn't see your car."

"In the garage. The storm was so bad I thought I'd better come out here and stay, especially since Mim and family are in New York." He closed the door behind Harry and the animals, who headed to their respective assignments. "When the help goes home she's out here all alone and those were nasty storms. One right after the other."

"Gee, I'm happy you're here. That's why I stopped by. I was worried about Tally being alone, too." She followed Herb into the huge kitchen.

Tally glanced up from yellowed hunt-territory maps, drawn in the 1930s. "I'm still alive, thank you."

"Never a doubt in my mind." Harry laughed. "Hey, those are something."

"Forgot I had them and then Herb and I were talking about the old Albemarle Hunt, which hunted the Greenwood territory. I was just a kid then but that hunt unraveled, odds and ends, and in 1929 Farmington took over the territory. Anyway, these old maps will show you."

Harry propped on her elbows to study the

maps. She loved old prints, photographs, aquatints. "I think people had better lives back then."

"Well, I'm inclined to agree — until you had a toothache," Aunt Tally sensibly replied.

As the humans enjoyed one another's company, Tally recalling her girlhood, Herb remembering the big jumps from hunt days gone by, the animals worked quickly.

Pewter, nosy anyway, quietly pulled open the pantry cabinets. They had glass window fronts so she didn't waste any time. She pushed the lids off the two sugar bowls, one silver and formal, one informal. Plain white sugar rested inside. She sniffed. Plain white sugar, pure and simple.

For good measure she inspected every small bowl, tureen, creamer. Everything was in order. Disappointed, she hopped down, pulling open the bottom cabinets that didn't have glass window fronts. Nothing in there but big pots and pans and serving dishes.

Mrs. Murphy had intended to prowl around the kitchen but with the humans in there she decided to join Tucker.

The corgi, diligent and intelligent, carefully started with the joinings between two boards, following it from end to end. Murphy walked in just as she reached the place where the table had been set.

The cat sat on her haunches.

Tucker stopped, checked out a spot, lifted her nose up, then put it back down. *"Murph, try this."*

The cat joined her friend and although her nose wasn't as refined as the dog's, a scent so faint as to be ethereal wafted up from a crack. *"Bitter."*

*"Smells like a bad poison, but we can't prove it."* The dog cocked her head, then put her nose down again, wrinkled it, bringing her head up. *"Not rat poison. I've never smelled this."*

Pewter sauntered in. *"Big fat nothing."*

*"Come here,"* Murphy said.

Pewter placed her nose where Tucker indicated she should. She sniffed, then blinked her eyes, jerking her head back. *"Nasty, what's left of it."* She turned to Murphy. *"You might be right."*

*"You two slept under the table. What I remember"* — the tiger jumped up on the fireplace mantel where she'd been sitting during the tea dance — *"is that Roger was already in the chair. Lottie came into the room. She'd been out dancing or in the garden. I don't know. The desserts had just been placed on the table. Everything was buffet style. People started to come in and crowd*

the table. They needed the coffee. Lots of drinking. Lottie picked up a piece of chocolate cake. She was in the line. Next she poured a cup of coffee from the silver samovar and then she put in three scoops of raw sugar. I remember it was raw sugar because she took a step back to put the sugar on the table, bumped into Thomas Steinmetz just as he reached for the sugar, and spilled it all over the floor. She apologized, he said it was his fault, and then she carried the cake and the coffee over to Roger, who was happy that she paid attention to him. I don't know what they said because I was, by then, watching the other humans." She thought a moment. "She'd made a mess of the sugar. Thomas cleaned it up before one of the kids hired to serve got there. He picked up the broken pieces of the bowl and swept up the sugar with his napkin. When one of the servers got there he handed it to him to put in the trash. He'd wrapped everything in his napkin. I didn't pay much attention to it at the time except to think that he was nice to do it because there was enough on the floor that someone could have slipped on it. Drunk as many were, I'd say that was a sound conclusion on his part. And, well, within ten minutes, Roger was dead. And quiet. No gurgling or choking. I was sitting right here. Quiet!"

*"Lottie Pearson gives Roger coffee and cake. She went with Don Clatterbuck to the dance that night."* Pewter frowned. *"Lottie Pearson."*

*"And she's not very happy with Mom."* Tucker flattened her ears.

*"Yes."* Murphy remained silent for a long time. *"I was thinking that Sean — but now I don't know. But what would Lottie Pearson have to do with three dead men, Wesley Partlow, Donny Clatterbuck, and Roger O'Bannon? Is she a black widow or something?"*

*"She could have been killing men before now, but thinking on it, maybe her animosity toward Roger was a big act,"* Pewter, suspicious, said.

*"If she isn't acting, someone around here sure is."* Tucker hit the nail on the head.

# 35

Harry, not knowing what her animals were thinking, was working from her own ideas. Satisfied that Aunt Tally flourished, she headed her truck toward the old folks' home, the highest building in Crozet, which wasn't saying much.

An expanse of asphalt surrounded the beige block building, still wet so the parking lot surface shone like mica. She pulled her truck to the back, cut the motor, and emerged followed by the "kids," Pewter shaking water off her paws at every step.

Harry walked around the building. Nothing unusual presented itself. She then stopped at the edge of the tarmac to study the railroad tracks that swooped right next to the building with a long curve. Wesley had been found near those tracks. The brush, already grown up at this time of year, could easily conceal activity. She pushed through the bushes and brambles, leaves spraying water on her. An old mud road pockmarked with huge holes filled with brown water followed the tracks. The hanging tree, a fiddle oak, sat just south of that road, maybe fifty yards. From the tree the distance to the tracks measured about two hundred yards.

Harry looked up at the strong, spreading limbs and shuddered. The sun peeked out from the clouds, then immediately disappeared again. Thunder shook the other side of the Blue Ridge Mountains. It was far enough away that it sounded like one of the gods, clearing his throat.

"Not more rain." Harry exhaled. "I tell you, it's either floods or drought these days."

*"You're exactly right. Let's go back to the truck,"* Pewter strongly suggested.

"H-m-m." Harry walked around the tree, searched the ground, then checked the tree bark. Her curiosity was getting the better of her, a condition her pets feared.

After ten minutes she returned to the truck, Pewter racing ahead of everyone. The skies grew dark gray rapidly. Harry opened the driver's door a crack, reached behind the seat, pulling out a towel. She wiped off each animal's paws before allowing them in the truck. Then she climbed in herself, opened the window about two inches, and sat. A fine mist slowly enveloped the old folks' building.

The front door opened. Sean O'Bannon, his hand under his mother's elbow, guided her to her car. The mist thickened, heavy with moisture.

"I forgot about that," Harry said to herself as she observed Sean slide behind the wheel of his mother's car, turn on the motor, and drive out.

*"What?"* Mrs. Murphy nudged her.

"Sean's grandmother lives here now. She's too old to properly take care of herself."

*"She understood you?"* Pewter's jaw dropped.

*"Coincidence."* Murphy laughed.

Harry thought out loud. "Seems Wesley was murdered at night, during the storm — of course, it's been one storm after another. Even without the cover of rain it would be pretty easy to get back in there without anyone noticing. But why back there? There's nothing there and even if there had been fresh tire tracks they'd been washed away by the time the body was found. Maybe going behind the home wasn't in the plan." The first raindrop struck the windshield, a circle of tinier droplets spraying upward after the contact. "Maybe this was an easy place to meet or maybe it was an easy place to jump the train as it slows for the curve to go through town. Plus easy to find if one doesn't know Crozet. Big parking lot. In the rain you could sit here with your lights off and who would notice, driving by? The question is, how long was Wesley alive after he was released from jail? I found the Mercedes star three miles from here. What was he doing out in the woods? There's nothing there."

*"Nothing that you know about,"* Murphy corrected her.

The rain arrived full force. Harry rolled up her window. The temperature dropped with the arrival of the rain, skidding into the low sixties so fast that the animals huddled together.

Harry reached behind her seat and pulled up an old sweatshirt, slipping it over her head.

"It's so raw."

*"Let's go home where it's warm,"* Pewter pleaded.

Finally, Harry turned on the motor, reached over, flipping the heat on — low — as well as the windshield wipers. She cruised by Miranda's. Tracy's car sat in the driveway. Although he now lived within walking distance, he must have decided it was going to rain.

She turned out toward O'Bannon's. The rain fell harder. She could barely see the wrecker's ball. She drove east for a few miles, then turned back for home.

The second she opened the passenger door, the animals flew from the truck to the house. She, too, dashed through the downpour.

No messages on her answering machine disappointed her.

Thanks to the constant rains she'd reorganized every closet, her library, the linens and towels, even the socks. The only indoor chore left to do would be to repaint the living room. She didn't feel up to that.

Restless, she rambled from room to room, then finally grabbed a county map from her map section in the library. She opened it on the coffee table, placing paperweights on each corner, shooing off Murphy and Pewter, who felt compelled to sit on paper, any paper.

She used a number four pencil, a light line, to trace the distance from the jail to the place at Marcus Durant's where she'd found Wesley's Mercedes star. Then she drew a line from there to the old folks' home. From the jail to Durant's would be a long distance to walk, close to twelve miles if you knew how to cut over meadows and pastures. Following Route 250 West to Route 240 West would increase the distance from the jail to Durant's by another two miles.

"Someone picked him up."

Murphy, back on the coffee table, but not on the map, peered down. *"Draw a line to Booty Mawyer's farm. Draw a line from the place where you found the star at Durant's to Mawyer's. Just for the heck of it."*

Pewter hopped up next to Murphy. *"Why not from the old folks' home to Booty's?"*

*"Could but I don't think that's the way it played out."*

Tucker, on her hind legs, studied the map also.

"I have an audience here." Harry smiled, then jumped when a loud clap of thunder exploded right over the house. "Big one." She sheepishly grinned. "Okay, what else? Murphy, get your paw off the map."

Murphy pointed from the river spot to Booty's. She did this three times before Harry caught on.

*"Do you think their minds just aren't wired right?"* Pewter wondered. *"They'd forget their head if it weren't attached to their neck."*

*"No, the problem is their heads are filled with junk. Whatever they see on TV or hear on the radio or hear at the corner store. Empty*

*stuff, eats up brain cells."*

Tucker loved Harry so she felt she should defend her. *"But Mother's better than most."*

"H-m-m. Booty's backs up on Durant's. He could have hidden in the shack. It wouldn't be that far to park the truck and walk to the shack."

*"Or to Donny Clatterbuck's!"* Pewter raised her voice.

Harry, believing the cat was afraid of the storm, petted her. "Wesley wasn't seen driving the truck by the time Coop was looking for it. Unless he drove the old farm roads, but for what?" She bent low over the map. "Railroad's not far." She sat up. "Doesn't compute." Then she stood to get the county map of Culpeper off the shelf. She unfolded it as the animals watched. "White Shop Road."

*"Right off Route 29. Easy to find,"* Pewter noted.

*"Easier driving from the south to the north than vice versa unless you know the road. See, it's at a sharp angle,"* Murphy pointed out. *"But once you know where it is, it's easy."*

"Back way to Bull Run Kennels," Harry said.

*"Hey, someone's coming down the drive. Intruder! Intruder!"* Tucker raced to the back

328

door, the fur on the back of her neck standing up.

A door slammed, feet could be heard running for the back door. The screened porch door opened with a creak and then a knock reverberated with the thunder at the back door.

*"It's Lottie Pearson,"* Tucker barked.

## 36

Harry hopped up, surprised to see who stood at her back door. "Lottie, come in."

Lottie stepped through, removed her coat, hanging it on a peg. "I'm sorry to barge in."

"It's a pleasure to see you," Harry replied, just as her mother had taught her. "How about a hot cup of coffee or tea? I have cider and hot chocolate, too. It's easy to take a chill in this kind of weather."

"Actually, I'd love a hot chocolate." She moved toward the kitchen table, remembered her cigarettes, and returned to retrieve them and a matchbook from her coat pocket, which she slid under the cellophane of the cigarette pack. "This is the coldest, wettest spring."

"Sit down. I'll have this ready in no time." Harry pointed to the kitchen chair. "We could go in the living room."

"The kitchen is fine. Everything important happens in there anyway." She dropped in a chair, Tucker sitting next to her, on guard.

*"Let's plop by our food bowls. We won't look as nosy there,"* Mrs. Murphy whispered to Pewter.

*"Good idea."* Pewter crouched, gathered steam, then soared up on the counter. Sitting by the food bowl was her natural position.

Lottie exhaled through her nostrils. "Do you get the Weather Channel?"

"Yes."

"Every blip is treated as though it's the beginning of some millennial trend. First there's a warming trend. Then it's El Niño followed by La Niña. Seventeen-year cycles more or less. How can anyone predict a trend? We haven't kept accurate records long enough."

"I wonder about that, too."

The milk warmed in the saucepan. Harry poured some cold milk for the kitties and gave Tucker a treat. When the temperature in the milk reached perfection, just before boiling, she poured the milk over the powdered cocoa, stirred it, grabbed a can of whipped cream out of the refrigerator, and spritzed a mound on top. Then she lifted an orange out of the fruit basket and skimmed a thin strip of orange peel. She placed that on top of the whipped cream, setting the concoction before Lottie.

"How pretty it looks."

"Give it a minute, still hot." Harry, with her extra-large mug of chocolate, sat down opposite her.

"I like the glaze on your mugs. They're almost big enough to be soup bowls."

"Bought them in the kitchen shop in Middleburg."

"Such a beautiful town. I wonder for how long." Lottie dipped her spoon into the whipped cream. "M-m-m." She grew serious again. "Washington encroaches. The big cities will swallow the entire East Coast in our lifetime."

"God, I hope not."

"West Coast, too." Lottie pressed on with her pessimistic conviction. "Everyone goes to the city then leaves the city and for whatever reason they all want to live in the beautiful countryside, which they immediately desecrate. If we were smart we'd restore passenger train service. Spur lines. Would cut the pollution by half if not more. Trains pollute eight times less than airplanes and four times less than cars. And you can read the paper while you commute. I can't read the paper while I drive. In fact, I can't do anything when I drive except drive. I'm so worried about someone slamming into me or jumping the meridian. You can't trust anyone these days."

"I suppose." Harry wondered how long it would take Lottie to reach the point of her impromptu visit.

Lottie fiddled with her cigarette pack, which she'd dropped into her lap. She couldn't light up until after the hot chocolate, much as she wanted to — wouldn't be proper to smoke and eat simultaneously.

*"We've heard about the weather and urban sprawl."* Pewter licked the milk off her lips. *"What's next?"*

As if in response to the gray cat, Lottie propped her right elbow on the table. It wasn't perfect etiquette but under the circumstances she thought Harry wouldn't mind. One can be too proper. "You know, Harry, that my position at the university requires a lot of socializing. I enjoy it. I enjoy meeting people and cultivating relationships. And," she quickly tacked on, "not all those relationships will result in major gifts to the university. Big Mim will never write us a check. Her money goes to her alma mater and I appreciate that. After all, when she was young the university was males only. Her son attended Cornell. So as I said not all of my socializing revolves around donations."

"That's nice to know." Harry drank half of her hot chocolate. She hadn't realized she was thirsty.

"I'm a people person." Lottie smiled.

"You'd have to be to be good at your job." Harry smiled back at her, wondering if she should heat more milk.

"I meet all kinds of people and I have to get along with all kinds of people. But mostly what I do is woo the wealthy. They are more alike than different." She drained her cup.

"I'm going to have some more."

"Oh, I couldn't."

"I bet you could and forgive me for not putting cookies on the table. I don't know where my mind is these days." She opened the cupboard, put some cookies on a plate, then heated more milk.

The rain drummed steadily outside; the night was blacker than black.

"Thank you. What I find is that most, now I said most, not all, people with money react to visual cues. They're quick to size other people up, if you know what I mean. What kind of earrings does she wear? What kind of watch does he have on and what does she or he drive? The cut of one's clothes. The cues are very, very important. The way in which one speaks. One's manners at the table. I swear that's why Southerners are so successful at fund-raising. We know how to act if nothing else."

"Good manners beaten into our skins." Harry laughed as she had heard a constant stream of corrections from her mother, aunts, adults as a child.

"That's one way to put it." Lottie turned in her seat toward the stove as the milk simmered. "You'd be amazed to know how much I spend on clothing alone. And I'm not really a clotheshorse but I have to look good."

"You're one of the best-groomed women I know. You, the two Mims, and BoomBoom, always."

"Boom's too flashy." Lottie waved her hand, dismissing even the thought of BoomBoom Craycroft. "It takes time, imagination, and money on my budget. After all, I wasn't born with a silver spoon in my mouth."

"I often wonder what life would be like if I had been," Harry mused as she finished making another delicious cup of hot chocolate. This time she shook a little powdered nutmeg on top, placing the orange rind on top of that. She'd forgotten the nutmeg the first time around.

"We'd both be in a better place." Lottie

turned back toward the table as Harry sat down. "It's grinding. I love what I do but it's exhausting to pay bills, keep up appearances, pay taxes. There's so little left for me."

"Yes, I know the feeling but we have our health, we live in one of the most beautiful places in the world."

"That's true." Lottie breathed in, lifted her heavy cup, then put it down. Still too hot. She spooned up some whipped cream. "Apart from your company, I dropped by to pose two questions to you. The first is, did you put Cynthia Cooper up to questioning me?"

"No," Harry abruptly said. "I didn't know she had questioned you."

"You two are close. You're a, what shall I say, amateur sleuth. She came to my office and that really upset me. She could have picked another place."

"I suppose she could have but if she was really worried or suspicious she probably would have met you somewhere else or simply hauled you in. If she came to your office it means she needed your help. I'd think that your superiors would know that."

"Maybe. It made me quite nervous."

"Lottie, two men have been murdered. I should think that would take precedence over any of us feeling nervous or put out."

*"Yeah, and Lottie may have poisoned one of them,"* Pewter catcalled.

*"Hush, Pewter. Don't call attention to us. Besides, the humans think Roger died a natural death and our smelling what we think is poison in the cracks of Aunt Tally's floor doesn't constitute proof. For all we know it could have been ant poison."*

*"It wasn't,"* Tucker rumbled.

*"Be that as it may, let's be quiet."* Mrs. Murphy half closed her eyes, pretending to sleep.

Pewter followed suit so Tucker walked a bit away from Lottie's chair and flopped down with her head on her paws. She never took her eyes off Lottie, though.

"It is gruesome. I know." She sighed. "I never even saw that hanged man. He didn't park my car. And as for Donald, well, it's too bizarre, just too bizarre."

"Okay, I answered your first question."

"Thank you. I feel better. I was terribly upset when Coop came in uniform and everything."

"Lottie, I assume you explained her presence to the people around you. You're making too much out of it."

"You work in the post office. It's different for you. I'm judged by a different standard and I'm telling you, people are not fair, not for an instant. Furthermore, women are judged more harshly than men."

"Oh, Lottie, I don't believe that."

"I do. We're held to a higher moral standard."

Harry considered this. "Do the Ten Commandments come with gender specifications?"

"No." Lottie frowned.

"Then it's the same for everyone, male or female. If people want to use gender as an excuse for their behavior, have at it. The rules are the same for everyone."

"Harry, you've been around Miranda Hogendobber too long. The real world doesn't work like that. The real world is still controlled by rich white men and it is in their self-interest to have their cake and eat it, too. So when Bill Clinton slept with every tart that came his way there was finger-wagging and fussing but finally people just figured that's what men do."

"Lottie, as I recall he nearly got impeached."

"I still maintain the standards are different. If I sleep around it's one thing. If Fair sleeps around, it's another."

"Lost him his wife," Harry coolly replied, then laughed.

"Uh — I'm sorry. Bad example." She blushed.

Harry leaned forward. "Lottie, what's the second question?"

"Oh, yes." She fiddled. "Do you mind if I smoke?"

"No."

She lifted her pack of king-sized filtered Salems from her lap, slid the matchbook out of the cellophane, tapped out a cigarette, and lit up, placing the pack and matches on the table.

Harry rose to fetch an ashtray, placing it to the right of her cup. "That's pretty." She picked up the matchbook. "Like a little work of art. Roy and Nadine's." She paused. "Roy and Nadine's." The matchbook Cooper had mentioned. "Lottie, where did you get this?"

"That? Oh, I don't know."

Harry turned it around. "Been to Lexington, Kentucky?"

"No. Let me think. I was at Aunt Tally's, needed a light. Uh — Roger. He wanted to light my cigarette; his hand was so shaky I had to hold his wrist. He gave me the matchbook." She paused. "Poor Roger. He was a pest but I didn't wish him dead."

"Lottie, this may be important. I'm going to call Coop."

"The matchbook?"

"Yes." Harry jumped up, lifted the receiver off the wall phone, and dialed Coop's home number. Luckily she was there. "Coop, hi."

"What's cooking? Or not cooking?"

"I'm sitting here in my kitchen with Lottie Pearson. She just lit up her cigarette with a Roy and Nadine's matchbook."

"Put her on."

Harry walked over to Lottie; the phone cord was long. "Here."

As Lottie repeated her story to Coop, Harry sipped her hot chocolate. Slender though the clue was, at least it was something. The other pack found in the Cowboys windbreaker could have belonged to either Wesley or Don, since the exact ownership of the windbreaker was undetermined. Identical matchbooks from Lexington, Kentucky, wouldn't just be floating around Crozet, Virginia. The connection could be something as simple and unsavory as Wesley selling Roger stolen hubcaps. She found the fact that Roger and Wesley must have known one another deeply disquieting. But what if the matchbook had been Don's? What else did they know? And what did Sean know?

Lottie's voice pierced her thoughts. "She wants you back."

Harry reached for the phone. "Well?"

"Interesting. Thanks for getting to me so fast. I'll drop by sometime when I get a minute."

"Okay." She stood to hang up the receiver, then closed the cupboard door that Pewter had opened when the humans were occupied. "Pewter, you're not getting that catnip until I say so." Harry closed the door.

*"Meanie."*

"She's going into a sulk."

"Cats are funny that way." Lottie sighed. "Everything is so strange right now. I'll drop this matchbook off at the sheriff's office on my way home. Odd." She pushed the matchbook around with her forefinger.

"Lottie, the second question."

"Oh, yes. I need a presentable date for the huge alumni dinner in two weeks. Someone very impressive, and I was wondering if you would mind terribly if I asked Diego. He'd be perfect at something like that."

"Yes, he would. I have no claim on him. If he wants to go that's his choice, not mine."

"Yes, but you like him. I don't want to step on toes."

"You're not stepping on my toes. It was good of you to ask me but it seems to me if a man and a woman aren't married they come and go as they please. Right?"

341

"It's not that simple. You see things in black and white."

"No, but I do think things are simpler than we make them."

"But you like him. You're attracted to him."

"I'll bet you just about every woman who sees that man is attracted to him." Harry smiled. "He's to die for, as they used to say."

Lottie puckered her lips, inhaled deeply, and exhaled. "There's been enough dying around here."

# 37

"I asked around if anyone had a recent photograph of Don," Cooper said.

"Any luck?" Rick checked his watch. He was due at a county commissioners' meeting in a half hour.

"BoomBoom had one from the parade. Here." She handed him the Polaroid of Don, his face half turned to the camera, and Roger O'Bannon, standing by the float. No hoopskirted belles were in sight, fleeing the float the second the parade stopped.

"Better than nothing. Mug shots of Wesley?"

"Got those. I faxed them off about an hour ago to the dealer in Newport News and the manager of Roy and Nadine's. That car dealership is huge, by the way, two hundred and five employees. That's a lot of payroll."

"Sure is." Rick shrugged. "My idea of hell is a committee meeting." He checked his watch again. "I wonder if you have to take an IQ test before being elected a county commissioner. You know, you can't run for office unless it's below one hundred." He checked his watch one more time.

"What is it this time?"

"The bypass. Same old, same old. I deliver the accident statistics on the highways, the locations, the times of the accidents, and the volume of traffic. They have the Department of Transportation statistics on volume but they want to hear what I have to say, and what I really have to say but I won't is that sooner or later the damned bypass will go through. If we work together I think we can limit the damage." He ran his palm over the side of his head above his ear. "Truth is it will make an ungodly mess wherever the state puts it."

"And we need it."

"Hell, yes, we need it. Traffic grows, people's tempers shorten, and we'll be in gridlock before you know it. The commissioners don't want to face facts. The bypass is a necessity."

He opened the long middle drawer of his desk, then pushed it shut after retrieving a rubber band, which he slipped on his wrist.

Cooper, recognizing his jog to his memory, the rubber band on his wrist, asked, "You could write yourself a note."

"Yeah, stick it in my chest pocket and

forget it. This way I don't forget." He snapped the band against his wrist.

"What do you need to remember?"

"Milk. The missus asked me to bring home a quart of two-percent milk. Well, I'd better push off. I'll see you in the morning."

"I've been thinking about the money in Don's safe. Would a merchant be able to get new money like that? A department store, a business like Wal-Mart, something with high volume?"

"I don't know. What would the purpose be? Money is money. Customers at Wal-Mart don't care if they get change in brand-new bills. We know the banks get new money supplies, the old money gets burned. I don't think I could stand to see that." He stood up, clapped his hat on his head. "Daniel into the lions' den."

"Boss, I'll say my prayers."

"You do that." He clapped her on the back, snapped the rubber band on his wrist, and left.

Paperwork had been accumulating on Coop's desk at a geometric ratio. She straightened up the piles, sighed, then gave in, sat down, and started sorting into three piles. The first one hit the trash can, the envelopes and letters making a little pinging sound in the metal wastebasket. The second pile was more urgent and the third pile was less urgent. She hoped that time would solve some of the questions and problems presented by the third pile. Her rule of thumb was if she waited three weeks, often she didn't need to answer. It wasn't the most scientific system in the world but it worked.

She e-mailed replies to the most urgent pile. For those individuals and organizations lacking an e-mail address she wrote out letters on the computer, then printed them.

In the background she heard the metallic grunting of the fax machine.

"For you," Yancy said as best he could, since his jaw was still wired shut.

She rose and grabbed the fax from the dealer in Newport News. No one at the dealership recognized Wesley Partlow. "Rats." She slipped the fax into her file box under her desk.

"No luck," Yancy commiserated through clenched teeth. He'd gotten pretty good at talking despite his handicap.

"Hell, no. Say, Yance, when do you get the wires out?"

"Next week."

"Bet you'll be glad."

"Yep."

"Does it ruin your sex life?" she teased

346

him.

"Nope."

She started to say something silly when Sheila at the front desk buzzed her. "Din Marks is here for you."

"Be right out. Yancy, your attacker is here. Maybe you'd better stay put."

"I'll get 'im in court."

"Right, buddy." She walked out front where a nervous Din Marks waited on a long wooden bench. An older man sat next to him.

"Mr. Marks."

Both men stood up so Cooper surmised the older man was Din's father.

"Officer Cooper, uh, Dad said I had to come down here."

"Pleased to meet you, Mr. Marks." She shook the older man's hand, rough with calluses. "Why don't we go in this room here? It's more private. Can I get you all a drink?"

"No, no, we're fine," the older Marks, rail thin, replied.

Once seated in the small room, Din squirmed in his seat. "I remember something."

"Let's hear it."

"Dad said I had to come on down."

"That's right, son." Mr. Marks was hoping his boy would make a good enough impression that perhaps the trial against him would not be so heavy to bear. Maybe Cooper would help Din.

"I remembered something that Wesley said. He said he was owed some money. Big money. He meant to collect it. Stealing hubcaps." Din shrugged. "Said it wasn't how he made real money. He said stealing was like, uh, pitching. You had to keep limbered up."

"Did he say who owed him?"

"No, ma'am."

"Did he say how much?"

"Fifty thousand dollars. Said he could make as much as he wanted. I didn't believe him but I was, well, you know."

"Did he say how he'd make more money?"

"No, ma'am, but I figured it wasn't in the stock market."

"Did he ever say what kind of work he did? Regular work? Like road work in the summer or roofing? Anything?"

"No."

"Well, you were right to come down here. Thank you, Din. Thank you, Mr. Marks."

As they stood up to leave, Mr. Marks, his eyes moist, said, "Will this help my boy?"

"Mr. Marks, the fact that he is cooperating with the sheriff's department can't hurt him. What can help him is if he goes to

AA meetings. If he repents in front of the judge and produces evidence that he is mending his ways, going to AA, I think, will make a favorable impression on the judge. Hear?"

Mr. Marks nodded vigorously. "Yes, ma'am, I hear." With that he put his hand in the small of Din's back, directing him toward the door.

They were no sooner out the door than Yancy, bright-eyed, strode into the front room. "Coop, Coop, will you look at this?"

She grabbed the fax he handed her. "Jesus, Mary, and Joseph. This changes things."

The fax from the manager of Roy and Nadine's read:

*Dear Deputy Cooper,*

*I do not recognize Donald Clatterbuck nor does anyone on my staff. However, we recognize the man with him. He comes in about once a month, usually in the company of a local businessman, Bill Boojum.*

*Let me know if I can be of further service to you.*

*Yours truly,*
*Tara Fitzgibbon*

## 38

"Are you sure we should do this?" Harry asked Susan.

"Someone has to" was the terse reply.

"Why not BoomBoom? She uses the salvage yard. I mean she has to get sheet-metal scraps."

Susan considered this. "Maybe all three of us should go to Sean."

"I don't want to go." Harry stubbornly dug her heels in.

*"Mother hates anything that might become emotional."* Mrs. Murphy sighed. *"I don't know why. Humans have highly developed emotions to keep them alive."*

*"When they lived in caves."* Pewter shook herself, then sat down for serious grooming.

*"What are you talking about?"* Mrs. Murphy edged toward the door. If the humans were going to the O'Bannons', she was going with them.

*"All that adrenaline worked when they lived in caves but I can't see how it does them*

*a damn bit of good now. Just gets them in trouble."*

*"I'm not talking about violence, I'm talking about the whole range of emotion."*

*"Piffle,"* the cat sniffed.

*"I don't think my emotions are any less developed than a human's,"* Tucker stoutly said.

*"Did I say they were?"* Murphy was irritated that her two cohorts missed her point and she thought they were being deliberately obtuse. *"What I'm saying is their emotions keep them alive. I am not saying those emotions are in the service of reality at this time in their evolution."*

*"They haven't evolved. That's the problem,"* Pewter sharply said. *"They're walking around in clothing but they're still the same animals who lived in caves, feared the dark, and smashed one another over the head for beans. Trust me."*

*"You have no faith."* The dog thought humans were better than that, some of them, anyway.

*"Faith, why should I have faith in human beings? You've got one man hung, one man shot, and we believe Roger was poisoned. That does not bespeak evolution."* Pewter stated her case succinctly.

*"I can believe Lottie Pearson would poison*

351

*Roger. Poison is a woman's weapon. But I can't believe she'd hoist Wesley Partlow over a tree. She wouldn't have the strength. I doubt Lottie could heave a hay bale. Now, Mom could do it."* Tucker quickly added, *"Never would, of course. Harry wouldn't kill anyone unless in self-defense."*

*"Hey, cut the gab. I'm not missing this."* Mrs. Murphy charged out the front door of the post office when Harry opened it.

"Girls, take your time." Miranda waved to Harry and Susan.

"You could go." Harry tried to wriggle out of this task one more time.

"I'm minding the store. And Susan asked you. After all, you all are closer in age." Miranda wasn't afraid of emotional outbursts. She truly believed Harry was a more suitable emissary.

Defeated, Harry opened the door to Susan's Audi station wagon. The three animals hopped in the back where the seat was down, making it pleasant for them. Susan had called BoomBoom so by the time they pulled into the salvage yard, BoomBoom was also there.

Three small pieces of sheet metal rested in the bed of BoomBoom's brand-new Chevy Silverado truck. Boom, contrary to her appearance, was a motorhead. She loved machines almost as much as Harry did. Driving her BMW provided her with true delight. She felt the same way about her half-ton truck, too, although the road feel was different. She liked sitting high up, she liked the huge V-8 Vortec engine, she liked the stereo system.

"Does he know we're coming?" BoomBoom asked.

"I called ahead. He's working. I called Ida first" — Susan mentioned Sean's mother — "she said he'd be at the yard. Work helps him."

"So many memories of Roger." Harry thought it must be painful, for she knew how it felt after her parents died and she took over the farm. Before that she'd lived in a small apartment in town.

"Well?" Susan raised her eyebrows.

The three trudged together to the main building.

*"I'm going to strangle Pope Rat."* Tucker scampered off to the garage.

*"She's a quart low."* Pewter indicated the dog. *"Why tangle with a rat? I'm going inside with the humans."*

*"I'm going to sit here and think."* Mrs. Murphy padded over to the marble section.

When the three women opened the door, Sean glanced up. "Hi."

"Hi," they said.

"Can I help you?"

BoomBoom spoke first. "We don't want to intrude but we want you to know that if you want to move the Wrecker's Ball from here, we've found a place to have it. The salvage yard in Louisa County agreed to do it and we'll do the work, send out a mailing."

He smiled. "Thanks. That's good of you and good of Jonathan." He mentioned the owner of the salvage yard in Louisa County. "But I'll have it here. Roger loved that party. I thought I'd have it in his honor and accept donations to establish a scholarship in his name at Virginia Tech."

"That's a wonderful idea." Susan meant it, too.

"Do you need extra hands?" Harry asked.

"No, thanks. My crew can handle it. We've got ten days. We're okay."

As the three women left the building, Harry saw Tucker streaking from the garage to the caboose on the siding. The corgi raced around the caboose because the first step was so high she couldn't climb up.

*"Pope Rat,"* Murphy told Harry.

*"Vermin!"* Tucker shouted.

*"Nipshit!"* the rat taunted from inside the caboose.

"Susan, I'm going to have to pick her up.

She won't come voluntarily." Harry ran over to grab her dog before the barking offended Sean and the customers. "Tucker, come on."

The dog's soft brown eyes pleaded, *"I can get him."*

"Come on." Harry, curiosity aroused, stepped on the platform. The door was locked and the shades drawn. "Make a neat restaurant or even a place to live."

Pope Rat put his eye to the opening he'd chewed in the door. *"Another nipshit."*

Harry scooped up Tucker, returning to the station wagon, where Susan and BoomBoom were talking. "Wouldn't you love to have that caboose? They've got wood-burning stoves in them and I don't know, I'd sure like to have one. Wonder why he locks it up."

"Going to clean it up, paint it, and use it as a coffeehouse, I think. At least that's what the plan was before Roger — anyway, I guess it's locked so people don't troop through and damage it." BoomBoom thought it would be a good place to gather. "And liability. I'm sure he needs to get everything perfect. What if someone fell off the steps before they're finished? Stuff like that."

"Yeah, I'm expecting someone to sue the

post office if they get a paper cut opening their mail." Harry grimaced. "Hey, here comes Coop."

As she pulled the squad car next to the Audi, Tucker squirmed out of Harry's arms, tearing back to the caboose.

"Damn you, Tucker." Harry ran after her, grabbing her again as the dog challenged the rat.

*"You're supposed to herd cows, not rats,"* Murphy dryly laughed.

*"He called me a nipshit. Called Mom one, too."* Tucker heaved, indignant.

*"He's like the blue jay. Born trouble."* Pewter harbored a plan to dispatch her tormentor. She wasn't telling anyone.

"So?" Everyone expectantly looked at the lean, long deputy.

"Can't tell you. Not until I speak to Sean." She picked her hat up off the passenger seat, then decided not to wear it.

Harry opened the driver's door for her. "I've been thinking."

"That's scary." Cooper laughed.

"Who knows that we opened Don's safe?"

"His mother and father. The sheriff. You. BoomBoom. I know his mother and father won't speak of it. At least, not for a while. It's too overwhelming. Who did you tell?"

"No one," BoomBoom truthfully replied.

"Harry told Miranda and Tracy but I was there. I guess in a way I told them, too."

"Susan. I told Susan," Harry stated.

"No one else?" Cynthia Cooper stretched her arms over her head. "Kinks."

"The older you get, the more getting out of bed in the morning becomes an athletic event." Susan shook her head in surprise at how rapidly the aches and pains mounted up and she was only in her late thirties, as were the others.

"What's your idea, Harry?" the officer inquired.

"Well, first let me ask you a couple of questions. Who had the combination to the lock? There wouldn't be a key to a lock like that, right?"

"Right. I thought when I first saw the safe that maybe there would be a key, you know, the big handles could be for show, but it really was a combination lock."

"A tough one," BoomBoom added.

"How do we know someone else didn't have the combination? The press doesn't know about the money. Rick withheld that information. Can it really be possible that all that money was Don's? And even if it was, whoever he was in business with had to know he wouldn't put a sum like that in the bank. That would be like waving a flag in front of a bull. So his partner or partners had to know Don's share would be in that safe. Which is exactly why Rick didn't tell the press even though they're hounding him for a development concerning the murder. He's hoping to flush them out," said Harry.

"Possible," Cooper drawled as Boom-Boom and Susan stared at Harry.

"I think I know what comes next." BoomBoom, no slouch, put her hands together.

"Put the lock back. Fill the safe with fake money. Maybe we can flush them out faster." Harry beamed.

"His partner will come back to take Don's share," Susan thought out loud. "Yeah, but how are you going to know when he comes back or if he comes back?"

"Can't we put a small surveillance camera in the shop, the kind they use in the bank? It can't be too expensive. I know Rick is worried about the budget." Harry warmed to the task. "No one needs to be there. You'll see who it is and nab him later."

"In the best of all possible worlds, yes, but what if he comes in with a mask? Or she? I shouldn't assume it's a man." BoomBoom rubbed her hands together. The talk of aches and pains made her joints hurt.

"Yeah, but any picture is better than no

picture and whoever this is knows no one is at Don's house. He won't even have to pretend to be a thief," Harry sensibly said.

Coop held up her hand. "Let me run this by the Boss. BoomBoom, can you weld the lock back?"

"If you all help me, I can. It's so heavy someone has to hold it in place. It's going to take a couple of hours to do it right. You don't want the seam to show, that's a big tip-off."

"How about Friday night? I have it off. Chinese." Coop meant bring Chinese food.

"I'll get the food." Susan thought this exciting. "We shouldn't park there."

"I've got to back up and drop off the oxygen. I need help with that, too. Harry, you're the strongest."

"Yeah, okay."

"We can park at the high school and walk over. There's so much activity there that our cars won't be noticeable," Susan said.

"Seven," Cooper said, then nodded toward the building. "I've got to get in there."

"Will you tell us later?" Harry couldn't stand not knowing something.

"Yes."

"Boy, it must be unsavory." BoomBoom,

sensitive, felt Cooper's reluctance, as did the others.

"Uh, yes."

Later that day, Cooper dropped by the post office to pick up her mail. She told Harry and Miranda that she had dropped off papers requesting to exhume Roger's body. Sean hit the roof. He called his lawyer and threatened to drag this case out as long as possible.

Cooper then visited Ida O'Bannon, again patiently explaining the new concern that Roger did not die a natural death. She knew this would be upsetting and she knew that Sean would call a lawyer but she hoped Ida could talk sense into him. This wasn't about violating Roger's corpse, it was about bringing his killer, if he was killed, to justice. He could then rest in peace.

Ida, tearful and shocked, said she would reason with her older son. Legally, this was her decision and she agreed to it.

"Coop, what — ?"

She leaned toward Harry, Miranda leaning in, too. "I sent photographs of Wesley and Donny to Roy and Nadine's."

Harry explained to Mrs. Hogendobber about the matchbook.

"And they recognized Don?" Miranda just couldn't believe this.

"No. The manager of the restaurant didn't recognize him but she did recognize Roger. She said he came in about once a month with a businessman named Bill Boojum."

"Who's Bill Boojum?" Harry asked the logical next question.

"He was easy to find. He's one of the biggest car dealers in Kentucky. He specializes in high-end car rentals and does a booming business with Thoroughbred trainers, jockeys, people who make money erratically. Sometimes it's a big paycheck, sometimes not. They find it easier to rent cars than to buy them."

"What did he say?"

"He seemed helpful enough. He said he knew Roger from college. They'd both gone to Virginia Tech. I checked that out with the alumni office. He told the truth. He said Roger was interested in getting into the racing game and he was putting him in touch with NASCAR people. He said Roger had already bought into a syndicate, a forty-thousand-dollar share."

"Forty thousand dollars — Roger?" Harry nearly fell over.

"I checked out the syndicate, too. Based in Lexington, Kentucky. Roger was, in fact, a member. They didn't know he had died.

The share passes to his mother. The lady on the phone, Mrs. Higgins, pulled it up on the computer and read it right off to me. I asked Boojum why Roger came out so often and he said he just loved Lexington. I can believe that. Who wouldn't? And he said he was besotted with racing."

"Loved cars." Harry rubbed her chin.

"It truly was his passion." Miranda found this troubling, the forty thousand dollars especially.

"An expensive passion, I reckon." Harry spoke a little too loudly, which made the animals jump. "What did Sean know?"

"He says he didn't know a thing about it. I had the presence of mind to ask him about the syndicate before requesting exhumation. He said Roger did drive to Lexington about once a month and he'd stay two or three days. Roger's reason was he wasn't having any luck with Virginia girls so he thought he'd try Kentucky girls."

"Does Sean know Bill Boojum?" Harry asked.

"Yes, but not well. He said he met him once or twice when Roger was in college. Sean, being older, ran with a different set of friends, plus he went to the University of Virginia."

"A sore point between them." Miranda

drummed her fingers on the countertop. "Roger in a car-racing syndicate."

"We'd better get that lock back on soon. All this talk of money takes me right back to Don Clatterbuck," Harry said, then told Miranda what they'd be doing that Friday night. "Oh, hell, I'm supposed to go to the movies with Fair. Coop, may I ask him to help us? He's stronger than the two of us put together and he'll never tell."

"Okay." Coop jiggled the handcuffs hanging from her belt.

"When do they dig up Roger?"

"Monday."

*"Wish I could be there."* Tucker wagged her nonexistent tail.

*"Tucker, that is so disgusting."* Pewter wrinkled her nose, gray like the rest of her.

## 39

Slowly the earth drank the rainwater. The ground remained muddy, the creeks little by little subsided. The scent of new blossoms began to overpower the odor of creek water.

Mrs. Murphy hastened to the barn at dawn as the owl returned from hunting.

*"Did you get a chance to fly over O'Bannon's?"*

*"Yes. There are lights on in the garage but the curtains are drawn."*

*"Any cars or trucks parked outside?"*

*"No, which I thought was curious."*

*"I do, too."*

*"Of course, it could be someone left the light on during the day or it's been on throughout the storms,"* the owl thought out loud. *"Still, you'd think someone would go in there."*

*"What about the caboose?"*

*"Your rat friend, an industrious sort, scurried from the garage to the caboose frequently. He had a bag of potato chips. When*

*he heard me — I swooped low for effect — he didn't drop the chips and run. A rough sort."*

*"If I could pour water in his hole, I bet I could get him to talk. I'd stop up the exits, of course."* Mrs. Murphy envisioned this to her enjoyment. She heard Simon snoring in his nest. He looked ratlike yet was so different from Pope Rat; two creatures could hardly be more different in temperament.

*"That rat has places and loot all over the salvage yard."*

*"No sounds from the garage?"* Murphy hoped for more clues.

*"Yes. I sat by the window and I heard human feet. I know someone was in there."*

Later as Murphy walked back to the house she wondered if someone was working late because of the Wrecker's Ball. Then again, why not park out front? And why not work in the new building where the dance would be held? If it was on the up-and-up why hide your car? Maybe Sean was in the garage. Maybe he felt closer to Roger in the garage. So many thoughts jammed into her head she had difficulty sorting them out. One thing did help her focus. She certainly didn't want Harry snooping around the salvage yard.

## 40

Sean's assistant, Isabella Rojas, disdained Lottie but had to be nice to her. The customer is always right even though in this case Lottie wasn't a customer. Sean would fire her if she behaved rudely toward anyone. The truth was that Isabella, like many a woman before her, had fallen in love with her boss.

"He's out back, Miss Pearson." Isabella forced a smile. "Statuary."

"Thank you." Lottie, with a supercilious air, swished back outside and found Sean carefully positioning chains around a massive recumbent griffin. "Sean." She waved.

"Hi." He held up his hand to the operator in the small crane ready to pick up the heavy object to place it on a flatbed.

"Who has bought this beautiful piece?"

"H. Vane Tempest." He named a wealthy Englishman who owned a large estate west of town and whose symbol was a griffin.

"But of course." Her eyes swept from the griffin to the crane to the flatbed and the large diesel semi that pulled it. "You must have a small fortune tied up in equipment. I never really appreciated how much. I guess you get quite good at leveraging your debt."

"Hey, I'm a junkyard dealer. I have a nose for finding equipment at good prices. Take that crane there. New it would cost one hundred and thirty-nine thousand dollars. I picked it up for nineteen."

"Fabulous," she purred. "But how do you do it?"

"Contacts and" — he stared off into the distance for a moment — "Roger. He'd give the equipment the once-over, tell me how much it would cost to bring a piece up to speed, and then I could make an informed decision. And we always looked for reliable brands like Caterpillar. You pay more but you get more. You know, Roger really was a genius with anything that had a motor in it. He even kept that old wrecker's ball in perfect working order."

"I'm so sorry about Roger. I know I've said that before, but I don't know what else to say." She played with the ring on her pinkie finger, right hand. "When you worked as closely as you did with Roger it must be doubly disastrous."

"The Lord giveth and the Lord taketh away," Sean replied. "At first, I was so shocked I wanted to sell the business and walk away. Mom talked sense into me. Running away doesn't solve anything. Three generations of O'Bannons sweated into this ground. With any luck there will be a fourth and a fifth."

"I certainly hope so." She smiled. "You can imagine yourself an old man watching your grandson move statuary."

"By that time they'll beam it up. You know, rearrange the molecules and send it without a crane and a flatbed."

"Maybe." She shifted her weight to her left foot. "I heard through the grapevine that you're going through with the Wrecker's Ball and I wanted to help."

"Thank you, Lottie."

"I thought perhaps I could perform some of Roger's chores."

"That's just it. I don't know the half of what he did. He'd burrow down there in the garage and I was up here. He took care of the catering. I did the decorations but there were so many things that just happened. I'm afraid I never closely examined Roger's contributions to the business, or my life. I feel so — so guilty."

"Sean" — she placed her hand on his forearm — "nobody does. It's not you. None of us knows what someone gives to our life until they're gone."

"Uh — thanks." He kicked the gravel path, then looked at her. "You'll be coming to the ball?"

"Of course. Well, I didn't mean to stay so long. I just wanted you to know I was available to help."

# 41

On a hunch, Cooper had sent out the mug shot of the false Wesley Partlow to all state agencies. At four-ten in the afternoon, she was sitting at her desk writing a presentation. Next Wednesday she was to give a speech at Western Albemarle High School about law enforcement as a career. Much as she loved her job, she was tired and drawing a blank.

Part of the exhaustion came from always dealing with people who were themselves under great stress. She'd received a blast from Sean about the exhumation next Monday. He was honoring his mother's wishes but he thought the request was ghoulish and would prove inconclusive.

Once he let off steam she asked him if he knew about Roger's purchase of a share of a stock-car syndicate for forty thousand dollars, a big chunk of change for a hobby, and Sean said it wasn't any of his business how his brother spent his money. He regularly visited the track at Waynesboro and it made sense that Roger would want to get involved at the higher end of the sport if he'd saved some money. Dale Earnhardt and Richard Petty were his heroes.

"You can't take it with you" is exactly what Sean O'Bannon had said.

Then Coop had to meet Don Clatterbuck's mother at the bank to open his safety-deposit box. The title to his truck, his birth certificate, a few stocks and bonds were in the narrow metal box along with the combination to the safe.

Mrs. Clatterbuck swore she didn't know the combination and thought the safe was another one of Don's finds. Sooner or later he might sell it. He liked to trade. She didn't know where he acquired that trait. Neither she nor her husband were traders.

No love letters were sheltered in the safety-deposit box.

Coop thanked Mrs. Clatterbuck, wrote down the combination, and finally returned to the office.

At four-twenty she wandered over to the coffeepot. A jolt of caffeine might trigger speech ideas. All she could think of was, "How would you like to pick up drunks, deadbeat dads, and squashed accident victims? For variety you could question a drug dealer with his jaw shot off." She knew if she continued in that vein she'd descend into the truly morbid. She no sooner had the coffee to her lips than Sheila buzzed her phone.

Returning to her desk, Coop picked up. "Deputy Cynthia Cooper."

"Louis Seidlitz, the bartender from Danny's."

"Yes, Mr. Seidlitz."

"I remembered that little puke's name: Dwayne Fuqua. It was driving me crazy."

"When I dropped by you said he didn't come in often."

"No, he didn't. Like I said, maybe once a month. Dwayne was on a mission."

"Sir?"

"Girls."

"Lucky?"

"No more than most." Louis laughed.

"Mr. Seidlitz, do you have a fax in the office there?"

"Yeah."

"Don't hang up. Give me the number and I'll fax you a photograph. Tell me if you recognize anyone."

He gave her the number. She faxed the photo of Donald and Roger.

She could hear the fax machine in his office grinding out the photo.

"Deputy?"

"Yes."

"The guy with his hands in his pockets. He'd hang out now and then. With Dwayne."

"Mr. Seidlitz, thank you so much. You've been a great help to me."

"Sure. Any time."

She hung up the phone, silently berating herself for being discouraged when she had first stopped by the bar. She'd felt she'd been sloppy. Well, Louis came through. He had just identified Donald Clatterbuck.

# 42

". . . Cool. A beautiful fall day." Diego described the day in Montevideo, for the seasons were reversed south of the equator.

"Raining here. When the animals walk two by two I'll worry." Harry laughed.

*"Can you believe they're talking about the weather?"* Pewter wrinkled her nose.

*"And you don't?"* Tucker felt a craving for bacon and wished Harry would make a bacon, lettuce, and tomato sandwich.

"So much has happened since you left." Harry didn't want to spend a lot of Diego's money on a long phone call. She had no idea how much money he really had but she certainly didn't want to waste any of it. "Don Clatterbuck was shot and killed. You might not remember him."

"Vaguely. Virginia sounds like the Wild West. Are you safe?"

"Sure. I'm of no importance to anybody."

"You are to me. I hope to see you again — soon."

"Thank you." She smiled, her voice lifted. "What do you have to do tomorrow?"

"Thomas and I fly over to Buenos Aires, which isn't far. If you look on a map you can see how the cities sit." A clock chimed behind him.

"Where are you now?"

"At my family's apartment in the city."

"I heard the chimes."

"A grandfather clock brought over from France in 1846. Oh, my father can tell you stories, but I didn't call to speak of my father. I called to tell you I will see you the weekend of the party, the ball." He paused. "I know you have a date for the ball. I will give him a run for his money."

"Please do."

"What can I bring you from Buenos Aires?"

"A picture of the polo grounds, where the Argentine Open is played. And you. I'd like to see you." This was about as flirtatious as Harry could bring herself to be.

"Sí!"

They said their good-byes, then hung up. Harry hummed to herself, then checked the kitchen clock.

"I'd better get moving."

*"Take us."*

## 43

*"What a crackbrained idea,"* Pewter complained.

*"Unfortunately, humans don't consult us before they go off on a toot."* Mrs. Murphy agreed with her friend's assessment of the situation. *"Silly of them, I know."*

*"In theory it's a good idea."* Tucker stayed on the other side of the room, away from the welding torch. The odor, the sparks, the flame bothered her more this time.

*"If whoever is doing this stuff is dumb, it's a good idea."* Pewter sniffed. *"But I doubt they're that stupid. They'll see the camera. It's like a bank camera."*

*"We know it's up there in the corner but the thief doesn't know it's there and it might work. There's an outside chance."* Tucker remained dimly hopeful.

*"We'll see. Also, I'd amend thief to killer,"* Mrs. Murphy said.

The animals watched as BoomBoom patiently restored the huge lock to its place.

Fair held it up but even his strong arms wearied. Harry took a turn to spell him.

As Boom worked, Cooper told the group about Dwayne Fuqua. " . . . on the fringes."

"What about a high-school counselor? He must have made an impression on someone," Susan said.

Cooper shook her head. "Not much. Didn't get his diploma. The father abandoned him. The mother turned to drink and drugs. No one knows where she is or even if she's alive. He lived in a room in a small house past the old Ford dealership, I mean before they moved. Checked with his landlady. She said he was quiet. She didn't know much about him except he'd be gone for days at a time. Paid his rent on time."

"Did he have a criminal record?" Harry called out as she was holding the lock.

"No. That surprised me."

"Odd." Fair stepped in as BoomBoom turned down the flame. "My turn."

"Thanks." Harry was relieved. "And he knew Don. That's really — I don't know. It confuses me. Waynesboro's just over the mountain. There's plenty of ways people can meet one another. I guess criminal intent doesn't have to be party to it." She shrugged. "But with both of them dead — well, what could they have known?"

"Or done?" Coop rested her elbow on the carton of phony money.

"I still say it's drugs. People don't have cash like that unless they deal drugs," Fair said.

Boom, mask up for a quick breather, added, "Diamonds. Gems. There's a lot of cash in that business."

Susan lovingly looked at the fake money, wishing it was real and wishing it was hers. "Well, what about rubies or sapphires?"

"Susan, what are you talking about?" Fair raised his voice over the sound of the torch.

"Okay, you intend to get engaged. You aren't sure what stone your fiancée would like. The jeweler shows you loose stones. You pick one and the others go back. Retail jewelers don't keep a lot of loose gems. Not here, anyway. We're too small a market. So Don could have illegal rubies. I mean it wouldn't have to be diamonds, given what Harry said about the dirty diamonds. I'd forgotten about that, the press calls them dirty diamonds."

"Gold, silver, platinum. Maybe it was metal." Harry was curious.

"Yeah, but the next question is, Where would Don Clatterbuck or Dwayne get the gold, who would buy it from them, and why?" Cooper sighed, her head spinning.

Harry smiled at Cooper. "What you're telling us is you don't think this money is about stones or precious metals."

"Right."

"Drugs," Fair persisted.

"The kingpin used Wesley, I mean Dwayne, and Don as mules." Coop rose to take her turn holding the lock in place. "That's more likely."

"Don could hide drugs in the animals he stuffed," Susan said brightly.

*"What an awful idea."* Pewter made a face.

*"What? You don't want to be stuffed when you die?"* Murphy laughed uproariously.

*"I'll outlive you!"* Pewter flared, flashing her fangs.

*"Who knows? Anyway, it doesn't do you one bit of good to think about death. There's nothing you can do about when you die but there's sure a lot you can do about living."*

*"Murphy, Pewter, let's not talk about dying."* Tucker hated the thought of dying.

The torch cut off, BoomBoom flipped back her face guard. "Done!" She inspected the seam as she tried not to inhale, because the metallic fumes made her eyes water. "Not bad if I do say so myself."

The others crowded round as the fumes dissipated.

"Let me clean up the floor." Harry had

brought a dustpan and hand mop with her, anticipating this. "It wouldn't do for someone to open the safe only to hear tiny metal bits crunch underfoot."

Once the floor was cleaned Coop stacked the fake money in the safe. "Okay, let's shut it, lock it, and then unlock it to make sure his combination works."

"No." Boom put her hand on the door to keep it open. "Test the combination before you shut the door."

"Right." Coop let BoomBoom twirl the handles, then stop them. Then she carefully rotated the center dial according to the directions found in Don's safety-deposit box at the bank.

The clicking of the tumblers filled the room as everyone remained quiet.

"Works." Boom smiled. "Want me to shut the door now?"

"Sure." Coop nodded.

The door shut with a satisfying, heavy sound.

"What do you think about my idea of Don hiding drugs in deer heads?" Susan reminded them of her idea.

"God, I hope there's nothing in my woodpecker." Harry wanted to get that woodpecker back from the Culpeper sheriff's department.

*"My woodpecker,"* Pewter corrected her.

"Nothing has turned up in your wood-pecker." Coop allayed her fears. "But hiding drugs in stuffed animals would be a good way to transport them. Maybe you're on to something, Susan."

"Wonder how Don got into it?" Harry asked.

"Greed. That's how everyone gets into it," Fair said.

"Where would they get that quantity of illegal substances to begin with?" Boom-Boom checked her tools.

"If they were selling marijuana that's not hard. It's grown here in the state and no amount of surveillance by helicopters at harvest time locates all of it. And people can grow it in greenhouses, too. If they sold cocaine, heroin, those drugs, they'd need a source in a big city. If that's what they were doing." Coop picked up the empty carton.

"What about legal drugs? Why couldn't they sell Darvon and Valium and Quaaludes?" Harry thought they were as bad as the illegal drugs.

"Sure, but they'd have to have a contact. Either a corrupt physician or a company salesman. You can't just go out and get your hands on a jar of muscle relaxers." Fair, being a vet, had a keen appreciation of legal drugs, since he was pestered by salespeople at regular intervals.

"What about steroids?" Susan wondered.

"Same difference." Fair picked up the heavy oxygen tank. "Even someone good at chemistry can't cook that up in the kitchen. Like I said, you'd have to have a corrupt source or steal them from a patient."

"Are there drugs you can make at home?" Harry innocently asked.

"Amyl nitrite," Coop answered. "But it's a liquid, wouldn't be that easy to transport. It's the kind of drug that someone with skill could cook up in the kitchen but your customer would come to the kitchen to buy. Liquids are too much of a pain to transport great distances and the profit isn't that huge. The profit margin on illegal drugs or designer drugs from the big drug companies is huge. Don isn't going to have five hundred and twenty-five thousand dollars in his safe from amyl nitrite."

"What if they stole frozen semen from high-priced stallions in Kentucky? What if the business was that? Some of those stallions stand for over a hundred thousand dollars. I know how the semen is cooled and shipped. If Roger kept going to Lexington he could be bringing back stolen semen.

With DNA testing he'd have to have the real stuff. But he could do it. Maybe the car racing was a cover."

"He could. I never thought of that but I don't associate Roger with horses." Fair put the oxygen tank down. "I guess he could have done it. Are we ready?"

The others nodded; they checked and re-checked the place, then turned out the light and left. Fair gallantly carried the oxygen tank up to the truck just as he had carried it down.

*"Strong bugger,"* Pewter said admiringly.

*"You didn't live with us when Mom was married to him. He really was worth his weight."* Mrs. Murphy remained neutral about whether or not Harry should get back together with Fair but she certainly appreciated his hard work on the farm.

Fair pulled Harry aside after he loaded the tank on BoomBoom's fancy truck. "Have you heard from Diego?"

"He called late this afternoon from Montevideo. He'll be in town next weekend. He's escorting Lottie to an alumni fund-raiser."

"Oh." Fair smiled.

"She asked him."

"Oh." His face fell.

"And?"

*"She's making it hard for him."* Tucker loved Fair.

*"He's gotten better at expressing himself."* Mrs. Murphy was proud of Fair's progress and although she wasn't a big believer in therapy she thought it had helped him. He liked structure even for his emotions, and therapy gave him the illusion of that. She knew one could never structure one's emotions but Fair's sessions helped him gain insight into himself.

"I thought we were going to the Wrecker's Ball."

"We are. I haven't changed my mind. You asked me at New Year's. As I recall you said, 'Plan ahead.' "

"I did, didn't I?" He was tremendously relieved, then he tensed again. "Is Diego coming to the ball?"

"He is and I'll dance with him. I dance with all the fellows. I even dance fast ones with Susan if you all are pooped out."

# 44

At eight o'clock Monday morning Roger O'Bannon was exhumed from his grave. As he hadn't been in the ground that long, he retained all his features and his digits but the body was filled with gas.

Rick detested exhumations. They were unpleasant affairs but he felt he had to be at this one in case Sean showed up. Although Sean had promised his mother he would comply with her wishes, people could snap, change their minds. Emotions were like quicksilver even in the best of times. This, hardly the best of times, called for extra vigilance.

Rick accompanied the body to Marshall Wells. As he worked, the new coroner said he couldn't promise when Richmond would return the results but he didn't think it would be longer than a week at most. Fortunately, this was a slow time.

As he drove away from the coroner's office, Rick called Coop, alone in her squad car that day.

"Coop, meet me at O'Bannon's Salvage."

"Trouble with Sean?"

"No. But I want to go over those grounds again."

"Might it be a good idea to wait for another day? I would expect Sean's a little raw today."

"In a perfect world, you're correct and sensitive. But if he is in on this or if he did kill his brother, he might drop a card, you know?"

"Okay. I'll be there in ten minutes. I'm at Route 250 and 240, want a sandwich?" A good deli was at that intersection.

"Not hungry."

"Sorry. I forgot." She was glad she wasn't at the exhumation.

Sean was curt but not openly rude. He told them to go wherever they liked.

First they walked the perimeter of the four acres. Rick liked to make sure he knew the terrain. Nothing unusual presented itself except for the fact that the business had room to grow physically, always a plus.

The few small outbuildings contained gardening tools or small pieces needing cleaning. Some salvage yards left the cleaning to the customer. Sean discovered if he cleaned, put in a little time, he could command bigger prices. It was worth the effort.

Then they pushed open the door to the garage. The large sliding door, big enough for vehicles, was locked but the small door, to the left of that, was open.

"Neat as a pin," Coop said.

"Yeah." Rick walked over to the hydraulic lift. "This is something."

"Nothing much here. I guess he wasn't working on anything. The books showed the last old car he sold was a week before his death. A 1932 Ford coupe. He got twenty-seven thousand for it. Deuce coupes. I'd love one."

"Yeah." Rick wasn't a motorhead but he appreciated old cars. They were more individual or so it seemed to him. "Nothing out of line. He picked up most of his old cars in South Carolina and Georgia. The sources checked out. Guess he was waiting to find the next one or two. He seems to have contributed to this business. He wasn't the front guy but he worked. For one thing, Sean wouldn't have put up with it."

"Here's a bag of popcorn." Coop bent over to pick up the empty foil bag. "That's the only debris." She tossed it in the trash.

They left, walking through each of the large outdoor piles of offerings. They tried the door to the caboose. Locked. Coop dashed back. Sean gave her the key. She dodged the puddles back to Rick.

She opened the back door, then ran up the shades on the windows. The light streamed in. "Cool."

A potbellied stove sat in the middle. The floor, hard oak, was clean and no dust was on the two chairs and the heavy desk in the corner.

"Sean's a neat freak, too," Rick noticed.

"This would make a neat restaurant. I hope he goes through with it," Coop said.

They opened the drawers of the desk. Nothing but an old cracked celluloid fountain pen.

"Well, that's it," Rick said. "I wish I knew what we were looking for."

"I'd have been happy with one marijuana plant in the window." Cooper sighed. As she walked toward the door, she said, "I feel bad, we're tracking some mud in here. I'll tell Isabella we did. I'll even clean it up."

"Coop, it's not as though we've brought in slops. If Sean is that anal retentive, he can sweep it out." As Rick headed for the door he looked down at the wet footprints. A beam of light shone on dried footprints, light mud. "Hey." He knelt down. "This can't be more than a few days old."

Coop knelt down with him. "Yeah." She followed the tracks: one person, big feet.

Two strides and then back out, footsteps overlapping the entrance footsteps. "In and out."

"H-m-m."

"Boss, you worried?"

"Yes."

"Me, too."

Pope Rat, observing them from his cozy quarters, growled, *"Nipshits."*

# 45

Coop sent photographs of Dwayne Fuqua and Donald Clatterbuck to Bill Boojum in Lexington, Kentucky. Bill couldn't or wouldn't identify either man. He'd never seen them with Roger.

Refusing to give up, Coop sent photos back to the dealer in Newport News. She asked him to show all his employees photographs of Dwayne, Roger, and Donald. Although none of those men ever worked at the dealership, it would have been possible that one or more of them could have dropped off a vehicle or picked one up to be delivered to Boojum's in Lexington, since a leasing agent would purchase cars from big dealers all over the U.S.

Within two hours of faxing the photographs she received a phone call from Fisher McGuire, the general manager. One of his office workers remembered giving Dwayne the registration papers for him to drive a Jaguar to Boojum's. He even remembered that the car was a three-year rental.

Large rental dealers like Boojum's would get a request for a specific vehicle, in this case a new Jaguar sedan, British racing green, tan interior. The salespeople at Boojum's would call their contacts at various Jaguar dealers until they found one matching their client. They would then pay for the car, have it driven to the dealership, and rent it to the customer. If the residual value of the car is accurately figured, a dealer can't lose on car rentals because the customer eats the depreciation, not the dealer. The customer is responsible for maintenance and is allowed a certain number of miles per year, usually twelve to fifteen thousand. Any mileage over that is charged at ten to fifteen cents a mile. If the wear and tear on the vehicle is excessive, the customer is responsible for costs when the lease term expires. Once the car is turned back in at the term of the lease, usually three years, the dealer sells it at retail value. The customer has the right to purchase the car at retail value.

The program works nicely for those people not wishing to tie up a lot of money in a car. However, since they don't own the vehicle it is never counted as an asset but only as a liability. The tax write-offs and depreciated value present another labyrinth of issues that only an accountant can decipher. A renter needs a lawyer before signing a contract. The renter might be able to write off the monthly rental fee if the vehicle is used for business. However, as is often the case, what you save with one hand the IRS steals from the other.

Cooper nabbed Rick as soon as he walked through the door. He listened intently to her findings.

"Boojum can't identify Dwayne?"

"No, but it's possible he never saw who dropped off the car. Dwayne may not have been a regular."

"True." Rick dropped heavily into his chair. "Who paid for the delivery?"

"It was prepaid by Boojum's. They didn't specify a driver. Fisher McGuire, the general manager down there in Newport News, faxed all the paperwork, including the release form, to Dwayne Fuqua. McGuire was under the impression that Dwayne was a driver for Boojum's. Bill Boojum says no one at his dealership has ever seen Dwayne Fuqua or Wesley Partlow, pick your name."

"I can guarantee you someone had seen him!" Rick slammed his hand on his desk out of frustration. His coffee mug rattled.

"Yeah, someone is lying through their

dentures." She held her hand on his coffee cup in case he lost his temper again. "So what's the deal? Are they running drugs in these rented cars? Each time over the mountain a different car is used. Maybe even a different driver. Lexington and Louisville are good drug markets."

"Hell, they're so rich in Lexington they can fly the shit in," he growled.

"Well, not everybody is that rich, Boss."

"It makes sense and yet it doesn't make sense. If Boojum is in on this he —" Rick stopped in mid-sentence, grabbed his address book. "Just one minute." He found the number he was looking for and dialed. "Sheriff Paul Carter, please." He waited a moment. "Paul, Rick Shaw from Albemarle County, Virginia. Buddy, I need a favor."

"What?" the sheriff, an old friend from Washington County, asked.

"I'm going to fax you three photos. Will you take them to Boojum's in Lexington, avoid Bill Boojum, and see if anyone can identify any of these men?"

"The big dealership there? Very high-end."

"High seems to be the operative word," Rick said. "That's it. I'm conducting a criminal investigation here and I have strong reason to believe that Bill Boojum may be involved."

"How criminal?" Paul laughed.

"Two murders and when the lab reports come back from an exhumation, I may have three."

"Jesus." Paul whistled. "I'll do it myself — out of uniform."

"I really appreciate it and, believe me, I'll return the favor if the opportunity presents itself."

"Don't mention it."

After hanging up the phone with Paul, Rick bounded up from his chair, striding over to his maps pinned on the corkboard on the wall. Coop followed.

"Boss, want a map of Kentucky?"

"Yeah."

Coop buzzed Sheila. "Hey, check the metal file cabinet out there for a recent map of Kentucky."

There was one and Sheila brought it in. Rick pulled extra pins out of the corkboard, opened and straightened out the map. He put it up as Coop, anticipating his next request, brought him a state map of Virginia. Once up they both stared at it.

"Here's what I don't get." Cynthia stuck her finger on Newport News. "Over a million people. A huge naval base. Wouldn't there be a big drug market there? Has to be. Why fool around with Lexington?"

"Organized crime owns Newport News. A small-fry could survive for a time but they'd be squeezed out eventually. Maybe mid-South cities are more open." He touched each of the pinheads representing the murder sites. "I'm not convinced this is about drugs, even legal ones as you've suggested."

"Whatever they're doing, it has to be easy to transport."

"No. Whatever they're doing simply must not call attention to itself. It doesn't have to be easy. They could be transporting stolen cars."

"Yeah, but we'd know if the cars were stolen around here. Besides, would Don have five hundred and twenty-five thousand dollars in his safe from stolen cars? These guys would have to be running one of the biggest rackets in America for that kind of money — and just for one guy. He probably wasn't even the head of it."

"I know. I know. That doesn't quite fit either. When we went to Roger's garage I was looking for a chop shop. Not a sign. Hauling in a car, stripping and selling off the parts, hell, there'd have been junk everywhere. That place of Roger's was immaculate."

Coop said, "His garage was cleaner than some people's houses."

"Scratch chop shop. I've even thought about counterfeit money. Unless there's a buried bunker or another place hidden, that's not going to work either. I know that drugs are the one logical piece in what is illogical right now but, Coop, I don't think it's drugs. I don't know if Don Clatterbuck and Roger could deal without dipping and that always shows."

"Roger liked to drink but remember Diana Robb says he did coke, too. I remember going over there to check on Mrs. Hogendobber's hubcaps and there was a line of beer cans to his shop. Never found a trace of drugs though." Cooper crossed her arms over her chest.

Rick paced in front of the maps. "It's difficult, hey, almost impossible to imagine Don or Roger organizing some kind of criminal business. Neither one struck me as that smart. Someone has to be on top, someone much more intelligent."

"Most murders occur within families or between people well known to one another. And most of those murders involve alcohol, drugs, or are crimes of passion. These murders are dispassionate, cool. The murder of Dwayne was opportunistic but not a crime of passion. The body wasn't mutilated, he'd been hit over the head; for whatever reason the killer couldn't finish him off with a blunt instrument so he strung him up."

"Maybe the weapon wasn't heavy enough or the killer wasn't strong enough. That points to a woman."

"Hoisting Dwayne over a tree couldn't have been light work."

"Push him on the back of a truck, throw the rope over the tree, and drive off. It rained so hard nothing was left. There could have been a truck in there or even a car, slide him over the trunk. It's messy but not all that hard."

"And Dwayne wanted more money. After Din Marks's talk with you that would appear motivation enough. If he wanted more now, he'd want more later. Or maybe he wanted promotion inside the company." Rick shook his head. "Greed leaches out every other emotion, doesn't it?"

"Yes, it certainly seems to do that. People become bloodless."

"I'm going to wait for the lab reports on Roger. If he was murdered then I must consider my first suspect Sean O'Bannon. He had the most to gain by his brother's murder, separate from whatever scam Roger was into. Sean inherits all of a lucrative business. Maybe he even inherits a lucrative illegal business."

"Maybe the safe full of money will lure the killer to put his foot right into the trap."

"A poster about selling off Don's goods might help. I spoke to his parents. They agreed and we won't put their phone number on there. Just an auction date, location, and time. Ought to light a fire under his ass." Rick's one eyebrow arched upward. He could be clever.

# 46

The daily sun and wind reduced the size of the puddles, the depth of the mud. Still not trusting the ground, Harry didn't drive her tractor to the creek. Large tree limbs were wedged along the banks; a few weak trees had crashed into the creek, their uprooted trunks looking like paralyzed squid tentacles. She needed to chainsaw the trunks into smaller portions, wrap heavy chains around them to drag them out. Once the wood dried she'd cut it for firewood, stacking it neatly on the porch. She'd also built a weather-tight woodshed next to the shavings shed. As spring and summer progressed she'd slowly fill the woodshed until full. That would hold throughout the next winter.

The mercury climbed to sixty-four degrees at noon, just warm enough to shed a coat but still cool enough for a midweight shirt. Harry took the opportunity before the weather shifted to hot and hotter to crimp a standing tin seam on her barn roof. The seams separate sometimes. You fold the longer piece over the shorter and squeeze them together. Her father had taught her how to do it. She wore sneakers, the rubber soles helping to give her traction on the roof pitch. Only one seam needed work, which made her happy.

Pewter and Murphy reposed under the large white lilac bush. Tucker slept under the lavender lilac bush. Both cats were awake but stretched on their sides to their full length.

*"Do you like bacon?"* Pewter reached out to bat at an ant, who easily avoided her.

*"You know I like bacon."*

*"If you had to choose between bacon and beef bits what would you choose?"*

*"Beef."*

Pewter rolled on her back. *"What about between beef and tuna?"*

*"Tuna."*

*"Tuna and salmon?"*

*"H-m-m, tuna."* Mrs. Murphy had to think about that one. *"Why are you asking me? Are you hungry again? You ate a huge breakfast."*

*"When I'm not eating I like to think about food. Food preferences are clues to person- ality."* This was said with great conviction.

*"Pewter, you need sunglasses."*

*"Huh?"*

"You're getting West Coast."

"Close-minded," she sniffed. "Figures. Tuna, a most conventional cat."

Mrs. Murphy lifted her head. "She's stopped."

Pewter lifted her head off her outstretched paw also. "What improvement will she tackle next? She's exhausting. She needs to learn to take naps."

Out of nowhere the blue jay screeched by them, shaking the lilacs. "Mouse breath!"

Pewter leapt up, shaking herself. "Death!"

"Don't go out. Move back. Let's see if we can draw him into the bush. Then we've got him."

The blue jay turned, flew around the walnut tree, diving for the lilac bushes, too smart to be lured in. He screamed, "Tapeworm host."

"That does it!" Pewter shot out of the bush but he'd already begun his climb.

To show off he flew in the center aisle of the barn and out the back side.

"If we find his nest we can climb up and kill him," Mrs. Murphy logically suggested. "If we can't get him or his mate we can push their eggs to the ground."

"I'd love to hear them splat, little tiny splats since they're little tiny eggs. Death to the next generation." Pewter's pupils en-

larged in excitement.

The only other excitement of the day was Diego calling Harry in the evening. He was back in Washington and looked forward to seeing her the next weekend. Since Fair was taking her to the Wrecker's Ball, he asked her to check her calendar so he could take her to the next dance, picnic, anything. Then he said they'd make their own picnic. She agreed. They'd enjoy a repast Saturday noon and if it rained, they'd eat in the barn just to be halfway outside.

She hung up the phone and began whistling.

*"What an awful sound,"* Pewter meowed.

*"It is,"* Mrs. Murphy agreed, running to Harry, begging her to stop.

"Sorry, girls, I forgot how sensitive your ears are." Harry laughed and stopped whistling.

*"Doesn't bother me,"* Tucker said. *"If you whistle I come running."*

*"Don't brownnose, Tucker, it's such an unattractive trait,"* Pewter grumbled.

*"You know, Pewter, you're so fat I bet there are shock absorbers on your cat box."*

That made Murphy laugh so hard she rolled off the sofa, hitting the floor with a thud.

"Murphy, you're supposed to land on your feet." Harry picked her up, kissing her forehead while Pewter, enraged, thumped down the hall into the bedroom.

The phone rang again. Harry walked into the kitchen to pick it up. On hearing BoomBoom's voice she squeezed her eyes shut for an instant.

"What worthy cause are you roping me into now?"

"Well — the Special Olympics need volunteers. They're going to be held at Wintergreen" — she named a local resort — "and we need people who know sports. I thought maybe you could be the starter for the races."

"Oh. Sure."

"That was easy."

"I like the Special Olympics." Harry smiled, then changed the subject. "Think our little trap will catch a mouse?"

"I hope so."

"I keep forgetting to ask you, how did you meet Thomas?"

"Big party at Vin Mattacia's." Mattacia had been Ambassador to Spain in the late 1970s. An urbane, outgoing man, he was at the hub of those people retired from the diplomatic corps who lived in the area.

"Oh."

"Great party. A Valentine's party. I enjoy him but I don't think the relationship will go anywhere. It's just — fun."

"Oh."

"I don't know if I ever want to marry again. Some days I think I do and some days I don't."

"It's a quandary."

After a bit more chitchat Harry hung up the phone, realized it was getting late, and took a shower.

Pewter, on the bed, ignored both Murphy and Tucker, who sat on the hooked rug by the bed.

*"Can you imagine standing in a shower? It's like standing in the rain,"* Mrs. Murphy asked the dog, settling down for a good night's sleep.

*"It's a human thing."* Tucker half closed her eyes. *"It's right up there with using a knife and fork."*

# 47

Coop breezed in the back door of the post office at seven-thirty in the morning. She tacked up the bogus auction poster on the bulletin board in the front part of the building.

Miranda and Tracy both knew what was afoot. Every single person who came into the post office commented on it that day.

Lottie wondered if the Clatterbucks were that hard up. She then sarcastically said she thought Harry would be in the first row of the attendees since Harry couldn't resist sticking her nose in other people's business.

Mim, just returned from New York, thought it much too soon. One needed time before sorting and selling.

Little Mim questioned who would want to buy bears' paws and the like.

Jim Sanburne merely shrugged. He accepted a broader range of behavior than did the women in his life.

The Reverend Herb Jones thought the whole thing was too sad.

Sean O'Bannon read the notice without comment.

At the end of the day, Rick Shaw listened to Marshall Wells on the phone. The lab report had come back with all due speed. Roger O'Bannon had been poisoned with quinidine, a drug which, taken in excess of one gram, kills within fifteen to twenty minutes. It can be administered in pill or powder form. Unlike most other poisons, this one kills without producing horrible convulsions. It is sometimes given to heart patients to suppress acute arrhythmias.

Coop, standing next to him when he hung up the phone, simply said, "Do we arrest Lottie Pearson?"

"She handed him the coffee. Can you prove she poisoned him? *Intentionally?*" He emphasized the word.

"Not just yet. She's not going anywhere."

At three o'clock that night, a car, lights off, glided down Don Clatterbuck's short driveway. The driver emerged, noiselessly closed the door, and walked to Don's shop. What no one had noticed when they left Don's shop after re-installing the lock was that the tiny red light on the video camera was reflected in the windowpane. The thief noticed and left.

# 48

The week roared by in a welter of chores, seemingly so important at the time yet quickly forgotten. Fortunately, mail volume was light, so Harry skipped out Friday morning to do her grocery shopping. Miranda, whose refrigerator remained full, gladly gave her the time. Tracy kept Miranda company at work.

"Have you decided what color dress you're wearing?"

"The magenta, the color of my peonies."

"You'll be the prettiest girl there." He smiled, deciding that either a white or pink corsage would complement her dress. "I don't remember Tim O'Bannon being so interested in charitable pursuits."

"Tim was tight as the bark on a tree. He used to embarrass Ida. When the boys took over the business they became involved in community affairs. I think they did it out of the goodness of their hearts but I don't expect it hurt business either. 'Each one must do as he has made up his mind, not reluctantly or under compulsion, for God loves a cheerful giver.' *Second Corinthians*, Chapter Nine, Verse Seven."

"What a memory."

*"We're back!"* Tucker announced gaily.

*"Mom drove home, put stuff in the fridge, gave us a treat, and now I'm ready for the mail cart."* Pewter hopped in, causing the cart to roll a bit.

"I bought pork chops." Harry sounded triumphant, up to the challenge. "I'm going to make stuffed pork chops according to your recipe. The only thing is, does Diego like pork? Some people don't."

"Feed him a loaf of bread, a jug of wine, et cetera. . . ." Tracy slapped her on the back.

"You men. All alike." She teased him for quoting the *Rubaiyat* because the next line was "and thou." Tracy assumed all Diego needed was Harry.

*"Gender wars!"* Pewter called out from the bottom of the mail cart. *"I pick women to win."*

*"Of course you'll pick women, you twit. You're female."* Mrs. Murphy jumped in the cart, too.

A loud discussion followed, after which Mrs. Murphy jumped right out, hit the floor front paws apart, and pretended to chase a mouse into an opened mail sack.

Tucker stuck her nose in the sack. Murphy batted at the dog, who snapped her jaws, appearing quite ferocious.

"Oh, to be a cat or dog." Harry admired their untrammeled joy.

"Your cat or dog." Tracy waved as Coop passed by in the squad car.

Within minutes she came through the back door. "Hi. Didn't want to park out front. I'll only be here a minute."

"More news, I hope?" Miranda offered her a cookie, which she took.

They knew about Roger. Rick had allowed Cynthia Cooper to tell them. After all, they were in on this mess. They'd helped with the safe and they'd not gotten in his way. He couldn't decide if he was mellowing or if he was too tired to bitch and moan.

"The sheriff from Washington County, Paul Carter, called. Two people at Boojum's recognized Dwayne Fuqua. Said he dropped off cars regularly. They also recognized Roger, of course, but what was interesting is that Roger would pick up Dwayne from Boojum's. Bill Boojum had to know."

"Hi." Susan popped through the front door followed by her youngest, Brooks.

"And why aren't you in school, young lady?" Miranda pointed her finger playfully at the high-school girl.

"Teachers' conference day." Brooks smiled.

"They didn't have those when I was in school." Miranda frowned. "I remember George Washington was good at math." She broke into a tinkling giggle.

"Oh, Miranda." Harry rolled her eyes.

"Brooks, I'm glad you're here. I was going to come over tonight and ask you some more questions. I wish they'd occur to me all at once but they don't." Coop leaned over the dividing counter as Brooks came up to lean on the other side.

"Will you stop running around," Harry commanded Mrs. Murphy, who had abandoned the mail sack to play tag with Tucker.

*"Spoilsport."* Murphy did sit down, though, as Tucker crashed into her, rolling them both over.

*"Sorry, my brakes don't work."* The dog licked Murphy's cheek to make up for the block.

*"Ha, a likely story,"* Pewter called out from the mail cart.

"When you brought sugar to the table, who handed you the sugar bowl?" Coop pulled out her small notepad.

"Chef Ted."

"Did anyone stop you on the way to table?"

"No."

411

"And it was a bowl of raw sugar?"

"Uh-huh." Brooks folded her hands, leaning harder on the divider. "I put it next to the silver creamer at the end of the table."

*"The broken sugar bowl was china."* Mrs. Murphy jumped up with a start. *"China. Oh, now why didn't I notice that at the time?"*

"And you weren't called in to clean up the sugar on the floor?"

"No. Someone cleaned it up. One of the guests, I guess."

"Thomas Steinmetz. Lottie backed into him." Coop had several eyewitnesses who corroborated that fact. "When you put the sugar bowl on the table, did you see who reached for it first?"

"Uh — Daddy. He was fixing a cup of coffee for Aunt Tally."

"Then why isn't Aunt Tally dead?" Susan held up her hands in frustration.

"You know, people have been asking that question for years," Harry devilishly replied.

*"But that wasn't the bowl!"* Murphy yowled.

*"Save your energy,"* Tucker advised.

*"I can't believe I was so stupid."* Murphy was distraught.

*"Don't be so hard on yourself, pussycat. Roger O'Bannon was sprawled on the floor*

with Little Mim yanking on his arm. That would get any cat's attention," Tucker soothingly said.

"Right under my nose." Murphy bent her head, putting her forehead on Tucker's chest.

"Hey, it's right under their noses, too. They haven't figured it out and they think their intelligence is superior to every other creature on the face of the earth." Tucker levelly offered that criticism.

"Ha," Pewter called out.

"Do you remember party guests walking into the kitchen?" Coop asked.

Brooks thought a moment. "Mrs. Sanburne, Little Mim, Aunt Tally, Sean —"

"Sean?"

"He came in to ask when the coffee would be ready. There might have been a lot of other people because I was carrying dishes out. Action central."

"I believe that," Miranda said.

"Anyone going into the kitchen passes through the large pantry for china and silver. The food pantry is on the other side of the kitchen." Coop was thinking out loud. "Brooks, do you remember if all the silver bowls were used?"

"No, ma'am."

Coop smiled. "Well, there's no reason for

you to have noticed. How were any of us to know what would happen? Sometimes I think solving a crime is like putting together a mosaic, it's thousands and thousands of tiny bits of information until finally a picture emerges."

"What an interesting thought." Miranda passed the cookie dish over the counter.

Brooks happily ate one. Susan resisted, willpower to the max.

"You've questioned the chef, of course?" Tracy asked.

"Yes. I was impressed with his memory for detail, especially about food." She smiled.

"Mind if I call Aunt Tally?" Harry asked.

"No," Coop said.

Harry dialed.

Tally picked up, greeting the caller. "Queen Bee and it better be good."

"Hi, Aunt Tally, it's Harry."

"Do I have a package?"

"No, I'm here in the post office with Deputy Cooper, Miranda, and Tracy, Susan, and Brooks."

"A little party."

"It would be much livelier if you were here."

"You're right about that." She laughed. "Now, what's on your mind, Mary Minor Haristeen?"

"When you hosted the tea dance, you used your own silver, china, and crystal, right?"

"Of course."

"How many silver sugar bowls do you have?"

"Two. One for white cube sugar and one for raw sugar. I use cubes because what people don't use that day I'll give to the horses."

"And both were in use at the tea dance?"

"My, yes, I think I had just about everything out there on that table."

*"Ask her about her china!"* Murphy hopped up on the table in the back and kept hopping, up and down.

"Calm down," Harry admonished the cat.

"I am perfectly calm," Tally answered.

"I'm sorry, Aunt Tally, I didn't mean you. Mrs. Murphy is pitching a fit and falling in it. Would you mind terribly going into your pantry and counting your sugar bowls, including china bowls if you have any?"

"No, but it will take me a minute."

"That's fine."

As Harry waited the others chatted. Mrs. Murphy anxiously ran over to Harry. She sat so she could hear Aunt Tally's response. As her hearing was acute she could hear if she was close to the receiver. She didn't have to have her ear smack on it.

"I'm back," came the authoritative voice. "I have two silver sugar bowls. Same as when I started. It's a good thing, too, because they cost far too much to replace. I also have only one china sugar bowl, my breakfast set of china. Does that help?"

"Aunt Tally, you've been a *major* help. I'll see you tomorrow night at the ball."

"Won't be the same without Roger. He'd get so loaded he'd start up equipment, make a mess, pass out on the railroad tracks. Everyone else will behave reasonably, I'm afraid."

"You never know."

Aunt Tally laughed. "Harry, in Crozet that's the truth, absolutely! Bye-bye."

Harry hung up. "Her two silver sugar bowls are there. Her china bowl is there yet the china sugar bowl broke. How could we have missed that? It means the broken china bowl wasn't Aunt Tally's." She smashed the palm of her hand to her forehead.

*"We all did,"* Murphy commiserated.

"That doesn't solve our problem but it gets us closer to understanding just how Roger was poisoned." Miranda sighed.

"Roger was poisoned!" Brooks's voice squeaked.

"Yes, dear, now keep it to yourself." Su-

416

san's tone ensured obedience.

"Are you going out to Lexington? Sounds like Bill Boojum needs a face-to-face interrogation." Tracy thought any transaction stood a better chance of success if conducted in person.

"Next week. We know the three murders are tied together. We know Boojum knows something he's not willing to share but we still don't know why. If we just knew why."

"Always comes down to that." Tracy nodded his head.

"Drugs. The setup was perfect but Rick's not buying that. At least, not yet." Coop drummed the countertop. "We need one little slipup, one tiny mistake. Just one."

She was about to get it.

## 49

A light southerly breeze carried the fragrance of honeysuckle over meadows and mountains. The bumblebees showed up in full force, as did the carpenter bees. Tiny praying mantis babies crawled over trumpet vines, greening up nicely but no deep-orange blooms as yet.

A curving hill at the back of Harry's land provided the perfect spot for a picnic. Still not trusting the footing, she didn't drive the truck back there but loaded up the hamper and cooler with drinks on the John Deere tractor. She made it in one trip, spread out the checkered tablecloth blanket, and put a spray of thyme tied with ribbon in the middle of the blanket. A votive candle in a clear glass holder was next to the spray.

When Diego arrived he sat in the tractor seat while she stood in front of him, driving.

Tucker ambled along since she didn't pop out of second gear. Mrs. Murphy and Pewter stayed back, laying a trap for the blue jay. They carried sweet feed in their mouths

to the lawn near the lilacs. They opened
their mouths, dropping it. Three trips and
they'd created an enticing pile. They repaired under the lilacs to wait.

Up on the hill, Harry and Diego chattered
away, never experiencing that awkward lull
that sometimes occurs when people are getting to know one another.

". . . swollen from handshaking." He re-
called how Lottie introduced him to anyone
and everyone at the alumni dinner.

"She was in her glory."

"She was and she's good at it. She'll pry
money out of those old men and maybe
even some of the middle-aged ones. Oh,
why does it take so long to make money?"
He laughed. "We need it most when we're
young."

"You think?"

"Oh, yes, while we're still open for adventure, before we become too accustomed to
creature comforts, before the children arrive." He surveyed the pastoral scene. "Perfect."

"That it is." She leaned against the maple
tree. "What adventures would you like to
have before settling down?"

His eyes sparkled. "Rafting the rivers on
the western side of the South Island of New
Zealand. Riding through Patagonia at

419

springtime. Hiking Wyoming's Grand Tetons and the Bighorn Mountains. Sailing throughout the Greek isles, although one could do that with children, I think. Ah, I'd love to play tennis in Cape Town, croquet in England, polo in Argentina. I want to see the aurora borealis and I want to have more picnics in Crozet, Virginia. What about you?"

"The Dublin Horse Show. I'd like to see that. I'd like to see the south of France and Tuscany and the opera house in Vienna. I'd like to see the Ostsee and then go over to Stockholm and tour the Swedish countryside. And I'd like to see the British Museum, but if I don't get to see any of those things I can read about them. Mostly, I'm happy with what I have. It isn't much by the standards of the wealthy and the powerful but it pleases me, and, Diego, how much does one need to be happy?"

"For some people, enough is not enough. They have cracks in their soul. No?"

She nodded. "Here I am, the postmistress in Crozet, Virginia. Most of humanity has never heard of Crozet and certainly not of me. But I think about the world. I wish people good lives and I know there's not much I can do to help them except take care of myself and not be a burden to others. I don't know if the human race can be helped."

"A very Protestant concern." He smiled, his teeth white against his tanned skin.

"I suppose it is, isn't it? This dreadful concern to improve one's self and the world. You'd think after all these centuries we would have learned to thank God for what we have and leave well enough alone." She smiled sadly.

"Do you believe in fate?"

A honeybee darted down on the mayonnaise while Harry considered this, then darted off again. "Yes."

"So long?" He laughed.

"I had to think about it. It drives my friends crazy. I'm not very spontaneous. I think things through and I don't know if I make fewer mistakes that way but it's just the way I am."

"I can see that. I'm the opposite, naturally. Opposites attract."

"I wonder." She laughed; his bubbling spirits delighted her. "Another sandwich?"

"Yes." He knew the ham sandwiches would make him too thirsty.

She handed him a sandwich, then pulled a small piece from her sandwich for Tucker, who devoured it instantly. "Forgot to light the candle." She reached into her jeans pocket.

"Oops, forgot to bring matches, too."

Diego fished in his pocket, pulling out a brightly colored matchbook. "Here."

Harry stared at the Roy and Nadine's matchbook in his hand. "Diego, where did you get those matches?"

"These?" He read the address. "Lottie's car."

Harry fervently hoped he was telling the truth. She knew the minute the picnic was over she'd call Coop.

"Have you ever been to Lexington, Kentucky?"

"No. I'll add that to my list of adventures."

Back at the house another small adventure was unfolding. The blue jay, perched on the weather vane on the roof, had observed the two felines laying the trap. He waited until the humans returned, Diego left, and the cats, disappointed, walked back into the house. Then he swooped down, gobbled up the grain, shouting in triumph. By the time the cats raced back out of the house half the sweet feed was gone.

*"I hate you!"* Pewter yowled at the top of her lungs.

*"Ha ha,"* the blue jay called from atop the weather vane.

Before dressing for the ball, Harry dialed

Cooper to report Diego's possession of the Roy and Nadine's matchbook.

"I'd call and ask her myself," Harry offered, "to save you the call but she'd think I was calling about Diego. It's as plain as the nose on your face she means to have him."

"You'd call because you're as curious as your cats," Coop responded. "However, I'll make the call. What time do you think you'll get to the ball?"

"Oh, seven. Starts at six-thirty, uh, wait, the invitation is on the fridge. Let me double-check. Okay, open bar at six-thirty, dinner at seven, dancing at eight. So I suppose we'll get there at six-thirty. Fair enjoys a drink. I'll pass."

"Did you ever really drink?"

"Not really, a beer here and there. Champagne at a wedding. What about you?"

"College."

"What time are you arriving?"

"Six-thirty." She laughed.

"Are you on duty tonight?"

"Yeah, but I'll be dressed to the nines. Rick, too."

"The minute you see me, tell me what Lottie said about the matchbook. I hope he picked it up off the floor of her car. If he didn't —"

"Yeah, I know."

# 50

The floodlights illuminating the old wrecker's ball shone cool blue. The lights on the sign for O'Bannon Salvage remained white but all around the edges of the yard that faced the road into the yard, lights cheerfully beamed in red, yellow, green, more blue, some pink, some white.

As celebrants drove in they cruised through an allée of light.

The new main building, the site of the dance, drew gasps of admiration from guests. Sean had built all his shelving on rollers so the shelves were rolled to the sides of the large building. In front of these, painters' spattered drop cloths were suspended from the ceiling to the floor. Beautiful salvaged objects, old fireplace mantels, marvelous huge coaching lights were arranged around the room or hung from the rafters. The centerpiece of the room, an Art Nouveau fountain complete with living nymph and satyrs, overflowed with flowers instead of water. Sean had filled the fountain with wisteria, hiring the gymnastics team from the university to display themselves in costume. The sculpted form of a stag stood atop the fountain, an unusual but dramatic symbol.

Each table's centerpiece boasted wisteria wrapped around salvage — a hand-carved finial, a porcelain wash pitcher, a mound of crystal doorknobs. People, drinks in hand, walked from table to table admiring the centerpieces, all of which were for sale for the benefit of the charity.

Other beautiful items, like old gold picture frames, had been bought by committee members and then donated for the charity ball. No one expected Sean to foot the bill for everything. As it was he'd gone to quite a bit of expense buying and painting the drop cloths à la Jackson Pollock. He and his staff cleaned the building, moved back the shelves, hung the cloths, and brought in the heavy statuary on a forklift. Fortunately, the floor was concrete. Plus he donated the fountain to be sold. He built the dance floor with a raised platform for the band. He told everyone he needed the work to keep his mind off Roger.

Miranda posed for a photo in front of the fountain with a satyr. The photographer was also paid by Sean. People bought the pictures, the proceeds going to Building for Life.

Aunt Tally was a sensation wearing a white tuxedo, a red rosebud in her lapel. Big Mim brought down a gentleman in his eighties to escort her aunt but Tally proved too much for him, ditching him for a forty-year-old lawyer dazzled by her wit.

Mim, herself swathed in St. Laurent from head to foot in colors as bright as a macaw, darted here, there, everywhere.

Harry and Fair looked as handsome together as they did when married. She wore her mother's beautiful classic Christian Dior dress and he wore a tuxedo that he'd bought from Bergdorf Goodman's over Christmas.

Susan chose lavender and Brooks chose white, for her first grown-up ball.

Lottie, sticking close to Sean, wore a simple but elegant off-the-shoulder black gown.

Diego escorted Little Mim, which set tongues wagging. Declaring independence from her mother, Little Mim was sponsoring a struggling designer in New York known as Mikel. He probably wouldn't struggle after the Wrecker's Ball because he made Little Mim look ravishing, not always the easiest task. Her emerald-green dress, exquisitely beaded, made a soft, unusual sound when she walked. It wasn't that Little Mim was bad-looking — far from it — but she was usually overshadowed by her mother. This dress ensured she wouldn't be tonight.

Coop, blond head towering above the other ladies, chose red for the simple reason that blondes usually don't. She felt like breaking rules tonight.

By seven, everyone was there, even a few uninvited guests. Mrs. Murphy, Pewter, and Tucker knew how to soften up Fair.

Fair had bought a new black Volvo station wagon. He grew tired of showing up every-where in his vet truck so he finally sprang for the Volvo. Harry told him to leave the pets home before she remembered the knocked-over lamps, shredded lamp shades, books on the floor. The depredations escalated with feline anger. A put-out puss might stop at knocking over a glass but to be left out of a big occasion called forth torrents of de-structive abuse. She agreed to allow them to attend the ball. After all, they knew their way around the salvage yard and it was far enough off the paved state road to pose no danger to them. Fair opened the back hatch so they could come and go as they pleased.

Harry put down a beach towel so they wouldn't get the beige car mat dirty.

*"Let's find Pope Rat,"* Tucker panted, eager to chase the rascal.

*"No."* Murphy reposed in the back of the Volvo. *"Let's sit here for a while and eavesdrop on conversations as people park or come back to their cars. I want to know if anyone comes back for a toot of cocaine."*

*"You're going with Coop's theory?"* Pewter happily snuggled onto the beach towel.

*"It certainly makes the most sense and yet — let's keep our eyes and ears open. No one expects us to be here. If they see us they'll make kitchy-coo sounds. They'll never know what we're up to — humans are dependable that way."* The tiger laughed.

*"But, Murphy, even if people do come back here or find a place outside for a snort that doesn't mean they're in on the murders,"* Tucker sensibly reminded her.

*"I know that. I'm hoping we'll glean something."*

*"Pope Rat knows."* Pewter scratched behind her ear. *"What a rat."* Realizing he *was* a rat, she burst out laughing.

Rick Shaw pulled up in the next lane of parked cars. He looked good in a tuxedo and his wife wore a white floor-length dress that was very becoming.

The animals could hear their discussion.

"Honey, if my beeper goes off I've got to go. The Reverend Jones said he'd take you home."

"I know, dear." She smiled, accustomed to his odd hours and sudden departures. "I'm just thrilled to be here."

They headed toward the strains of the string quartet. The dance band would rock out after dinner.

The chimes sounded, signaling that dinner would be served. Guests checked their table numbers, moving to their assigned seats.

Sean, as host, sat with the director of Building for Life. Lottie sat on his right. BoomBoom, who'd been head of publicity on this one, sat with Thomas, who was a darker shade of tan than he had been at the Dogwood Festival.

As Diego guided Little Mim to their table, number two, he winked at Harry, who winked back. Fair chose not to notice.

Liberally lubricated by the open bar, the conversation flowed, the volume rising with the courses of wine attending dinner. The nymph and satyrs in the fountain, having sampled drinks offered them by admirers, became friskier than intended, the satyrs most particularly. It wouldn't be long before they took their mythology literally.

After dinner, liqueurs were served along with a staggering array of desserts, fruits, cheeses, and sherbets.

Sated, the guests sat, eyes glazed with happiness.

As the tables were cleared, Sean stood up. "Excuse me, folks, I'm going outside for a smoke."

"I didn't know you smoked." Lottie stood up, too.

"I didn't until now. They can say what they want about nicotine, it really does soothe the nerves." He smiled wanly.

"I guess a little puff can't hurt you too much." Lottie smiled indulgently.

Other people filtered out. Thomas, chest pocket filled with divine Cuban cigars, trailed men behind him. They resembled penguins following the Big Penguin.

Lottie ducked off into the ladies' room before joining the smokers. Harry was in there brushing her teeth.

"Harry, I can't believe anyone is that obsessed with their teeth." Lottie turned up her nose in disgust.

Harry rinsed out her mouth. "Those nuts on the chocolate cake got stuck in my teeth. It drives me crazy."

"H-mmph." Lottie marched off.

As Harry emerged she bumped into Aunt Tally. "Isn't he divine?"

"Who, Aunt Tally?"

"The Marine." She indicated with her eyes a fit man in early middle age wearing his Marine uniform for just this occasion, a carryover from the nineteenth century and one that delighted ladies. His short waist-length tunic fit him tightly, his medal ribbons, four rows deep, bedecked his left chest. His blue-black closely fitted trousers carried a thin red stripe on the outside. His patent leather dancing shoes gleamed.

"What happened to your date?"

"Harry, too old. I can't stand old men." Tally flicked up her cane.

"Well, what about that other guy?" Harry hadn't met the lawyer.

"Uh." She shrugged. "Dull. But now this one, he's a man all right." She covered her mouth with her gloved hand and looked exactly as she must have looked at seventeen at her coming-out debutante ball — minus the wrinkles, of course.

Harry lowered her voice conspiratorially. "I know you can't be good but go slow."

"At my age, sugar, there is no slow. Get it while you can! And I will, I will!" Tally giggled, then hurried into the ladies' room.

Rick, dying for a smoke, had been waylaid

431

by Jim Sanburne. As they were talking Rick's beeper went off.

"Excuse me. I'd better take this." A little printout read DON. Rick's face registered no emotion. "Jim, I've got to go." He briskly walked to Coop, herself walking outside for a smoke. "Come with me."

Hoping not to call attention to themselves they walked fast but not frantically to Rick's car.

*"Something's up,"* Mrs. Murphy noted.

# 51

Pulling into Don Clatterbuck's, they grabbed their guns and opened the car doors, crouching behind them. Coop dearly wished she weren't in a ball gown.

Rick moved away from the door, running low. He stood outside the shop door, reached over, and opened it. He flattened himself against the building. Nothing.

Coop, keeping as low as her dress would allow, joined him on the other side of the door.

Rick reached in, flicking on the light switch.

No sound. No movement. He ran inside, diving for the workbench. Nothing.

"Coop, come on." He scrambled to his feet, brushing off his tuxedo.

The door to the safe hung wide open. It was empty.

"Our birdie can't be too far away." Coop grabbed a chair, placing it under the camera. She turned off the camera, removing the tape inside.

Yancy had set it up, locking the tiny TV playback box in Don's broom closet. Coop hiked her long skirt up, stepped down as Rick opened the closet. They quickly plugged in the small monitor.

"Dammit!" Rick exploded.

A masked figure. A black cloth covering the face, slits for eyes and mouth, wrapped in what could be a black bedsheet or long cloak, it stopped in front of the camera after emptying out the safe to give them the finger.

"I'd like to see his face when he discovers the money's no good."

"Won't discover that until he gets it in a bright light." Rick slipped his gun back in his chest holster. "Whoever did this knew we'd be at the ball tonight."

"Boss, that's no surprise. Everyone's at the ball tonight."

"Maybe, but we know this — he knows that we're here. I think we've just been suckered." He sprinted for the car, Coop right behind him. She turned out the lights as she ran out.

"Boss, Boss, I can't run as fast as you."

He waited the extra twenty seconds it took for her to fold herself into the car. "Coop, I wouldn't give you a nickel right now for Sean's life or Lottie's."

"We'll nab them."

"That's not what I mean. One of them is going to be dead." He peeled out, spewing stones everywhere.

## 52

Mrs. Murphy stretched herself. Out of the corner of her eye she saw Pope Rat, scurrying from the direction of the caboose, carrying a bag of popcorn toward the garage. *"Hey, Tucker, there's the rat."*

Tucker vaulted off the Volvo, racing toward the large, glossy rat.

*"She can move,"* Pewter admiringly said.

*"Yeah, maybe we'd better provide backup."* The tiger paused. *"Here come Rick and Coop."*

"You cover Lottie. I'll cover Sean," Rick ordered as they raced back to the ball.

*"H-m-m, Mom's in there."* Murphy gazed after the dog, who ran after the rat, unwilling to part with the popcorn. Instead, Pope Rat turned and scooted back into the caboose. He had cleverly gnawed an entrance right over the coupling and just to the right of the human-sized door.

Tucker had hit this impasse before, so she ran around and with great effort pulled herself up on the first step and was at the caboose door in the rear, the last thing one sees as the train rides by. But this time it wasn't locked. She pushed it in, surprising the foul-mouthed creature who was sitting in front of the wood-burning stove.

Pope Rat bared his fangs. He picked up the popcorn bag, slowly backing away toward his hole.

Tucker stopped for a moment. A gunnysack of money sat in the middle of the floor. Much as she wanted to break Pope Rat's neck she turned and bounced down the steps, running flat-out for the Volvo. *"Murphy, Pewter, the play money is in the caboose!"*

*"We'd better get Mom."* Murphy moved toward the main building, great purpose in her stride. They had noticed cars coming and a few going while lounging in the back of the Volvo but nothing had captured their attention as out of the ordinary. Now all three animals wished they had climbed on the roof of the car to see exactly who was driving in and driving out.

The band played old tunes, new tunes. The dance floor was crowded. Rick and Cooper entered the building a few moments apart. Mrs. Murphy, Pewter, and Tucker followed Cooper in.

Harry, sitting this one out to drink a cup of tea, saw her three pets. "Oh, no." She got up but noticed Cooper's face. "Are you all right?"

"Yes."

"Hey, you never told me about the matchbook."

"Diego told you the truth." She scanned the room for Lottie, out on the dance floor with the Marine, much to Aunt Tally's disgust.

"I'm so glad." Harry exhaled in relief. "All right, you varmints, we're going back to the car."

She walked out, the three following her much too obediently. As she reached the car all three took off toward the caboose.

"Dammit." Harry felt the cool night air, wishing she had a wrap. She trudged in her high-heeled shoes, those instruments of torture, to the caboose.

Tucker and the cats pushed open the door, driving Pope Rat back into his hole one more time.

*"Nipshits,"* he taunted.

*"Who cares about you?"* Tucker's voice carried great self-importance.

Harry slowly climbed the steps, walked into the caboose. Her eyes took a moment to focus, adjusting to the dim light. She then saw the opened sack. Kneeling down, her knees cracked. She winced, reached in, retrieving a neatly bound stack of one-hundred-dollar bills.

Holding them close to her eyes, she whistled. "The fakes? Jesus."

Slipping one fake bill into her cleavage, she hurried back to the ball. She had sense enough not to burst in. A few people called to her, she smiled and called back. Her entourage followed behind her, Murphy in the lead.

Fair came up. "I've been looking for you."

"Fair, Cooper is on the dance floor. You can push through that throng better than I can. Will you bring her to me? It's important." She lifted the hundred-dollar bill from her cleavage.

"I guess it is." His long strides carried him to the dance floor in a second, although he had to dodge an amorous nymph.

Cynthia Cooper, dancing with the Reverend Herb Jones, kept Lottie in her field of vision. Rick, dancing with his wife, did the same with Sean.

Fair whispered in Coop's ear, she hesitated, he whispered again, she thanked Herb for the dance, disengaged as subtly as possible, then joined Harry, who showed her the money.

Coop tried to catch Rick's eye but he was glued to Sean. "Fair, ask Lottie to dance. Keep her tied up," Cooper ordered the vet. "Tell Rick I'm going to the caboose."

"I'll go with you," Harry happily volunteered.

"You keep Lottie tied up." Fair didn't want Harry in danger. "Coop, I'd better go with you."

"I'm not asking her to dance," Harry stubbornly said as she pushed a none-too-compliant Fair toward the dance floor.

The two women hurried out, the animals again going with them, but before Fair could reach Lottie she had quietly disengaged from the Marine, walked behind the band, and walked out the back door. She saw the animals and humans going to the caboose. Looking over her shoulder, Lottie walked to her car.

*"Over here."* Tucker excitedly circled around the gunnysack in the caboose.

*"What is this, Grand Central?"* the rat complained from his quarters. As he had finished the popcorn his mood was improving considerably. The only reason he was taking the popcorn to the caboose in the first place was that he was tired of the music, of hearing the humans. He had resigned himself to staying in the caboose until the ob-

noxious pet threesome left him in peace.

Harry, a step behind Coop, knelt down beside her. Neither one had a flashlight but Coop fished a lighter from a small hidden pocket on the side of her dress. She clicked it on and the cheap plastic light shot out a long flame.

"It's our little bag of tricks all right."

"You think he knows it's fake?" Harry asked.

"I don't know but whoever threw it in here didn't lock the door, either because they knew this money was worthless or because they didn't have the key."

Moving at a slow trot, Fair came out of the main building. He scoured the parking lot, finding Lottie as she opened the door to her car.

"Lottie."

"Fair, you getting your exercise?" She smiled.

"I was hoping you'd dance the next dance with me."

"Of course." She put a fresh pack of cigarettes in her evening purse, closed the door, and walked back with him.

Back at the ball they started to dance when the band stopped. Jim Sanburne strode up to the raised dais, taking the offered microphone from the lead singer.

Thomas groaned in BoomBoom's ear, "Spare us a long-winded speech. I hear enough of them."

"As mayor, I will say a few words. I'm never too talky. Now if Little Mim, as vice-mayor, gets the mike we might be here for a while." He winked at Little Mim as everyone laughed.

"I'm going to slip out for a smoke." Thomas kissed her on the cheek, stood up, then adroitly moved along the edges of the crowd until he walked out front. He inhaled the cooling night air and reached in his pocket, pulling out an aromatic Portages cigar.

He could hear Jim laud the charity's director, then continue. "I am grateful for so many of you coming to support Building for Life. Those of you who have attended the Wrecker's Ball in the past know that anything is possible . . ."

*"Footsteps,"* Mrs. Murphy warned.

*"Come on."* Tucker nipped Harry's ankle.

Harry opened her mouth to chastise the corgi when she, too, heard the crunch of footsteps on the pea gravel. Putting her finger to her lips she motioned for Cooper to follow her. They quickly opened the door on the coupling side of the caboose, grabbed the long iron handrails, cold now as

442

the temperature continued in its plunge, and swung themselves out, Harry flat against the caboose on the right side, Coop on the left.

The footsteps passed them, the metallic steps vibrating as the individual stepped up onto the back platform, then opened the door to enter the caboose.

Mrs. Murphy and Pewter jumped down with ease. Tucker hit the ground with an *oomph,* rolled over, scratched to her feet, and followed the cats under the caboose as Harry and Coop dropped to the ground. The two women quietly crept along the side of the caboose opposite from the main building. It was even darker on that side.

They heard someone else walk toward the caboose, coming from the direction of the party.

Both women looked at each other. They hoped their feet wouldn't show.

Mrs. Murphy peeped out from under the caboose. *"Sean."*

*"I knew it,"* Pewter crowed.

Not a moment later, Lottie's voice called out, "Sean, where are you going?"

Whoever was in the caboose froze.

"For a smoke. Thought I'd walk around the yard."

Fair walked out trying to shadow Lottie,

but it's difficult for a six-foot five-inch man to be unobtrusive.

Lottie turned toward him, "Fair, what's going on?"

"We never had our dance."

"Oh." She faced Sean. "For some inexplicable reason I've become attractive to Fair." This was said with irony.

"May I have this dance then?" Fair persisted.

"Let me smoke a cigarette with Sean and I'll be right back in."

Fair beat a retreat toward the ball, all the while racking his brain for a place to hide so he could spy on Lottie. Rick, meanwhile, leaned against his car for a smoke, his eyes darting back to Sean from time to time. Diego came out, asked Fair where Harry was. Fair shrugged. He had no intention of helping Diego. Diego returned inside.

"Would you like to walk with me?" Sean evenly asked Lottie. "My first stop is the caboose. I don't believe I've ever showed it to you."

"That would be lovely." She raised her voice in that falsely feminine way.

Cooper and Harry heard whoever was in the caboose tiptoe to the coupling door in the back, the same one they used. The door opened and closed but no footfall followed.

Whoever it was was hanging on the hand-rail. The two women looked at one another. Cooper silently cursed herself for leaving her evening purse in Rick's car. A small pistol was in it.

Just as Sean and Lottie reached the caboose steps, Lottie said, "Sean, I'm just freezing. Let me run back to the car for my wrap."

"I can go faster than you can. High heels." He smiled, pointing to her feet, then headed toward Lottie's car about one hundred yards away.

No need for her to describe her car. In Crozet everyone knew everyone else's wheels.

With lightning speed, Lottie climbed up the steps, pushed open the door, grabbed the sack, and walked back out again, the sack over her shoulder. She shoved it under the caboose and as she did, she saw Harry's and Cooper's shoes. She started running for her car.

Whoever was hanging on the caboose dropped.

*"Thomas!"* Pewter exclaimed.

"No, you don't." He tackled Lottie just as Sean opened Lottie's car door, unaware of the drama at the caboose.

"The money's under the caboose." She

hissed a whisper, hoping that Cooper would nail him. He let her go. She hurried for her car, Tucker right behind.

Thomas bent down and grabbed the sack just as Coop stepped out from behind the caboose.

"Hands up, you're under arrest."

He saw Cooper was unarmed, hit her in the midriff with the sack, and tore after Lottie, who pushed Sean out of the way as she was plucking the keys out of her bag.

*"Stop."* Tucker bit her on the ankle.

Lottie howled but managed to shake the dog off, hitting Tucker in the head with her purse. She slipped in the car, slamming the door shut while Tucker barked for all she was worth.

"You okay?" Harry bent over Cooper.

"Stop them," the tall woman gasped.

They could hear more running footsteps and hoped some of them belonged to Rick and Fair.

Harry, unarmed, heard a gun fire, felt wind by her temple, and hit the ground.

The cats were right with her. A sensible person would have rolled under cars for cover. Not Harry. She ran for all she was worth to the front of the main building.

*"What's she doing?"* Pewter kept up with the human. As humans aren't that fast, the

cat didn't have to overexert herself, but she was out of shape.

*"There's only one way out. She's going to block it."* Mrs. Murphy knew how her human thought.

*"They'll blow through that chain-link gate."* The gray cat was really worried now. She had visions of Harry being run over and then realized that same fate could apply to her as well.

At the gate Harry rolled it shut, then climbed up on the crane. She sat high in the cab. She could see Sean crawl out of the way, Tucker helping by tugging at Sean's collar, as Lottie started her engine. She was ready to run them both over.

Thomas had sprinted to his car, a Mercedes sports car. He shook his fist as Lottie roared by him.

They would have to drive around the full car lot, around the side of the building, and then out the front drive to the gate.

Rick figured that out. He ran through the cars toward the front gate.

*"Push over flowerpots, Pewter, anything to slow them,"* Mrs. Murphy hollered.

Tucker, rounding the corner at warp speed, heard the tiger, and started slamming into the wooden trellis, whiskey kegs, empty, old wooden milk cartons. *"I bit her on the ankle!"* the mighty little dog barked.

Fair Haristeen also figured out where the crisis would be. He, too, was running through the parked cars as fast as his legs would carry him.

"Got it." Harry fired up the crane, the heavy diesel motor rumbling.

People, hearing the commotion, began to pour out of the building. A few were unsteady on their feet. Those might have thought it was the ghost of Roger O'Bannon, loaded again, creating another memorable drunken scene.

Harry, nervous, forgot exactly which calipers controlled what. She swung the ball over the festooned building, causing those outside to scream and hit the dirt.

"Dammit!" Harry cursed, took a deep breath, gently squeezed the correct calipers, and swung the ball back.

Big Mim, back on her feet, realized what Harry was doing.

The roar of car engines and squeal of wheels were heard from behind the building. People scattered again.

Harry ran the ball up to the nose of the crane, positioning it directly above the gate. She blessed Sean for putting out the colored floodlights.

She didn't know the exact time it would

take from when she squeezed the calipers to when the ball would hit, dropping straight down vertically. She prayed she'd get it right as she kept her hand on those calipers.

Lottie took the corner around the main building on two wheels. She crushed the trellis. Tucker dodged out of the way. The cats fled to the safety of hiding under the crane.

*"Hurry, Tucker, Thomas will be right behind,"* Mrs. Murphy called to her dear friend.

Tucker ran for all she was worth.

Rick, gun in hand, reached the corner of the building, too. He fired at Lottie's tires but she saw him and swerved. Thomas, not ten feet behind her now, also saw Rick and he turned his vehicle straight at the sheriff, who tucked and rolled as Thomas swerved to miss the side of the building, narrowly missing Fair, who leapt on top of a car hood, then onto another one.

The guests, mesmerized, watched.

Diego, realizing Thomas was part of the drama, stepped away from the crowd as he edged toward the parked cars closest to the gate.

Tucker made it to the crane in the nick of time.

Cooper, shoes off, ran over the pea gravel

in her stocking feet. She'd grabbed her gun. She hurried around the other side of the building.

"My God, she's going to ram the gate!" Big Mim screamed.

Just as the nose of Lottie's car hit the gate, Harry squeezed the release calipers and down dropped the wrecker's ball.

Smash! The ball hit the hood, driving the engine out the bottom. Lottie, no seat belt on, flew through the windshield with such force that she catapulted into the caved-in gate, killed on impact.

Harry picked up the ball and swung it toward Thomas. She lowered the ball. He had little room to maneuver with Lottie plastered in front of him. The ball crashed into the passenger side of the Mercedes with a metallic splintering sound.

Diego Aybar ran to the car, pulling out a dazed and bloody Thomas.

# 53

Monday morning, Rob Collier tossed the mailbag through the front door of the post office. "Harry, way to go, girl." He held his thumbs up.

"Thanks." She sheepishly smiled.

By then most of Crozet had filtered into the post office for their mail and to talk over events.

*"I figured it out. I don't know why people are complimenting her,"* Pewter groused.

*"Yeah, yeah."* Tucker, tired from greeting everyone, sat by the table.

Miranda must have hugged and kissed Harry ten times. Every time she thought of the younger woman's quick thinking and cool head — after all, Lottie or Thomas could have shot her right out of the crane if they had kept their wits about them — Miranda had to hug and kiss her again.

A tired Coop finally rolled in at eleven. "Hey, partner." She smiled. "I think we've dotted the i's and crossed the t's."

451

"Will Thomas live?" Miranda asked, always concerned even when people were worthless.

"His face is a mess. He's full of broken bones but amazingly that's all."

"It was Lottie who opened Don's safe, wasn't it?" Harry figured that out.

Coop curled her upper lip. "Thomas blanched when I gave him a wad of bills to inspect. He's blaming everything on Lottie and she's not here to give her version of events."

"Was it drugs?" Miranda offered Coop a cup of steaming tea which she gratefully accepted.

"No. No, it wasn't. It was a lot more sophisticated than we realized. They were selling stolen cars in Uruguay. A four-year-old Mercedes sedan can bring as much as two hundred and twenty thousand dollars, a new car brings three hundred thousand. Thomas, thanks to his job, could ship stuff down there very easily."

"Cars, entire cars. Wouldn't the airlines or the shipping companies check the registration numbers?"

"That's where Roger and Dwayne came in. Roger would grind out the number on the inside of the front door and make a new plate. Who's going to check the engine number? He'd repaint the car. Rick and I thought he might be running a chop shop but this was less work and more profit thanks to Thomas. People in Uruguay and Paraguay will snap up expensive cars like candy. Thomas, of course, knew everybody, as did Lottie. It was Lottie who brought Thomas to Roger."

"I'll be, poor Roger."

"He said one time too many that he was a rich man, trying to win Lottie. The more he drank, the more he boasted. Roger was becoming a liability. She put on a big show, too big a show of disdaining him. Both she and Thomas figured Roger'd blow it somewhere soon. In time they'd find someone else to punch out new plates. Roger was dispensable. Thomas put the poison in a china sugar bowl along with a handful of raw sugar. Thomas's mother, sick, was on quinidine. We think he simply pilfered her prescription. They had a china bowl. It wasn't Aunt Tally's. He said Lottie was in charge of putting the bowl in the pantry. He picked it up. It was hidden behind plates. I don't know how she did it. He says he doesn't know but their plan was to kill Roger in front of everyone. The more people around the safer they'd be. Lottie made the coffee for Roger and she backed into Thomas as he was reaching for the bowl. It hit the floor and broke as planned. They wanted his death to appear natural. Sean's views on honoring the dead were well known."

"Bold though. They were certainly bold," Miranda acclaimed.

"What about Dwayne?"

Coop answered Harry. "He stole stickers, license-plate registrations, titles. Bill Boojum, on the Kentucky end, had someone doing the same thing at their Department of Motor Vehicles."

"He funneled stolen cars through the business?"

"Boojum, like all the big dealerships, had a body shop. What they stole from Louisville or Lexington or across the river in Indiana, they'd quickly paint over. Dwayne would drive it back and hide it in Roger's shop. Roger took care of any details left unfinished from Boojum. His drop-offs to Boojum from the Virginia end were legitimate."

"What Dwayne occasionally stole from Newport News, Richmond, and Staunton, Roger would paint, grind out registration numbers, and so forth. It was a lucrative setup and Thomas paid everyone in cold cash."

"Did Sean know?" Miranda wondered how wide their net cast.

"He swears he didn't know."

"Why didn't Sean recognize Dwayne?"

"He was out of it but I think Dwayne might have threatened him. I don't know and I'm not one hundred percent convinced that Sean didn't know more than he's letting on. If it turns out he was an accessory, well, he'll be needing a good lawyer." Coop shrugged. "It might come down to 'Am I my brother's keeper.' Maybe Sean did know and was trying to get Roger out of the business."

"Why did they kill Dwayne?" Harry asked.

"He wanted more money. He said he was taking the most risk in driving the cars and stealing them. He wanted more, a lot more. Thomas said he'd give him fifty thousand cash and arranged to meet him at the eldercare home. He had to act fast because Dwayne knew he killed Roger. That didn't take a rocket scientist to figure out. He was pushing Thomas and Lottie hard. Fifty thousand dollars was no longer enough." She mused, "I guess Dwayne wanted to move up, so to speak, in his profession. Boy just couldn't stop stealing, little things, big things. He was a born thief."

"I don't know if I would have ever figured it out," Harry thoughtfully said. "What did Don have to do with it?"

"He could repair damage to upholstery. He could change the whole color of an interior if need be but he also stole cars. The money was good — Thomas swears he didn't kill Don. He said it was Lottie. I think Don was delivering something to Lottie or Thomas — cash, fake titles, something. And before Dwayne was killed he may have been back by Durant Creek with Don. He probably stayed in the cabin back there. How he lost his Mercedes star — could have been a fight with Don. He was probably putting the screws to all of them. My hunch is once Don realized Roger was murdered he was scared shitless — a liability in crime. Dwayne wasn't scared. Thomas said he never acted scared, just greedy."

"Cooper, was all that five hundred and twenty-five thousand dollars Don's?"

"Yes. It's what he acquired over the last three years. Thomas, by the way, believes he has diplomatic immunity. He thinks he won't have to stand trial. We are pretty sure the business raked in close to four million a year."

"Does Thomas have immunity?" Miranda asked.

"Yes." Coop put her cup down. "But his government promises to prosecute him in his own country. For all I know he'll walk free."

"What a scam!" Harry shook her head.

"Lottie fell into it. She met Thomas at a party held in Washington. She'd make the rounds but that's part of her job. He sensed she was bright, cold-blooded, on the make. And she was."

"Coop, what an awful story." Miranda sighed. " 'And He said to them, "Take heed, and beware of all covetousness; for a man's life does not consist in the abundance of his possessions." ' *Luke*, Chapter Twelve, Verse Fifteen."

"I'm glad Diego wasn't in on it — was he?" Harry's voice dropped.

"We don't think he was but his career will be tarnished by it. That's the way the world works." Coop accepted a refill. "His government has already called him back to Uruguay. He'll have to testify at the trial."

"Their families are old friends. I wonder what pressures will be brought to bear on Diego?" Harry sadly said.

"You know," Coop mused, "Rick and I found the registration blanks and the title blanks. They were in Roger's files in his shop. We went over those files, so they had to have been moved there after we combed the shop. Funny thing, a monster rat, absolutely unafraid, watched us."

*"Bet we know what he called them,"* Tucker laughed.

"Oh, Harry, I've got something for you." Coop walked out the back door, returning with the pileated woodpecker, which she placed on the table. "Released from jail."

"Isn't he beautiful." Harry admired Don's work.

"And so big." Miranda had never seen a woodpecker up this close. "I'd stay on the good side of him."

*"I can't wait until she takes him home. I am going to shred him. It's my woodpecker. Feathers everywhere,"* Pewter promised.

*"You wouldn't."* Mrs. Murphy tilted up her head.

*"Just wait and see."* The gray cat puffed out her chest, laughing.

Dear Reader,

My big news is I've found three fox dens, two reds and one gray. I watch from a distance. Foxes and cats are natural enemies since we compete for the same game. However, there are enough field mice this year to keep us all busy.

Oh, I've seen more hawks, falcons, and raptors than I can ever remember. And green herons as well as the big blues. Birds make me cackle, I can't help it.

Thank you again for the photographs you send me. Even horses send their photos.

It's been a good time on the farm. The hay crop was really good. Next year comes the timber harvest, all things being equal. Mom still can't afford to build a new bridge but she did patch up the old one. John Morris and Robert Steppe used the big tractor and did a pretty darn good job with Dana Flaherty directing all. Really fixing the bridge is about a $15,000 task but we all did our patch job for $1,700 worth of stone.

Part of the roof blew off in high winds. That hurt. Poor Mom. She was able to fix up the roof but she still doesn't have the money to repair the inside of the house and it does look pretty awful.

But we all have each other. We're all healthy. The fences are strong. The cattle are fat and the horses are so happy, they're silly.

Farming is a hard life if your goal is to be wealthy but I agree with Mom and Harry, it's the only life for us. When the sun rises and the Blue Ridge Mountains turn scarlet, the roosters wake up, the horses, too, and I can smell the earth, oh, I tell you, this is as close to paradise as a kitty can get. Sometimes, I climb into the big wisteria twining on the front entranceway to the house. The leaves flutter over my head, the praying mantises are everywhere, birds dart in, and sometimes they don't even know I'm there! It's the best of the best and I hope you are having half as much fun in this life as I am.

Yours in catitude,

Sneaky Pie
www.ritamaebrown.com

APPLE OF MY EYE

Library of Congress Cataloging-in-Publication Data
Hanff, Helene.
Apple of my eye / Helene Hanff.
p.   cm.
Reprint.
Originally published: London: Deutsch, 1977.
Includes index.
ISBN 0-918825-73-3 (pb) 0-918825-88-1 (cl)
1. Hanff, Helene—Homes and haunts—New York (N.Y.)
2. Authors, American—20th century—Biography.
3. New York (N.Y.)—Description—1951-1980.
I. Title.
PS3515.A4853Z462    1988
917.47′1′044—dc19
88-11998
CIP

Printed in the United States of America

DESIGN AND COMPOSITION BY THE SARABANDE PRESS

When New York City went bankrupt (became poor?), its Department of Civic Affairs and Public Events was closed down, and all the duties formerly shared by several executives devolved upon one small Assistant to the Mayor, still in her thirties, named Arlene Wolff.

Arlene creates mammoth street fairs and city-wide holiday celebrations at almost no cost to the city. She does it by commandeering the services of New York's business community, hotels, airlines and public relations firms, and the Police, Fire, Sanitation and Parks Departments, and galvanizing all of them into a work force to brighten the lives of New Yorkers all year round.

She does this in addition to her routine duties of planning and managing all official entertainments and receptions for distinguished visitors, given by the Mayor at Gracie Mansion, and arranging all citations and awards given by the city to individuals and organizations.

Her awesome talents in the performance of these duties and her selfless devotion to the City of New York, are equaled only by her talent for selfless and devoted friendship.

This book is for her.

TO ARLENE FROM HELENE. WITH LOVE.

Christmas 1976.

This book about New York was written in 1976 and therefore mentions conditions (bankruptcy), places (Gimbel's and Brentano's) and one amenity (the Culture Bus) which no longer exist; and it omits all the new sights which have sprung up during the past decade. I've tried to correct both these problems in a postscript chapter labeled simply "P.S." And I've added an index and a few maps that were crucially missed by readers of the original edition.

However, there was one additional omission which caused foreign visitors acute distress and I hasten to include that item before we go any further:

### "WHERE'S THE T—L-T?"

Unlike European capitals, New York has no public toilets indicated by signs on its main avenues and streets. This discovery causes foreign visitors distress enough.

But there's a related problem which makes their plight more difficult, which I was made aware of by Miss Jean Marsh, coauthor and star of the famous English TV series, "Upstairs, Downstairs," who told the following story at a party at which I was present.

Just before she was to make her first trip to the U.S. to do a promotional tour for PBS, Miss Marsh was briefed on one prissy American peculiarity by a London authority on American manners and customs.

"It is very bad form in the States," she was told, "to use the

word 'toilet.' We've made a list of the euphemisms Americans use instead." And Miss Marsh memorized the list: Ladies Room, Powder Room, Rest Room, Lounge. Thus armed, Miss Marsh left for New York.

She was met at the airport by a PBS official who drove her to the TV production center of its Channel Thirteen studio in Manhattan. They arrived at the back door which opened directly into a floor-to-ceiling forest of wires and cables. Never having seen this bewildering technical side of television before, Miss Marsh was staring at it when a little man hurried around the edge of the forest, introduced himself and welcomed her to Channel 13. Then he said:

"Before I take you on a tour of the studio, would you like to use the facilities?"

And Jean Marsh said:

"Oh no, I'm not mechanical at all, I'd be afraid to touch anything!"

"Use-the-facilities" was so far-fetched a euphemism for "toilet," her mentors in England had never heard it.

(I explained to her where the phrase came from. Back in the 1880's or '90's, the owner of a new luxury New York hotel advertised it as the first hotel equipped with "indoor sanitary facilities." Other new hotels across the country followed his lead, and we've all been using-the-facilities ever since.)

WHERE DO YOU FIND THE LADIES ROOM, POWDER ROOM, REST ROOM, LOUNGE, MEN'S ROOM, GENTLEMEN, GENTS? (Alan, my neighbor up the hall, says that in the better hotels and restaurants, the men's room is identified merely by a male silhouette.)

You'll find one of the above euphemisms listed on the Floor

Directory of every Fifth Avenue department store—and at Macy's and Bloomingdale's, of course. It's likely to be on the floor plan and on wall signs, in every museum. Hotel lobbies rarely have signs posted, but if you walk through the lobby with your eyes open in all directions, you're sure to see the door you're looking for, with the appropriate sign on it.

Churches will always take pity on you in an emergency. Restaurants will not unless you're lunching or dining there. But you can always walk into a coffee shop, order coffee and *then* ask for "the washroom." And if you stumble on a branch of the New York Public Library—and you're likely to be near three midtown branches, one at 41st and Fifth Avenue, one on 53rd between Fifth and Sixth Avenues, and the Music and Drama branch which is part of Lincoln Center—you know the day is saved.

# PROLOGUE

On April Fool's day, I came home from a meeting with a publisher, hurried through my apartment-house lobby and told all the tenants waiting at the elevator:

"I've got the dream assignment of all time! I'm going to write copy for a book of photographs of New York City!"

Everybody congratulated me. Riding up in the elevator everybody assured me that a book of photographs with copy by a knowledgeable New Yorker like me would help to counteract the city's unfortunate image.

As soon as I had my coat off, I phoned all my friends and told them the news.

"If I'm an expert on nothing else," I said, "I'm an expert on New York, New York!"

Everybody agreed.

Confining the book to "New York, New York" ("So nice they named it twice," it says on T-shirts all over town this season) meant I wouldn't have to do research on Brooklyn or Queens, both of which are out on Long Island, or on the Bronx, which is up on the New York state mainland, or on Staten Island which is off the coast of New Jersey. All I was going to have to worry about was the original City of New York on Manhattan island, where I've lived all my adult life and which, as I told my best friend on the phone, I know like the back of my hand.

That was on Thursday. On Friday, I hurried round to my local branch of the New York Public Library and brought

home three books about New York. They were old books but I thought they'd give me the facts and figures I ought to have. I got paper and pencil, carried all three books to the desk, opened all three to page one and began dipping into all three at once.

Each book had a list of Must See sights and I began copying out those that had made all three lists:

> The Statue of Liberty
> Wall Street and the Stock Exchange
> Times Square
> Empire State Building
> Rockefeller Center
> United Nations
> The Cloisters
> Grant's Tomb

Grant's Tomb?

I put the pencil down, closed the books and stared at the list. I'd never been to the Statue of Liberty. I'd never been to Wall Street or the Stock Exchange. I'd been to Times Square, and while it's admittedly a sight it's not the kind you put on anybody's Must See list.

I'd been to the top of the Empire State building, but the Empire State building was no longer the world's or the city's tallest building and it no longer had the best view of the New York skyline. It had been superseded by the 110-story World Trade Center, and I'd never been to the World Trade Center.

I'd been in and out of certain Rockefeller Plaza buildings several hundred times, but I'd never taken a tour of the entire

Center. And while I had been to the Cloisters once, years ago, I had only a hazy memory of it.

If I have to add this, I'd never been to Grant's Tomb.

I stewed over this for a few hours. Then I remembered that Patsy Gibbs was coming to lunch on Monday, and with great relief I put the whole problem out of my mind till then. Patsy Gibbs was not only a native New Yorker, she was a Radcliffe graduate married to a Harvard graduate and their son and daughter were both currently Harvard students. Nobody else I knew combined a native's knowledge of New York with access to two generations of Harvard brains.

Patsy and I had met and become friends back in the early sixties as members of the same neighborhood Democratic club. Then she had moved to the West Side and in recent years we'd seen each other very rarely. I considered it providential that we'd run into each other on Fifth Avenue the week before and had made a lunch date for Monday.

Patsy arrived promptly at one. (She's generally called "Pat" but to me, the name "Pat" suggests somebody tall, cool and unruffled. Patsy Gibbs is small, excitable and enthusiastic, with a face that registers emotions like a silent movie heroine and I've always called her Patsy.)

"Listen, I need your help," I said as I took her coat. "I'm writing copy for a book of photos of New York and I've just discovered I've never been to any of the tourist attractions! Would you believe I'm going to have to take a boat to the Statue of Liberty next week?"

I was about to ask her what I ought to know about the Statue when the look on her face stopped me. Patsy was staring at me with intense, imploring eagerness.

"Can I come with you?" she pleaded. "I've never been there!"

"You've never been to the Statue of Liberty?" I demanded. "But you were born here!"

"My parents took me when I was five but I don't really remember it," said Patsy. "And when my kids were old enough, they went with their grandparents so I never got to go!" And again with that beseeching look: "Can I come with you? Would you mind?"

I did not ask her whether she had an equal craving to tour the New York Stock Exchange or stand on the 110th Floor Outdoor Observation Platform of the World Trade Center, and I did not ask how she felt about Grant's Tomb.

"Of course you can come with me, Patsy," I said kindly.

"I keep telling you it's Pat!" she said impatiently. "Patsy doesn't suit me!"

Believe me, it was about to.

APPLE OF MY EYE

# Friday, April 9

PRIDE GOETH.

During the rest of that week, I copied information industriously out of the library books. At the end of the week I knew how long the Statue of Liberty's right arm was, how many tons the George Washington Bridge's cables weighed and how many acres of floor space were occupied by the American Museum of Natural History.

I also had a page of earnest *Instructions for Tourists*. (1. Stop at the nearest bank or subway station and buy bus-and-subway tokens. 2. Stop at the Convention & Visitors' Bureau for sightseeing brochures and maps.) And I had made a tentative list of sights to see and trips to take. On the night before our scheduled trip to the Statue of Liberty, I was feeling in complete command of the entire project, and studying the Yellow Pages, when Patsy phoned.

"We have to take different subways down there!" she said in a panicky voice. "We've never been around Battery Park! How are we going to find each other?"

"We're not going by subway," I said. "I've drawn up a list of *Instructions for Tourists* and Item 3 on the list is: 'Don't take subways, take buses.' You can't see New York from a subway window. So I thought we'd take a regular Sightseeing Bus down to Lower Manhattan, to see what it's like, and then get off the bus at Battery Park and go out to the Statue."

"Oh, great!" said Patsy enthusiastically. "I've always wanted to take a Sightseeing Bus. Where do we get it?"

"Well, I'm looking at the ads in the Yellow Pages," I said. And Patsy said: "Wait, I'll get the phone book." When she came back, I said: "Page 1671," and we studied the bus company ads.

"The Port Authority has the biggest ad," said Patsy. "You want to take that one?"

"The Port Authority Bus Terminal," I said, "runs from Eighth Avenue to Ninth, they don't have signs to tell you which way is Eighth and which is Ninth, and there are always thousands of people streaming in and out of both entrances and up and down the escalators. You and I are both small, I'm nearsighted, we both panic easily and we'd never find each other."

We settled on a smaller bus company in the west Forties and arranged to meet on the sidewalk in front of the bus office at nine-thirty a.m. for the ten o'clock tour of Lower Manhattan.

We met on time. (I got off the Fifth Avenue bus and ran half a block to the bus office and was just in time to see Patsy running half a block from Sixth Avenue; it turned out we're both fanatically prompt.) We bought our tickets and then went up the block to a drug store, climbed on counter stools and ordered coffee. I took out of my shoulder bag the large Composition book I'd bought for note-taking and showed Patsy my collection of Facts-and-Figures.

Patsy looked impressed as she read them.

"This is going to be a very heavy tourist guide," she said a little nervously.

"Well, I want to do it right," I said complacently. At which moment a fat woman in a fur coat sitting on the counter stool next to me turned to us and demanded:

"Where's Cartier's?"

I stared at her blankly. I don't live a Cartier life.

"It's on Fifth Avenue," Patsy told her.

"Yes, I know that, dear," said the fat woman. "Where on Fifth?" No answer. Patsy doesn't live a Cartier life either.

"Have you ever been to Tiffany's?" I said. "It's a beautiful store, it's—"

"Tiffany's is on the south-east corner of Fifty-Seventh and Fifth," said Patsy. "It's a very famous—"

"No dear. Cartier's," said the fat lady firmly. "Never mind, I'll find it."

We walked back to the bus depot in subdued silence. Ten or twelve tourists were boarding the bus and we filed in after them. The bus had a heavy roof, narrow windows and poor visibility. We took seats in the back and the bus moved out of the dingy side street and rolled down a West Side avenue past more dingy West Forties streets. I stared out of the dirty window, very tense.

"Why does he have to drive through the dreariest streets in New York?" I said to Patsy. "Why can't he go down Fifth?"

"This is a two-hour bus trip and you're not allowed to smoke and there's no john," said Patsy morosely. "Write that down, it's the kind of information people need."

The bus rolled down into the garment district and the guide called everybody's attention to the fur trolleys and heavy racks of dresses being pushed along the sidewalk. I went on fuming. The garment district wasn't pretty. Anything that wasn't pretty I didn't want visitors to see.

At Thirty-Fourth Street the bus turned east, and as we came to Fifth Avenue the guide announced dramatically:

"Straight ahead, on your right, folks, is the Empire State building!"

And everybody looked out the right-hand windows and saw the restaurant on the ground floor of the Empire State building. What else can you see out of a narrow window on a solidly roofed bus?

Patsy slid way down in her seat and twisted sideways and peered up through the dirty window.

"Lie down," she advised the other passengers. "If you lie down and look up sideways you can almost see the top."

"They ought to open these windows so people can lean out and look up," I said loudly. "In New York, you have to remember to look Up."

The bus proceeded down the only dull stretch of Fifth Avenue and then turned east again and the guide announced joyfully:

"We're coming to the Bowery, folks! New York's Skid Row! Watch out your windows for the Bowery bums. Sometimes you can see 'em layin' right in the gutter sleepin' it off!"

This galvanized the passengers. They half rose out of their seats and pressed their noses to the windows. As the bus moved slowly along the Bowery, a wide avenue lined with missions, some of the passengers ran across the aisle to peer out the opposite windows in the hope of seeing bums in the gutter.

"Bowery bums are a big draw!" Patsy murmured in surprise. As luck would have it, there were only two or three bums out that morning and they were standing up.

The bus made its first stop in Chinatown and we all got out and filed into a Buddhist temple and then into an adjoining

curio shop, full of the usual cheap souvenirs-of-New-York and some fine jade jewelry. Then we came out and stood on the sidewalk for a few minutes, looking up and down Pell Street at the huge Chinese signs that hung from upper-story tenement windows and dwarfed the Chinese vegetable markets and restaurants huddled below them. After this we were herded back in the bus, which rolled on down toward Lower Manhattan.

On the way, we passed a huge construction site with a giant sign above it reading CONFUCIUS PLAZA; and Patsy and I were so absorbed in speculating about this that we didn't notice much else along the way. As the bus careened down along the eastern edge of Lower Manhattan to the bottom of the island, Patsy said uncertainly:

"Do you get the feeling we're missing something?"

"I get the feeling we're missing everything," I said. "This is no way to see New York."

At Battery Park, the passengers were invited to leave the bus again and walk along the river's edge for a few minutes. As I stepped down from the bus, Patsy, ahead of me, spotted a ticket booth with a sign reading: Liberty Island Ferry. Statue of Liberty.

"Come on!" she called, and we raced for the ticket booth and bought the last two tickets for a boat which was just about to pull away from shore. Clambering aboard it, we felt as if we'd been let out of school.

We made our way to the far rail of the ferry and hung over the edge, staring out at the statue. Liberty stood with her back to us.

"I should have known that," I said. "She's facing the

immigrant ships that sailed in from Europe, she's holding the torch up for them, not for us. She can afford to turn her back on us; we have it made."

"Look back!" said Patsy sharply. And I turned and looked back at the Lower Manhattan skyline. DO NOT DO THIS. You'll have plenty of time to stare at the skyline on your return trip. On your way out to the statue you have to keep your eyes on her; you'll have only one chance, as the ferry rounds Liberty island, to see her face, the torch in her hand, the Declaration of Independence in the crook of her left arm and the broken shackles at her right foot. And just once, you have to see her, face to face. Not because she's a work of art; for all I know, she isn't. You have to see her face because if you're an American, she's the symbol of what you're supposed to be. Looking at her, I had a sudden memory of Franklin Roosevelt beginning a formal address to a convention of the D.A.R. with: "My fellow-immigrants."

Across the water from Liberty island we could see the abandoned, ruined buildings of Ellis Island which the Federal government closed down years ago. Looking from those buildings to the statue, I felt a fierce pride that my city was still making room for the "huddled masses" nobody else wanted, even when it went bankrupt caring for them.

The ferry guide told us the boat would be back to pick us up in an hour and a quarter, and Patsy said: "What are we going to do with that much time?"

Neither of us knew, till we saw it, that inside the pedestal of the statue there's a remarkable Immigration Museum.

The exhibits include photographs of the tense, hopeful faces of immigrants peering out at us from under their Old Country shawls, and photographs of the involuntary, hopeless

immigrants chained together in the holds of slave ships, staring at us with bewildered eyes.

There's a room containing twelve talking statues, mostly of Revolutionary War heroes, each of whom describes his contribution to his adopted country in English heavily accented by his native France, Poland, Germany, Scotland or Ireland.

Patsy charged up to every statue, listened to its recital and then charged back to me like a gnat:

"Did you hear that? Write that down! Did you hear the ones on this side? Are you writing down what each one did?"

I used to write American history books for children, so I said with annoyance:

"I don't need to write everything down! I know who James Wilson and L'Enfant were!"

"You do?" said Patsy, round-eyed. "I never heard of most of these people!"

So much for Harvard, I thought smugly.

I pointed to the statue of one Tadeusz Kosciuszko and said graciously:

"I will tell you about him, because every New Yorker knows his name. More or less."

"I don't," said Patsy meekly. "How do you pronounce it?"

"Koshoosko," I said. "He was a Polish engineer, he came over here to fight for the American cause and General Washington put him in charge of building West Point. Now: have you ever listened to a New York City traffic report in the morning? Have you ever heard the New York City Police Department give you the traffic conditions on the Kosky-Osko bridge?"

"Sure," said Patsy.

"Well," I said, "the Kosky-Osko bridge was named for

Kosciuszko, the Polish engineer who built West Point. Kosky-Osko is the closest a New York cop can get to Koshoosko."

"How do you know all that?" Patsy marveled. I could have answered honestly: "We had a Polish super in our building who told me how to pronounce it," but I didn't, I just glanced around to see whether any other tourists were impressed by my story—and that's how I discovered we were the only two tourists left in the museum. We bolted out of there and had to run the length of the island at top speed to catch the ferry which was just about to pull away without us.

"You didn't take the elevator to the top and stand under the statue's face," said Patsy, when we'd caught our breath. "You should have done that for the tourists."

"Why didn't you tell me?" I demanded. "What do I have you along for?"

"I mentioned it," said Patsy. "You didn't hear me and I wasn't going to repeat it. My only childhood memory of the statue is of standing on that outdoor platform, three hundred and five feet above sea level, terrified out of my mind. I'm afraid of heights."

We were hanging over the rail staring at the Lower Manhattan skyline at the time. And since the skyline is dominated by the twin towers of the World Trade Center, I realized I had a problem. I'd read somewhere that the World Trade Center's 110th floor Observation Deck is a quarter of a mile above the ground, and sooner or later I was going to have to get Patsy up there. It's an absolute Must for tourists, and I certainly wasn't going up there alone; I'm afraid of heights myself.

The ferry deposited us at the dock alongside Battery Park and we looked around for a restaurant. We didn't see any.

Lower Manhattan, just ahead of us across an intersection, was full of restaurants but we didn't know where to find them.

"Where's Sloppy Louie's?" I asked Patsy. "Isn't that around the docks somewhere?"

"I think it's further up," said Patsy vaguely. If we'd had a map, we'd have seen that we were only a few blocks from Fraunces Tavern, which was not only a restaurant but one of the tourist sights on my list. But we didn't have a map. (Why would we have a map? We lived here.) We had lunch at the only place we could find, which was a dirty, dockside cafeteria.

"You'd think there'd be a downtown restaurant mentioned somewhere in that four pounds of information you copied out," said Patsy, as we slurped lukewarm instant coffee out of paper cups.

"There was," I said. "Fraunces Tavern, but I don't know where it is."

"Has that reopened since the Cubans bombed it?" Patsy asked.

"I thought it was Puerto Rican nationalists," I said. "I don't know whether it's open or not, I'll check it out."

After lunch we toured Battery Park, a broad green strip along the bay at the tip of the island and one of the places guaranteed to bring out the historian in me.

"President Washington," I told Patsy—though I knew from experience that the minute you start a sentence with "President Washington" everybody stops listening—"used to stroll here on summer evenings with his wife and the members of his Cabinet and their wives, back in 1789 when New York was the nation's capital."

By this time, Patsy wasn't even within earshot. There are

memorial stones in Battery Park, honoring immigrants who died in their adopted country's wars, and Patsy was darting from stone to stone, rapping out: "Who's on this slab? Did you write him down? Who's on that slab over there? Did you read this one? Write it down. You're not writing anything down!"

"What do I want with every name on every stone?" I demanded.

"Well, I just think you're being very haphazard about this!" said Patsy. "Somewhere in this book you'd better write: *Everything in this book is half-accurate.*"

It was mid-afternoon when we finally left the park, crossed the broad intersection and walked up into Lower Manhattan to look for a subway to take us home. But except for occasional jury duty—when you take a subway down to your designated courthouse, spend the day indoors and take the subway home—neither of us had ever really been to Lower Manhattan. Now, as tourists, we were seeing it for the first time and it struck us full in the face.

Lower Manhattan, which contained the original City of New York (and before that, the city of New Amsterdam) was once a town of small, upright houses on narrow, curving streets. The houses are long gone but the narrow, curving streets are still there, transformed into toy canyons by the row on row of jutting skyscrapers along them. And on every narrow street and alley, early skyscrapers have been joined by newer and higher ones, so that glass, steel and chrome towers rise above and behind the stone skyscrapers of the fifties, which themselves rise above the brick buildings of the twenties. The result is so dramatic that as we walked, Patsy would clutch my arm every few minutes and say: "Look up there!"

And I'd look up and see three skyscrapers rising in a single

vertical line, each built a generation later than the one below it, all three in wholly unrelated architectural styles, yet the three together somehow forming a single, harmonious composition.

We didn't notice what streets we were wandering along or what ones we passed; we just walked, open-mouthed, gawking upward. We did stop once. We came to a huge, heavy new building and stopped to stare at it, impressed, because etched in the stone was the name ONE WUI PLAZA.

"The Chinese are really booming!" said Patsy. "One Wui Plaza is finished and Confucius Plaza is going up. Write that down."

I was writing it down when I happened to notice, above the name of the building, the zigzag symbol used to denote electricity.

"Let me ask you something," I said. "Is Western Union an international company?"

(One Wui Plaza did a lot for my morale later on. It kept me from feeling guilty when I didn't write something down every single time Patsy ordered me to.)

We stopped at a Chock Full O' Nuts and climbed on stools and ordered coffee and Patsy ordered a doughnut. We were sipping our coffee peacefully when Patsy said:

"Were we on Wall Street?"

The question filled me with mild hysteria which I hoped I kept out of my voice.

"Of course we were on Wall Street!" I said. "It was that canyon!"

"They're all canyons," said Patsy absently, chewing her doughnut. She broke off a corner of it and handed it to me. "Taste that."

I tasted it.

"Ambrosia," I said.

"So's their coffee," said Patsy. "Write it down." I looked at her and she said: "I'm serious! All tourists aren't rich. They'll see Chock Full O' Nuts places all over town; they should know you get great coffee and doughnuts there, and good sandwiches, and the service is quick and the places are always clean."

"I'll use it." I said, "I just hope it doesn't go to their head."

We found a subway we could both take as far as Grand Central, and as we went down the steps, Patsy said:

"You'll have to come down here again; we didn't see anything."

"Of course I'm coming down again!" I said as we put tokens in the turnstile and joined the people on the platform. "I have to do Wall Street, I have to do Fraunces Tavern—and I certainly have to go to the top of the World Trade Center! That's the one Must in a *new* tourist book about New York!"

Patsy studied the subway floor.

"I'm afraid of heights," she said.

"So am I," I said.

"No, I mean really afraid," said Patsy. "It's a phobia."

"I'm just as afraid as you are. Don't give yourself airs," I said. Then it occurred to me that she didn't have to go there with me if she didn't want to, and I added hastily: "I probably won't get to it for a while. There are so many other places I have to see."

"Where are you going next?" Patsy asked.

I had no order of preference, and I was so anxious not to press the World Trade Center that I fled clear to the other end of the island.

"The Cloisters," I said.

"Oh, I haven't been up there in years, I used to love that place!" said Patsy.

"I thought I'd go next Thursday," I said casually.

Patsy looked stricken.

"I can't make it, Thursday," she said.

The subway screeched into the station and there was no way I could shout "How about Friday?" without seeming pushy. We squeezed into a subway car and rode to Grand Central without trying to talk. As she left me to change to a West Side subway, Patsy mouthed "I'll call you." During the rest of the ride home, I looked over my notes and discovered I'd taken no notes at all on Lower Manhattan. That discovery marked the beginning of a very moody weekend.

On Friday night at two in the morning I got out of bed to look up Cartier's in the phone book. (It's at Fifty-Second and Fifth.) On Saturday, as I cleaned the apartment, I seesawed between deep gloom and high panic. Instead of being in command of a large project with an admiring Patsy at my side, I saw myself taking solitary trips to places I knew nothing about and—if Lower Manhattan was any criterion—wouldn't know anything about after I'd seen them.

On Sunday, I tried to bury myself in the *Sunday Times* as usual. But it's the *New York Sunday Times,* and everything I read pointed an accusing finger at some New York sight I'd forgotten to include in my plans. On Sunday night came the climax. I went to sleep and dreamed I was in the publisher's office. My finished manuscript lay on the desk between us as the publisher, with a sorrowful look, handed me a large, beautifully bound volume, its title in gleaming gold letters reading: BROOKLYN BOTANICAL GARDENS.

On Monday morning, I got out the 1975 World Atlas and just in case my editor should ask why I hadn't researched all five boroughs, worked out the following reply:

Brooklyn has a larger population than the entire state of Kansas, or the state of Oklahoma.

Queens has more people than the twin cities of Minneapolis/St. Paul combined.

The Bronx contains more people than the cities of Cleveland and Boston combined.

Staten Island has almost as large a population as the city of Birmingham.

That leaves New York, New York, the city jazz musicians first dubbed "the Big Apple," situated on a strip of island twelve miles long by less than two miles wide at its widest, which contains more people than live in greater Seattle with all its suburbs included, and that's enough territory for one book to cover.

Over lunch I calmed down. I reminded myself that I'd been hired to write copy for photographs which somebody was collecting for me and would eventually send me. The Cloisters was way up at 186th Street, and I had no guarantee the book would include a photograph of it. (I was prejudiced against the Cloisters anyway.) I decided to postpone the trip, and all other sightseeing trips, till the photos came; and after lunch I fled thankfully back to the safe haven of my library books.

At five o'clock, Patsy phoned:

"Hi," she said. "Listen, I changed my dentist date, I can go, Thursday. Where do you want me to meet you?"

# Thursday, April 15

PATSY CAME EAST, I WALKED NORTH AND WE MET ON THE corner of Seventy-Ninth and Madison for coffee before taking a Madison Avenue bus up to the Cloisters.* It was a sunny April morning and we ordered coffee-to-go and carried our containers over to Fifth, to the Seventy-Ninth Street park entrance. We sat on one of the benches beside the lawn that rolls up to Dog Hill. We were therefore sitting with our backs to the Metropolitan Museum of Art, which is the only way I will ever consent to sit.

The Metropolitan Museum of Art is one of the world's great museums. It is also a sprawling, ugly pile of grey stone, which you won't realize when you go there because you'll enter through the front doors on Fifth Avenue, and the museum's Fifth Avenue façade is impressive. It extends from Eighty-First to Eighty-Fifth Street and is New York's answer to Trafalgar Square: on any fine day, you'll see fifty or sixty people sunning themselves on the broad front steps. Flanking the steps are fountains, and at night when the façade and the fountains are illuminated, the museum looks seductively beautiful.

The Metropolitan Museum has great European and American collections, great Egyptian collections, Greek and Roman collections, medieval collections and Far and Near East collec-

*The Metropolitan Museum now runs a mini-bus to the Cloisters. Telephone for rates and times.

*17*

tions. It has a concert hall, courtyard cafeteria on the ground floor and a private parking lot. All of this occupies thirty-seven acres, and I don't know how many additional acres the museum will occupy when its two new buildings, one to the north of the main building and one to the south, are completed.* What I do know is that all of its acres were torn out of Central Park, which does not belong to the Metropolitan Museum of Art, it belongs to me. Me and a million other New Yorkers for whom life in New York would be unthinkable without it.

Wherefore, when Patsy glanced over her shoulder at the museum, barely visible behind the ugly wall around its huge construction site, and asked: "Have you been in the Lehman Wing?" I said: "I have not. I spent a solid year watching the museum's bulldozers and derricks trample down old trees and rip huge, gaping holes in one of the loveliest park stretches to put that wing up. Now I'm watching a newer and bigger demolition starting all over again."

"Do you ever go to concerts in the Grace Rainey Rogers?" Patsy said. "It's a perfect size for chamber music, I love that hall. And I love the Islamic collections. And the costume exhibits. I guess I love a lot of it."

"Most people do. So would I, if it had a heart," I said. "Will you tell me why, in this skyscraper city, a three-story museum can't build *Up?* Why does it always have to build on the ground, destroying more and more of Central Park?"

"The Cloisters," said Patsy neutrally, "is part of the Metropolitan Museum."

"I know it is," I said. "And I consider it very broad-minded

*See pp. 165-7, P.S.6.

of me to be going on a day's outing just to visit it."

We went back to Madison and got on a Number 4 bus and looked out the windows at the shops. Madison Avenue is an incredible street; there's nothing you can't buy on it, from designer clothes to housewares, from pastry to paintings. The most expensive stores are in the Sixties and Seventies, but there are shop windows to look at out of a bus window all the way up through the Nineties.

It wasn't till the bus crawled up through the early hundreds that I said to Patsy:

"I don't work on weekends—Saturdays I clean and Sundays I lie down—but I should've made an exception for the Cloisters. The Culture Bus would have got us up there much quicker."

"Does it go up as far as the Cloisters?" asked Patsy. "Wait a minute!" And she darted down to the front of the bus and spoke to the driver, and came back with the Culture Bus Loop I folder in her hand. She was right: the Culture Bus doesn't go uptown as far as the Cloisters. But it will take you everywhere else mentioned in this book, and it's the greatest New York invention since the Mets.*

At 110th Street, the bus turned west along the northern boundary of Central Park and as it turned north up Riverside Drive, Patsy got galvanized and started rapping out sights for me to write down.

"Hundred-and-Twelfth Street! If they sit on the right, and look over that way, they can see the spires of the Cathedral of St. John the Divine . . . Hundred-and-Fifteenth! Columbia University. Well, you can't see much of it from here but put it

*See Foreword.

19

down anyway . . . Hundred-and-Twenty-Fifth! Riverside Church. No, wait. Tell them to look out the back window till the bus gets to . . . to . . . One-Twenty-Eighth. If they look out the back window at a Hundred and Twenty-Eighth, they can see the Riverside Church bell tower."

I didn't say anything. The Columbia-Riverside-St. John's-Grant's Tomb area was a separate day's outing and I had no intention of going on that dreary safari by myself.

The bus rolled on up into Washington Heights and Patsy said:

"Hundred-and-Seventy-Ninth! George Washington Bridge!"

"Listen, I'm supposed to make a big thing out of that bridge, it's a Top Ten Sight," I said. "It's beautiful at night, but what else can you say about the George Washington Bridge?"

"It gets you home from Jersey," said Patsy.

An hour and a half after it had left Seventy-Ninth Street the bus turned in at a parking lot at the foot of the Cloisters. We stepped out and had to crane our necks to look up at the rambling stone structure. The museum is set on a high eminence overlooking the Hudson, and from the bus parking lot it is only reached by several flights of high, steep stone steps. We were halfway up them when Patsy suddenly said: "I'll be right back," and shot back down the steps and disappeared. I went on climbing and waited for her at the top. Standing there, looking through the entrance to an ancient monastery, it occurred to me that the Cloisters would be preposterous anywhere in the world but in a country as new as my own.

Financed in the nineteen thirties by John D. Rockefeller,

Jr., the museum contains a thirteenth century cloister from an abbey in the south of France; a chapter house from a twelfth century abbey in Gascony; a reconstructed twelfth century cloister from the eastern Pyrenees; a thirteenth century Gothic portal from Burgundy and stonework from a twelfth century church in south-western France. All of these sections and fragments of ancient buildings were pulled down, stone by stone, shipped across the Atlantic, reassembled and reconstructed and set on a high hill in New York, New York. To Europeans watching the dismantling of ruined abbeys and chapter houses, it must have seemed a Mad Scientist project only an American billionaire would finance.

But no European can imagine being born in a country which was a wilderness three hundred years ago, in which a building seven hundred years old is literally unimaginable. John D., Jr. knew that millions of Americans had no hope of seeing Europe, but might manage to see New York. Since his countrymen couldn't travel abroad to see medieval architecture, he brought medieval architecture to them.

Patsy came running back up the fifty or sixty stone steps and when she had caught her breath, said:

"I talked to a guard. People driving up don't have to worry about the steps. There's a ramp for cars that goes up to the Cloisters. Anybody coming by bus who can't climb steps should call in advance, and somebody here will meet them and take them up in an elevator."

We went through the entrance hall and up to a desk where a woman sat behind a pile of folders. Next to the pile of folders was a sign. Patsy and I stared at that sign.

Most New York museums these days are reduced, by inflation and rising costs, to asking a small admission fee or

voluntary contribution. The Cloisters, like the Met, is listed in the Convention & Visitors' Guide as requesting a voluntary contribution. "Pay what you wish," says the Visitors' Guide. But what the sign on the desk said was: Suggested Contribution: $1.75.

Patsy was shocked.

"That's too much!" she said. "Suppose a tourist family comes up here? Say a man drives up with his wife and three kids and maybe the kids' grandmother. He could get all the way up here thinking it's a free museum and then get cleaned out of ten or twelve bucks! For the smallest museum in town."

I was too angry to answer. I took out two one-dollar bills and laid them down on the desk. The woman behind the desk looked at them, and then coldly at me, and then coldly at Patsy.

"Is this for *both* of you?" she asked.

"It is," I said, stonily refusing to let her intimidate me. But I live here and I hate the Metropolitan Museum with a passion and she couldn't intimidate me. She could intimidate you. DON'T LET HER. The Cloisters is a free museum. If you want to make a contribution, it will help the museum to stay open. But remind yourself that your contribution is voluntary. If the woman at the desk forgets that, remind her.

The dark monastic interiors calmed us down. The chapels are starkly bare, their ancient stone walls, altars and tables unornamented except for a few sculptured figures of saints, and high, narrow stained-glass windows. On a few of the walls were medieval French and Flemish tapestries borrowed from the museum's Tapestry Room. The arched doorways of the chapels led out into the cloister gardens and the airy grace of the gardens accentuated the austerity within.

There was one exhibit which rather haunted me. Referred to in the official booklet only once, by the unamplified word "reliquaries," there stood on display on the bare floor of one chapel several ancient stone coffins. Each coffin bore on its lid a full-length effigy of the man or woman buried in it. One, for instance, bore the effigy of a young woman identified as:

MARGUERITE

d. 1277

daughter of Robert

Second Baron of Neuberg

Normandy

She was probably laid to rest in a monastery near her father's estates. And you suddenly think how bizarre it is that seven hundred years later, she should have been uprooted and transported thousands of miles to a continent she never knew existed, to be put on public display in a city and civilization she could never have imagined. I'm very grateful to John D. Rockefeller, Jr. But is she?

It was one-thirty when we finally left the main building to look for the cafeteria Patsy remembered was somewhere on the grounds. We asked a guard for directions and he said:

"Just walk down that way about a quarter of a mile. You can't miss it."

And he pointed the way. But he was pointing to two parallel paths. The inner path, next to the Cloisters, was crowded with tourists, so we took the empty, outer path nearer the river. (The inner path was crowded because it led to the cafeteria; but that was the kind of horse-sense conclusion

neither of us in all our travels ever managed to reach, let alone jump to.)

People tend to think of this island as being level ground. It is not. In New York, "downtown" and "uptown" are literal words, and if you're a walker you're well advised to remember that "downtown" is downhill and "uptown" is uphill. You won't notice this in midtown Manhattan where the incline is very gradual. In uptown Manhattan, the incline can, without warning, become surrealistic. Patsy and I, being deep in conversation as we walked, didn't notice that our path was running gradually downhill while the adjoining path was running gradually uphill. We were still gravely discussing the significance of the Cloisters and I was making a few more notes, when Patsy said:

"Something's wrong. We've been walking for half an hour and he said it was only a quarter of a mile."

We peered ahead and saw nothing that looked like a cafeteria. Then I happened to glance to our right.

"Where's the other path?" I said.

The inner path had entirely disappeared. We were walking along a single path by the side of a fifteen-foot-high stone cliff. A man came walking toward us on the path and Patsy stopped him.

"Can you tell us where the cafeteria is?" she asked him.

"What cafeteria?" he said.

"They told us there was a cafeteria on the Cloisters grounds," I said.

"Oh, the *Cloisters!*" he said. "The Cloisters is up there." And he pointed up at the top of the cliff.

"How do we get there?" Patsy asked him.

"You're walking away from it," he said. "The Cloisters is

back that way." And he pointed us back the way we'd come. We turned around and went back to Square One and started over, along the inner path, and by the time we finally reached the cafeteria we'd had a healthy two-mile hike.

We revived over sandwiches and coffee, at an outdoor table in the sun, and then set off on a tour of Fort Tryon Park.

"This must have been an old fort," I said. "It's named for William Tryon, he was one of the British governors of New York."

Fort Tryon park is a pleasant green rectangle overlooking the Hudson, with recessed stone benches along stone paths. Today, the benches were all occupied by elderly women reading or knitting in the sun. Most of them probably remember the park long before the Cloisters arrived in it. The land surrounding the fort was owned by the Rockefellers who gave it to the city for use as a park, back at the time of World War I. By the early thirties it included a promenade, a playground and a pool. Then in 1938 came the Cloisters, and took up most of it, and the park is now very much smaller. (See Metropolitan Museum.)

Across the Hudson from us were the opulent new apartment houses perched along the cliffs of the Jersey Palisades, built not to attract Jerseyites but to attract New Yorkers.

"People in this town are crazy," I said. "Thousands of them work in New York all day long, and then trek all the way up the Hudson and across the river to New Jersey, just to look at New York at night."

"Well, the views are spectacular," said Patsy.

"I know, but isn't that going a little far for a view?" I said. "You don't have to move to another state to get a good view of New York City!"

For a second, Patsy didn't answer. She was looking tense.

"All right," she said finally. "If you're determined to go to the top of the Trade Center we'd better go there next, before I lose my nerve."

"Tuesday?" I said. "It's supposed to be less crowded early in the week."

"All right," she said, and as we headed back to the parking lot, she added: "I warn you I'm not going to like it."

"Neither am I," I said.

Throughout its construction, the World Trade Center was cordially detested by all New Yorkers. The unpopular Rockefeller brothers were so closely involved in the financing that for a while, the twin towers were known as Nelson and David; the giant buildings are owned by the even more unpopular Port Authority, which wasn't created to build and own huge office towers. Plus which, the financially desperate city didn't need two new 110-story office buildings and couldn't afford to supply them with services. And to cap it off, the rumor among the fifty thousand office drones who worked in the buildings was that the elevators shook, especially up around the 85th floor (a rumor I did not think it necessary to pass on to Patsy).

The bus followed the same route back and Patsy said:

"Make a note: they can take a subway home from the Cloisters."

"They have to take one subway ride anyway," I said, "just for people-watching." (The variety of human sizes, shapes, colors and faces you'll see on one New York subway car is a living, breathing World Atlas.) "Listen, should we make a list of one-way Avenues? Fifth-Avenue-buses-go-down, Madison-buses-go-up and so forth? — so visitors won't stand on an Up avenue waiting for a Down bus?"

"If they're standing on Fifth Avenue they'll see the traffic's all going one way," said Patsy. Then she said: "What are you going to do if you have to mention Sixth? What are you going to call it?"

"I'm going to call it Sixth Avenue," I said. "Did you ever hear anybody call it anything else?"

"Then you'll have to explain it," said Patsy.

"Okay, I'll explain it," I said.

The late, great Mayor of New York, Fiorello H. LaGuardia, once remarked: "When I make a mistake, it's a beaut."

Well, Hizzoner's most enduring beaut was committed against Sixth Avenue. Back in the forties, Fiorello got carried away one year by Pan American Day—or maybe it was Week—and announced that in honor of Pan America, Sixth Avenue was henceforth to be known as The Avenue of the Americas. Nobody thought he meant the change to be permanent, but he did.

All the Sixth Avenue street signs came down and new signs went up reading: AVE. OF AMERICAS. Every place of business on the avenue had to change the address on its stationery and in the phone book. A couple of decades later, when new skyscraper office towers went up along midtown Sixth Avenue every corporation in every building naturally had to list its address as *Avenue of the Americas.*

But somehow the name didn't take. To the people who lived here, Sixth Avenue flatly declined to be known as the Avenue of the Americas. It went right on being Sixth Avenue. Thirty years later it's still Sixth Avenue, and it's obviously never going to be anything else. The chief sufferer from Fiorello's beaut, therefore, is the hapless visitor.

You'll come to New York one day and go shopping in Saks

Fifth Avenue, and when you come out of Saks you'll stop a passerby and ask him if he can direct you to Radio City Music Hall. And the passer-by will point west and say: "One block over, on Sixth Avenue."

And you'll walk one block over, and when you get there you'll check the street sign, and the street sign will say — AVE. OF AMERICAS. So you'll stop another passerby and say: "Pardon me, can you tell me where Sixth Avenue is?"

To which there is no possible answer except: "You're standing on it."*

---

*I'm gratified to report that all its street signs finally read "6th Ave." again, though a few retain their "Ave. of Americas" sign as well.

# Tuesday, April 20

THE NIGHT BEFORE WE WERE TO GO DOWN TO LOWER Manhattan, I called Patsy and gave her the itinerary:

"Wall Street, Trinity Church, the World Trade Center and Fraunces Tavern," I said, slipping the Trade Center in as if it were just one more ground-level attraction.

"How do you want to go down?" Patsy asked. "We've taken one West Side bus. Do you want to take an East Side bus down and see the Lower East Side?"

"I have to do that on foot," I said. "I want to go down to Orchard Street on a Sunday, it's one of those sights I've heard about all my life and never seen."

"Oh, great!" said Patsy. "And we can walk down and see Wall-Street-on-a-Sunday, it's supposed to be a ghost town. Make a note."*

And I made a note, laying the groundwork for what we would look back on as Blockbuster Sunday.

"What about tomorrow? You want to take a Second Avenue bus anyway?" Patsy asked. "Is there anything for tourists to see on Second?"

"Not much," I said. "It's mostly for people who live on it or near it. You know: supermarkets, neighborhood stores, thrift shops."

"Nothing else?" Harvard probed.

"OTB parlors," I said.

*See pp. 152-3, P.S. 1.

OTB stands for Off-Track Betting. It's a legal way for New Yorkers to bet on the horses, and was devised by the city as a painless way to extract from its citizens the extra dollars it so badly needed. (Then the state discovered OTB was profitable and took it over, and now the state runs it and hogs the money.) OTB parlors are store-fronts and some neighborhood block associations wage battles to keep the gambling parlors from opening in their neighborhoods, and while I don't mind them that much, they don't exactly beautify the landscape.

"Let's save time and take a subway down," I said to Patsy, "and get off at the Wall Street station so we won't miss Wall Street again."

We got off at Wall Street and when we came up the subway steps we found ourselves on the sidewalk in front of Trinity Church. The church, on Trinity Place, faced the beginning or end of Wall Street, we weren't sure which.

Trinity was one of the city's fashionable Anglican churches back in pre-Revolutionary days (becoming Episcopal after the war). The building has been twice destroyed and rebuilt since then, and is a simple Gothic church, with a narrow steeple that was once the city's tallest spire and tranquilly refuses to look either shrunken or out of place among the towering skyscrapers. But it wasn't the church, it was the churchyard I'd come to see. Alexander Hamilton is buried there. So is Albert Gallatin, whom I'm much fonder of. (He was Jefferson's Secretary of the Treasury.) So when we came out of the church and I tried the churchyard gate and found it locked, I was very disappointed and glad I hadn't told Patsy who was in there. (I keep assuming other people *care* where dead statesmen are buried.)

"Would One Wall Street be at this end?" I asked Patsy.

"I don't know," she said. "What's there?"

"Wall Street got its name from a wall Peter Stuyvesant built to keep out pirates. We all know it never did keep out pirates and it was torn down a couple of centuries ago, but there's a plaque on the building at Number One Wall Street marking the spot where the wall began."

"Let's find it," said Patsy, starting across the street.

We found the building on the corner directly opposite Trinity Church. It was a huge bank building, home of the Irving Trust (and I hope Washington Irving had nothing to do with the founding of it). Next to the name was the address: Number 1 Wall. We hunted along the walls for the plaque and didn't find it. But on the side wall, we found a large, pale square in the stone, with four holes at the corners, marking the spot where the plaque had been.

"Somebody stole it," I said.

"Let's go ask," said Patsy, and sprinted around the corner and in through the imposing front doors. I followed her as she stepped up to the first desk she came to, and asked the dignified gentleman behind it if he knew anything about the missing plaque.

"Vandals took it, I'm afraid," he said regretfully.

"How long ago?" asked Patsy.

"Oh, quite some time ago," he said.

"Well, the plaque had no historical value," I said. "It was just a plaque. Couldn't the bank afford to replace it?"

He gave me a gently reproving look.

"I'm sure that's being done," he said.

When we came out, Patsy said: "Make a note to come back next month and see if the new plaque is up."

"You mean you believe him?" I demanded. "You think a

bank is going to run out and have a new plaque made? A *bank?*"

"Make a note," said Patsy implacably. "We'll come back down and see."

I made a note.*

One thing about the World Trade Center: you don't need a map to find it. With our eyes on the severe twin towers jutting skyward, we steered a zigzag course through winding streets until we came to an intersection seething with traffic, across the street from it. As we waited for a green light, we looked across the street and saw, in front of the Trade Center and blocking the entrance to it, cement mixers, mounds of earth, piles of wooden boards and the rest of the construction mess out of which the Center's landscaped plaza will have emerged by the time you read this.

"You know the problem with this book?" I said to Patsy. "I want to write about the Trade Center Plaza and I can't because it isn't there yet. I want to write about Radio City Music Hall and I'm not sure it'll still be there when the book comes out. No other city on earth has such a mania for tearing down the old to build the new—which I approve of. My theory is that since New Yorkers mostly come here from somewhere else, they have no interest in the city's past, they come with big plans for its future. And on a narrow strip of island, you can't build the future without tearing down the past first; there isn't room for both. But it's a headache when you're writing a book about it."

We crossed the intersection and picked our way through the mess to the unfinished door of World Trade Center Two,

*See p. 152, P.S.1.

where the Observation Deck is. We walked into the lobby and I said: "Welcome to the Twenty-first Century." (And what's startling about that, is that in the next two weeks I was to read the same words in two descriptions of the Center lobby.)

The lobby is mostly white marble and seven stories high. Far up on the walls are Gothic oval windows, bizarrely church-like; and the height and depth, and the whiteness and the church windows, create the effect of a science-fiction interior. Two or three stories above the lobby floor is a mezzanine deck which encircles the lobby; you take an escalator up there to buy tickets to the 107th Floor Observatory, from which an escalator takes you on up to the tallest outdoor observation platform in the world, on the 110th floor.

It was a cloudy day and the sign over the ticket booth warned: Visibility—5 miles. There were very few people on line and I said to Patsy: "Should we wait and come back on a clear day?"

"We're here," said Patsy grimly. "We're going through with it."

Fifteen or twenty of us were herded into an elevator, and the door slid shut. The elevator shot up to the 107th floor in a matter of seconds—and they're right, it shakes; and your ears pop. At the 107th floor the door opened and relief flooded us: the vast floor was enclosed by an unobstructed expanse of heavy windows that ran clear round the deck. Hand in hand, bravely, we approached the windows.

There's a bench inside every window. Between the bench and the window is a heavy brass railing you can hang onto as you look down (and you'll hang onto it). Stencilled in each window is a small map of the street below it, with the sights and buildings labelled. You grasp the railing and look straight

down a quarter of a mile, into Wall Street or Battery Park or whatever is below your particular window. And then you look up and out, at eye level, at all five boroughs and all five great bridges, but mostly at the city itself. From this bottom-most tip of the island the whole of New York is spread out before you, its thousand skyscrapers fused into a single, improbable vision of "topless towers." For us, they shone against the grey sky as if the sun were on them.

Seen from those windows, the New York skyline was more an entity than Wren's London or L'Enfant's Washington. No one could look at it without asking: "Who built it?" If you consult the library books, you'll be told that the Empire State building was designed by Shreve, Land & Harmon, and that Rockefeller Center was created by Corbet, Harrison & Mac-Murray, Hood & Foulhoux, Reinhard & Hofmeister. Yes, but who? What senior member of the firm drafting plans for the Lever building said: "Suppose we used green glass . . . ?" Who of the Seagram architects first said tentatively: "What about bronze . . . ?" Whose pencil drew the spectacular sweeping curve of 9 East 57th Street? Who built it? Anon, that's who. Nobody built the New York skyline. Nobody by the thousands.

We stared out with no sense of height, just awe.

"That's some dying city," I said.

And suddenly, irrationally, I gloried in the high-handed, high-flying, damn-your-eyes audacity that had sent the Trade Center's twin columns rising impudently above the skyline at the moment when New York was declared to be dying, and so deep in debt it couldn't afford workers to dispose of the Center's trash, police its plaza or put out its fires.

We moved from window seat to window seat, silently

gawking, except when Patsy, sitting before a window map that included Fraunces Tavern, announced that she had studied the location and knew exactly how to find it, so the afternoon would present no problems.

There are telescopes by the windows and several tourists were glued to them, probably hunting the block in Queens they lived on. (Locating Uncle Harry's house in Connecticut would have to wait for a clearer day.)

Next to the elevators was the steep escalator which led up to the 110th floor Observation Deck. Patsy circled it warily and said: "Let's wait and get on behind other people."

We stepped on behind a broad-backed man and his broad-backed wife. Patsy was so ashen with terror that I forgot my own in my obligation to reassure her.

"Did you know," I said conversationally, "that in 1770, New York City went bankrupt? Governor Colden had to write to London for permission to float a loan."

"Keep talking," said Patsy.

"The Crown," I said, "vetoed the loan."

"Oh, right," said Patsy.

"Well, what with all the taxes New York was paying to London, the town got very worked up," I went on, "and the Crown grudgingly reconsidered and said: "All right, you can have a loan. But just this once. After this, if you're still in trouble, you can drop dead." Well, after that, the Revolutionary War broke out and the Crown lost all its colonies."

We stepped off the escalator onto an outdoor platform sensibly designed to prevent suicides and provide a needed anticlimax to the Observatory three floors below. The platform we stood on reminded both of us of a resort boardwalk. It's a broad wood and cement floor, the railing hidden behind

thick shrubbery. A few feet below it is another broad board-walk extending further out on all sides, so that when you look down, the lower boardwalk is all you can see. Then you look out, and the splendor of the city smites you all over again with "astonishment of the heart," as it says in the Bible.

It was one-thirty when we finally took the elevator back down to the lobby to look for a restaurant open to the public. A new restaurant had just opened on the 107th floor of Tower One, but we knew we wouldn't be admitted to it. (That restaurant— "Windows on the World"—is now New York's most celebrated restaurant. But it was an added source of irritation when it first opened, because it opened as a private club from which the general public was excluded at lunch-time. This caused such public fury that the restaurant backed down later, and today, non-club members are admitted to lunch on payment of a steep cover charge in addition to the cost of the lunch. At night, dinner at the restaurant is like a ticket to a Broadway hit musical: you have to reserve your place months in advance. If you're not rich, go there for Sunday brunch, when there's no cover charge; or better still, stop at the cocktail lounge after dusk—it's open from four to seven—and see the diamond-studded night city.)

We found an attractive coffee shop in one of the two lobbies, I forget which. It had small tables along cushioned banquettes. We found an empty table and a waitress brought us menus. After studying mine, I was happily watching attractive lunch platters go by on trays when I realized that Patsy, her menu unopened, was staring at me.

"What's the matter?" I asked.

"You're writing this book for tourists," she said. "We can not eat lunch in the basement of the world's tallest building."

"It's not the basement, it's the ground floor," I said.

"It's the basement," said Patsy. "We are sitting in the basement of the tallest building in the world."

"The 110-story Sears building in Chicago is taller," I said.

Patsy went on staring at me like a stony conscience.

"In Toronto," I said, "there's a Needle that's taller than the Sears building in Chicago."

Nothing. Patsy's accusing eyes never left my face. So I sighed and gave in and put my shoes back on, and we left the coffee shop and went past a maze of lobby shops and on into the other lobby and up to the information desk, and then around to a bank of elevators which would take us up to the 44th floor "Sky Lobby" where, we were told, there was a restaurant.

There is definitely a restaurant on the 44th floor. I'm told it's very pleasant and you will probably find it without difficulty. We couldn't find it. We went down a long hall which turned more corners than I thought there were. We went past rabbit-warren office doors and past two of the Center's seven banks of elevators. Finally, when an office worker came along, Patsy stopped her.

"Do you know where we can eat up here?" she asked. And the office worker said:

"One flight down, through that door."

We pushed open the door and walked downstairs; and that's how we happened to have lunch in the dirtiest, dreariest office-workers' cafeteria that ever closed for the day just as we were ready for our second cup of coffee.

And of course, when we got out on the street, Patsy, not having the stencilled window map with her, didn't have any idea where Fraunces Tavern was. However, on our walk from

Trinity Church to the Trade Center, we had noticed the wall maps which are a charming feature of the Lower Manhattan landscape. On lamp-posts and on the walls of buildings, at three- or four-block intervals, is a small map of the immediate area with all the chief points of interest marked, and a bright, black arrow pointing to one spot on the map, with the legend: YOU ARE HERE. We found one such map near the Trade Center and Patsy studied it.

"This map," she said finally, "is upside down. I think we go that way."

We went that way, through small streets we hadn't been on before, and I began to wish somebody we knew would come along. There are two groups of professionals who work in Lower Manhattan: 1. the stockbrokers, bankers, underwriters and accountants who work in the financial district, and 2. the city officials, judges, law clerks and attorneys who work in the City Hall and Courts district. We knew a sprinkling of people in the second group, but of course none of them came by. Finally we stopped a man hurrying by with a briefcase.

"Can you tell us where Fraunces Tavern is?" Patsy asked him.

"I'll be glad to," he said. And he put down his briefcase, took his wallet out of a breast pocket and extracted from the wallet a small map. As he studied it, I was comforted to realize that Lower Manhattan was just enough like London for even the regulars to carry maps. So Patsy and I weren't as dimwitted as we felt.

"Here we are," he said finally, and pointed us down toward Battery Park and then east of it.

We walked down till we came to the broad intersection where, from the Battery Park side, we had first seen Lower

Manhattan. But the approach from the upper side was dramatically different. With the skyscrapers behind us, we looked across the intersection to a row of eighteenth-century houses on a street that was like a little island standing by itself, a forgotten relic of the past. Fraunces stood on the corner nearest us. Being both a historical museum and a popular restaurant, its red brick and white molding looked freshly painted, and its windows, brightly clean, were flossy with white curtains. By contrast, the four houses alongside it looked decayed and abandoned and there was something touching about them, empty and neglected but still stubbornly standing where they had always stood. Then we noticed the last house in the row. Dingier and more dilapidated than its neighbors, it had a sign of life in its bleary ground-floor window. The sign read: OTB.

And Patsy was waving at it wildly and I was laughing and crowing "I love this town!" and we almost got run over crossing to Fraunces.

All traces of the bomb damage were gone, and the tavern seemed intact. It's an attractive restaurant, "restored" and self-consciously charming like the Dickens pubs in London.

We went upstairs to the celebrated room from which General Washington said farewell to his officers. According to an eye-witness, Washington "filled his glass and lifted it and said: 'With a heart full of love and gratitude I now take leave of you.'"

"The officers who were present at the leave-taking," I told Patsy, "very probably included Kosky-Osko."

The museum contains military despatches, and a few letters and artifacts from the Revolutionary War, as well as the history of Samuel Fraunces, the West Indian who owned the

tavern before, during and after the Revolution.

("Race prejudice is a remarkable thing," I said to Patsy. "When the British invaded New York and the patriots fled, the British confiscated all patriot property. When the British marched out and the patriots returned, they confiscated all Tory property. But neither side ever confiscated Sam Fraunces' tavern: he was black so he didn't count as Tory or patriot. You get the feeling nobody ever thought to ask him which he was.")

It was ten minutes to five when we left Fraunces, so we were just in time for the five o'clock subway rush hour. Maybe, just once, you ought to take a New York subway during the five o'clock rush, to see how the other side of insanity lives. Every subway car is wall-to-wall people. I was pushed nearly to the middle of the car by the crowd entering behind me; and though I had nothing to hang on to, and the train lurched round every bend, the solid wall of bodies kept me upright. I finally managed to work my right arm through enough coats and elbows to get three fingers around the center pole and I counted eleven unrelated hands or parts of hands above and below mine on the pole. Then the train stopped at Grand Central and two thousand more people pushed into the car and I lost my hold entirely. It's not an experience I am up to twice in one week, so when Patsy phoned on Wednesday and said: "I've got tomorrow free. Where to next?"

I said: "Midtown Manhattan. We're entitled to a nice easy one. We're going to spend the day with millionaires."

# Thursday, April 22

"WOULD YOU BELIEVE," I SAID TO PATSY WHEN I MET HER the next morning, "that there are forty-five museums listed in the Manhattan telephone book?" I consulted my notes and added: "In addition to the Irish, Chinese, Jewish, Hispanic, American Indian, Black, Primitive and Folk, there are museums of Firefighting, Numismatics, Sports, Jazz and Oceanography. And that's not counting any of the art museums, not even the most famous ones—the Met, the Guggenheim, the Whitney and Moma." (The Museum of Modern Art is on Fifty-Third Street, and when you pass it you'll see an enormous navy blue banner floating in the breeze with the acronym MOMA on it.)

"How many do we have to go to?" Patsy asked dubiously.

"I picked out four," I said. "Three have a common denominator: even tourists who are bored by museums have to see them. They can ignore the museum when they get there. It isn't the museum I want them to see."

"Oh," said Patsy. "Like this one."

We were standing in front of a mansion on Thirty-Sixth Street between Park and Madison. Its official name is the J. P. Morgan Library. It's a two-story mansion built by J.P., to house his private library and his priceless collection of art objects. And let's say you have no interest in J.P.'s rare porcelains, illuminated medieval manuscripts, Gutenberg Bibles or early children's books, and that since you're not a scholar or collector, you won't be admitted to the reference

library. Go anyway. Go there to meet J. Pierpont Morgan.

The mansion was designed as "a Renaissance palazzo built of fitted marble blocks in the classical Greek manner," it says in the brochure. Inside, however, the house abandons the Renaissance and classical Greek in favor of Queen Victoria and Edward VII. You enter a dark, airless hall with heavy mahogany doors opening into two exhibit rooms. After you've seen whatever interests you—the medieval manuscripts in glass cases or the portable Flemish altar on the mantel—climb the dark, heavy mahogany stairs to the second floor, to the East and West Rooms. Do the East Room first. This was J.P.'s private library.

The long gallery above the room is lined with rare and magnificently bound books (which you can't go up the gallery stairs to look at, because you're not a scholar). You'll find a few more books in glass cases and more rare art objects on display. Then go into the West Room, which was Morgan's private study and has been preserved just as he left it. In the West Room, you are in the palpable presence of the owner of the house.

The room is suffocating with mahogany and red plush: heavy dark mahogany tables and chairs, red plush sofa and drapes, and red silk wallpaper. The carved ceiling was imported from a Florentine cathedral. The stained-glass windows were imported from a German cathedral. I don't remember where the massive fireplace was imported from. Dominating the room, extending from the ceiling down to the mantel above the fireplace, is a huge, standing portrait of J. P. Morgan, wearing a red dressing gown that matches the red silk wallpaper. Beneath the enormous canvas, several small items on the mantel pale into insignificance, including a

priceless miniature portrait of Martin Luther. Straight-backed mahogany armchairs are set at a respectful distance from the imposing desk they face.

"From behind that desk," the guard on duty informed us proudly, "Mr. Morgan made all the major financial decisions for the Allies in World War I." Kings and queens and heads of state, he told us, came to this room, hat in hand, to negotiate loans with the great J.P.

The room gave me the cold horrors. But history, as somebody once remarked, is not a rummage sale. If you come to New York looking for the history of the United States, the pretty candy-box of Fraunces Tavern is not chiefly where you find it.

It was a relief to get out of that oppressive mausoleum into the sunny April morning again.

"Did you know that J. P. Morgan was born in Hartford, Connecticut?" I asked Patsy.

"If that's the beginning of one of your long-winded stories I don't want to hear it," said Patsy. "Let's start walking toward the Frick even if we don't make it." The Frick Collection was nearly forty blocks away, up at Seventieth and Fifth. "We can stop for coffee on the way."

"Of course we're stopping for coffee on the way," I said. "We're going to Paley Park. I told you we're spending the day with millionaires, I didn't say they were all dead."

Paley Park is on Fifty-Third Street between Madison and Fifth, but it's not the open green space the word "park" implies and you have to look sharp or you'll pass it by. It's a narrow hole-in-the-wall park, sandwiched in between two dark buildings, a green oasis where you can get coffee and a sandwich to eat at one of its picnic tables, or just sit on a park

bench and enjoy the greenery and the waterfall which is the back wall. I read somewhere that William Paley (whose CBS building is only a couple of blocks away on Sixth Avenue) built it for the city's midtown office workers. Those who brought their lunch from home needed a pleasant place to eat it; those who didn't, needed to buy sandwiches and coffee at a place less dreary than the cafeterias they could afford. As we got our coffee and took it to a table, I told Patsy:

"William Paley was born in Philadelphia, like me."

She wasn't listening. She was fishing two newspaper clippings out of her handbag. She pushed them across the table to me and said:

"I thought you might have missed these."

Both were from the *Times*. I hadn't missed them, I'd ignored them. One was about the house down in the Twenties somewhere, where Teddy Roosevelt was born. The other was about the Morris-Jumel mansion up at 160th Street and St. Nicholas Avenue. Looking at those clippings I realized that Patsy's Harvard background could be something of a problem.

"With all there is to see in New York," I said, "do you really think tourists are going to want to run down to the Twenties to see Teddy Roosevelt's birthplace? FDR had a town house on East Sixty-Fourth Street and I wasn't even going to bother with that."

"Herbert Hoover," said Patsy thoughtfully, "had a suite at the Waldorf Towers. Well, all right, I guess you can skip presidents' houses. But the Jumel mansion is a landmark, it was Washington's headquarters during the Revolution."

"I know," I said. "He was there just long enough to lose the Battle of Harlem Heights and abandon New York City," and I changed the subject. I thought I'd disposed of the Jumel

mansion and when we rose to go, I left the clipping on the table. But Patsy, with one of her stony glares, picked it up and stuffed it into my shoulder bag and I knew I hadn't heard the last of it.

The Frick Collection was the finest private art collection in the country, when Henry Clay Frick died and left it—and the mansion that houses it—to the people of New York City. (He was born in Pittsburgh.) It's another "palazzo" but entirely white—white stone outside, white stone and marble inside. And as often as we'd both been there, entering it today was almost a shock, coming to it as we did from the somber darkness of the Morgan. The Frick house is all light and air.

You enter a foyer where an oblong stone pool of very clear green water is flanked by white garden benches and potted trees. You go on into a central hall, the white marble floor as spacious as the gallery rooms opening off it. At the far end of the hall, there's a great marble staircase with the pipes of an organ on the landing. (The keyboard is in a niche by the foot of the staircase.)

I read in S. N. Behrman's "Duveen" that Frick used to hire an organist to come and play to him on Saturday afternoons. Frick sat in his long gallery, reading the *Saturday Evening Post,* while the organist played "Silver Threads Among the Gold." Never mind: today, you can hear lovely chamber music concerts at the Frick on Sundays at four.

We entered the gallery rooms where white walls leave all the color to the paintings—and even if (like me) you know nothing about painting, the blaze of colors on the Frick walls will dazzle you.

"Harry Truman," I said, "once said that the Carnegie

libraries were steeped in the blood of the Homestead steel workers."

"Did you see the Goya over the mantelpiece?" said Patsy. "It's incredible."

"The steel workers at the Homestead plant had gone on strike for a union contract. So of course the plant hired scab labor," I said.

"Look at the little Memling," Patsy murmured. "The light takes your breath away."

"The manager of the Homestead plant brought in three hundred armed Pinkerton guards to protect the scabs. He smuggled them in at night by boat. When the Pinkerton guards' guns weren't enough to break the strike, the governor sent in the state militia."

"Where's the Rembrandt self-portrait?" asked Patsy.

"The guards and the militia cut down the steel workers in cold blood, and that finally broke the strike," I said. "And for years afterwards, the steel companies didn't have to pay union wages; and Carnegie and the Homestead plant manager lived happily ever after."

"Why do you have to tell me a story like that when I'm trying to see the most fabulous collection in town?" Patsy demanded.

"Because that's how this fabulous place got built," I said. "The manager of the Homestead plant was Henry Clay Frick."

We left the Frick and when I said: "Next stop: the Cooper-Hewitt Museum of Interior Design," Patsy gave me a sour look.

"I love the Cooper-Hewitt," she said. "I love the Meissen china and the antique wallpaper and the antique textiles — and after your terrible story, I won't be able to enjoy it!"

The Cooper-Hewitt museum is at Ninetieth and Fifth, in the Carnegie mansion.

As we walked up Fifth Avenue, passing all my favorite East Side streets at intersections on the way, I said:

"How can I get visitors to turn off Madison or Fifth and walk East and explore the side streets in the Sixties and Seventies? When my friend, Nora Doel, came here from London she was bowled over by them. She said the only pictures she'd ever seen of New York were of skyscrapers; she couldn't believe the rows of beautiful houses along the East Side streets."

"I gather," said Patsy politely, "you're not planning to include the West Side in your book."

"I'm doing the West Side next, as a matter of fact," I said virtuously. "I'm going to do Rockefeller Center."

Patsy stopped in her tracks.

"Do you mean to stand there and tell me you call Rockefeller Center the West Side?" she demanded. "Your idea of the West Side being the west side of Fifth Avenue?"

"Rockefeller Center runs west of Fifth almost to Seventh," I said. "And you didn't let me finish. We're going to do Rockefeller Center and Lincoln Center, and I'll mention the theatre district. I'm not chasing all the way over to Duffy Square just to look at it, but I'll mention that Duffy Square is at Forty-Seventh and Broadway, and there's a booth there called TKTS where you can get half-price theatre tickets for any show on Broadway that isn't sold out for that day's performance. And unless you really insist on dragging me through the Natural History Museum to stare at reconstructed dinosaurs I don't know what else there is to see on the West Side."

"If you can lower yourself to come to my house," said Patsy, "I'll show you."

We turned into the side entrance of the Carnegie mansion, to be met by a locked gate and a huge sign telling us the museum was closed for the summer "for renovation" and would reopen as a branch of the Smithsonian Institution. By the time you read this, it will have become a much larger and more impressive museum of interior design, with medieval and Byzantine textiles and collections of drawings, ancient and modern. And maybe the remodelled Carnegie mansion will have an interior less grim and forbidding than it used to be.*

"Okay, now where?" asked Patsy as we turned away from the locked gate. "Gracie Mansion?"

Gracie Mansion, up in the Eighties next to the East River, is not a museum, it's the official residence of the Mayor of New York. Technically, it's a tourist attraction but it's surrounded by a wall.

"What can a tourist see of Gracie Mansion but the wall and the driveway?" I said. "Do you want to know the only way an ordinary citizen can get a really good view of Gracie Mansion? Have a baby. A couple expecting a baby should reserve a room at Doctors Hospital and ask for a room with a river view. As soon as the baby's born, the parents can hang out the window and watch the goings on in the Gracie Mansion garden and living room and dining room and even a couple of bedrooms."

And we went on up to 104th Street and Fifth, to the Museum of the City of New York.

It's a small, manageable museum in a brown-and-white brick house, recording the city's history from the Dutch days onward in four floors of engaging artifacts.

*See p. 167, P.S. 6.

---

Everybody's favorite exhibit is the display of antique toys and dolls, together with a group of marvelously detailed dolls' houses, complete down to handmade linens in the hope chests. Patsy, being a rabid theatregoer, had to be dragged away from the Broadway theatre exhibit. (It changes every few months and may deal with an era or just a single personality in the theatre, and is always complete with three-sheet posters, programs, costumes, photographs and recorded songs.)

There are period rooms from every quarter-century, and until you see the life-size mannequins in each room, you don't know how tall mankind has grown in three hundred years.

There's one exhibit which I love and which ruined my day. It's a group of dioramas depicting the history of the New York Stock Exchange, from the famous first meeting of merchants under a buttonwood tree to the nineteenth century day when ticker-tape replaced runners, and including a spectacular three-dimensional view of Wall Street during the Blizzard of '88. And it was as we were peering into this one that the hideous oversight struck me. I must have turned a sickly color because Patsy asked:

"What's the matter?"

"I made sure we saw Wall Street because it's on every book's Must See list," I said. "And I forgot that the reason *why* it's on every Must See list is it's the home of the world-famous New York Stock Exchange. Which we didn't even look for, much less take a tour of."

"Oh, right," said Patsy. I looked at her and she looked pleased. "I guess we'll have to go back down there," she said.

"To tell you the truth," I said, "I was going back down anyway. Alexander Hamilton and Albert Gallatin are buried in Trinity churchyard and I want to see their graves. The

cemetery was locked when we were there but I thought I'd phone Trinity and ask when it's open."

"It wasn't locked," said Patsy. "The side door was open. I wondered why you didn't want to go in."

I had two martinis that night before dinner instead of my usual one and a half. I didn't mind having to go back down to Lower Manhattan again (and wouldn't have minded if I'd known we'd have to go back down there not once more but twice). What I minded was the discovery that I was no more in command of the project than I'd been when we started.

# Wednesday, April 28

LIKE MOST CITIES, NEW YORK IS A COLLECTION OF SMALL neighborhoods. I live in Lenox Hill, surrounded by colleges (Hunter, Marymount Manhattan, Mannes Music), singles (young and old), monster new apartment houses and dogs. Above Lenox Hill is Yorkville, old and formerly German, with a main street—Eighty-Sixth Street—that looks like any small town Main Street except that the bakeries, restaurants and small stores along it are German, Swiss and Hungarian as well as American. Below me is Sutton Place, small and rich and quiet, and below that Beekman Place, even smaller and richer and quieter. Then, you come to Murray Hill and then to Tudor City—a compact small town built above the city and reached by high stone steps—and then Madison Square and Gramercy Park, and so forth. Most of these neighborhoods have their local free weekly newspaper, their political clubs, block associations and Community Planning Boards.

Patsy lives on Central Park West, in a section of it which is also a neighborhood: a row of old and famous apartment houses, now cooperatively owned by the families who live in them. Above her neighborhood and slightly west of it is the Riverside Drive neighborhood, thick with Columbia professors' families, and above that is Morningside Heights. (See next chapter.) Below Patsy's, there is Lincoln Towers—an apartment house complex behind Lincoln Center which is its own self-contained community—and below that you come to Chelsea and Clinton and the Village, and so forth. They, too,

have their throwaway newspapers and political clubs and block associations and Planning Boards.

BUT: all the neighborhoods above and below and including mine, are strung together into a psychological unit and share a common attitude and common rules of behavior. And all the neighborhoods above and below and including Patsy's, are strung together into a psychological unit and share a common attitude and common rules of behavior. And the two units are poles apart and don't understand each other. Because unlike other cities, New York is literally split down the middle by Fifth Avenue, into East and West Sides. And never the twain shall meet on any common ground but Saving New York City.

Fifth Avenue itself, which runs through the center of town from Seventh Street to a Hundred and Tenth, is neutral territory. But the street signs at intersections along the Avenue mark off the separate sides for you. Say you're standing in front of St. Patrick's Cathedral and you see a sign on the downtown corner reading: E. 50 St. Cross the avenue and you'll see a sign on the corner reading: W. 50 St.

And just so you'll know what Side you're on at any given moment, if you're on Fifth and you walk East, you'll come to Madison, Park, Lexington, Third, Second and First, in that order. If you're on Fifth and you walk West, you'll come to Sixth, Seventh, Broadway, Eighth, Ninth and Tenth. That's in midtown. When you go up to Fifty-Ninth, where the park begins, you'll see that Central Park itself separates East from West, being bounded on the East by Fifth Avenue and on the West by Central Park West (an extension of Eighth Avenue) where Patsy lives. Both Fifth Avenue and Central Park West have fine views of the park, which is very even-handed. Today,

the East Side is basically richer than the West; fifty years ago it was the other way round, which is also evenhanded.

What the West Side has always had, that the East Side has never had, is a concentration of the city's great performing arts centers: the Broadway theatres, Carnegie Hall, Lincoln Center, the giant television network centers in skyscrapers along Sixth Avenue, and Rockefeller Center, which begins at Fifth Avenue and mushrooms west.

That's the background. The underlying differences between East and West Siders can wait till we get over to Patsy's.

Patsy and I met that morning at 30 Rockefeller Plaza ("30 Rock" to the people who work there) and went up to the tour desk in the lobby and discovered there are two separate tours: Tour 1, a guided tour of Rockefeller Center and Tour 2, a backstage tour of NBC's radio and television studios. Tour 1 tickets were available. Tour 2 was on strike.

"Should we do the Center tour now and come back for the NBC tour when the strike is over?" I suggested.

"—and we'll get home tonight and hear on the six o'clock news that the strike's just been settled," said Patsy. "Let's wait a week."

So we left Rockefeller Center and walked up to Fifty-Seventh and then turned west, toward Lincoln Center which starts at Sixty-Fourth Street. We turned west on Fifty-Seventh partly because it's a beautiful street to walk along: it has fine shops and art galleries and Carnegie Hall. But there was another reason—and I promise this is the last time I'll bore you with street directions, but this one is something nobody ever warns visitors about, and it always gets them into trouble.

If you're standing in front of One East Fifty-Fourth Street and you're looking for One West Fifty-Fourth Street, you'll find it right across Fifth Avenue or, as they say, right-across-the-street. But if you're standing in front of One East *Sixty-*Fourth Street and you're looking for One West Sixty-Fourth Street, it's not across the street, it's clear across Central Park, and you ask somebody where you get a crosstown bus to take you over to the West Side. Patsy and I avoided this by turning west before we got to Fifty-Ninth where the park begins.

"We get the tour tickets at Avery Fisher Hall," I said, as we came within sight of the Lincoln Center buildings.

"Philharmonic Hall," Patsy corrected grimly.

We got our tickets for the tour which took us through most of the main buildings—a two-level theatre for stage plays known as the Vivian Beaumont Theatre upstairs and the Mitzi Newhouse Theatre downstairs; the New York State Theatre (home of the New York City Ballet and the New York City Opera companies); Avery Fisher/Philharmonic; and the Metropolitan Opera House. (The best Lincoln Center tour is the backstage tour of the Met which you can only take during the opera season, October to March, and which includes rehearsals.) The tour didn't include the Julliard School of Music and its adjoining concert hall, alias Alice Tully Hall.

"The trouble with this tour," said Patsy as we hung over the rail of one of the Met's promenade decks, "is that it's in the daytime, and these buildings have to be seen at night. You have to be part of the audience. You have to see the chandeliers lit, and the promenade decks during intermission—when you look down at all the marvelous people in the lobby, all looking the way you'd like to look."

"I'll tell you a story about this place," I said. "My friend

Arlene ran a political fund-raising party here a few years ago. There's a lobby on the Met mezzanine big enough for a cocktail party for two hundred people and that's where she had it. I was volunteer ticket-taker—the party was for a candidate our club was backing—and my ticket table was at the top of the grand staircase. The party was on a rainy winter Thursday, at five, and people came direct from their offices without going home to dress. You know how they look—the lawyers and law-clerks and local officials and club workers who go to that kind of party. I sat at my table at the top of the staircase and watched them push through the Met doors in bunches, in a hurry to be out of the rain, all of them looking wet and frazzled and out of sorts. When they started up the sweeping marble staircase they were all hunched forward, the way people do when they're climbing steps.

"But when they reached the third or fourth step, they began to change. Coming up that staircase they straightened, almost imperceptibly at first. They became erect, they began to climb more slowly—and about halfway up, every man almost unconsciously took the arm of the woman next to him. By the time they reached the top, the men were stepping aside to let the women pass, and the women were sweeping regally up to my table and smiling at me and saying 'Good after-noon,' which they don't normally say to a ticket-taker. It was extraordinary."

Outside the Vivian Beaumont theatre, on a wall beyond the long reflecting pool, there's a plaque honoring John D. Rocke-feller III, identified as "the prime mover" behind the creation of Lincoln Center back in the early sixties. On the plaque is a statement by Rockefeller which begins: "The arts are not for the privileged few but for the many."

"That's what's special about New York," I said. "The concern for 'the many' that people have when they come here, or acquire after they get here. That's why a handful of rich men and women have done so much for the city."

"Like Frick," said Patsy.

"Like Frick and Carnegie," I agreed. "This overcrowded city is where they lived; and it's the hordes of people of all kinds, which Rockefeller delicately called 'the many,' that they left their great collections to and built concert halls for. In view of which, we shouldn't resent the new names on all these buildings.

"Personally," I said, "I wish Avery Fisher had declined to have Philharmonic Hall renamed in his honor, no matter how much money he spent to have the acoustics corrected. And I wish Alice Tully had said: 'No, no, just call it Julliard Hall.' But let's face it: you and I both know that while art may be for 'the many,' it always has to be financed by the few. And fair's fair: readers of a book about New York have a right to know what Avery Fisher and Vivian Beaumont and Mitzi Newhouse and Alice Tully have in common."

After lunch we walked up Central Park West to Patsy's apartment house, passing side streets lined with large Victorian brownstones and greystones as we went.

Back in the early years of the century, the West Side was a middle- and upper-income residential area. The East Side in those days was most famous for its slums, where railroad laborers lived and died in Old Law and New Law tenements. (Old Law tenements had air shafts; New Law tenements had to have windows.) Those were the days when the West Side was the opulent New York of Lilian Russell and Diamond Jim Brady, of majestic hotels and fine town houses. Today most of

the hotels are ancient and decayed and house welfare families. The rows of Victorian houses, having long since become moldering rooming-houses, are still largely rooming-houses; but more and more young families have begun buying them, ready to spend years remodelling and rewiring to convert them into modern one-family homes. The old houses have high ceilings, fireplaces, long halls and spacious rooms all reminiscent of an earlier age which, to West Siders, is the secret of their charm.

"A friend of mine lived over here for ten years," I told Patsy. "She had a floor-through in an old brownstone. Then I met her in my supermarket one day and she told me she'd moved into a new building up the block from me. She said: 'I got up one morning and thought: Enough of this Old Charm, I want a modern kitchen.'"

Patsy nodded.

"We lived on the East Side for six years," she said, "before I suddenly knew I didn't care if the molding peeled, I wanted to live where I could feel roots and a sense of the past around me."

By this time we were approaching the American Museum of Natural History which runs from Seventy-Seventh to Eighty-First Street and has a 67-foot long, 16-foot high, 30-ton reconstructed brontosaurus in Brontosaurus Hall, if that interests you. Also stuffed elephants, stuffed lions and stuffed rhinoceroses.

"Do we have to do the monsters?" I asked.

"They have a fabulous jewel collection," said Patsy. Then she said: "No, forget it, you could spend a month in there and not see everything, and not find your way out again."

"I'll tell you what," I said. "We'll skip Natural History and go see the Hayden Planetarium Sky Show. There's a show at

---

three, I made a note of it. We can just make it."

Patsy threw me a noncommittal look.

"Our class went there when I was eight," she said. "My kids both had to go with their classes when they were eight."

"Well, I've never been," I said—and we went.

We were ushered into the Sky Theatre, where the ceiling was a simulated sky full of stars, and we took seats among the twenty or thirty school children waiting for the show to begin. A lecturer came out on stage and welcomed us. Then the theatre darkened, the overhead sky-ceiling brightened and the show began.

"Twinkle, twinkle, little star, How I wonder what you are!" said the lecturer, and then proceeded to explain what a star was, in terms nobody without an M.S. in Astronomy could understand.

The children squirmed and looked up at the star-studded ceiling with relief whenever the patterns changed. At the end of an hour, the lecturer recited triumphantly: "Twinkle, twinkle, little quasar, Now I know what YOU are!" and the houselights came up and we got out of there.

"You could have warned me!" I said. And Patsy said: "Well, you go back every fifteen years thinking maybe it's got better." We adjourned to her house for coffee. And you need only walk into her foyer to know why families live on the West Side.

My own apartment is listed by the landlord as a "2½-room studio" and is actually a living room with a small alcove. The living room counts as one room, the alcove is a second room because it has a window, and the kitchen is half-a-room because it doesn't have a window. The bathroom they throw in free. Real estate arithmetic. And the statement I am about to make is not an exaggeration and not meant to be humor, it's a

flat fact: You could put my entire apartment in Patsy Gibbs' foyer. In the *foyer*. Opening off the foyer are more rooms and bigger rooms than you'll find in a modern ranch house. There's a large living room, an equally large library, a dining room that seats twelve easily (eighteen if it has to), three bedrooms, three baths, a large bedroom for the housekeeper (remodelled from two small rooms), and a kitchen, which includes a former butler's pantry, where eight people can sit down to breakfast.

"Anne Jackson and Eli Wallach have an apartment the size of yours, if you'll pardon my name-dropping," I said, as Patsy made coffee. "I got lost in theirs once. I could hear Annie calling me and I went from room to room and couldn't find her; she had to come and get me."

"When we first moved in, we had a babysitter coming one night," said Patsy, "and we waited and waited for her, and finally I called her house and her mother said she'd left forty minutes before. So we went looking for her. She'd been sitting in the library for half an hour."

Though living space is mainly what families move to the West Side for, you find singles and childless couples over there, too; and living space and charm are not what chiefly attract them. The real difference between the East Side and West Side is in the people. They not only think and behave differently from each other; they look different.

Generally speaking, West Siders look dowdy, scholarly and slightly down-at-heel, and the look has nothing to do with money. They look like what a great many of them are: scholars, intellectuals, dedicated professionals, all of whom regard shopping for clothes as a colossal waste of time. East Siders, on the other hand, look chic. Appearances are impor-

tant to them. From which you'll correctly deduce that East Siders are conventional and proper, part of the Establishment and in awe of it—which God knows, and God be thanked, West Siders are not.

I'll give you an example. Suppose tomorrow's New York *Times* prints the news that JFK airport is building new runways for supersonic jets. The West Side Democratic clubs will charter buses, ride out to JFK and march around the airport with placards reading: NO SST FOR NYC and SAVE THE ENVIRONMENT FOR OUR CHILDREN. They'll sing fight songs, have a couple of clashes with the police and turn up on the eleven o'clock TV Evening News. The East Side clubs will hold a dignified debate and then send a telegram to the governor telling him they're against air pollution.

But since families need living space and may move to the West Side to get it, and since singles want modern kitchens and may move to the East Side to get them, both Sides have a certain number of fish-out-of-water. Which explains why Patsy and her husband never joined a West Side club when they moved over there and why I periodically drift away from mine. I love the East Side streets and buildings; but my Establishment neighbors occasionally drive me up the wall and I read wistfully about West Side demonstrations because, psychologically, I belong over there. And Patsy, who loves the West Side for its space and charm, has never set foot in a noisy West Side Democratic club because, psychologically, she belongs over here. (Though Patsy is special: she was born on the West Side, so it's not a Side to her, it's her Old Kentucky Home.)

Still, the Side you live on influences your thinking and behavior if you live there long enough. I've accepted the

Establishment name of Avery Fisher Hall. Patsy will call it Philharmonic Hall for the rest of time.

We had coffee in the living room, before picture windows looking out over Central Park with a breathtaking view of the Central Park South skyline beyond. Then I said:

"It's after five, I have to get home."

"We have one more stop to make," said Patsy.

"Where?" I asked.

"Zabar's," said Patsy.

I'd heard about Zabar's from all my gourmet friends but I'd never been there, so I said:

"I'll go there with you some time. Not today. I'm tired."

Patsy's face registered instant outrage.

"Zabar's is one of the most famous Sights on the West Side!" she said. "Do you realize people like Frank Sinatra have pastrami and bagels flown to them in Europe so they won't starve? You are going to put Zabar's in your book!"

"I'll tell you what I'll do," I said. "I have to tour Morningside Heights—Columbia, Riverside, Grant's Tomb, all that—which is another West Side tour. If you go with me, we'll take a Broadway bus back down and stop off at Zabar's on the way home."

"All right," said Patsy, "but this time you're not going to weasel out of it."

And just like that, I had her committed to the only wearing uptown junket left on my list.

# Monday, May 3

I'LL SAY THIS FOR OUR TOUR OF MORNINGSIDE HEIGHTS: every sight we saw bore the unmistakable stamp: Made in the USA.

We got off the Broadway bus at 112th Street, at the (Episcopal) Cathedral Church of St. John the Divine which is "the largest Gothic cathedral in the world," according to the church booklet. It is a permanently unfinished cathedral.

The cornerstone was laid in 1892, and for three decades the work went steadily forward, until the completion of the great bell tower in 1930. Then came the Depression, followed by the war decade and war shortages, and in the fifties the great middle-class exodus to the suburbs. By the sixties, the neighborhood had changed from rich to poor, and today there are no plans to finish St. John's. As a clergyman we met there said simply: "You don't spend millions on a cathedral when people around you are hungry."

The magnificent church seats ten thousand, but since it's a bishop's seat and has no parish, the nave is roped off for great occasions and the average Sunday congregation of three hundred worships in a vestibule chapel inside the front doors.

Patsy and I went down the side aisles to look at the rare tapestries hanging from the scaffolding which still supports one church wall. Then I moved down to look at the stone pulpit, and Patsy went out onto the altar floor to look at the three fine chairs, two white ones flanking the bishop's red one, all three set against the righthand altar wall. Suddenly she

turned and beckoned me violently, her face purple. I went up and joined her, and Patsy pointed to the wall behind the three chairs. Halfway up the wall hung a telephone. Next to the phone was an intercom board. On the intercom board was a list:

1 Console
2 Power Amp. Room
3 Panel Room
4 Dean
5 Precenter
6 Pulpit
7 Organ
8 Bishop's Throne
9 Recording

"Operator, gimme the Bishop's throne."

There may be an equally efficient intercom system operating off the wall of the high altar at Chartres or Westminster Abbey but somehow you doubt it; it just reeks of American knowhow.

We left St. John's and started walking toward 115th Street and Broadway and the entrance to the original quadrangle which once contained Columbia College and now contains a fraction of Columbia University's undergraduate buildings. Since Morningside Heights is also the home of the Union Theological and Jewish Theological seminaries, it's very much a Town-and-Gown community; and what startled Patsy and me, in view of all the horrific crime stories we'd read about the area, is that a Town-and-Gown community is exactly what it looked like.

We were walking in a spacious neighborhood of tree-lined avenues, the solid, substantial fronts of old brick houses hiding the poverty and desperation of both the black and Puerto Rican newcomers and the elderly white holdovers who live there. The lovely green stretch of Riverside Park along the Hudson concealed the fact that the park is considered one of the city's most crime-ridden. Maybe crime only comes out at night there. All I can tell you is that Patsy and I wandered all over the area all day long, and saw only students, professors and clergymen hurrying by, a class of small boys filing into a church school, black and white children playing at the foot of Grant's Tomb and elderly men and women sitting on park benches.

Entering the Columbia quadrangle was like stepping into the set of a nineteen forties college movie. The ivy-covered buildings and flagstone walks, the students lying on manicured lawns with their noses in textbooks (it was final-exam season) seemed unreal.

We were walking along a stone path, with college buildings on both sides of us, when Patsy announced:

"I have to find a ladies' room."

We stopped a passing student who pointed to an administration building and said:

"Right over there."

We went into the building and wandered about without seeing a washroom. Patsy stopped another student, who sent us through a courtyard and into an annex where we were directed up a flight of steps to an elevator and told to get off at the seventh floor. We went down the seventh floor hall and around a corner and there at last was a washroom. When we came out, we saw an elevator next to the washroom and we

rode down to the ground floor and went out into the quadrangle, unaware that while we had entered the building through the front door we'd left it by the back door and that furthermore it wasn't the same building.

You remember those parallel paths at the Cloisters? Well, the Columbia quadrangle also has parallel paths. But since the paths are on opposite sides of college buildings, you only see the one you're walking on. Patsy and I went our way along a flagstone path, looking at the buildings; and if the path was taking us gradually uphill, we didn't notice it. We just strolled on, admiring the academic scenery, until, with great suddenness, we saw the end of the quadrangle looming ahead and apparently suspended in space. We found ourselves on an open parapet above a fifteen or twenty-foot drop to a stone courtyard below. If you're afraid of heights, this is not a good place to find yourself. Looking around, I discovered that we were entirely alone. There wasn't a student in sight and the only building near by presented its windowless back to us. Next to the building I noticed the top of a flight of steps leading down from the outside of the parapet and, without looking at Patsy, I made myself walk over to it and look down.

"It's okay," I called to her. "It's a short flight of steps going down to a landing and there's a building down there."

We ran down the steps, our eyes glued to the landing so they wouldn't stray off to the side and see the twenty-foot gorge.

On the landing we found a large glass door and peering in, we saw that it was the back door to a gym. The gym was empty. The door was locked. We turned to go back up the steps and saw, for the first time, that they were open, ship's ladder steps. Patsy went white.

"I can't go up there," she said.

Since the only alternative was to throw ourselves off the parapet, I heard myself say:

"I'll go first."

Sheer guilt drove me up those steps: it was my book we were up there researching (if that's the word for what we were doing). I started up the steps, Patsy close behind so she could keep her eyes on my back. I could hear my breathing. Patsy had stopped breathing altogether; she held her breath till we got safely back up onto solid stone ground. By this time I was too far gone for fear, and throwing off caution I walked close to the end of the parapet—and saw a long, steep but solid flight of stone steps leading down to the courtyard.

Columbia University has new science buildings and playing fields down on the courtyard level, and there was new construction going on which we ought to have investigated, but by that time we'd lost our taste for Columbia.

What Columbia does not have, as far as we could discover, is a place where non-students can eat. Anything. We wandered up and down Broadway and up and down the side streets and finally Patsy stopped a girl going by with books under her arm, and asked if she could tell us "where there's a place to eat around here." The girl recommended Mom Somebody-or-Other's Delicatessen.

"It's the best deli in town," she said earnestly, and pointed us a few blocks further down Broadway.

"Do you want to try it?" Patsy asked when the girl had gone on her way.

"I just want to sit down," I said. Since most delis don't have tables, I thought this meant "No," but Patsy decided it meant "Yes," and she started back down Broadway toward the deli. I

followed her, repeating every now and then: "I just want to sit down."

In every New York neighborhood there's one deli which the local residents believe is the best in town. Since all of Morningside Heights, including the entire populations of Columbia, Union Theological and Jewish Theological, believed Mom Whatsername's to be the best deli in town, there was a long line of customers waiting for service. The line was jammed in between grocery shelves on one side and glass cases of cold meats and salad on the other. Everybody on line was waiting to step up to the glass cases and give one of the two countermen a lunch order for sandwiches and coffee. To go. There weren't any tables.

Patsy streaked back to the end of the line, I followed her fuming, and as the line inched forward, she turned to me now and then to say brightly:

"The line's moving very fast, considering."

After twenty minutes of Considering, we finally got our sandwiches, cole slaw, one milk and two coffees and then carried the bags two blocks to a Riverside Park bench. I was carrying the bag with the cole slaw in it, and the cole slaw dripped all the way over.

We sat on a bench and I chewed my turkey-on-rye-with-Russian in simmering silence until Patsy turned to me, hesitated, and then asked tentatively:

"Do you want me to keep on with this? This sightseeing?"

My bad humor dissolved in shock.

"What kind of question is that?" I demanded. "Here I'm in the middle of giving birth to this important book, and the midwife asks if I want her to keep on with what she's doing!"

"Well, I just realized this morning it's May," said Patsy.

"We go away in June, when the kids come home from college. I thought I'd better ask how much time you want me to save this month."

"All of it!" I bleated. "We haven't seen anything yet! We have all the major tours to do!"

After lunch we stopped at Riverside Church—known colloquially as "the Rockefeller church" because John D. Rockefeller, Jr. supplied the funds for it. Riverside is another beautiful Gothic church, less ornate and imposing than St. John's. It's probably no more beautiful than the big midtown churches—St. Patrick's, St. Thomas's and St. Bartholomew's—but then, it isn't the building that makes Riverside Church the pride of New York.

As its brochure proclaims, Riverside is "an interracial, interdenominational and international" church. Along with the standard church groups, its three thousand parishioners include a Black Christian Caucus and a Chinese Christian Fellowship. From the days of Harry Emerson Fosdick, its most celebrated preacher, to the present, Riverside has involved itself in every battle for human rights from anti-war protests to migrant labor legislation to prison reform. And since Martin Luther King graced its pulpit as guest preacher in the sixties, we weren't surprised to find that its current roster of ministers includes a woman.

"And I'll bet you," I said to Patsy, "that men who've never had any trouble at all saying 'charwoman' or 'cleaningwoman' will find it absolutely impossible to say 'clergywoman'."

Catty-corner from Riverside Church is the tourist attraction which dominated the landscape of Morningside Heights, Grant's Tomb, with its immense granite dome, sat on its hill above the Hudson looking impressive, beautiful and de-

serted, and we trudged staunchly across the street to it. We went up the broad marble steps and in through the imposing doors, to pay our respects to Ulysses Samuel Grant, the great Union general who won the Civil War, whose military memoirs have been compared with Caesar's, and who as President of the United States a century ago presided over the most corrupt and scandal-ridden administration in the country's hundred-year-old political history.

You enter a vast, empty white marble hall, feeling dwarfed by the huge dome above you. You walk to the center of the floor to the rim of a great marble basin. You peer over the rim of the basin down to a floor below, and see two bronze coffins containing the mortal remains of U.S. Grant and his wife, Julia Dent Grant. This is the sight you've come to see, and almost all there is to see.

"It looks like Les Invalides," said Patsy. "Napoleon's tomb."

"I don't know whether that makes it more preposterous or less," I said.

"Well, at least there are two of them in here, instead of just one," said Patsy, looking on the bright side.

Beyond the great hall were two small rooms and we went back to investigate them. On the walls were framed newspaper clippings recounting the history of Grant's life and career, and framed newspaper photographs of the family. And it's nobody's fault that the bearded general and his wife were angular and rawboned, and stared woodenly into the newfangled camera with expressionless faces, but today they look like characters in an Ozark cartoon.

There was one photograph in particular, in which Grant and his wife and children were all sitting bolt upright on the porch of a bolt-upright frame house which, if it wasn't falling

down, could at least have used a paint job. Underneath the photograph was a typewritten caption: *President Grant and his family on the porch of the Summer White House at Long Branch, New Jersey.*

Patsy and I had to support each other out of there.

A solitary guard was on duty at the door and when we came out, Patsy asked him if there were many visitors to the Tomb.

"Oh, yes," he said. "Every year there's a big ceremony on General Grant's birthday."

"How many people come to it?" Patsy asked.

"Well, the Union Army vets always turned out big for it," he said. "We'd have three to four hundred vets come every year."

"How many people came this year?" asked Patsy.

"Well, they've all died off now," he said. We waited, but he didn't add anything. We thanked him and went down the broad steps and left the deserted shrine and walked over to the Broadway bus stop. And the photographs had been funny and the tomb outlandish, but old lines were running in my head:

> The tumult and the shouting dies.
> The captains and the kings depart . . .
> Lord God of Hosts, be with us yet,
> Lest we forget—lest we forget!

Going from Grant's Tomb to Zabar's (pronounced Zaybar's) was going from the sublime to the ridiculous or from the ridiculous to the sublime, I'll never be sure which. And if Grant's Tomb was Made in the USA, Zabar's was Made in New York City. Definitely no question.

I don't think anybody's ever counted the number of delicatessens in New York, but there are four within less than two blocks of my apartment house and it's not an unusual number. Every neighborhood has a string of delis and almost all of them make excellent sandwiches, sell good rye bread and pickles and the usual cole slaw, pickled beets, potato, chicken and tuna salad. But Patsy was right: none of them can be remotely compared with Zabar's.

You go in through the front doorway and duck under ten or twelve different kinds of salami hanging on hooks from the ceiling. Way in the back, there's a cheese department it would take two jars of Air Freshener to neutralize. Between front and back, on the walls and on tables well away from the exotic food cases, there is every item of expensive gourmet kitchen equipment on the market, at considerably less than the market price.

None of which begins to convey the essence of Zabar's. Patsy went looking for the manager and conferred with him, and then came back to me, her arms full of outsized Zabar brochures. When I got home I culled from the brochures the following very incomplete summary of what you can buy at Zabar's, the pride of the West Side, at Eightieth and Broadway:

Fourteen kinds of salami; eight kinds of pâte; nine kinds of cooked fish; twelve kinds of salad; seven kinds of Hungarian sausage; thirty kinds of bread.

Also smoked beef jerky, fresh caviar, sturgeon, stuffed vine leaves, Hungarian peasant bacon, Polish and Yugoslav mushrooms, Romanian pastrami, and cheese "from every country in Europe."

Not forgetting eleven kinds of tea from every country that grows it, and coffee from Jamaica, Hawaii, Kenya, Tanzania, Guatemala and Mexico.

There's one more attraction to Zabar's. It is New York's only genuine *haute monde* delicatessen. A Zabar's shopping bag is a recognized status symbol. It tells the world you're a cultivated and discriminating gourmet, instead of just another New York shlemiel buying a hot pastrami on rye and a sour pickle to go.

# Thursday, May 6

THIS WAS OUR ONLY RAINY DAY. AND THE RAIN CUT SHORT A tour we weren't all that crazy about, and sent us indoors on a tour we had both taken countless times and which somehow never palls.

Now that Patsy had committed herself, I dispensed with diplomatic overtures and phoned her and said bluntly:

"Thursday we're doing the Village."

"Yich-ch," said Patsy.

Greenwich Village is more than a neighborhood, it's a way of life. People who live there would be miserable living anywhere else. People who don't live there, see the Village as a kind of continuous theatrical performance interesting to visit for an evening.

Since the Village is on the West Side (the brief life of a potsmoking neighborhood called the East Village having begun and ended with the sixties), I said to Patsy: "I'm taking a Fifth Avenue bus down, just to check out any Avenue sights I need to mention. Do you want to go down by subway and meet me?"

"Where?" said Patsy. "Not in the Village?!"

"Meet me on the steps of the church at Twelfth and Fifth and we'll do Lower Fifth and the Square first," I said.

"Oh, great, I love it down there," said Patsy and we hung up.

It was sunny enough when I left home and walked to Fifth to catch the bus. One day while you're here, you ought to get

on a Fifth Avenue bus up around the Carnegie mansion and ride all the way down to where the Avenue ends below Eighth Street; it's the best sightseeing bus I know of. You'll ride down along Central Park with all the museums and mansions on your left until you come to the Plaza Hotel at Fifty-Ninth Street, which marks the beginning of the midtown shopping district and from there on, you have to try looking out the windows on both sides of the bus at once.

Most of the famous shops are in the Fifties: Bergdorf-Goodman, Tiffany, Bonwit-Teller, I. Miller, Gucci, Cartier, Mark Cross, Saks. (Lord & Taylor is down at 37th Street, B. Altman is at Thirty-Fourth and if you walk two blocks west of Altman's you come to R. H. Macy and Gimbel Bros., she-added-so-as-not-to-slight-anybody.) Spread through the Fifties and Forties you'll see the avenue's five mammoth book-stores: two Doubleday, one Scribner, Brentano and the beautiful Rizzoli.*

The newest avenue sight at the moment is the glittering Olympic Tower, midtown Fifth Avenue's first apartment house. Olympic Tower, as Patsy succinctly put it, "has apartments nobody can afford to live in, over stores nobody can afford to buy in."

At Fifty-Third on the uptown corner on your right you'll see St. Thomas's Episcopal church, once New York's most fashionable church; now better known for its wonderful Wednesday noon choral concerts. Don't miss them on any account, if you're in town at Christmas or Easter time. Don't worry about how you're dressed. You'll see students pile into the church in blue jeans with their arms full of books, and

*See p. 160, P.S.4.

women with their shopping bags flapping. The rector, John Andrew, is genuinely pleased to see the church jammed and gratified that you like his men's and boys' choirs, and he couldn't care less how you look.

Down below Thirty-Fourth I saw one place I'd forgotten. It's just off Fifth, at One East Twenty-Ninth Street. This one's also an Episcopal church with the official name of The Church of the Transfiguration. And the story has been told a hundred times but I feel like telling it again.

Back in 1871, when theatre people were beyond the pale of respectable society, a celebrated actor named Joseph Jefferson wanted to provide a funeral service for a fellow actor who had died penniless. Jefferson went to a fashionable Fifth Avenue church to consult the minister about arrangements.

"I'm afraid we couldn't possibly hold funeral services at our church for that sort of person," said the minister, "but there's a little church around the corner that might help you."

So Jefferson went to The Little Church Around the Corner, and the church gave his friend a Christian burial and has been marrying and burying actors and other disreputable folk ever since. If you stop in during the day and find a wedding in progress, you're welcome to assist at it. After six p.m., the weddings are private.

The church at Twelfth and Fifth, where I was to meet Patsy, and another below it at Tenth and Fifth, are both old-fashioned neighborhood churches and typical of Lower Fifth, a small, quiet residential neighborhood running from Thirteenth Street down to Eighth, with its side streets extending into the Village.

I got there a little early, which was what I'd hoped to do. When I first came to New York, I used to go down to the New

School on West Twelfth Street and the neighborhood is nostalgic for me. The New School—officially The New School for Social Research—is a college for adults. You can earn a B.A. or Ph.D. there and you can take day-time courses; but the New School's early fame stemmed from the fact that it was primarily an evening college for people more interested in an education than a degree. In the forties, its faculty was a haven for scholarly refugees from the universities of Hitler's Europe. Which may, or may not, be what led Senator Joseph McCarthy to label the school "Communist-dominated" in the fifties. This embarrassed the Eisenhower administration somewhat: it turned out John Foster Dulles had once taught at the New School.

I used to go down there two nights a week, for courses in such practical, everyday subjects as Ancient Greek and the Philosophy of Religion. (Our Greek professor was a German and like most Germans he couldn't pronounce *th*. So when pointing to the Greek letters zeta and theta, he'd say: "Zis is a zeta, and *zis* is a *zeta*." And somebody in the class would pipe up: "But professor, you said *that* was a zeta," and he'd say, "Yes, yes, quite right, zat is a *zeta* but *zis* is a *zeta*!") I was wandering along Twelfth Street remembering all this pleasantly, when Patsy came steaming toward me from Sixth Avenue.

We walked down Lower Fifth toward Washington Arch, stopping at Ninth Street to poke into Washington Mews, a cobblestone square lined with former carriage houses once attached to Washington Square mansions. The mews houses are quaint and charming and looking at them you know you're in, or near, the Village.

"Who owns these?" Patsy asked me.

"NYU," I said, meaning New York University which is a private, not a state-owned, university. "The only way you can get to live in a Washington Mews house is to be a big name on the NYU faculty."

We went on down to Washington Square, created as a park setting for Washington Arch. The Arch was built in 1889 to commemorate the centennial of Washington's inauguration — because if Paris had an Arch and London had an Arch, why shouldn't we have an Arch? I-imagine-somebody-said.

We walked along Washington Square North looking at the fine houses of Henry James's day and trying to decide which of them the heiress, Catherine Sloper, lived in. These houses are also now owned by NYU.

"I was in one of them once," I told Patsy. "They have one horrendous feature. They're all connected by interior doors. By which I mean you can be sitting in your living room in your underwear on a Saturday morning when a door in your living room wall slides open, and your next door neighbour walks in from his-or-her living room and says "Hi, you busy?"

We crossed Fifth Avenue to Washington Square West and walked on over to MacDougal Alley — "where the effete meet," said Patsy — which is another mews lined with quaint and charming carriage houses, these privately owned. At MacDougal Alley, you are in the Village and you walk west to reach the heart of it.

With its center of activity around Seventh Avenue, the Village is a maze of short, narrow streets radiating in all directions, some of the streets cutting into each other and then disappearing to reappear a few blocks later way over that way. Patsy had brought a Village map along and she looked up from it to inform me:

"There are two West Fourth Streets, one below Eleventh Street and one above Eleventh Street."

So she put the map away and from then on we just wandered in and out of all the side streets, stumbling by accident on the more famous ones—Bank and Christopher and Morton and Waverly Place—all of them old and quiet with rows of small houses, looking as remote from the skyscraper city as if they'd been set down in it by mistake.

One of the most attractive streets we saw was St. Luke's Place, the locale of the Audrey Hepburn film, *Wait Until Dark,* with neat four-story houses behind wrought-iron railings and high front steps. If you walk along it in the evening, you'll see glimpses of private libraries through the lighted windows of high-ceilinged living rooms. We missed one famous house on West Eleventh Street but as far as I know it's still there, if you want to look for it. A gold plaque identifies it as the Greta Garbo Home for Wayward Children.

Scattered along the avenues and through the side streets are the Village shops, all of them remorselessly quaint-and-charming. I was taking notes on the items for sale in the shop windows—hand-woven Mexican rugs, Indian sandals, unisex haircuts, Taro cards, astrology charts, handmade ceramics, handmade leather belts and shoes—when Patsy, reading over my shoulder, advised me:

"Just say the whole Village is handmade."

On Bleecker Street there are boutiques named "Elegant Plumage," "Second Childhood" and "Marquis de Suede." Also on Bleecker Street, a Spanish restaurant, an Italian, a Mexican, an Indian and a Moroccan restaurant—and that's on a side street. On Seventh Avenue we passed Greek, Indian, Chinese,

Turkish, Japanese and Italian restaurants, all within a span of a few blocks.

HOWEVER: at noon it started to rain, and we thought we'd wait out the shower over an early lunch, and that's how we discovered that most Village restaurants open at five p.m. You have to walk to Sixth Avenue to find a restaurant open for lunch. We found a Greek restaurant open and crowded with NYU Law School students.

"We made the same mistake with the Village that we made with Lincoln Center," I said to Patsy as we waited for a table. "The Village is another place that has to be seen at night. What tourists ought to do is come down late in the afternoon while it's still light enough to see the houses and shops, and then have dinner and go on to one of the off-off Broadway coffee-house theatres."

"They don't serve coffee," said Patsy gloomily. (She doesn't drink.)

"Well, whatever they're called," I said.

Off-Off Broadway theatres (which differ from Off-Broadway less in professionalism than in the price of the ticket) specialize in new, experimental plays performed in any loft or hole-in-the-wall available. But the ones that are the most fun are those in the back rooms or upstairs rooms of Village restaurants and bars, where the audience sits at small tables and watches the play while sipping Sangria or New York State wine. The play may bore you; the audience won't. Which is to say that the real sightseeing attraction of an evening in the Village is Villagers.

On a warm evening, Seventh Avenue and the streets near it are alive with Villagers, and with the young who live uptown

and come down to the Village in the evening. The people—especially the not-so-young—seen on a Village street in the evening look completely unlike all other New Yorkers. They are colorful, flamboyant, unconventional and uninhibited. The atmosphere is of a friendly, integrated, liberated democracy, or an arty, intellectual Sunset Boulevard, depending on your point of view.

We got a table, and after the waitress took our order for a Greek shishkebab, Patsy fished out of her handbag a folded newspaper article from the Sunday *Times* and handed it to me. It was written by a *Times* architecture critic and was a lecture on How to Look at Buildings.

"I read this one," I said. "I did not think highly of it."

Every time a new building goes up in New York, some critic condemns it in the *Times,* and every time an old building is to be torn down, the Landmarks Preservation Commission issues vehement demands that it be Preserved. Well, the chief New York building the *Times* writer had lectured me on How to Look At was Grand Central Station, which every now and then somebody suggests tearing down, only to be met with screaming objections from the Landmarks Commission.

"Do you know any New Yorker," I asked Patsy, "who personally looks on Grand Central Station with affection?"

"I hated that place when I was a kid," said Patsy. "We went away to camp from there. Going away you couldn't find the counselors, and coming back you couldn't find your parents."

"Exactly," I said. "You've put your finger on the difference between the experts who want to Preserve old railroad stations and the people who have to use them."

Grand Central Station is a huge, squat stone building sprawling from Forty-Second Street to Forty-Fourth and from

Lexington past Park Avenue and halfway to Madison, to a small avenue called Vanderbilt. It was built early in the century when architects believed that every building had to have a decoration on top. You see manifestations of this where Patsy lives: fine, tall old apartment houses with fancy cupolas and decorated Cupids on top. The author of the *Times* article admires that kind of architecture and is particularly fond of the statuary group on top of Grand Central Station, he says it pulls the entire station together. The central figure is a Greek god (it might be Eros) wearing a hat, a loincloth and wings. He's standing by himself on top of the Grand Central clock. Near by, on both sides of him, reclining pseudo-Greeks are looking up at him. All of them sitting around on the roof of a mammoth railroad terminal, pulling it together.

"Do you remember the furor when the old Penn Station was torn down?" I said. "That station was a gloomy horror of a building to come into at night, heavy and dark—and the lights so high overhead they threw deep, gaunt shadows on the stone floor. The Landmarks Preservers had a fit when it came down and a new, clean, light, easy-to-find-your-way-around-in station went up. What was it to them if the old station was a nightmare to people who used it? They didn't use it, they just rode around it in their cars staring learnedly at the architecture and advising us peasants to Preserve it."

So now we're Preserving Grand Central Station. You'd better go look at it while you're here. God knows it's a sight.

We dawdled over lunch hoping the rain would stop, but it didn't.

We phoned Rockefeller Center and the NBC tour was still on strike.

"What other indoor tours do you have on your list?" Patsy asked.

"Only the UN and that's one tour I don't need to take," I said. "I know that place by heart. I love it."

"So do I," said Patsy. "I take out-of-towners there first." She sipped her coffee and added: "I wonder how the new hotel is coming?"

"What hotel?" I said. "Are they building a hotel over there?"

So we went out to the street and hailed a cab and told the driver to take us to the United Nations.

"A cab and a restaurant in one day?" Patsy said with an eyebrow raised. "We're ruining our record."

That was the only cab we ever took. But as we settled in the back seat, I said to Patsy:

"I'm tired of cafeteria lunches. From now on, we're going to eat restaurant lunches like respectable tourists." And the cab driver must have heard this because he called back to us:

"You girls wanta see Bowery bums? You wanta see lesbians? I can show you everything! Where're you girls from?"

We told him we lived here and he spent the rest of the ride complaining about City Hall.

"Do you live here?" Patsy asked him as we got out of the cab.

"Nah!" he said. "I live in Brooklyn."

I never got to the UN without stopping first on the sidewalk to feast my eyes on the original buildings—the Secretariat and the General Assembly—with the hundred-odd member-nation flags flying in front of them. The UN occupies sixteen acres of land (mostly donated by the Rockefellers) and the years have seen the addition of a UN Library

building, Dag Hammerskjold Plaza and the Eleanor Roosevelt Memorial. Across the way, we saw the construction mess which, by the time you read this, will have opened as One UN Plaza, New York's newest luxury-hotel and office building, in sloping blue-green glass.

As we got our tickets at the tour desk, I looked up at the Foucault Pendulum swinging above the grand staircase and told Patsy: "Every time I come here, I make up my mind that this time I'll understand how that thing gives me 'visible proof of the rotation of the Earth,' as it claims in the booklet. And every time I come here, I don't."

"If you come here early in the morning, the pendulum will be swinging one way," said Patsy, "and if you come back late in the afternoon it'll be swinging the opposite way. And you know the pendulum didn't turn around, so the Earth must have turned around."

"Thank you," I said. "It pays to go to Harvard," and we joined the tour.

Every time you go to the UN, you see something new. Every new country admitted to membership presents a gift to the UN. We hadn't been there since the admission of the People's Republic of China and our tour started with a look at China's spectacular gift. On a table almost the length of a wall, stood a replica of a railroad system winding through the mountains and cities of China, done entirely in hand-carved ivory, with every tree, house and inch of track intricately detailed.

Every time you take the tour you also learn something new. The young guides have fifty times as much information in their heads as they can convey in a one-hour tour, and each guide is free to choose which features of each room and which art works to tell you about. The guides, drawn from all the

UN countries, speak perfect English and are awesomely well-informed.

"How do you know so much? How do you remember it all?" Patsy asked the attractive young woman from Sweden who was our guide; and the guide told us that all UN guides are required to attend a daily briefing on current debates and keep abreast of all the literature dealing with "the Economic and Social Council's seven thousand projects, the UNESCO projects on behalf of children in one hundred countries and the administrative work of the Trusteeship Council."

Unless a meeting is going on in one of them, the tour takes you into all the main rooms—the Security Council chamber, the General Assembly room and the meeting rooms of the Trusteeship Council and the Economic and Social Council. They're still the most beautifully designed and constructed assembly rooms I've ever been in.

At the end of the tour, you're deposited in the basement, free to spend time and money in the UN Bookstore, Gift Shop and Souvenir Shop. The unique feature of the book store is its English translations of children's books from all the UN countries. And don't buy ordinary souvenirs in ordinary shops till you've seen the UN souvenir and gift shops. The shipments of gift items from member nations are continuous and unpredictable. One month you'll find Israeli jewelry and African wood carving, the next month silk scarves from India and moccasins from Iceland.

Patsy got carried away by all the exotica and bought a set of cushions labeled "Four Peas in a Pod": four round green cushions shaped like peas, fitted into a long, split green cushion shaped like a pod.

Made in Vermont.

# Wednesday, May 12

EVEN IF YOU'RE NOT NOSTALGIC ABOUT HOLLYWOOD, YOU have got to take the Rockefeller Center tour, the highlight of which is a tour of Radio City Music Hall, the super-colossal Zenith of movie palaces.

(The NBC strike hadn't ended, we'd just got tired of waiting. When it was finally settled, we went back and took the NBC tour and found it dull. Since television production is based in Hollywood, the NBC tour was confined to looking through glass windows at news rooms, soap-opera stages and the studios of NBC's local radio station. The only mild diversions were a demonstration of old-time radio sound effects and a chance to walk onto a TV stage and see yourself on a monitor.)

"Rockefeller Center" originally meant the group of low buildings clustered around the central seventy-story RCA building fronting Fifth Avenue at Forty-Ninth Street and extending back to Rockefeller Plaza. Today the Center has grown to a mammoth complex of some twenty-odd buildings (they keep adding) mushrooming west from Fifth past Sixth almost to Seventh. The main buildings are connected by an underground concourse, and if you can find your way through the concourse—which mostly you can't—you can go from building to building and see most of the Center's two hundred shops, twenty six restaurants and eighteen banks without ever going out in the rain.

But to most New Yorkers, "Rockefeller Center" still means

the original grouping, and you can see it best from across the street outside the doors of Saks: a group of buildings of graduated heights around a green plaza with the RCA building ("30 Rock") rising in the background. Cross the avenue to the Center and walk through the plaza and you'll see the two-level sunken plaza below it. The lower level is an ice-skating rink in winter and an outdoor restaurant in summer; the upper level is a kind of kibitzers' balcony from which to stare down at the skaters or diners, an essential amenity in a city where People-Watching is a favorite sport.

"Did you know," I said to Patsy as we waited in the RCA lobby for the tour to start, "that when Rockefeller Center first opened, it caused as much outrage as the World Trade Center? It opened in the thirties, and everybody said the city didn't need a huge office complex in the middle of a Depression."

"Where'd you read that?" Patsy asked skeptically.

"They said," I continued, "that nobody'd rent enough office space to pay for the upkeep, nobody had the money to open shops, and nobody could afford to buy in them if they did open. And they said who needed a movie palace seating sixty-two hundred people, when every neighborhood movie theatre had to give away dishes to lure families into buying tickets?"

"Who told you all that?" Patsy demanded.

"Cole Porter even wrote a line about it in a song," I said. "Sung by Fred Astaire. Nobody told me. I remember it. I was going to school in Philadelphia and I read about it in the *Evening Bulletin.*"

Patsy was regarding me with detached interest.

"You must be ninety!" she said pleasantly.

The tour took us through the RCA building first, and we stopped at a small, unlikely garden built outside the seventh

floor windows and visible only from the upper floors of the building we were in and the upper floors of nearby office buildings.

"This garden is never used," the guide told us. "It is here for the psychological relief of office-workers on high floors."

We were also, of course, taken to the Seventieth Floor Observation Roof with its marvelous skyline views. Which reminds me: if you can't get a reservation at "Windows on the World" (the World Trade Center restaurant), the next best place from which to see New York at night is the Rainbow Room on the sixty-fifth floor of the RCA building. BUT BE WARY: unlike "Windows on the World," the Rainbow Room has tables at narrow corner windows with almost no view. If you're stuck at one of these, get up and walk to the nearest broad window before you leave, and look out and see what Thomas Edison and New York's anonymous architects have wrought in the way of an incandescent miracle.

We went through the concourse and into the lobbies of the famous original buildings: the Italian building, with Atlas holding up the world on its façade; and the French and English buildings—and I would have been just as happy if the guide hadn't told us that the plaza gardens are officially named the Channel Gardens because they have the French building at one end and the English at the other.

From there, we proceeded to Sixth Avenue to the Largest Indoor Theatre in the World, containing the Largest Indoor Stage in the World, Radio City Music Hall.

The tour began in the great lobby from which we descended a sweeping staircase to the Lounge, a full city block long, thickly carpeted and furnished with chairs and sofas, and ceiling and wall decorations in the grand Hollywood style.

"Do you remember a ladies' room here where the toilet seat sprang up and glowed with violet light when you rose from it?" I asked Patsy. "Ultraviolet disinfectant was common for a while later on, but at the time no other toilet in town lit up lavender and it unnerved me."

"No, the one I remember," said Patsy, "had mirrored walls on all sides. It was terrifying: you not only saw yourself from all angles but on into infinity."

The tour guide's talk was entirely devoted to weights and measures: how many feet wide and high the stage was, how many tons of cable it took to raise the whale-sized orchestra from the pit to the stage on an electronic platform; how many acres of seats the theatre's vast tiers held; how many tons the World's Largest Indoor Organ weighed.

(The plans for the Music Hall were drawn up in 1929, when organ music accompanied silent films; and either the management was already stuck with the World's Largest Organ when the theatre opened, or didn't think the talkies would last.)

Patsy and I moved away from the tour group to wallow in our memories of Radio City Music Hall stage shows. And if I speak of them in the past tense, it's less because the Music Hall may have been converted to other forms of entertainment by the time you come, than because the place itself is so firmly part of a long-gone past for both of us.

Traditionally, New Yorkers have gone to Radio City Music Hall only at three stages in their lives: 1. when they were children; 2. when they were young and dating; 3. when they had children of their own to take to the annual Christmas or Easter or Fourth of July extravaganza. Patsy, who grew up in New York, was awash with memories of the annual Christmas

show which had been the high point of every childhood year.

"First the lights went down and you'd hear the organ. You wouldn't see it, you'd just hear it. Then a purple light would come up over on the side, and you'd see the organ and the organist sliding slowly out of the wall in a purple glow. Then, while the organist played, you had to wait—the wait was absolutely endless because you were so excited—for the show to begin. Then, while the organist was still playing, you'd look up at the side boxes and they'd be full of Biblical statues. And then, slowly, the statues would move, and you'd see they were people, and they'd come down from the boxes and march slowly up the side aisles and onto the stage. They were marching," she explained, "to Bethlehem. And then all the manger animals would file up on stage, marching to Bethlehem, and then a star would appear and lead everybody to the manger for the big tableau."

Then the hundred and fifty piece orchestra rose slowly up out of the pit and the stage show began.

"First came the acrobats who threw each other around," said Patsy, "and then the men with the animal acts who threw the animals around. I always worried for fear one of the dogs would make, right there on the stage. And then the soloist—it was always some terrible singer—would sing Christmas carols. And then came the ballet. And finally, just as you thought you'd die if they didn't come soon, the Rockettes. And they were wonderful."

All Radio City Music Hall stage shows followed that format. They were all spectacles, sumptuously costumed and performed against a background of half a ton of resplendent scenery.

"Did you ever see the Fourth of July show, with the elec-

tronic fireworks going off at the end?" Patsy asked me. "The Rockettes wore red-white-and-blue sequin shorts and sequin tap-shoes and sequin Uncle Sam vests, and they all snapped their heads to the left at the same second and when they went *tap,*-ta-ta-*tap,* ta-ta-*tap-tap-tap,* every knee was in an exact line with every other knee. And four hundred men would march down from the boxes in sequin Uncle Sam suits and sequin stove-pipe Uncle Sam hats, singing 'You're a Grand Old Flag,' and the electric fireworks would go off and make a huge flag for the final tableau." And she added thoughtfully: "It was so terrible it was remarkable."

I'll tell you an old joke that will sum up Radio City Music Hall for you.

It seems a man and his wife went to the Music Hall one Sunday afternoon, arriving toward the end of the film. When it ended, the house lights came up for a few minutes before the stage show and the man rose, murmuring to his wife: "I'm going to the men's room."

He located an exit on his floor—orchestra, loge, mezzanine, balcony or second balcony—but he couldn't find a men's room on it. He descended a staircase and looked on the next floor and couldn't find a men's room and descended another staircase. He walked along corridors and pushed open doors, he went along dark passages and up and down steps, getting more and more lost and more and more frantic. Just as his need became intolerably urgent, he pushed open a heavy door and found himself on a small street lined with houses, trees and shrubs. There was no one in sight and the man relieved himself in the bushes.

All this had taken time, and it took him additional time to work his way back up to his own floor and locate his own aisle

and section. By the time he finally reached his seat, the stage show had ended and the movie had begun. The man slid into his seat, whispering to his wife: "How was the stage show?"

To which his wife replied: "You ought to know. You were in it."

We came out on Sixth Avenue, and maybe because the Music Hall had evoked the past so vividly, we both looked at the avenues with new eyes. The transformation of midtown Sixth Avenue over the past ten or fifteen years has been extraordinary. Back in the fifties, it was one long honky-tonk row of shooting galleries, cheap souvenir shops, third rate second-hand bookstores and dingy cafeterias. Today, from Forty-Eighth to Fifty-Ninth Street, Sixth Avenue is so opulent a row of office towers set in landscaped plazas that if you put a few flags and trees around, you could almost start calling it The Avenue of the Americas. The best time to see it is early in the evening when you're on your way to a Broadway theatre. At dusk every skyscraper is blazing with light, the plazas are illuminated and walking down the avenue is dazzling.

We had lunch at a Japanese restaurant near the Music Hall; and not till we'd worked our way through both tempura and sukiyaki and the waitress had brought our second pot of tea, did I push across the table to Patsy a typewritten itinerary for Blockbuster Sunday:

*St. Mark's-in-the-Bowery*
*The Lower East Side (Orchard St.)*
*Chinatown*
*City Hall*
*Wall Street-on-a-Sunday*
*Trinity churchyard.*

Patsy didn't bat an eye. She just shot me a sidelong glance and asked:

"Why did you leave it off?"

"Well, I did think about it," I said, "because we did go on a very cloudy day, the visibility was only five miles, and I thought I'd wait and see if it's very clear on Sunday."

"You know we're going back up there," said Patsy, and added "WTC" to the bottom of the list.

We poured ourselves more tea and lit cigarettes. Then Patsy staring into her teacup somberly said:

"Do you realize what we owe the Rockefellers?" And she ticked the debt off on her fingers. "The Cloisters. Riverside Church. Lincoln Center. Rockefeller Center. The UN."

"Rockefeller University," I said. "It's around the corner from me. It's beautiful." Rockefeller University is a scientific graduate school, it graduates only Ph.D's. "I read somewhere that its faculty has won nine Nobel prizes in the last five years."

"From the top of this island to the bottom," said Patsy soberly, "and from the East River to the Hudson with Rockefeller Center in the middle, we owe them so much!"

"Harry Truman would tell you that the Rockefeller fortune was built on the blood of Colorado miners," I said.

"I know, I read Merle Miller's book, too," said Patsy. "I know it's blood-money."

"Still, —" I said.

Patsy nodded.

To the Rockefellers, living and dead, whose blood-money has so greatly enriched the landscape of New York City and the lives of New Yorkers:

Thanks for everything.

# Sunday, May 16

ONCE UPON A TIME, WHEN THIS CITY WAS THE DUTCH TOWN of new Amsterdam, a new governor arrived from Holland named Peter Stuyvesant. He was a moral man and choleric, and he took a fit at what he found here: one unfinished church, one unfinished school, fifty decaying houses and seventeen taprooms.

Peter Stuyvesant went to work and over the next two decades transformed the town into an orderly and prosperous community of houses, farms and shipyards. He was a bad-tempered man with a dictatorial manner and he stumped around town on his peg-leg quarreling with everybody. He was also a bigot who wanted to ship all the Quakers to Rhode Island. ("They have all sorts of riff-raff people there," he explained.) Every now and then, the Staats General sent him peremptory orders to stop harassing minorities.

Stuyvesant built himself a large farm along the East River—a *bouwerie,* as the Dutch called it—where for twenty-four years he lived the good life of an autocratic governor. Then, in 1664, the Duke of York's troops invaded New Amsterdam. Knowing that resistance would get him nothing but a bombed city and slaughtered inhabitants, Stuyvesant surrendered without firing a shot. The Duke of York, not content with renaming the entire province of New Nether-lands "New York province" after himself, also named the city after himself. New Amsterdam became New York City and Dutch rule came to an end.

Stuyvesant was seventy-two years old by then, and the Staats General in Holland sent him a kind letter saying, in effect:

"You've earned a peaceful retirement. Come on home."

And Peter Stuyvesant wrote back saying, in effect:

"I am home."

Whether you called it New Amsterdam or New York, this was his town. What was it to him if (like millions to follow) he had come here from somewhere else? Peter Stuyvesant withdrew to his *bouwerie* and lived out his old age as a private citizen of the city he had governed for twenty-four years. He died peacefully at home, and was buried in a vault in the family church.

Stuyvesant's farm and church are long gone. But a church was later built on the property, in that part of it which is still called the Bowery. And it was at this church—St. Mark's-in-the-Bowery, at Tenth Street and Second Avenue—that Patsy and I met that Sunday morning, to pay our respects to the first New Yorker.

What we had gone there to see, we found in a side wall of the church: an old stone vault with an inscription which read:

In this vault lies buried

PETRUS STUYVESANT

Captain General and Governor-in-Chief of
New Amsterdam in New Netherlands
now called New York,
and the Dutch West-India Islands
died Feb. 4, A.D. 1672
Aged 80 years

"I have suppressed my poor-man's-historian instincts on other tours," I told Patsy as we left the churchyard, "but today we're doing Old New York. Here and there I just may remember a fascinating historical note which I will want to share with you."

"After talking my ears off about Peter Stuyvesant for half an hour, did you think you had to tell me that?" said Patsy.

We walked down along the Bowery and found the sidewalks empty on both sides of the avenue.

"Not a bum in sight," I said. And Patsy said reasonably: "I guess like everybody else, Bowery bums sleep late on Sunday."

We walked down to Houston Street (pronounced How-ston instead of Hew-ston, no book I ever read could tell me why) where the Lower East Side officially begins. But we had to walk on down to Orchard Street to see the real Sunday action.

The Orthodox Jews of the Lower East Side shut their shops early on Friday afternoon for the sabbath, and reopen them on Sunday morning. And if you think the street scenes in the movie *Hester Street* depicted a bygone era, go down to Orchard Street on a sunny Sunday morning and correct your impression.

The street was closed to traffic when we got there, and a large banner strung across the street from the tops of tenements proclaimed: ORCHARD STREET MALL. On Orchard Street, the word "Mall" is about as appropriate as it would be for a street market in downtown Calcutta. We joined a dense mob of people inching along the middle of the street, looking to left and right at the merchandise jamming every inch of sidewalk on both sides of the street.

There were long racks of women's dresses and men's and

women's pants, and graduated wooden platforms stuffed with rows of shoes and hats. Sandwiched between the racks and platforms were mountains of T-shirts and ties piled on a piece of blanket spread on the sidewalk. Down the street we passed heavier racks with thick bolts of upholstery fabric, dress wools, and opulent rolls of gold and silver brocade, positively blinding in the sun.

But that was only on the sidewalks in front of the shops. The shop owners obviously felt the need of more display space. Men's shirts on wire hangers hung from awnings and from the fire-escape railings of every tenement. Dresses on hangers hung from flagpoles, handbags hung from hooks driven into the brick walls, and a couple of hundred T-shirts dangled from a clothesline strung along an entire block of third-story tenement windows. In the dizzying welter of merchandise cramming the sidewalks and hanging in midair from every available anchorage, the shops themselves — where uptown New Yorkers buy designer clothes at half price — were almost invisible.

A woman was coming toward us, pushing her way expertly through the solid sea of bodies in the center of the "Mall," and passing out handbills as she came. We took one. Under the name and address of the store, the handbill advertised:

PARIS IMPORTS
Yves Saint Laurent     Valentino     Pierre Cardin
Gucci     Pierre D'Alby     Anne Klein
Calvin Klein     French Jeans

"Tell them," said Patsy as I wrote all this down, "the difference between Sunday and Monday. You come down here

Sunday to sightsee; you come down Monday-through-Thursday to shop."

When we came abreast of Fine & Klein, the most famous of the cut-rate clothing stores on Orchard Street, we inched our way over to the sidewalk to look at the Gucci bags and Cardin suits in the window, and I saw what Patsy meant. The store was so jammed with shoppers that an employee stood in the doorway barring entrance to any more customers till some of those inside departed.

This is how you shop down there. Go to a Fifth Avenue store and find the Cacharel suit or Hermès bag you want. Copy down the number on the tag and take the number with you to Orchard Street. Designer clothes are never on display on the sidewalk, and only a few are displayed in the shops themselves. Most of them are kept packed away in boxes. But produce the number of the item you want, and the difference between Fifth Avenue and Orchard Street prices will stagger you.

We passed two stores, close together, which were testimony to the overlapping neighborhoods around us. One was the A-ONE NACHAS KNIT SWEATER SHOP. ("Nachas" is the Yiddish word for "joy," so if you want and A-1 sweater knit with joy, that's where you'll find it.) The other was a religious artifacts store, its windows crammed with Catholic statues and medallions and an assortment of Christmas creches. The older generation of middle European Jews still clings to the Lower East Side; older Italians still cling to adjacent Little Italy; and below both, new waves of Hong Kong immigrants cling to overcrowded Chinatown. And the extent to which the three neighborhoods spill over into each other is visible on Sunday on Orchard Street. We saw boys wearing *yarmulkas* eating

Italian ices, and Jewish and Chinese men deep in conversation. If you're here in September during the biggest of the city's Italian street fairs, the San Gennaro Festival on Mulberry Street, you'll see more Chinese than Italian faces looking down at the fair from tenement windows. And you won't believe it, but on Allen Street there's a Kosher Chinese restaurant where the Chinese waiters wear *yarmulkas.* The truth is that the faces you see down there would stick out like sore thumbs in Rome or the Warsaw Ghetto or Hong Kong; they aren't Italian, Jewish and Chinese faces, they're New York faces.

We walked all the way down Orchard Street to Canal. We had passed famous Lower East Side streets at intersections all the way down. I managed to control myself as we crossed Rivington Street, famous for its huge sidewalk barrels of Kosher pickles. But one block below Rivington, we came to Delancey Street.

"Did I ever tell you about Oliver Delancey, the Outlaw of the Bronx?" I asked Patsy.

"Oh, God," said Patsy.

"He was a sort of commando raider," I said. "The Delanceys were rich Tories, their sons were educated in England and so forth. Well, during the Revolution the Delancey men became officers in the King's Loyal American regiment and fought bravely for the King's cause and they were all due to be knighted after England won the war. So was Jimmy Rivington. He published the Tory newspaper in New York during the British Occupation. The British thought very highly of Jimmy, he was presented to the Prince of Wales when the Prince came to New York. Jimmy Rivington and the Delancey men all expected to be among the first American

Knights of the British Empire. Instead of which, they wound up giving their names to the two most famous lower-class immigrant streets in the world."

"Write that down," said Patsy automatically.

At Canal Street, we turned west to Mott, one of Chinatown's narrow streets, clotted with restaurants, vegetable markets, curio shops, a Chinese book store, all of them on the ground floors of appallingly ancient, decayed tenements, but with a new modern Chinese Community Center rising hopefully in the middle of the block.

Since 1963, when American immigration laws were finally amended to include "orientals," overcrowding in Chinatown has become more and more severe. A *Times* story identified Confucius Plaza as a publicly-financed housing project, and to walk along Mott Street is to see how desperately it's needed.

It was nearly two o'clock by the time we got there and we were both ravenous; but as far as I'm concerned, there's no better street in New York for handling an appetite. The new Hong Kong immigrants of the sixties brought their Szechuan cuisine with them. They opened restaurants in Chinatown, to which New Yorkers who like hot food—chili pepper hot— became addicted. As the immigrants learned enough English to move uptown, Szechuan restaurants sprang up in all New York neighborhoods; but walking along Mott Street, I happened to see the first Szechuan restaurant I'd ever tried and which I remembered with special pleasure.

"Do you like Szechuan food?" I asked Patsy.

"I like all Chinese food," said Patsy innocently.

"Well, I haven't been there in a long time," I said, "but Mandarin Inn used to be wonderful. Shall we try it?"

"Why not?" said Patsy. And we crossed the street to

Mandarin Inn, where a sign in the hall informed us that Chef Wong demonstrated the preparation of lemon chicken on the second Sunday afternoon of every month. We didn't wait around for the demonstration, but we ordered the lemon chicken, and shrimp with garlic sauce, which were the Specialties of the Day. I ordered a side dish of Szechuan string beans from memory.

"Do you want your shrimp starred?" I asked Patsy as the waiter took our order.

"What do you mean?" she said.

"When a dish is starred or has a red check next to it, it means it's extra hot," I said. "Do you like hot spicy food?"

"No," said Patsy.

So I ordered my shrimp hot, she ordered hers mild. The lemon chicken is always mild, but I forgot to warn Patsy about the string beans. Being deep green, they looked cool. Patsy speared one, dropped it negligently into her mouth, and then began to claw the air. She drank her glass of water, and mine, and a cup of tea before she managed, still gasping, to push the dish of string beans over to my side of the table.

I liked the lemon chicken better than the highly-touted version served at a fashionable uptown restaurant where it's so saturated with sugar you can't taste the lemon.

"In my extremely limited experience," I said to Patsy, "every over-priced, super-chic restaurant in New York, where you can't get a table unless they *know* you, turns out to have disappointing food when you finally get there. Whereas every neighborhood in New York has good, unpretentious restaurants where they'll feed you just as well, for half the price and none of the aggravation."

"Tourists should do what we did at Columbia," said Patsy.

"Ask somebody going by on the street: 'Where's a good place to eat around here?'"

So you do that. Don't stop a man with a briefcase, he's probably a commuter. Wait till a man or woman comes along with groceries, a bike, a baby-coach or a dog and ask him-or-her to recommend a restaurant.

We walked down Mulberry Street after lunch and passed a Chinese Teahouse and Pastry Shop. I had Sunday brunch in one of those shops once. Trays of hot filled pastry puffs were brought to the table, the pastries on one tray stuffed with shrimp, others with meat and vegetables, with a tray of sweet puffs for dessert.

On Mulberry as on Mott Street, the vegetable stores were open on Sunday, and through the open doorways we could see bok toy, the mustardy lettuce, fresh ginger and black, hundred-day-old duck eggs.

Ahead of us, at the end of Mulberry Street, rose the first towers of Lower Manhattan and we walked on west to City Hall at the upper end of the old city. On a deserted Sunday, you can appreciate the grace of the low white building, its Colonial columns and portico and domed clock tower tranquilly at home among the skyscrapers, thanks to City Hall Park which keeps them at a respectful distance.

"You see that turret window up there on top?" I said, pointing up at the small window under the clock tower.

"What about it?" said Patsy.

"There's a little man who sits up there by himself in an office behind that window," I said. "He's been sitting up there for forty years and he's a human encyclopedia of New York City. Anybody in the City Administration who needs a New York fact or date or place-name origin, phones the little man

up in that turret. He's been sitting up there through eight or nine administrations with his encyclopedic head, every mayor finds him indispensable and he outlasts them all."

City Hall Park being the center of a radius of Lower Manhattan streets, we had to decide which exit would take us down to Trinity Church. Patsy studied several YOU ARE HERE maps and then informed me that they were all upside down, but that Broadway should take us down to Wall Street. We crossed an empty, silent intersection and started down Broadway into the financial district.

The absolute quiet and emptiness of Lower Manhattan on a Sunday spreads it out before you like a model city, giving you a chance to see it first in perspective and then, as you walk, in a series of small, clear-cut pictures.

At the corner of Broadway and Liberty, in the shadow of the huge Marine Midland building, Patsy clutched my arm and said: "Look down there!" And I looked down a long curving canyon as dramatic as Wall Street's.

At the next corner, Thames Street, she seized my arm again and ordered: "Look up!"

On opposite corners of a narrow alley, two buildings rose maybe forty stories above the street, and on what might have been the thirty-fifth floor, a foot-bridge connected the two buildings. Somebody obviously got tired of taking an elevator all the way down, crossing the narrow alley and taking another elevator all the way up, and built a bridge outside two thirty-fifth floor windows to save steps.*

We went on down to Wall Street, and there was Trinity Church with the churchyard gate standing open. We found

*See p. 152, P.S. 1.

Hamilton's impressive monument, and Gallatin's, and what I consider a fitting monument to Robert Fulton: an enormous, pretentious tomb—but empty. (His remains are buried elsewhere.) And we came upon a gravestone which touched me very much.

The stone must have been recently restored because the legend on it was plain and easy to read from the outside path on which we stood. What touched me, however, was not what was on the stone but what I could read between the lines.

The inscription noted that the deceased had been a "merchant of New York" until 1783, when he had "removed to Newfoundland where he established a new home," and where he had died fifteen years later.

"I promise I won't bore you with any more stories if you'll just listen to this one," I told Patsy. "First, read the stone."

Patsy read it and then asked obligingly:

"Who was he?"

"I don't know. Nobody. Just a merchant," I said. "But he was a Tory. 1783 was the year when the British left New York, after seven years of Occupation. They left in November, and most Tories left at the same time. Some of them were afraid of reprisals from the returning patriots, and some of them just didn't want to live under a rebel government; they wanted to stay English. So England offered them free passages to Newfoundland, and they became pilgrims all over again, sailing off to another wilderness—in winter—to start a new life. Well, here's one of them. He 'removed to Newfoundland and established a new home there' and died there. Only he must have left instructions in his will for his body to be carried, by ship, all the way back to New York to be buried in Trinity churchyard—because here he is."

"That's a nice story for a book about New York," said Patsy judiciously. "Use that."

It was after four when we left the churchyard. We had been walking steadily since ten that morning. My shoes hated two of my toes and a bone in my right foot; Patsy's kept mutinously dropping off behind her. But it was a sunny day and in the absence of exhaust fumes, the air was sharply clear. The World Trade Center towers looked closer than they were and we pushed on toward them without bothering to discuss it. If you're gung-ho about New York, and you're that close to that view on a bright, clear day, you're going back up there whether your feet want to or not. But we were very thankful when our feet finally made it to the World Trade Center entrance and we walked into the surrealistic lobby. Then we looked up at the mezzanine.

The line of people waiting to buy tickets ran clear around the mezzanine; everybody in New York had discovered it was a clear day. But the sign on the ticket window said "View to the Horizon," and we'd passed the point of no return anyway, so we went all the way around the mezzanine and got on the end of the line, where we stood, inching along, for twenty-five minutes. Then one of the two elevators took us up, and we sat in one window seat after another gawking out and down in blissful silence, the long wait forgotten.

"If it were six instead of five," said Patsy, "we'd be able to watch the sunset."

"Does this building face west?" I asked.

"It faces everywhere," said Patsy positively. "It does everything."

When we'd sat in every window seat, we finally rose to leave. And I don't know why it didn't occur to us that if two

elevators took twenty-five minutes to get all of us up there, they would take at least that long to get all of us back down. Standing on line all over again I was getting a backache and I leaned backwards to relieve it. Whereupon Patsy inquired: "What are you doing?"

"I have a backache," I said.

"That's not what you do for a backache," said Patsy. "Bend forward with your arms stretched out and then bend down till you touch the floor."

I leaned over and as my fingertips touched the floor, a hand began thumping my head down to meet them.

"Relax your head," advised Patsy. Which is how I discovered that your head is not like your arms or legs, you can't relax it, or stiffen it, you can't do anything with it. Like Mount Everest, it's just there. And all this time, Patsy's two hands industriously pushed my head down and Patsy's voice commanding authoritatively:

"Relax your head."

How we looked to the rest of the line it didn't occur to us to consider; we were too busy with what we were doing.

By the time we got back down to the ground floor we were so tired I needed a new definition of the word. Patsy supplied it.

We had a long subway ride still ahead of us, and we had to locate our separate subways through a network of unfinished corridors. Before embarking on this final lap, I fished out my cigarettes and lit one. Patsy usually prefers her own brand but she was just standing, swaying slightly, staring at my pack in a kind of vacant stupor.

"You want a cigarette?" I asked—and took one of mine out of the pack and extended it to her. Patsy stared at it a moment.

"No," she said finally. "I wouldn't have the strength to draw on it."

That's tired.

I didn't hear from Patsy till Wednesday evening.

"I've been paralyzed for three days," she said when she phoned. "Both the shoes I wore Sunday have holes in them."

"Don't complain to me, I've got two corns and a bunion," I said.

"Well, you told me to save Thursday," said Patsy, "but I'm warning you: I'm only up to something very easy and midtown."

"So am I," I said—and wondered how to tell her what I had in mind.

"Okay," said Patsy. "As long as we don't have to do it this week, I'll tell you why I called you. There's a black-owned Sightseeing Bus company that does a three-hour tour of Harlem. We have to reserve seats in advance. You want me to call /them and book seats for next week?"*

"Fine," I said. "Any day you can make, I can make."

"Right," said Patsy—and couldn't resist adding: "Guess where their first stop is?"

"Where?" I said.

"The Jumel mansion," said Patsy. "I told you we'd see everything! Now, what's for tomorrow?"

"We'll only need a couple of hours," I said cautiously. "You want to meet me at Bloomingdale's at three?"

"I don't like Bloomingdale's," said Patsy.

"I went to Zabar's; you can go to Bloomingdale's," I said. "Meet me at the Lexington Avenue entrance."

*See p. 171, P.S.8

Considering our mutual fear of heights, I saw no reason to tell her in advance, that I considered it our duty as tourists to get on a cable car suspended over midtown Manhattan, and ride across the East River and back on it.

# Thursday, May 20

A FEW BLOCKS FROM WHERE I LIVE, THERE'S A PEDESTRIAN
walk along the river, above the East River Drive. If you're
strolling along it, you'll see on the opposite bank a small
island, two miles long, running parallel with the East Side
from Forty-Second Street to Seventy-Ninth.

The city bought the island from a man named Blackwell
back in 1823 and for years it was known as Blackwell's Island,
but in the twentieth century it became better known as
Welfare Island because of the free hospitals-for-incurables the
city built and maintained there. In the early years of the
century the island also had a very jazzy jail. Boss Tweed had "a
magnificent cell" there, according to the brochure, with a
picture window to give him a view of the city he'd robbed
blind. And Mae West spent ten days there for appearing in a
play she wrote called *Sex*.

By the early sixties, when I first became aware of it, Welfare
Island was occupied only by two hospitals for the severely
handicapped. The hospitals had large, permanent populations and the patients were citizens with voting rights. And
since Welfare Island ran parallel with our neighborhood, it
was included in the Assembly district represented by our local
Democratic Club. So during every political campaign, our
club leaders climbed into a car, with our State Assembly or
City Council candidate in the back seat, and drove across the
Queensboro Bridge, and then back through part of Queens,
to visit the voters on Welfare Island. The trip took fifteen

minutes without traffic, thirty minutes with traffic.

This year, the club leaders drove over as usual; but they saw ten times as many voters as ever before and they probably made the trip by car for the last time. Because this year the island has been transformed; it is now Roosevelt Island, a new suburb built to house 2200 families in mini apartment houses. And the island's residents will commute to their New York offices not in fifteen to thirty minutes, but in four. A tramway has been built to carry them back and forth across the East River by cable car, for the price of a subway token. The tram made its first run last Monday.

The cable cars leave from a specially constructed depot above Sixtieth Street and Second Avenue. Which is why I told Patsy to meet me at Bloomingdale's. Bloomingdale's occupies a square block from Fifty-Ninth to Sixtieth and from Lexington to Third. But if I'd told Patsy to meet me on the Third Avenue side, she might have got there before I did, she might have looked toward Second and seen the tramway depot — and guessed — and bolted. So we met at the Lexington Avenue entrance to Bloomingdale's.

"Put this in your shoulder bag, but don't forget to read it later, it's funny," said Patsy, handing me the inevitable clipping.

"Why don't you like Bloomie's?" I asked as we went into the store (where I was going to walk her through to the Third Avenue exit).

"It's too big," said Patsy. "I can't find anything."

"If you just remember that Bloomingdale's was once a cheap department store on Lexington Avenue," I said, "that's all you need to know — because it's still, basically speaking, a cheap department store *on Lexington Avenue.* When the Third Avenue

El came down and Third Avenue became beautiful and expensive, Bloomingdale's naturally added a beautiful and expensive Third Avenue side. So you take the Lexington Avenue escalator up to the cheap-clothes floors, and the Third Avenue escalator up to the designer-clothes floor. But they have a great furniture department, a great housewares department and a sensational gourmet food shop in the basement, so don't say you don't like it."

By this time, we had come out on Third Avenue, Patsy following me absent-mindedly. But as we started walking toward Second, she saw the new Tramway depot looming overhead at the corner of Second, and stopped cold.

"We're not going up in that ski-lift!" she said.

"We owe it to my readers," I said.

I kept on walking and she followed me in silence. At the corner of Second Avenue, a flight of stone steps led up to the tramway platform. We reached the foot of the steps and Patsy halted again. She waved an arm toward the cable wire overhead.

"Do you see what you're going to be riding on?" she demanded. "It's a piece of string!"

"I couldn't do it alone," I said piously. "Together, we can do anything."

She followed me up the stone steps to the platform, where we stood and watched the cable car glide toward us from the island, swaying gently as it crossed the river.

"Will you look how it's shaking?" said Patsy. "Why do we have to try this thing the first week it's operating? They haven't got it safe yet!"

The car landed, and the people who stepped out of it were smiling, which gave me the courage to push Patsy into it

ahead of me. We were joined by a dozen other thrill-seekers with nothing better to do in the middle of a Thursday afternoon.

The cable car, a glass bubble with standard bus seats, runs alongside the Queensboro Bridge, and since we were level with the cars going by on the bridge we had no more sense of height than we'd have had in an ordinary El train. What we did have, as the car stood poised over midtown Manhattan at the edge of the river and then started slowly on its way, was a goggle-eyed view of present-day transportation.

Below us, on land, was the usual Second Avenue traffic jam of buses, trucks and cars. On the water were a couple of barges, a commuters' motorboat and a Circle Line Sightseeing boat taking tourists on the time-honored trip around Manhattan island. Above us, planes flew in the distance, and as we crossed the river, a helicopter went by on its way to one of the airports.

And Patsy, who had been shaking when she stepped into it, was darting back and forth from one side of the car to the other, barking: "Look down there! Look over here! Look out that way!"

The tramcar landed at the new suburb, unfinished and sparsely inhabited as yet, though the rental offices were busy. We walked nearly the length of it, admiring the small six and seven-story apartment houses, the new streets and park, the new school and swimming pool, the very old church and the old Blackwell house on its way to becoming a community center.

"It's pretty now, like a toy city," I said to Patsy. "But you can visualize the fast-food stores and parking lot and they've already got space set aside for the suburban shopping center. Riding a cable car over the East River is something tourists

might want to try. But once they get here, all they'll see is one more standardized suburb."

(Two days later, riding a cable car over the East River turned out to be something half of New York wanted to try. On the tram's first weekend, twenty thousand New Yorkers converged on it, bringing their children and a picnic lunch, prepared for a day's outing on Roosevelt Island, which had no picnic facilities. The families picnicked all over it and, when the trash baskets overflowed, littered all over it. The island also had no public toilets, and the results of that were so horrendous that the beleaguered islanders threatened to close down the tramway if the weekend invasion continued. It didn't. Within two weeks, the novelty had worn off and the tram trip to Roosevelt Island joined the list of sightseeing tours New Yorkers are definitely going to take some day, like the trip to the Statue of Liberty.

That afternoon when I got home I dug Patsy's clipping out of my shoulder bag. It was from the *Times* and featured a photograph of Trinity churchyard and the intelligence that the graveyard had become a favorite lunchtime meeting place for young pot-smokers. I phoned Patsy.

"I forgot to tell you," she said. "We're booked for the Harlem tour at ten a.m. Monday. Penny Sightseeing Bus, 303 West Forty-Second, write it down."

I wrote it down, and said:

"I read that clipping. Do you really think a story about pot-smoking in Trinity's graveyard belongs in a book for tourists?"

"It's a modern sidelight. Put it in," said Patsy. "Now listen. I've been thinking about that story you told me. About the Tory who left New York after the Revolution and fled to Buffalo."

"NEWFOUNDLAND," I said. Buffalo. I was losing all my respect for Harvard.

"Well, wherever it was," said Patsy. "What exactly did the stone say?"

I went to get my notes and came back and reported:

"I didn't take his name. What I took verbatim was that he was 'a merchant of New York who removed to Newfoundland in 1783 and established a new home there,' and I must have looked at the birth and death dates because I made a note that he died up there fifteen years later."

"Was it a gravestone," asked Patsy, "or a plaque?"

"A gravestone, I think," I said.

"I think so, too, but you'll have to make sure," said Patsy. "Because it occurred to me: if it was a plaque, then he's buried in Newfoundland and somebody just put up the plaque in his memory."

"You've just ruined a beautiful story," I said. "But the lettering was very clear, I could read it easily from the outside path, so it might have been a plaque."

"Is it worth going back down to check it?" Patsy asked. "Or do you just want to phone them?"

"We have to go back down anyway," I said. "We still haven't toured the Stock Exchange."

"Oh, right," said Patsy. "And I want to check up on that bank; I want to see if they've put up a new wall plaque. All right, just put the Tory's gravestone on your list or we'll forget it."

As things turned out, we were to be in no danger of forgetting it. Ever.

## Monday, May 24

THIS DAY STARTED WITH A MYSTERY, AND PATSY AND I aren't sure it didn't end with one.

We'd been having unnaturally hot weather and a month earlier than usual, New York City was air-conditioned to death. To give you an example — and a warning: two friends of mine landed in hospitals with pneumonia, in July, from the icy, air-conditioned offices they worked in. I get frozen out of restaurants and movie theatres all summer; and since the buses to Jersey resorts always delivered me to the beach with a sore throat and a sinus cough, I began to worry about the Harlem sightseeing bus. On Saturday, therefore, I phoned the Penny Bus Company. A man answered the phone.

"I'm booked for your Monday morning tour," I said, "and I wondered whether your bus is heavily air-conditioned and whether we'll need to bring sweaters."

And he said:

"You must be Mrs. Gibbs."

My mouth fell open.

"I'm coming with Mrs. Gibbs," I said.

"Oh, that's right," he said. "There are two of you. We do have one air-conditioned bus, but the air-conditioning doesn't work very well so it's never very cold."

I thanked him and we hung up; and I called Patsy. I told her that the man who answered the phone had said immediately: "You must be Mrs. Gibbs," and I went on: "We must be the only passengers on the bus. Will you mind that?"

"No, it means we can ask a lot of questions," said Patsy.

We met in front of the bus office and went upstairs to the ticket office. There was a man behind the desk and he smiled and said good morning, and Patsy said:

"We have seats reserved on the ten o'clock bus."

And he said:

"You're Mrs. Gibbs."

But when we paid for our tickets, he got out a list of names and checked off ours at the bottom of a long list.

"The other passengers have all gone downstairs to the bus stop," he said. "You'd better go right down; the bus'll be along any minute."

As we went downstairs, I said to Patsy:

"Maybe he knows we're the only whites on the bus."

We got down to the bus entrance and found the other passengers assembled on the sidewalk. There were thirty-five of them. All thirty-five were white.

"It's a Group," Patsy murmured. "We're the only ones not in the Group."

But we examined our fellow-passengers furtively and, except for a couple here and a threesome there, they were obviously strangers to each other.

The bus arrived, the door opened, and as we filed into the bus, the driver, who was also white, beamed at us and greeted us individually with "Good morning," and "Hello, how are you?"

We found seats and settled ourselves and I got out my notebook. Then the tour guide came aboard. The tour guide was a handsome, middle-aged man and the only black on the bus. As the bus pulled away and headed uptown, the guide said, in a resonant baritone voice:

"I want to welcome you, and to ask you to tell me whenever I'm going too fast for you. Mrs. Penny, the owner of the bus company, tells me you all speak English, but wherever we stop, there will be information sheets available in your own language. According to my list, you're all from Germany, France or Australia, but sometimes the list is incomplete, so if you need information sheets in some other language, just tell me."

The man I talked to on the phone had said, "You're Mrs. Gibbs," as soon as he heard my American accent. Patsy and I were the only Americans on the bus.

The guide told us he had been in show business for twenty years and that conducting sightseeing tours was something he did in his spare time.

"I do this because I enjoy it," he said. "I like Harlem and I enjoy showing it to people."

(The bus wasn't air-conditioned and as I sat happily by an open window, Patsy, perspiring freely, muttered in my ear: "Make a note: No smoking, no john and no air-conditioning," and declined my offer to trade seats with her. "I don't want that hot air blowing on me," she said.)

The bus was rolling along Central Park West and the guide, who had been pointing out the sights along the way, suddenly paralyzed us by pointing to the building Patsy lives in.

"That is one of the city's finest old apartment houses," he announced, and added: "Steve Lawrence and Edie Gorme live there."

"They moved out," Patsy hissed at me. "Should I tell him?"

"Have you got any celebrities to substitute?" I asked her.

"Margaret Mead?" suggested Patsy. "Abe Burrows? Helen Gurley Brown?"

"Fine," I said. "We'll tell him later."

The bus drove on up to 116th Street where the guide pointed upward to a back of beyond view of the spires of St. John's Cathedral and part of the Columbia quadrangle, the buildings so far above us on a cliff we had to crane our necks to see them.

"Do you see where we were?" Patsy squeaked. "On that parapet? We had to be crazy!"

We were in Harlem now, driving through a neighborhood of sharp contrasts. On our left were huge modern housing projects with ground-floor playgrounds and landscaped walks; on our right, directly opposite the projects, rows of indescribably decayed and crumbling five-story brownstone tenements. But as we rolled on upward, past the graceful stone entrance gate to New York City College and then past the Grange, Alexander Hamilton's home, we were on a wide avenue driving through an attractive, middle-class Harlem neighborhood where old shade trees on front lawns framed bay-windowed Victorian houses. We passed a modern Episcopal church building which the guide told us had been built by its black parishioners in 1970, after the old church building had burnt down, and which had won prizes for its architect.

I was taking frantic notes on all this when Patsy turned to me abruptly and demanded:

"Why?"

"Why what?" I said.

"Why are we the only Americans on the bus?"

"I don't know," I said. "Maybe Americans don't know about the tour. I didn't."

"Then how did the foreigners find out about it?" said Patsy. "They can't all have read the fine print in the Convention &

Visitors' guide the way I did. I was looking through it to see if we'd missed anything or I'd never have known about it either."

The bus drew up outside the Morris-Jumel house and as we piled out, I said to Patsy:

"When the guide isn't too busy, I'll ask him."

One of the curators met us at the door and she obviously knew the Penny operation well because she stood ready with mimeographed information sheets in German and French, and four in English for us and two young men from Australia.

The house was built before the Revolution by Roger Morris, a Tory who abandoned it to emigrate to England. During the war it served as headquarters first for Washington, then for the British and finally for the Hessians; and the military documents and letters on display around the walls dealt mostly with the British-Hessian Occupation. Years later, the house was bought by a Frenchman named Jumel, whose chief claim to fame was that his widow was married to Aaron Burr for four months; and a few Burr portraits and letters were also on display, along with a great many Jumel possessions, none of them particularly interesting.

Patsy and I found the house and its contents dull; what the German and French tourists thought, we didn't know. When you're in a Revolutionary War museum and the only comments you hear around you are in French and German, you feel a little weird. So it was a relief when one of the Australians pointed to the date on a military despatch and said to his companion: "That was the year Australia was first settled!"

Patsy and I went outside for a cigarette and a look at the view: the Jumel house is on a hill above the Harlem River. As we looked across the river to the woods drifting northward along the opposite bank, I said:

"That wood over there once belonged to a very sociable Dutch burgher named Jonas Bronck. He came to New Netherlands and bought a stretch of farmland over there and he built a big farm and a big farmhouse for his family. But they got bored living up there by themselves, and Jonas started inviting New Amsterdam families out to his place for a week or two. So you'd be walking along Wall Street or the docks, and you'd see a family piling their children and their clothes-boxes into a boat and you'd ask them where they were going. And they'd say: 'We've been invited up to the mainland, to visit the Broncks' or 'We're going up to see the Broncks.' I don't know who changed the *ck* to an *x*."

The guide came out with the rest of the tourists and led us all around the corner to a narrow street, a cul-de-sac two blocks long that was probably once a mews attached to the Jumel house. On both sides of the street were trim lines of small, upright houses with front steps that ran parallel with the sidewalk, rising to a landing where they turned a right angle to the front door. But you could only see the steps by walking around a barrier. In front of each house, a tall, left-handed triangle of brightly painted wood hid the steps and the landing from view. One barrier was dark green, one bright yellow, most were white. The line of houses with their brightly-painted shields seemed to have dropped into twentieth century New York from another world.

"This street is Sylvan Terrace," the guide told us. "The houses are very expensive; only wealthy black families can afford them." And as he led the way back to the bus, he told the foreigners:

"There was a time when black New Yorkers had to live in Harlem because they were excluded from housing everywhere

else. Now that they can live in other neighborhoods, when wealthy black families buy houses in Sylvan Terrace, it's because Harlem is where they want to live."

We drove along Edgecomb Avenue, an attractive residential street. Then we turned down Eighth Avenue and were abruptly on a depressed, dirty main street lined with shabby tenement storefronts. But as the bus approached 139th Street, the driver pointed to the block of it opening off Eighth Avenue.

"This block," he said, "and the next one — 138th Street — are special. I want you to look at them."

We looked down 139th Street and saw a line of tall, handsome brownstones on a street that was scrupulously clean.

"These two blocks are very famous," said the guide. "They're called 'Strivers' Row.' The houses were built by Stanford White, back at the turn of the century. The name 'Strivers' Row' may have come from a West Indian named Striver who lived there. But the people of Harlem love their myths; and the Harlem folk tale is that the name comes from the fact that Strivers' Row is where all the poor people of Harlem are striving to get. For years, Strivers' Row had the only fine housing open to black people. The houses are still fine and they're still expensive. And like Sylvan Terrace, the Strivers' Row houses are owned by people who don't have to live in Harlem but want to."

At 135th Street and Seventh Avenue, the foreigners heard the name of Harlem's favorite son for the first time. At that corner, Seventh Avenue becomes Adam Clayton Powell Boulevard ("though they don't acknowledge the name-change downtown," the guide added dryly). Powell was elected to

Congress in 1945 and steadily reelected until his death in 1972. But he was also a preacher, and the bus made its second stop at the Abyssinian Baptist church which Powell made famous. At the height of his ministry, church membership stood at 18,000. Today it may still be the largest church congregation in the country with 12,000 members.

We were welcomed to the church by an aide to the minister who gave us a brief history of it, pointed out the church's chief ornaments and then took us into the Powell Room, which might once have been a large social hall and is now a Powell museum. The photographs, plaques and testimonials, including one from the Late Emperor Haile Selassie of Abyssinia (now Ethiopia), form a visual biography of Powell. He was a handsome man and the photographs of him are strikingly alive. More than that, they point up the singular fact of his life. Powell was expelled from Congress for precisely the same kind of political corruption for which a white Senator had his wrist slapped by the same Congress in the same year. And the life of prejudice and hatred he endured, in and out of Congress, he could have avoided. Adam Clayton Powell could have passed for white and chose not to.

I was sorry we saw the inside of no other church. And when we drove past a Muslim mosque, I'd have liked knowing whether it was the one from which Malcolm X first proclaimed to the people of Harlem that black was beautiful; but his name was never mentioned by the guide.

The tour made its final stop at a horribly dilapidated building on 135th Street which houses the Schomburg Collection, the largest collection of black history and art in the country, if not the world. But another Penny bus was parked in the only legal space available in front of it so our tour bus

had to bypass the collection. We learned later that we'd have seen very little of it even if we'd gone in. Most of the valuable art objects and manuscripts are packed away in crates, waiting for the new Schomburg museum building which was to have been built this year. The architect's plans were complete and the site selected, when the city's financial collapse put an end to the Schomburg's hopes of a decent home.*

The bus rolled on down to 125th Street, Harlem's main shopping street (the guide told us that one of its two black-owned banks was founded by Johnny Mathis) and then on down through the terrible slums which were the only Harlem we'd ever read about: the burnt-out buildings and uncleared piles of rubble that look like a bombed-out city, the inhabited tenements as desolate and unfit for human habitation as the abandoned buildings crumbling away beside them. It was a relief, at 116th Street, to turn east to Lexington Avenue, to the gaudy bedlam of the main shopping street of Spanish Harlem.

"It looks a little like Orchard Street," said Patsy as we peered out the window at the racks of dresses and cardboard packing cases overflowing with wigs and sweaters that filled the sidewalks. What was definitely not Orchard Street was the atmosphere: the Spanish signs above stores the Latin music blaring from radios up and down the block and the staccato, stentorian Puerto Rican voices raised in the Puerto Rican English known as "Spanglish."

The bus turned down Fifth on its way back to Forty-Second Street and the driver invited passengers to say where they'd like to be let off along the way. The two Australians wanted to

*See p. 171, P.S.8.

get off at Seventy-Ninth Street to visit the Natural History Museum, unaware that it was clear across the park on the West Side.

"They'll never find it," said Patsy. "I'm going to get off with them, I'll walk them across the park, I'd walk home that way anyway."

"Ask them how they found out about the tour," I said. All four of us got off at Seventy-Ninth, Patsy and the Australians went west through the park, I walked down through it to Seventy-Second and then home. On my way home, I bought a New York *Post*. I read the *Post* over lunch and then I phoned Patsy, knowing she'd have got home by then.

"What did you find out from the Australians?" I asked her.

"They're architecture students," she said enthusiastically. "They're over here on a six-month tour of the country, the Australian government's helping them. They've covered a thousand miles of this country in three months, they told me all about New Orleans and St. Louis!"

"What did you find out about the Harlem tour? How did they know about it?" I prodded.

"Oh," said Patsy. "I forgot to ask."

"Never mind," I said. "I have to call the tour guide anyway and give him the new celebrities in your building. Now then. Have you read the *Post*? Did you see what's opening to the public for the first time on May 29?"

"What?" asked Patsy.

"Ellis Island," I said.

"Oh, God," said Patsy. "My grandparents came to this country through Ellis Island. When can we go?"

"Monday?" I suggested.

"Monday's Memorial Day! We'll be away," said Patsy.

"Let's give it a week for the first crowds to thin out anyway," I said. "How's Friday, June 4? We'll get an early start and do the Stock Exchange, and stop at Trinity to check out that gravestone, and have lunch at Delmonico's and finish up at Ellis Island."

"It sounds like another blockbuster day," said Patsy.

"It should be," I said. "It's our last."

"Oh," said Patsy, sounding subdued, and we hung up.

The next morning I phoned the Penny Sightseeing Bus Company and got the name and telephone number of our guide and phoned him. I gave him Patsy's new list of tenants ("Margaret Mead?" he said. "Oh, my! Thank you very much.") and then I said: "Will you tell me something? How did all the foreign tourists know about your tour?"

"Mrs. Penny has had fantastic publicity in European papers," he said. "Back in 1967, the AP ran a story on the tour and it was picked up by some European newspapers. And people over there who read about it took the tour when they came here, and then went home and wrote to their home-town newspaper: 'You were right, it's a great tour' and that got her more publicity. And it just keeps mushrooming."

"Didn't the AP story run in American newspapers?" I asked.

"Oh yes," he said. "And the New York *Times* ran a story on us; the press has been very good to us."

"Then Americans do know about it," I said. And he said "Oh yes."

I thanked him and hung up, still mystified. Two weeks later, when Patsy's son came home from college, he and a friend took the Penny tour, and they, too, were the only two Americans on a bus crowded with foreigners.

"I think I understand it," I said to Patsy when she relayed this information to me. "Foreigners are curious about our racial troubles so a tour of Harlem attracts them. White Americans don't like thinking about our racial troubles so they avoid the tour."

"And black Americans?" Patsy inquired. "They come to New York as tourists, too. Why don't they take the tour?"

Mystery unsolved.

## Saturday, May 29

FROM MEMORIAL DAY WEEKEND IN MAY TO LABOR DAY weekend in September New Yorkers divide into two groups: 1, those who always leave town on weekends, and 2, those who never leave town on weekends. Those of us in Group 2 have the standard negative reasons for staying home: we hate traveling on crowded highways and trains, and if we work all week and count on weekends to do our housekeeping chores, we hate coming home tired on a Sunday night to a dirty apartment, an overflowing laundry bag and an empty refrigerator.

But there's a positive reason that's equally potent. New York has a special charm for us on a summer weekend, when the town empties out, when the trucks and commuters and commuter cars are gone. The air is cleaner, the city is quieter, and the peaceful, empty avenues seem especially wide and beautiful. When we've had enough of the peace and quiet, we head for Central Park where the action is.

On weekdays, the park itself is the town's only quiet, peaceful oasis. The playgrounds will be busy, and you'll pass a few baby-coach brigades, dog-walkers and teenage ball games; but there are vast, green empty stretches and I love it that way. On summer weekends, the park is jammed and jumping and I love it that way.

So on Saturday of this first holiday weekend, I got up early to get my cleaning and marketing done by early afternoon and then headed for the park. Alone. On weekday afternoons, I go

with my true love, a worried-looking, doe-eyed German shepherd named Duke, who lives on the sixteenth floor with parents who are out at work all day and a brother who's in college. The park is more fun with a dog, and these days safer. I have never personally seen anyone or anything menacing in Central Park in all the years I've been going there, with or without a dog, you understand, but the newspapers' lurid accounts of muggings have made me cautious. If the newspapers printed—which they never do—equally lurid descriptions of car-crash victims, you'd learn to be cautious about your killer car. As it is, you probably know that cars kill and maim six hundred times as many people as muggers do, but you go on driving your car. I go on loving Central Park.

Today I went alone, partly because on a holiday weekend the park is too crowded for Duke. He's the longest German Shepherd you ever saw, and if he chased a stick across a park lawn on a holiday weekend he'd wreck ten picnics. But mostly my mind was on this book, and on the secret of Central Park which only New Yorkers know about, and I went over there looking for signs of that secret.

There was the usual holiday jam at the Seventy-Second Street entrance: crowds around the ice cream and pretzel stands and a tangle of bikes and baby-strollers, as cyclists and parents tried to work their way through the crowd and into the park. Just inside the entrance on my left, Nancy's playground was crowded with holiday fathers. Its bright red and yellow poles are faded and weatherbeaten now.

Nancy's playground (which doesn't have her name on it) is one of the small, pre-school playgrounds you'll find at four- and five-block intervals throughout the park. One young mother used to call hers "The Snake Pit" because she was stuck

in it all day every day, summer heat or winter snow, till her toddler graduated to one of the school-age playgrounds and could go without her. Well, about ten years ago, my friend Nancy was stuck in the Seventy-Second Street playground with her two-year-old son. It was the usual antique playground with iron swings and a sandbox, and Nancy decided it ought to be modernized.

Nancy became Chairwoman of a Mothers' Committee to raise funds for the project. She ran a big movie benefit and a fundraising cocktail party, and finally the committee had enough money to hire a designer and finance the construction of new playground equipment. And one fine spring day the new playground opened, with bright red and yellow poles and a tree house and a turret house and stone picnic benches and tables alongside the miniature wading pool.

But during the winter, Nancy had gotten pregnant again, and she and Ed needed a larger apartment. By spring, when the new playground opened, they'd moved up to the Eighties over near the East River and Nancy was taking her two sons to Carl Schurz park instead. And every time she rode downtown on a Fifth Avenue bus and saw the bright new playground from the bus window, she felt like Moses riding past the Promised Land.

On my right, across the road from Nancy's playground, a broad lawn slopes down to the Model Sailboat Pond, with the Model Boathouse (a gift of the Kerbs family) beside it. Press your nose against the boathouse door and when your eyes have got used to the dark interior, you can see all the elaborate boats in dry-dock: Columbus's fleet, pirate ships, whaling vessels, all fully rigged, and Spanish galleons complete down to the galley slaves at the oars. The hobbyists who built them

hold a regatta on a Sunday in June, and if you're here on the right Sunday it's something to see.

At the far end of the Pond is the Alice in Wonderland Statuary (a gift of the Delacorte family) depicting the Mad Tea Party in bronze. A gigantic Alice presides over the tea table where the Dormouse, Cheshire Cat and March Hare are dominated by the Mad Hatter, or at least by the height of his mad hat. Older children climb to the top of Alice's head and sit on it, younger ones climb to the top of the Mad Hatter's hat, and toddlers crawl or stagger in and out among the giant mushrooms under the tea table.

(Alice in Wonderland is equaled in popularity only by the Children's Zoo down at Sixty-Fifth in the park, the gift "To the Children of New York" of the late Governor and Mrs. Herbert Lehman. The Zoo buildings—including Noah's Ark and Old McDonald's Farm—are brightly colored and have entrance gates no higher than a five-year-old. You can see them from a Fifth Avenue bus window.)

On the western rim of the Sailboat Pond opposite the Model Boathouse, is Hans Christian Andersen. The great bronze figure sits at ease, leaning forward slightly, a book open on his left knee. His nose is worn shiny by the thousands of children's hands that have used it as a lever by which to hoist themselves up to sit piggy-back around Hans Christian's neck.

But to see him properly, you have to visit Hans Christian with a child who has just learned to read, and who will climb up on Andersen's right knee and read aloud to you, from the open book on his left, the story of the Ugly Duckling. The duckling himself sits at Andersen's feet, listening with permanent bronze attention. This statue isn't as popular with

children as Alice. But if you're a parent or grandparent watching a child read from Andersen's book, or a group of children sitting on the ground at his feet listening to the Story Lady from the New York Public Library read one of his fairy tales, you'll find the expression on Andersen's face very moving as he looks down at the children.

(At the back of the statue, an inscription in the stone explains that the statue was a gift to the children of New York from the children of Denmark.)

When Duke is with me, we walk north from the Sailboat Pond toward Dog Hill, and we usually pass the Clown on our way. Nobody seems to know who he is. All anybody knows is that on weekday afternoons he'll turn up in the park in a clown's motley and makeup, to sing and tell stories to the children who collect around him. I see him usually near Alice-in-Wonderland; friends of mine have seen him at other stations. Rumor has it he's a Wall Street stockbroker. But one Sunday when Duke and I were on our way to Dog Hill with our friends Richard and Chester-the-Sheepdog, we passed the Clown and I said:

"I've never seen him here before on a Sunday."

And Richard said:

"I thought he was taller. Are you sure this is the same Clown?"

The foot of Dog Hill is at Seventy-Sixth Street and the hill slopes gradually upward to Seventy-Ninth, rolling backward in a broad sweep as it rises. We claim it's the largest canine social hall in the world. On a sunny weekend afternoon, there'll be forty or fifty dogs charging around, two or three of whom always appoint themselves a welcoming committee and streak all the way down to the foot of the hill to greet every

new arrival. It's the dream of my life to make enough money (which I won't) or leave enough money when I die (which I might) to donate a dog drinking-fountain to the Hill. If there's room on it for an inscription, it'll read:

TO THE DOGS OF NEW YORK CITY

FROM AN ADMIRER.

This town has got the friendliest, most sociable dogs you'll ever meet.

From Dog Hill, Duke and I usually push west to the Ramble, a small wood with winding paths and streams, and on over to the Rowboat Lake where he goes swimming. Then we may walk up along the western bank and above it to see how Shakespeare's garden is coming along.

A month ago, the once-beautiful garden was a wasteland of dead flower beds and weeds, the decaying footbridge crumbling into the empty moat. The city has had no money for gardeners or workmen for several years. But during the past month, anonymous volunteers have been working in the garden, early every morning and on weekends. They've cleared out the debris, and weeded and replanted and watered, and spread leaf-cover over the worst-damaged plots, and the garden isn't what it was but it's beginning to grow again.

The garden is set on a high hill overlooking the Shakespeare theatre, and Duke and I generally circle the theatre coming back over to the East Side. Officially, it's the Delacorte Theatre. But I suspect the Delacortes would agree that it ought to be called the Joe Papp Theatre instead.

Joe Papp began putting on free productions of Shakespeare, in a clearing in the park back in 1954. Robert Moses was Czar

of the parks in those days and he demanded that Papp charge admission and use the money to pay the city for damage to the grass. Papp went to court, to sue for the right to present Shakespeare free of charge. He won the suit. Moses asked the city to appropriate funds for a proper theatre, to save the surrounding lawns, and the Delacortes—and thousands of anonymous New Yorkers—contributed the rest of the money. The theatre opened in 1961 and seats three thousand people at free Shakespeare productions every summer, nightly-except-Monday.

Coming back east from the theatre a couple of months ago, Duke and I passed a grove of newly-planted pine trees at the far end of the lawn behind the Metropolitan Museum. The trees were planted by a man whose name I wish I remembered. I read about him in the *Times* a few days afterwards. A *Times* reporter saw the man planting trees and asked him why he was doing it, and the man said he'd just happened to notice a bare stretch of ground at that end of the lawn and he thought a grove of evergreens would be nice there.

Since Duke wasn't with me today, I didn't walk north from Seventy-Second, I went a little south and west instead, to Central Park Mall. There's a bandshell at the entrance to it where there are free concerts on summer evenings—and on holiday afternoons, which I didn't know till I got there today.* There was an all-Mozart concert in progress when I went by, and the benches which seat a thousand people were almost completely filled. There are band concerts there, too. And I don't like band music but I'll have to go to the June 10

---

*These days there are opera and dance performances in addition to concerts at the bandshell during the summer.

band concert, out of apartment-house loyalty. There's a Russian refugee couple in my building named Litkei. Mrs. Litkei is a retired ballerina; her husband is a musician. And this morning, they put handbills under all the doors in our building (and all over the neighborhood on street-light poles and lobby tables) which read in part:

In the Name of All Foreign-Born Americans
in Grateful Appreciation to the United States of America
Erwin Litkei
proudly presents
The 26th U.S. Army Band . . .

How can you not go to that?

Beyond the Bandshell, the Mall itself runs through the park for several blocks. Today's warm weather had brought out the food vendors—and I don't mean the usual pretzel, Italian ice and hot-dog vendors. Along with the shish-kebab stands and Italian sausage stands presided over by enterprising families, two young men were broiling chicken and corn on the cob over a charcoal fire, a middle-aged couple was cooking tacos and four young people sat behind a long table with two signs, one advising SMILE! BE HAPPY! and a smaller one advertising Magic Foods to Turn You On! The magic foods were apples, bananas, peaches, watermelon slices and coconuts. At one table, two girls were selling their homemade date-nut and pumpkin breads. Knowing they had potential customers in my building, I asked:

"Are you here every weekend?"

"I don't know," one of them answered uncertainly. "This is our first day."

Entertainers were performing to small crowds on the lawns beside the Mall. Two college students were doing rope tricks, a Puerto Rican band was playing Latin music and at the far end, three students were playing a Haydn trio. A collection plate at their feet bore a sign explaining that classical music lessons cost money.

From the Mall I went west to the Sheep Meadow, where the Philharmonic and the Metropolitan Opera give performances on summer evenings, one Philharmonic concert drawing 250,000 people. The Sheep Meadow has an elastic seating capacity. There aren't any seats. You sit on the grass and keep inching over to make room for one more. (The concert and opera performances are paid for by private citizens and corporations, both usually anonymous.)

The size of the park—it's twice the size of Monaco—is a great boon on summer evenings. Down at the Wollman Skating Rink (gift of the Wollman family) the Schaefer Music Festival features rock-and-roll concerts (sponsored by the Schaefer Beer Company). And loud as they are, the rock concerts are so far away that they never interfere with Mahler or Puccini holding forth on the Sheep Meadow—which in turn can't be heard by the actors or audience at the Shakespeare Theatre—which doesn't interfere with the sounds of the free Jazz Festival or Harlem Dance Theatre performance going on up on the Harlem Mall.

Circling the Sheep Meadow and coming back east, I noticed the new green trash baskets. There are several hundred of them in the park now. The Central Park Community Task Force keeps adding batches of them with money raised by the Central Park Community Fund. Both organizations are composed of New Yorkers whose names wouldn't mean anything

to you. They're trying to do for the park what the city can no longer afford to do. But there's a much older organization of volunteers called the Friends of Central Park. Which brings us to Estelle, a fellow-member of the Democratic club where Patsy and I first met and the guiding spirit behind the Friends of Central Park.

For years, Estelle has been the chief thorn-in-the-side of every city official, parks commissioner and private enterprise threatening her park. She has stood on picket lines outside the Metropolitan Museum of Art through one losing battle after another. And she fought harder than anyone else in the heartbreaking losing battle against the Metropolitan Transportation Authority, which is now engaged in ripping up whole acres of the park clear through from East Sixty-Fourth to West Sixtieth, to build a commuter's subway.* Through Central Park. It's because of the yawning craters and the old trees uprooted and destroyed to make room not only for a subway but for an MTA office building in the park, that I have described nothing in the park below Sixty-Fifth Street. When you drive down Fifth Avenue, you'll see the ugly grey construction wall, the crude building and a glimpse of the havoc being wrought by the subway construction. And I can write "You'll see" with grim confidence—though I don't know when this book will be published or when you're coming to town. The office building, the wall, the subway construction and the ravaged park land will still be there. Count on it.

We thought Estelle would never recover from that blow, but she did. Fighting such juggernauts as the Metropolitan and the MTA, she loses more battles than she wins, but she

See p. 164, P.S.5.

keeps bouncing back. She keeps on organizing picket lines and mass protests, raising money for a Tree Restoration Fund and demanding action from every new parks commissioner.

In recognition of which, there's to be a birthday party in Estelle's honor on July 21. Patsy's in charge of it. More than a hundred of Estelle's friends have been invited to a Bring-Your-Own-Picnic Supper at the Central Park Lake boathouse which is where Estelle wants it. Before the party, she'll receive an official Citation from the Mayor, to be presented to her by the Commissioner of Parks (if she's speaking to him). The party is in celebration of a milestone birthday of one of the most devoted of those unsung friends of Central Park who are the secret of its glory.

On July 21, Estelle will be ninety.*

---

*As this edition goes to press, Estelle has just celebrated her 102nd birthday.

# Friday, June 4

SINCE THIS WAS OUR LAST DAY, PATSY CAME OVER EAST AND we took the Lexington Avenue IRT down to Wall Street together. We came up on the sidewalk in front of Trinity Church and I said:

"Let's get the inscription off that Tory's gravestone first. It'll only take a minute. The stone's at the edge of the cemetery; I read it from an outside path."

"I know," said Patsy. "It's on the Gallatin side." (The graveyard has two sections; Hamilton is buried in one, Gallatin in the other.)

We opened the gate and entered the churchyard, and stopped and stared with pleasure. The cemetery had been transformed by new plantings: flowering bushes where none had been before, even new trees where none had been before, and everywhere on the ground thick patches of green leaf cover.

"They've dressed it up for the Bicentennial!" I said.

We started along the outside path of the Gallatin side and Patsy, ahead of me, stopped at the spot where she remembered I'd read the inscription. There was no stone there. What *was* there, was a large patch of green leaf cover backed by a flowering bush.

Some facts in this world you can accept. Now and then you're faced with a fact you can't accept.

"It must be further along," I said.

We moved along the outside path slowly reading every stone. We circled the entire path. My Tory merchant wasn't there.

"He's on the Hamilton side," I said. And we went over to the Hamilton side and walked slowly along the outside path reading every stone. My Tory wasn't there.

We entered the cemetery grounds and picked our way among the inner paths where we hadn't set foot before. We did every path, inch by inch, kneeling to read every stone, in a silence that got more and more pregnant. We did every path in both sections of the cemetery and it was a long time before we finally straightened and stared at each other.

"All these new bushes and leaves," said Patsy tentatively.

"Exactly," I said. "They've covered that poor slob's stone with green leaves!"

"Let's go ask somebody," said Patsy.

We went into the church, but nobody was around at that early hour. There was, however, a rack of books and pamphlets inside the doorway, including a book labelled *History of Trinity Churchyard*. We carried it to a nearby bench and sat down to examine it.

Since we didn't know my Tory's name or birth and death dates we couldn't find him. But reading a few pages, we did come upon mention of a deceased parishioner whose remains had been moved from the west section of the cemetery to the south, or maybe it was from the west to the north. And the book also contained a reminder that while Robert Fulton's opulent crypt was in Trinity churchyard, Robert Fulton wasn't.

We returned the book to its rack and left the church and walked through the churchyard in silence. But as we passed

the spot where we were certain the plaque-or-stone had been, Patsy stopped. She stared down at the leaves and the flowering bush, and shook her head in disbelief.

"It's remarkable," she said in an awed tone. "In this town, you not only get pushed around all your life, you get pushed around after you're dead!"

"I'm getting to the bottom of this," I said. "Tomorrow morning, I'm phoning Trinity Church."

(The next morning I looked up Trinity Church in the Manhattan phone book. I stared at the listing for several minutes. Then I pulled myself together and phoned Patsy. "Go look up Trinity Church in the phone book," I said. "I'll wait." And we gawked at it together for five minutes before we hung up.

I defy you to find another city in which a church parish takes up half a column in the phone book, with a total of forty-seven separate phone numbers. Forty-six are for the Rector, Associate Rector, Deputy Outreach & Planning, Parish Administration, Parish Resources, Parochial ministries, also Accounting, Administration, Budget, Buildings, Camp & Conferences, Cemetery Ofc., Chapels, Clerk, Communications, Food, Maintenance, Personnel, Purchasing, Real Estate and Schools. The forty-seventh is for All Other Business, of which it's a little hard to think of any. Not wanting to be transferred from Cemetery Ofc. to Administration to Outreach, I abandoned the phone and wrote a letter to the rector, asking politely whether my Tory had been moved elsewhere or just covered with leaves.

I received a charming reply but not until the rector had worn himself out trying to locate my merchant's name and stone-or-plaque for me. Without success. Letters flew back

and forth between us, and finally he wrote to say that while Trinity had, in former times, moved gravestones from section to section when it wasn't sure where they rightly belonged, this practice had been discontinued a generation ago, and my Tory was therefore probably under the leaves and the rector himself hoped to search for the gentleman on the first winter day when the leaves were gone.)

We left Trinity, and Patsy headed across the street to check the side wall of the Irving Trust. There was no new plaque, only the pale square of stone where the old one had been. Patsy went into the bank to inquire, innocently, about the missing plaque. I reached her side just as the bank official was saying regretfully: "Vandals stole it, I'm afraid."

"It was only a plaque, it had no historical value," I said as if I'd never said it before. "Couldn't the bank afford to have a new one made?"

And he said, with as much huffy reproof as if he'd never said it before: "I'm sure the bank is doing that."

As we left the bank Patsy, glancing from the blank spot on the bank wall to Trinity churchyard across the street, said morosely:

"One thing about the Stock Exchange: it'll *be* there."

The Wall Street entrance to the New York Stock Exchange is for members and employees only. Tourists go around the corner to 20 Broad Street and up to the third or "Visitors' " Floor.

We stepped out of the elevator and a receptionist waved us toward the Visitors' Gallery, a long hall to the right of the reception desk. A plate glass window runs the length of the hall and we went up to the window and found ourselves looking directly down into the Floor of the Exchange two

floors below. Other visitors were lined up alongside us and a guide was explaining the functions of everything we saw below us: the "Big Board," with its listing of stocks traded, the electronic ticker which has replaced ticker tape, the trading stations and the men and women whose blue, maroon or grey jackets identified them as brokers or assistants or runners. A few customers stood behind the entranceway to the Exchange, their eyes on the electronic ticker panel.

"You know what brokers call this?" a man standing next to me said to his companion, pointing down to the Floor. "Ulcer Alley."

From the gallery, the guide led us down the opposite hall, and after seeing a few exhibits there we filed into a small theatre to see a cartoon film entitled: *One-Man Band Goes to Wall Street.* The cartoon story of how a small company grows large enough to be listed on the Big Board was entertaining; but its high-school textbook explanation won't give you any practical grasp of how the stock market works. The difference between the film's theory and Ulcer Alley's practice was underscored by the contrast between the gay insouciance of the cartoon and the grim, unsmiling faces on the Exchange Floor. As I remarked to Patsy when we left: "It's a nice place to visit but I wouldn't want to live there."

Delmonico's restaurant (not to be confused with the restaurant in the Hotel Delmonico on Park Avenue) is at the corner of Beaver and South William Streets and we were going there for our final celebration lunch because an article in New York Magazine suggested it might be a tourist attraction. It is.

One of Patsy's clippings said that the original Delmonico's had gone bankrupt and closed in 1917. But walking into the present restaurant, we found that hard to believe. Where

Fraunces Tavern has been "restored" with self-conscious charm, Delmonico's seems never to have changed at all; it looks exactly as it must have looked a hundred years ago. To walk through the vestibule into the grandiose saloon with its heavy mahogany bar, and then push through the swinging doors into the restaurant, is to walk back into the 1870s. From the patterned brocade wallpaper and heavy iron sconces to the ornate chandeliers with their load of small green lampshades, everything seems to be just as it always was. If you remember *Life With Father*, you find yourself glancing at the door, half-expecting to see Father Day shepherding the family and Cousin Cora in to his accustomed table.

My friend Richard has a cookbook entitled *The Epicurean*, compiled by the Delmonico chef and published in 1920, which I covet and can't get him to part with; and the cookbook requires 1180 pages to hold the laborious recipes and gargantuan menus which made Delmonico famous, in the gluttonous Edwardian days when it was the scene of ten-course testimonial dinners to President Grant, the Grand Duke Alexis of Russia, Charles Dickens and Ferdinand de Lesseps.

The modern menu has shrunk to fit modern stomachs, though the food is still good (and still expensive). But it's less the food than the evocation of a bygone era that makes lunch at Delmonico worth the price.

When we came out, we could see Battery Park a few blocks below us, and we walked down to the park ticket booth where, on our first sightseeing day, we had bought tickets for the ferry to the Statue of Liberty.

"We've come full circle," said Patsy.

The Ellis Island ticket booth was next to the Liberty Island

booth and we bought tickets and waited with other tourists to board the ferry. A guide rode to the island on the ferry with us and warned us, on the way, that twenty-odd years of disuse had left the island's buildings badly eroded by water and weather. The wooden beams above the main hall, he said, had so rotted away that fences had to be thrown up to prevent injury to tourists from falling beams, before the island could be opened to the public. (The National Park Service, which oversees Ellis Island, has had its budget severely cut by Congress.)*

As the ferry drew alongside the dock, we saw the hulk of the original ferry, the *Ellis Island,* still at anchor. The *Ellis Island* had met the immigrants as their ships docked in New York harbor, and ferried them to Ellis Island for medical and legal processing before they were allowed to set foot in the New World. Those who failed the medical and legal examinations never would set foot in it.

We were taken to the Main Hall, a vast room where the immigrants were separated into national groups, and tagged, before they were sent on to the examination rooms. Opening off the room we saw ancient lavatories—and heard an elderly man behind us say: "That's it! That's where we washed!"

We saw the dormitory rooms where the immigrants slept, and the medical examination rooms where those found to have tuberculosis or trachoma, or any other incurable or contagious disease, were denied entry. When the breadwinner of a family had bad lungs or a faulty heart, the whole family might be rejected since they might become public charges without

*Now that times are better, Ellis Island has been closed for extensive repairs and is due to reopen in the fall of 1989.

him. More terrible still was the plight of a healthy family in which a single child was found to have TB. The family had to decide whether to give up its chance at a new life in America and return to Europe, or send the child back to the Old World alone.

The legal examination consisted of questions: "Can you read and write? Have you got a job here? Who offered you the job? Who paid for your passage?"

These last two questions were designed to weed out the "undesirables": prostitutes, spies, revolutionaries and strike-breakers. Strike-breakers were the most numerous. The island's peak years were 1892 to 1929, when labor was organizing its first major strikes for decent wages and working conditions. The great steel companies and railroads went to lengths to import cheap immigrant labor with which to break the strike. (See the Frick Collection, Carnegie Hall, Rockefeller University . . .)

Rejected immigrants were isolated in a special building on the island to await the ships that had brought them to America and were now required to pick them up and return them to Europe. But most of the immigrants had nothing to go back to. They'd sold everything — house, land, farm tools, possessions — to raise passage-money for the trip. There's a tower above the main building on Ellis Island. And during the night when no guards were on watch, rejected immigrants climbed to the top of the tower and jumped to their deaths. Five thousand bodies of immigrants were burnt in mass cremations on the island, since there was no money for burial. How many more immigrants were drowned and their bodies never recovered, nobody will ever know.

Such stories were bearable to us because we were told that

the overwhelming majority of immigrants—98 per cent of them—were accepted. After days of harrowing uncertainty, they were given legal and medical clearance, were put aboard the *Ellis Island* once more, were ferried past the Statue of Liberty into New York harbor where they stepped ashore, home free.

As we were leaving, I looked back at the great, empty Main Hall, more dilapidated but probably no more grim and forbidding now than when the immigrants were herded into it, tense and frightened, to await the all-important examinations. Standing there with Patsy Gibbs at my side, —granddaughter of Ellis Island immigrants, whose children will be second-generation Harvard graduates—it seemed to me that every New York sight we had seen, from one end of the island to the other, was insignificant compared with the gaunt and crumbling wreck of Ellis Island.

It was after five when we finally stepped ashore at Battery Park and walked once more, as we had on our first day, up to the broad intersection leading into the city. As we waited for a green light, the canyons and towers of Lower Manhattan stretched ahead of us; and every street and skyline grouping was familiar.

"We own this city now," said Patsy. "Do you feel that way?"

"I've been defensive about it for so long," I said. "Every TV newsman tells me the city is dying, every newspaper story harps on crime and bankruptcy—and then you see a headline reading FORD TO NEW YORK: DROP DEAD. It gets to you, without your realizing it. I'll never be defensive about it again. It's a marvelous city."

Patsy was standing rooted to the sidewalk, her mouth open, her eyes wide with shock.

"Defensive!" she repeated in a scandalized voice. "Are you crazy? This is the most fabulous city on earth!"

And we walked on peacefully through the narrow streets toward the subway we could take together as far as Grand Central.

"I don't see how this can be our last trip," said Patsy. "There have to be places we didn't see!"

"A few," I said. "Four hundred art galleries. Forty museums. Two hundred-and-something landmark houses. SoHo. Astor Place. We never got down to see Washington Market at five in the morning. We never took the helicopter trip from Thirty-Fourth Street up over Central Park. But I've got a deadline on this book, and all I've written so far is a thick book of notes and a prologue."

We went down the subway steps and put our tokens in the turnstile. The platform was crowded—it was the five o'clock rush hour—and we stood off to one side by ourselves. I looked at Patsy's face and wondered if mine looked the same.

"You know," I said, "we can come down here again. It's probably slipped your mind but we live here! We can do the whole tour over again, any time we want to!"

But we knew we never would. We'd been on a holiday and the holiday was over. I was on my way back to my typewriter; Patsy was on her way back to her family. In a few days, we'd have settled back into the routines of our separate lives.

The subway train roared into the station, splitting eardrums as usual. As it screeched to a halt, Patsy turned to me and shouted:

"It was the best two months I ever had!"

"Me, too!" I shouted back.

The doors opened and we squeezed into a car jammed to the doors with rush-hour riders. But the densely packed bodies somehow shifted, willing, as always, to make room for two more tired New Yorkers on their way home.

## IN MEMORIAM

In June of 1980, Patsy Gibbs died of breast cancer at the age of 47. After that, I was profoundly grateful to have "Apple of My Eye" on a bookshelf, for the illusion it gave me that Patsy was still alive and in the house with me. But when I set out to see the new sights to be covered in a new P.S. chapter, "the presence of that absence was everywhere."

I did the best I could without her.

# $\mathcal{P.S.}$ 1

## THE SOUTH STREET SEAPORT—AND THE BIG CHANGE IN LOWER MANHATTAN

IF I'VE GOT IT RIGHT, THE SEAPORT RENAISSANCE OF THE '80's began in Boston when the city hired a company to convert its depressed waterfront area into a restaurant-and-shopping mall. The project proved so successful that the same company was hired to transform the waterfront areas of New York, Philadelphia, Baltimore and points further south and west, in the same way.

Normally, New York City would not have been in crucial need of more shops and restaurants than it already had. But its waterfront mall, known as the South Street Seaport, was created at a moment when there was a dramatic change in the surrounding area of Lower Manhattan.

There had always been a scattering of small neighborhoods down at the tip of the island, most of them poor and working-class. But in the 1980's, two new neighborhoods were added, both upper-income and Yuppie. The first and smaller was TriBeCa (a *Tri*angle of streets *Be*low *Ca*nal Street) where old housing underwent "gentrification" and new luxury housing was added. The second was a monster complex of 40-story apartment towers mixed with a few low condominiums, all built on Hudson River landfill at the edge of Battery Park and named Battery Park City. Its astronomically expensive co-ops, condos and rental apartments are 90% occupied, with more buildings going up, each sold or rented as fast as it rises. I have no idea how many thousands of people it will eventually

house but it has already doubled the population of Lower Manhattan, if you throw in TriBeCa.

The new residents of the neighborhood are chiefly Yuppies who work in the Wall Street financial district. Relieved of their long subway rides and commutation tickets, they can not only walk or jog to work, they can now dine well and dress well without making long trips uptown, thanks to the South Street Seaport's shops and restaurants—and spend lunch hours, cocktail hours and long summer evenings in the Seaport's large open square.

To uptown New Yorkers, the Seaport is a pleasant place to spend a warm evening, and somewhere new to take out-of-town guests. What it may be to you, the tourist, I thought I'd better haul myself down there to find out.

I began this P.S. project in the autumn and on a bright Saturday in early November, at high noon, my friend David and I took the subway down to Lower Manhattan. David is a young Philadelphia architect but as a recent graduate of Columbia's School of Architecture (and a Yuppie) he knew the Seaport well and had offered to show it to me.

It's on the East River a little below Brooklyn Bridge. David and I walked into the large open square with its standing sign at the entrance reading WELCOME TO THE SOUTH STREET SEAPORT. At the far end of the square we saw a large lunch crowd at outdoor tables belonging to an adjoining restaurant. In the near half of the square two small crowds had gathered, one around a juggler, the other around what appeared to be a race between two toads.

Bordering the square were old cobblestoned streets lined with early 19th century brick houses, four or five stories high. Pointing across the square to our right, at one prim little row

of houses, David said it was called Schermerhorn Row and he wanted to show me a sign above it. But first I thought we ought to tour the square's main building, the old and newly rejuvenated Fulton Market.

The ground hall was a huge food exhibition hall, with food displays on both sides of a wide central aisle. On our left as we walked, we passed a coffee corner where David counted more than fifty kinds of coffee beans in open sacks, tables piled with great mounds and slabs of cheese, barrows with layers of fresh-caught fish, onion bins, salad stalls and vegetable stalls. Across the aisle and stretching the length of the floor was what seemed to be a mile-long display of breads and pastries on counters and in cases. Upstairs, on the mezzanine and second floors, the Seaport's most famous restaurants were empty or maybe closed for the winter.

We came out and David led the way across the cobblestones to Schermerhorn Row. At the far end, a store window on the ground floor had a flossy sign reading "Laura Ashley," and its two or three dresses looked somehow forlornly fashionable in the ancient waterfront house. But it was the sign over one of the houses at the opposite end David wanted me to see. It proclaimed that the row of houses had been built in 1812 "for Peter Schermerhorn, ship chandler, on newly-filled land."

"They were in such a hurry to get the houses up," said David, "they didn't give the land time to settle." And he pointed to the bottom row of bricks just above the window ledge, tipping drunkenly downward till the last brick on the row disappeared entirely under the ledge. I thought of Battery Park City, also built on "filled in land" and hoped it wouldn't start sinking into the Hudson at one end.

We strolled past the shops and restaurants leading to Pier

17, we walked past the maritime museum—a gallery of photos and artifacts from the great ocean liner days as well as earlier times—out to Pier 16 where the three sailing ships permanently at anchor are part of the museum's tours. But it was clearly off-season. No one was out in the Seaport boats which will serve you lunch on their ninety-minute cruises, and the great upper deck of Caroline's restaurant where you can watch the yachts and sailboats go by as you dine, was closed for the winter.

Before taking the subway uptown to see another new sight on which I needed David's architectural expertise, we walked across town to Wall Street. The financial district had always been a ghost town on weekends and I wanted to see if that had changed. Just before we came to Wall, I stopped David at a little alley called Thames Street (p. 102) where two skyscrapers, one on either side of the alley, are connected by a small footbridge—way up on their 30th or 35th floors. I pointed up to it.

"Patsy and I wondered who built that bridge up there," I said. "Well, last month, the Sunday after the stock market crash, the New York Times Sunday Business section ran an article about New York University's Graduate School of Business because it's the only business school in the heart of the Wall Street financial district. It didn't say how many floors of these two buildings the school occupies, but it did mention the footbridge. That bridge takes students and professors from one set of classrooms to another."

When we came to Wall Street, I was gratified to find that Peter Stuyvesant's bronze plaque is finally back in place on the bank building at One Wall—but the street itself was full of pedestrians—and litter—and noisy with construction drills.

From which I conclude that the famous ghost town which was once "Wall Street on a Sunday" is also a thing of the past.

On Sunday I phoned my friend Arlene (see Dedication). Arlene no longer works for the city but in recent years she has done political fund-raising parties at the South Street Seaport, usually in May and June. My problem was that the new edition of this book would have gone to press by then.

"Suppose tourists are down in Lower Manhattan some day next summer," I said. "They've come back from the Statue of Liberty and Ellis Island, and it's six o'clock on a summer evening and they go over to the South Street Seaport. What will they find?"

"Food," said Arlene. "Every restaurant has sidewalk tables—or street stands which are even better. I mean you buy clams at one stand and french fries at the next—and a zillion kinds of deli, and chili and hoagys and icecream cones and Gus's pickles from Orchard Street. Or you go to Sloppy Louie's or Sweet's for crabs and lobsters.

"Or you can eat at one of the Yuppie restaurants—there's one on the mezzanine of the Fulton Market where they kill for a table—or you can eat on the Robert Fulton steamboat in the harbor. Or you take your finger food into the Square. There's always something going on, a jazz concert or a bunch of street entertainers—clowns, jugglers, what the Yuppies call 'buskers.' I mean it really jumps down there on a summer night!"

So if you're down in Lower Manhattan for a day's sightseeing, try an evening at the South Street Seaport. The river breeze has got to be a pleasant change from an air-conditioned movie.

And speaking of movies, the next change taking place in town is over in the Broadway theatre district. . . .

# $\mathcal{P.S.}$ 2

## FAREWELL TO BROADWAY

BACK IN 1904, THE NEW YORK TIMES BUILT AN OFFICE tower in an open square at 42nd Street and Broadway which it promptly named Times Square. Years later the Times moved out and Allied Chemical moved in, but by that time the square had become known throughout the world as Times Square, the hub of the Broadway theatre district. That district, dubbed "The Great White Way" because of the bright lights of its theatre marquees and huge neon advertising signs, now extends up Broadway through the forties and into the fifties. Elastically known as "the Times Square area" it has been the subject of a bitter controversy in which no New Yorker is neutral.

What happened was that over the past two decades Times Square and "the Times Square area" have become more and more seedy and crime-ridden, with porno shops, drug-dealing and massage parlors moving in among the theatres in rows of dilapidated buildings. The city decided the time had come to rebuild the area and asked real estate developers to submit plans for the wholesale renovation and reconstruction of the Times Square area. And the plan finally approved has had at least half the city up in arms. (Including me.)

The plan is to tear down all the old buildings and replace them with forty-story office towers and a few mammoth hotels. The first new building—which replaced two old theatres—is a bulky hotel occupying the entire block between 45th and 46th Streets. The rest of Broadway is scheduled to

become a long line of impersonal office towers—like Sixth Avenue in the 50's and Park Avenue in the 40's—cold and remote by daylight, with no shop windows and no pedestrians, and however landscaped and floodlit, silent and deserted at night. New York's Landmarks Preservation Commission is trying to save the old theatres by designating them historic landmarks, but this attempt is being fought not only by the real estate developers but by the theatre owners, who claim that the old theatres are outmoded and uneconomic.

For us ordinary citizens, what's really at stake is all that's connoted by the word "Broadway": the neon signs, the crowds, theatres, ticket agencies, restaurants, still holding their own among the sleazy sex shops—all the noise, light and life of the most famous theatre street in the world.

So you'd better visit it one evening while you're here. In a few years, "Broadway" may be a thing of the past.

Meanwhile, if you can't afford Broadway ticket prices, you'll find a small, new Off-Broadway theatre district along 42nd Street, west of 9th Avenue. It's called Theatre Row, it's housed in a few refurbished theatres reclaimed from their movie-theatre past and renamed for theatrical personalities running a gamut from Samuel Beckett to Douglas Fairbanks. You'll see highly professional productions of new comedies and dramas—one of which occasionally surprises everybody by being a hit—for a fraction of the cost of a play on Broadway. And around the corner on 9th Avenue from 43rd to 45th Streets, you'll find a string of attractive, inexpensive restaurants ready to feed you well and get you to your theatre on time.

So that's what's new in the West Side entertainment district. Farther up, on Patsy's Upper West Side, the affluent

'80's have brought a gentrification boom, with more and more brownstones being reclaimed from their roominghouse past and restored as one-family town houses, and expensive new apartment towers going up alongside them. And of course, on Columbus Avenue and Upper Broadway, the Mom-and-Pop stores have disappeared, forced out by skyrocketing rents, replaced by boutiques and chic restaurants for the Yuppie trade.

But I'll tell you an interesting thing. I've gone over there of an evening, with friends, to a concert at Symphony Space (a converted neighborhood movie palace) or to an off-Broadway play at the Promenade Theatre (ditto) and we usually have dinner at one of the new restaurants before the performance; and listening to them talk at nearby tables, looking at them and listening to them in the lobby at intermission or strolling along Upper Broadway at the end of the evening, it seemed to me that the character, flavor, appearance, and point of view of Upper West Siders haven't changed a bit.

And on over to a couple of new sights on the East Side. . . .

# *P.S. 3*

## MIRACLE AT 54TH STREET (AND LEXINGTON AVENUE)

BEFORE I FORGET: BACK ON P. NINETY-THREE, THERE'S A note about Bloomingdale's still being a cheap store on the Lexington Avenue side. Well, of course, as soon as the ink was dry on that statement, Bloomingdale's redecorated and rebuilt the entire Lexington Avenue side, including the ground floor which now boasts a glittering atrium of black glass and chrome lined with perfume and cosmetic counters.

Let's say you've finished your shopping at Bloomingdale's and you have half an hour free, or even fifteen minutes. Please walk down Lexington a few short blocks to 54th Street and see the sight I dragged my young architect friend David to see. What I'd read about it, David verified for me.

What you'll find at 54th and Lexington is the enormous skyscraper headquarters of Citicorp and, directly in front of it, the chastely elegant St. Peter's Lutheran Church. But your eyes deceive you. The church is not in front of the massive Citicorp tower, it's an integral part of it. The two buildings share one solid wall.

Citicorp had wanted to buy the land on which the church stood but St. Peter's had served its parishioners from that location for years and didn't want to leave. So Citicorp said: "You don't have to leave. Sell us your land, let us tear down your old building and we'll build you a new one to your specifications. It'll be part of our office building but as separate and quiet as if we weren't there."

How perfectly the plan worked I meant to demonstrate to

David at the end of our tour of the church. Citicorp's grand façade and busy shopping-mall atrium (every building's got an atrium these days) face Lexington Avenue. St. Peter's Church has its entrance on 54th Street and I led the way around the corner. (I'd been to the church several times, though I'd never toured the building.)

We entered the vestibule where a young woman sat at an information desk, and we helped ourselves to brochures describing the church. Then we opened a door that led into the small chapel famous for its "Nevelson environment," a group of five sculptures by Louise Nevelson commissioned by the church. The chapel, described in a brochure as an "inviolate space" for prayer and meditation, was so profoundly silent that David and I found ourselves talking in hushed whispers, though there wasn't anyone in there meditating at the time, and we were trying to decode the abstract sculptures.

We came out and went down a flight to the church proper, called "the sanctuary," with its stone ceiling, polished red oak pews and austerely beautiful modern altar. As at St. Thomas's, there are concerts held in the sanctuary at St. Peter's and the pews, which looked rooted, are all moveable.

We went down another flight to a large conference room and a small Off-Broadway theatre. We were the only visitors on every floor, and on all three the silence was so profound that our footsteps and low voices sounded loud in our ears.

When we got back up to the vestibule floor, and before I could lead the way, David asked the woman at the desk for directions to the men's room. She pointed to a door next to the chapel door, and David disappeared through it. He reappeared a few minutes later, in a state of shock. The door had led directly into the Citicorp atrium and, as I had once done,

David had stepped unwittingly from the absolute hush of St. Peter's into the noisy traffic of shoppers and office workers swarming through a busy midtown atrium in one of the city's biggest skyscrapers.

One door—and one perfectly constructed shared wall—had separated, and protected, two clashing environments.

So you go see that while you're here. As befits a church-related building, it's a genuine modern miracle.

Which is a little more than I am personally prepared to say for the far more famous new sight at the top of the Fifth Avenue shopping mile.

# 𝒫.𝒮. 4

## THE GLAMOROUS GLITZ ON FIFTH

BEFORE COVERING THE AVENUE'S NEWEST ATTRACTION, there are a couple of changes to be noted. Of the five book-shops along the shopping mile, Brentano's is gone, and the beautiful Rizzoli's has moved around the corner onto 57th Street and halfway up the block toward Sixth Avenue, but they've been replaced on Fifth by two huge newcomers, Barnes & Noble and B. Dalton.

Which brings us to the main event: the glittering glass-and-steel structure between 57th and 56th Streets but soaring up into the stratosphere. It's called Trump Tower and its where multi-million-dollar apartments are owned by the likes of Arab billionaires, multinational corporations and Johnny Carson, on high floors remote from the Trump Tower atrium, five stories high with a sixth level below ground. Spectacular as it is, I am solemnly informed by my friends that the atrium is not what it once was.

Certainly the doormen are not what they once were. When the building opened, the doormen were two black giants, in uniforms reminiscent of the British Royal Guards complete with high beavers or bearskins, I never got close enough to see which. And when they weren't opening the impressive doors they patrolled back and forth in front of them like sentries. I'd heard about the shops that lined the atrium and since I knew I couldn't afford them, it never occurred to me to walk into the place. Friends who did phoned to tell me what was going on inside.

"You won't believe this," one friend reported, "but at ten o'clock this morning, a piano player in white-tie-and-tails was sitting at a white baby grand piano, in the middle of the Trump Tower atrium, playing Cole Porter."

And my friend Arlene phoned to report an added development:

"You know that shoe store in the atrium where you can't buy a pair of shoes for under two hundred dollars?" she asked. "Well, there's a row of benches outside it. And this morning the benches were full of New York bag ladies, come in out of the cold—sitting listening to Cole Porter."

The piano, pianist and bag ladies are all gone now, and the present doormen are normal-sized, affable looking gents in inobtrusive uniforms opening doors instead of parading in front of them—leaving you free to concentrate on the atrium itself. I got my first view of it by accident; it was an aerial view and I still think it's the best way to see it, especially the first time. It's the view you get coming down into it from the second floor of Bonwit's.

Bonwit Teller is an old Fifth Avenue women's store, and when its new building opened I read that its five stories were (like St. Peter's and Citicorp) part of Trump Tower's atrium. But the entrance to Bonwit's is around the corner on 57th Street and Tiffany's still occupies its corner building at 57th and Fifth, separating Bonwit's from Trump Tower, so you have to stand back and look up, to see that the two new buildings are really one. I didn't do that the first time I went to Bonwit's new building to find out whether my old Bonwit's charge account was still valid.

I went in through the main entrance on 57th Street (the only one I knew of). I walked past the cosmetic and handbag

counters to the escalator at the back, rode up to the second floor and got the information I needed. Then I toured the floor, looking at blouses and suits, going up a few steps here and down a few there. After which, I saw a Down escalator and stepped onto it—and then saw that it wasn't taking me back to Bonwit's ground floor. As I rode slowly down into the Trump Tower atrium, I gawked above and below me at the spectacular panorama of its height and depth, its glittering shop windows and below-ground restaurant, all of which, to my nearsighted eyes, seemed bathed in a pink-and-gold glow. I found it overpoweringly rich and glitzy and I had no desire to see more of it, till I had to cover it for this chapter. Then I phoned my friend Carole.

"If you take me on a tour of the Trump Tower atrium, I'll buy you tea there afterward," I said. "I presume they serve tea somewhere?"

"They do indeed," said Carole, and we set a date.

You notice I didn't ask her whether she was intimately acquainted with the place. I assumed it. Carole has an air of absolute assurance that told me she'd be perfectly at home in astronomically expensive surroundings and was attracted to them. The assurance has nothing to do with money. If I were suddenly to become a millionaire, I would still wear the "I'm-a-peasant" expression which is an indelible part of my face. Carole can be chic and broke at the same time, so that if she turns up on an Unemployment Insurance line, she appears to be slumming.

We met and walked into the atrium and for the first time I noticed the pink marble floor and towering pink ceiling reflected in the polished brass bordering the mirrored eleva-

tors and the shop windows, causing the golden-pink glow that nearly blinded me till I got used to it.

The atrium runs straight back from Fifth Avenue clear to Madison—useful to remember on a rainy day—and is lined with expensive shops as far as the escalator. Just beyond that, if you look left you'll see an open doorway leading into Bonwit's ground floor, and looking straight ahead you'll see a sign pointing to the IBM Plaza. So let's detour a moment to see it.

The IBM Plaza, on Madison Avenue at 56th Street, is one of several new plazas along Madison in the fifties and Third Avenue in the forties, all of them under towering skyscraper office buildings. Most of them have tables-and-chairs and refreshment stands. The IBM is the most popular, partly because of its location and partly because its glass roof and doors make it usable even in wet or icy weather, and protect its bamboo trees and the seasonal flower displays in its broad low pots so that it never looks or feels wintry. That November day the plaza glowed with yellow and orange 'mums and great branches of autumn leaves—which were the last normal sight I was to see for an hour. We went back into Trump Tower and Carole led the way up the steep, narrow escalator.

Ascending the Trump Tower escalator you rise, not to Bonwit's upper floors but to the atrium's "terraces"—one thickly carpeted balcony after another, each one lined with shops. The higher we rose, the more New York seemed to have vanished, replaced by a never-never land of Palm Beach opulence and Hollywood extravagance, where window displays of jewelry, cashmere, fine leather, *haute couture,* all seemed to exist that day in a soundless, empty planet. Not a soul in sight, not

a whisper to be heard. No one joined us on the escalator, no one appeared on any of the plush landings. Carole kept glancing at me and asking tentatively. "Are you all right?" And I wasn't. By the time we stepped off onto the atrium's top floor, "Terrace Five," entered the restaurant where the super-rich dine, and ordered tea, I was suffering from genuine Culture Shock. Which Carole explained to me.

"Those stores aren't American and they're not for the American trade," she said. "Cartier's—and the Italian leather shop and shoe store—they're almost all European-owned and they cater to the Arabs and foreign investors who live here or visit here."

"We didn't see a living soul go into any of the stores," I said. "They must phone for what they want."

"Or they have it sent up to their suite on approval," said Carole. "I want you to know that even the week before Christmas, all those stores close promptly at their regular six o'clock closing hour. How you can tell is, the escalator shuts down."

Tea on Terrace Five was far less elegant than tea at the Plaza, the only advantage being that at Terrace Five you don't have to wait in line for it. The long tea lines at the Plaza wear me out. But afternoon tea—now that the English have given it up—has become very popular in New York and you"ll fine it served at all the new hotels. And if the new hotel teas are too expensive and the Plaza line is too long, there's always good old Rumpelmayer's, on Central Park South, where you can get a table without waiting.

One more Trump Tower story before I close it out. This one was told to me a couple of Christmases ago by a friend who went to the atrium to a concert of Christmas carols one

afternoon. For their final selection, the choristers, grouped near the foot of the escalator, struck up the old carol, "We three kings of Orient are." As they did so, what to my friend's wondering eyes should appear but the kings themselves, bearded and costumed to the teeth, riding in majestic state down the escalator.

# $\mathcal{P.S.}$ 5

## SOMETHING NEW IN CENTRAL PARK

WELL, THERE'S A GREAT DEAL THAT'S NEW IN CENTRAL PARK, now that I think about it. For one thing, the staid New York Times recently published an editorial announcing to prospective visitors that Central Park is once more safe. "Fear is now forgotten," it solemnly stated—and went on to urge tourists to explore its green acres, now that the long-neglected trees and lawns are flourishing again.

And the lovely fact is that the park has been transformed, thanks to the affluence of the past few years. The gardeners are back at work, and a new and prosperous volunteer group, The Central Park Conservancy, has been reclaiming damaged lawns, repairing statuary, rebuilding rustic bridges and best of all, planting new groves of trees and new flower beds the length and breadth of the park.

One vast lawn that was in dire need of rescue was The Sheep Meadow, so worn down by the thousands of feet and rumps assembled there every summer for Philharmonic concerts and Metropolitan Operas, that it had to be cordoned off for a year for repairs, and the concerts moved to the Great Lawn inside the West 81st Street park entrance. When the Sheep Meadow was finally restored, it was restricted to gentler use and the concerts and operas continue to be performed on the Great Lawn. (Which will one day be so damaged that it will have to be cordoned off and the concerts and operas moved to. . . .)

Which brings us to the park's celebrated new sight, a five-minute walk from the Great Lawn, just inside the West 72nd

Street park entrance and across the street from a prestigious and very old apartment house called The Dakota. (It seems that back in 1890 when it was built, the apartment house was so far out of town that New Yorkers derisively dubbed it "the Dakota Territory"—and either the name stuck, or the builder blithely made it official.)

The Dakota is where John Lennon lived and where his widow, Yoko Ono, still lives. After Lennon's death, Yoko Ono paid for the cost of landscaping a small plot of park land, encircling the 2½ pear-shaped acres with exotic trees and shrubs and naming it Strawberry Fields; after which she gave the city one million dollars for the permanent maintenance of the memorial. If you walk over to see it, you'll also see, set in an adjoining path, a circular black and white marble mosaic depicting a giant starburst radiating out from the central word "Imagine." It was a gift from the stonecutters of the city of Naples.

Moving over East to the Fifth Avenue boundary of the park, if you're walking along Fifth in the sixties, you'll see another new sight over the park wall: the new Rustic Playground, complete with child-sized wooden bridges, wooden catwalks, slides built into the side of a hill, and rock climbs for the intrepid.

Which reminds me. Somewhere I voiced the gloomy prediction that the subway excavation damage would never be repaired. I'm overjoyed to be wrong: there's not a trace of damage visible any more. (The subway itself was a total disaster. By the time inspectors discovered its tracks were flooded, they were beyond repair.)

And we move further uptown to the park's last new sight— and a monstrous ugly one it is, too.

# $\mathcal{P.S.}$ 6

## THE MET MUSEUM UNDER GLASS

THE "NEWER AND BIGGER" PARK DEMOLITION NEXT DOOR
to the Metropolitan Museum, which I mentioned way back on
page 18, finally resulted in the construction of two new
museum buildings, one behind the Met's southern end (at
80th Street), the other behind its northern end (at 84th).
They are identical two-story glass tents, more egg-shaped
than tent-shaped and truly grotesque as "wings" of the Met's
massive 19th century stone structure. But both glass tents are
carefully hidden beyond and behind the original building so
as not to spoil the museum's beautiful Fifth Avenue façade.
Invisible from the avenue, the two glass tents are intrusively
visible only to the users of Central Park.

Mindful of my duty to you, I asked Carole to take me on a
tour of both tents. (She was startled to learn I'd never set foot
in either of them and surprised that I cared how many acres
had been torn out of the park to build them, and we had an
amiable argument about whether future generations would be
gladder to have the museum or the park.)

When you've walked into the museum and paid the fee, ask
for a floor plan; the place is now so gigantic it's easy to miss
some of the small collections without it. Carole stuck one in
my shoulder bag but she was at pains to ask directions to every
exhibit, from every guard we passed.

"I hope you're going to mention," she said, as we headed for
the Lila Acheson Wallace Wing (the south wing), "that no

matter how many questions I asked, the guards were friendly and patient and knowledgeable."

They were.

The Lila Acheson Wallace Wing is named for the wife of the founder of the Reader's Digest, and her collection of 20th century art—some American, mostly European, occupies most of the wing. But there is room for a small Michael C. Rockefeller Wing on the first floor that contains the African and Pacific islands art and artifacts collected by a young son of Nelson Rockefeller. In 1961, Michael Rockefeller went out to New Guinea "to record and preserve the art of a disappearing culture." He was lost in the jungle, and despite land and air searches that went on for years, no trace of him was ever found. The collection was formerly housed in a small museum. I hope it doesn't get lost in the vastness of the Met.

The Museum's American Wing has been moved from the old building to both floors of the new North Wing, and it now includes probably the best collection of American portraits. The first floor also houses the Met's famous Egyptian Wing and includes its most publicized recent acquisition, the Temple of Dendur. According to the brochure, the temple was built in 15 B.C. by the Emperor Augustus for the goddess Isis. By the year 1963 it was in such a state of decay that the Egyptian government asked the United Nations to adopt it. In 1967, the U.N. made a gift of it to the United States, and the U.S. "awarded" it to the Met.

The temple and a reflecting pool occupy a large unadorned room; they are the only objects in it and they endow it with a special serenity.

"This is a lovely room," I said to Carole. And she said:

"It's a great room for parties. You can rent it."

---

"You can what?" I said.

"You can rent it for private parties."

I phoned the Met later to check this. You can rent the Temple of Dendur for a private party only if you are a "Corporate Patron" who has made a $30,000 contribution to the Met.

To anyone who, like me, finds huge museums overwhelming, the original Met was intimidating enough. Add two new ugly glass tents and I was in no condition to see—or appreciate—its treasures. Among which, tucked away in a corner of the Wallace Wing on "the mezzanine"—a landing a few steps above the first floor—is the Berggruen Klee Collection which I hurried past, not knowing it contained Klee's poster for "The Comedians" which I love with a passion. I'll go back and see it one day, but on that autumn afternoon I'd had all I could take of the glass tents and their plethora of nearly empty rooms which I presume are to be filled eventually by newly acquired collections. One of them made me grind my teeth. Billed as a "Chinese Garden Court" it contained two narrow flower beds buried in leaf cover, with a miniature pond between them. And nothing else.

Two flower beds without flowers, and a toy pond—in Central Park whose autumn glory flamed all around us through the glass walls.

When we left the Met we walked on up Fifth to the Carnegie mansion where the former Cooper Hewitt Museum (p. 46) seems unchanged though it's now The Smithsonian Institution's National Museum of Design. I was hoping you'd see something of the old mansion but all that's left now is an oak staircase and oak paneled walls. The house has been so gutted and remodeled, nothing of the original interior re-

mains. You can get a brochure with photographs of the house as it once was, but they won't give you the sense you get, at the Frick Collection and redoubled at the Morgan Library, of walking back into the past and into the private world of a self-made colossus.

And we'll move on uptown for some good news at the Cathedral of St. John the Divine.

## THE TOPLESS TOWERS OF ST. JOHN THE DIVINE

BACK ON P. 62, THE CATHEDRAL OF ST. JOHN THE DIVINE was described as being "permanently unfinished," because, in the words of one of its clergy, "You don't spend millions on a cathedral when people around you are hungry." Much as the unfinished cathedral towers worried Bishop Moore and his redoubtable right hand, Dean Morton, the appalling poverty in the depressed neighborhoods surrounding the cathedral—Harlem and Morningside Heights—worried them more. Then one day in the late seventies, Dean Morton announced his brainstorm: the unemployed young men and women of the area would be trained and paid to complete the cathedral towers.

"We will resume building this great house of God, and revive the dying art of stonecraft by teaching it to the young people of the neighborhood," he said.

And in 1982, under the direction of a master stonecutter imported from England, thirty young men and women (including a single mother of four living on welfare) began a course of training in the art of stonecutting and the finer art of carving gargoyles and saints out of limestone blocks. (The mother of four worked on a pinnacle, a four-foot-high miniature castle complete with turrets and windows, to be set in place at the top of a tower.)

It takes four years to turn out a fully trained artisan and the cost of tools and training for one mason or carver is $23,000 a year. But by the year 2000—with luck, prosperous times and

Metropolitan Museum of Art, 17, 18, 168–170
Metropolitan Opera House, 54
I. Miller, 74
Mitzi Newhouse Theatre, 54, 56
Model Boathouse. *See* Central Park
Model Sailboat Pond. *See* Central Park
MOMA. *See* Museum of Modern Art
J. P. Morgan Library, 41–43
Morningside Heights, 51, 62, 63, 68, 172
Morris-Jumel Mansion, 44, 118, 119
Mott Street, 99, 101
Mulberry Street, 98, 101
Murray Hill, 51
Museum of the City of New York, 48
Museum of Modern Art, 41

Natural History Museum, 47, 123
NBC radio and television studio tour, 53, 85
New Amsterdam, 93, 94
New School for Social Research, 76
New York City Ballet, 54
New York City Opera, 54
New York State Theatre, 54
New York Stock Exchange, 49, 140
New York University, 77

Off-Broadway, 79
Off-off Broadway, 79

Off-Track Betting, 30, 43
Olympic Tower, 74
One UN Plaza, 83
One Wall Street, 30, 31, 152
Orchard Street, 29, 95, 97, 98, 153
OTB. *See* Off-Track Betting
Paley Park, 43
Penny Sightseeing Bus Company, 114, 121, 124, 174
Philharmonic Hall, 54, 56, 61
Plaza Hotel, 74, 164
Port Authority Bus Terminal, 4

Radio City Music Hall, 28, 85, 87–90
Rainbow Room, 87
RCA building, 85, 86, 87
Riverside Church, 20, 68, 92
Riverside Park, 64, 67
Rizzoli, 74, 160
Rockefeller Center, 34, 47, 53, 85, 86, 92
Rockefeller Plaza, 85
Rockefeller University, 92
Roosevelt Island, 109, 112
Rumpelmayer's, 164
Rustic Playground. *See* Central Park

St. Luke's Place, 78
St. John the Divine, Cathedral of, 62, 63, 117, 171, 172, 174
St. Mark's Church-in-the-Bowery, 94
St. Peter's Lutheran Church, 157, 158

St. Thomas's Episcopal Church, 74
Saks, 74
San Gennaro Festival, 98
Schaefer Music Festival. *See*
  Central Park
Schermerhorn Row, 151
Schomburg Center for Research
  and Black Culture, 174
Schomburg Collection, 121, 174
Schomburg Museum, 122
Scribner, 74
Shakespeare Garden. *See* Central
  Park
Shakespeare Theatre. *See* Central
  Park
Sheep Meadow. *See* Central Park
Smithsonian Institution's
  National Museum of
  Design, 170
South Street Seaport, 149, 150,
  153
Spanish Harlem, 122
Statue of Liberty, 7, 142, 145,
  153
Stock Exchange, 141
Strawberry Fields. *See* Central
  Park
Strivers' Row, 120
Sutton Place, 51
Sylvan Terrace, 119, 120
Thames Street, 102, 152
Theatre Row, 155
Tiffany, 5, 74, 161
Times Square, 154

TKTS, 47
Tramway, 109, 110
TriBeCa, 149, 150
Trinity Church, 30, 31, 49,
  102, 103, 112, 137–140
Trump Tower, 160–163, 165
Tudor City, 51

UN. *See* United Nations
Union Theological Seminary, 63
United Nations, 82, 83, 84,
  92

Vivian Beaumont Theatre, 54,
  55, 56

Wall Street, 29, 30, 49, 102,
  137, 140, 150, 152, 153
Washington Arch, 76, 77
Washington Heights, 20
Washington Mews, 76, 77
Washington Square, 76, 77
Welfare Island, 108
Windows on the World, 36
Wollman Skating Rink. *See*
  Central Park
World Trade Center, 10, 26,
  32, 104

Yorkville, 51

Zabar's, 61, 70–72

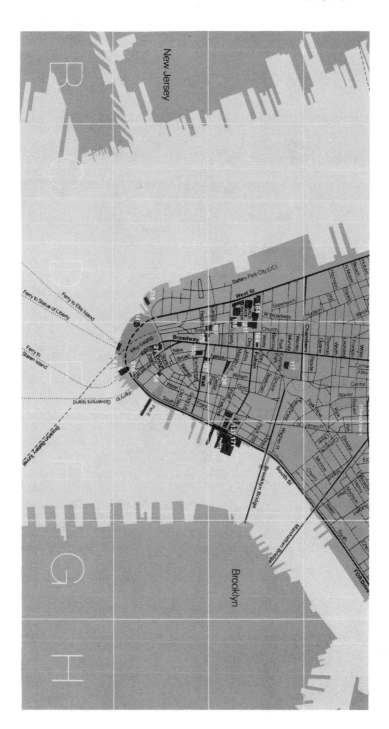

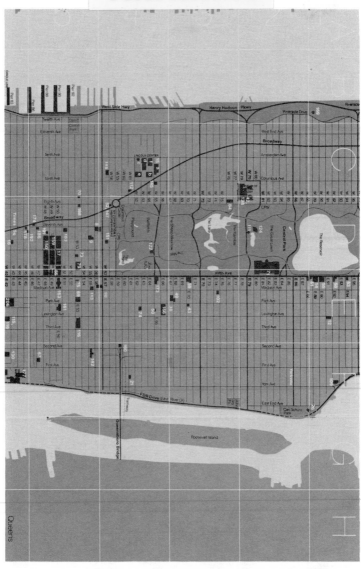

Maps are details from the New York City Visitors Guide and Map provided by the New York Convention & Visitors Bureau. Numbers refer to sites. For more information, contact the New York City Convention & Visitors Bureau, Two Columbus Circle, New York, NY 10019, 212-397-8222.

REPRINTED WITH PERMISSION OF THE NEW YORK CONVENTION & VISITORS BUREAU, INC.